MR. DARCY'S
LITTLE SISTER

C. ALLYN PIERSON

sourcebooks
landmark

Published by Sourcebooks Landmark, an imprint of Sourcebooks, Inc.
P.O. Box 4410, Naperville, Illinois 60567-4410
(630) 961-3900
FAX: (630) 961-2168
www.sourcebooks.com

Originally published in 2008 as *And This Our Life*

Library of Congress Cataloging-in-Publication Data is on file with the publisher.

Printed and bound in the United States of America
VP 10 9 8 7 6 5 4 3 2 1

This book is dedicated to my mother, who loved to read.
Barbara Pierson
March 25, 1933–December 7, 2009

Prologue

Pemberley House
21 September, 1813
Miss Elizabeth Bennet
Longbourn, Hertfordshire

My dearest Sister-To-Be,—

I cannot even begin to tell you how delighted I am to know that you are making my brother the happiest of men! I look forwards with joy to the prospect of our relationship and trust that you will soon consider me a true sister and not merely a relation in law. All of the residents of Pemberley are completely distracted by their happiness, knowing that there will finally be a mistress to adorn and command Pemberley House; and Mrs. Reynolds has been extolling your beauty and grace to those who were not fortunate enough to see you when you visited all too briefly in the summer. I believe that she takes a great deal of credit for this happy event since it was she who spent so much time showing you and your aunt and uncle around that my brother arrived while you were still touring. I must make this note very short as I wish to send it off with one to my brother by return post, so I will put off further expressions of my delight until later, and merely sign myself,—

Your loving sister,
Georgiana Darcy

To save thy secret soul from nightly fears.

—THOMAS GRAY, "THE BARD, A PINDARIC ODE"

GEORGIANA FINISHED FOLDING HER LETTERS AND QUICKLY sealed them before she had time to think about them further. Mrs. Annesley, her companion of just over a year, looked up from her book and smiled.

"Are you finished with your letters, Miss Darcy?" Her voice was soft and low, with just a hint of the music of Scotland, although Georgiana would never consider mentioning this linguistic idiosyncrasy to the woman she considered a friend as well as a paid companion. Mrs. Annesley was a native of Derbyshire but had spent a number of years in Edinburgh, where her husband held a minor position as a tutor at the great university there. She called those years "the Babylonian Exile" and felt that the cold, damp winters of Scotland had injured her husband's health and hastened his early death. Not that she talked of these things. Mrs. Annesley would never discuss anything that she felt would cause melancholy thoughts in her charge, and Georgiana generally appreciated her reticence.

"Yes, I am done. I should like to post them before I think of a dozen pages of additional thoughts. If I do they will never reach my brother and his fiancée before the wedding, and I do not want Miss Elizabeth Bennet to think that I do not welcome her into the family."

"I have always found that it is better to post my letters immediately, with the exception of comments which are angry—those it is better to hold until the next day and reread in the cold light of morning before posting."

Georgiana gave her a wide smile. "Well, these hold only happy thoughts. Do you think we could post them yet today?"

The older woman glanced at the watch pinned on her bodice. "It is a pleasant day for a drive and it is only two o'clock; we should easily be able to drive into Lambton and post these and return in time for a cup of tea before changing for dinner. I also need another skein of silk for my embroidery—perhaps we could get that as well. Would you order the carriage, my dear?"

Georgiana flushed slightly and rang the bell. When Smithfield answered, she gravely said, "Please order the carriage, Smithfield. Mrs. Annesley and I are driving into Lambton."

Smithfield bowed with all the solemnity of an archbishop and answered, "Yes, Miss Darcy. Would fifteen minutes be suitable?"

"Quite suitable, thank you, Smithfield."

Georgiana slumped back in her chair with a sigh and a brief frown. "Another comportment hurdle crossed. We shall label this one 'giving orders to servants.'" She sat up abruptly and grinned at her companion. "I know! Let us take Pilot with us. He enjoys a ride in the carriage."

Mrs. Annesley winced briefly as she looked at the gigantic Newfoundland dog who had been the constant companion of Georgiana's father and who was now lying calmly at his mistress's side.

"How you can bear to be around that drooling monster, I do not know. As far as the orders to the servants, as you know 'practise makes perfect.'"

"I just wish I could have practised more before Miss Bennet's visit last summer. I did not exhibit stellar comportment on *that* occasion. The surprise of my brother's introduction of a young lady of whom I had heard not a word beforehand and the gimlet eyes of Miss Bingley watching our second meeting the day after were too much for me to bear with equanimity. But Miss Bennet was lovely, was she not?"

"A very sweet-tempered and well-bred young lady, as well as very pretty. I am sure you will be good friends when you are better acquainted."

"I cannot imagine why Miss Bingley brought Wickham's name into the conversation on that occasion. That was the topic that completely destroyed my composure. You do not suppose she knows about my past indiscretion with Wickham, do you?"

"Well," Mrs. Annesley paused to consider her words and then said, "I suspect that Miss Bingley is jealous of Miss Bennet. After all, Miss Bingley would have been as aware as you were of the significance of your brother introducing you to the young lady."

Georgiana gave her a sardonic smile and drawled, "Yeessss, I am quite sure she was."

Smithfield entered and her smile faded, replaced by the austere courtesy which she had been taught to use when interacting with the servants.

"The carriage awaits, Miss Darcy."

"Thank you, Smithfield." She rose and called Pilot, and they left.

Two days later, Georgiana was practising a difficult Mozart sonata when she was interrupted by Smithfield, who announced, "Colonel Fitzwilliam, Miss Darcy."

She jumped up and tipped several music books off the pianoforte in her haste. Her face flushed over her clumsiness, but she retained enough composure to bob a quick curtsey to her guardian and say, "Colonel! What are you doing here?"

The colonel, his blue eyes crinkling in amusement, answered, "What a lovely greeting from my little cousin. I could leave if you prefer."

Georgiana could feel her blush deepen. *What an idiot you are, Georgiana. Can you not behave with a modicum of poise even with your closest relations?* She forced herself to smile graciously and say, "Of course I am delighted to see you, Colonel Fitzwilliam. I am, however, surprised to see you at this time of year. I would have expected you to be off with some of your fellow officers killing birds."

"Your brother has interrupted my pursuit of grouse and eligible young ladies with his wedding plans. He sent me to bring you and Mrs. Annesley to Netherfield. Have you not received his letter?"

Her eyes sparkled at the news and she forgot her pretence of maturity. "Not yet. I sent him one asking to go only two days ago. I see my brother has anticipated me." She suppressed her eagerness and added astringently, "Why did he not just send a servant? I would think a colonel would have better things to do than act as errand boy."

"Undoubtedly, Miss Darcy. However I was already planning to visit Pemberley to check on my little cousin. I am such a responsible guardian. Now, if you will excuse me, I will run upstairs and change out of my dusty travel clothes." He smiled at her and kissed her on the top of her head before heading for the staircase, patting Pilot as he went through the hall. Georgiana noted with a prick of annoyance how similar his attitude was towards her as the dog.

Later, while Georgiana and Mrs. Annesley were awaiting the colonel in the drawing-room before pouring tea, Georgiana crumbled a teacake idly until her companion noticed.

"Are you well, my dear? You do not seem yourself this afternoon."

"Mmm. I am just… concerned."

"About what?"

"I am nervous about meeting all the Bennets. I have been thinking about it most of the afternoon. What if they do not like me, or they think me an awkward boor?"

"My dear girl, you must relax and not worry so much over the opinions of others. You are a pretty girl who is both accomplished and intelligent. Why should they not like you? Miss Elizabeth is marrying your brother, after all, and what family could object to him? And it is my understanding that Miss Elizabeth has no dowry, so her marriage to your brother must be cause for both happiness and relief for her family; and you are his sister. They will most likely be exerting themselves to the utmost to impress you."

A smile twitched involuntarily at Georgiana's mouth at the picture Mrs. Annesley had conjured. "I suppose so."

"Trust me, dear girl, it will be so. It was quite clear last summer that Miss Elizabeth is as gentle and well bred as anyone could want. She is not as sophisticated as the ladies of the haut monde, but that is not to be mourned in the least."

"I wonder if Miss Elizabeth is as nervous about facing me as I am about seeing her once again."

"It is quite possible."

Georgiana grinned wryly to herself at the picture of the two of them, Miss Elizabeth and herself, sitting in silence for hours, flushed and embarrassed and unable to find a word to say. Of course it would not happen. Miss Elizabeth had already shown her mettle with Miss Bingley the previous summer. She would not be easily cowed.

The colonel soon joined them, and he conversed easily with Mrs. Annesley. Georgiana sat silently, her eyes moving back and forth between them as they spoke, but her mind was fixed upon the coming meeting with the Bennet family. Her reverie was interrupted by the sound of a carriage on the sweep and, soon after, the sound of Smithfield greeting a visitor. They were not long left in suspense over the identity of their guest, as Smithfield immediately announced Mr. Jonathan Walker.

Georgiana blushed. Mr. Walker had been very kind and attentive during the past summer and she knew that she was the reason for his call. What ill luck that the colonel was here! Having her guardian watching the both of them while she tried to carry on a conversation with a gentleman was disconcerting, and she could not think what to say. Fortunately, Mr. Walker was as perfectly comfortable in the drawing-room at Pemberley as he was at The Yews, his father's manor, and when his conversation with Georgiana died a quick death he talked to the colonel and Mrs. Annesley for thirty minutes then excused himself and left. As soon as their guest left the colonel commented, "How often does Mr. Walker visit, Georgiana?"

She reddened again but tried to be offhand in her answer. "Oh, I think about once a week, or so. I have not noticed particularly." She turned to Mrs. Annesley. "Do you not think that is correct?"

"I believe so, my dear."

"Mmm." The colonel's right brow was lifted in an expression she knew well.

"And why do you ask, Colonel?" She knew her voice sounded irritable.

"I am just wondering who this young man is. I do not recall meeting him before."

Georgiana's eyes glittered hotly. "For heaven's sake, Colonel Fitzwilliam, his father is the squire of Lambton and they have been the squires of Lambton for the past three hundred years or more. He is a neighbour, and that is all."

She put down her teacup and stood up. "If you will excuse me, sir, I am going upstairs," she said coldly. "I have some French grammar to study." She stalked to the door, closing it behind her with a too-careful click.

The colonel looked at Mrs. Annesley for a long moment, his eyes wide with astonishment, and then shook himself and blinked. "Well…" His voice faded and he tried again. "If you will excuse me Mrs. Annesley, I believe I will take a stroll down by the stream with Pilot before the light fades."

"Of course, Colonel." She paused and then added tentatively, "Colonel?"

He stopped halfway to the door and turned.

"Yes, Mrs. Annesley?"

"I apologise for Miss Darcy's behaviour. She is very nervous about the upcoming Season and has been very… well… her spirits have been very unequal in the past few weeks. She is at a very difficult time in her life; ordinarily I have found her to be a most thoughtful, caring young woman."

"Yes, so have I. She seems to have lost her sense of humour somewhere along the way between childhood and adulthood, however. She used to be able to laugh at herself."

"Some days she is as merry as a lark, and others she is more like a hedgehog, all prickly spines. If you would like, I will have her apologise to you. She should not be speaking to her guardian in such a manner."

"No, no. I do not want to give the incident more importance than it should have." His voice faded as he glanced towards the staircase where Georgiana had disappeared.

"As you wish, Colonel Fitzwilliam."

He bowed and left the room, whistling for Pilot, and she heard Smithfield close the hall door behind him.

Georgiana came down for dinner, trying to behave as if nothing had happened, but the conversation at the table was stilted. Colonel Fitzwilliam had a bland expression on his face and asked Georgiana very general questions about what she and Mrs. Annesley had been doing. As they rose from the table to have their coffee in the drawing-room, he said, "I hope you will play for me tonight, Georgiana."

She bowed her head in acquiescence and played the pianoforte for almost an hour before excusing herself and going upstairs.

That night, as she lounged on her bed—using Pilot (illegally smuggled up to her room) as a backrest—Georgiana read through some of the earlier pages of her diary before writing the day's events.

23 July: Mr. Walker called again today. He is very easy to talk to and has many amusing stories about London society, but he is also a student of history and we had a most interesting discussion about the political situation in France. He thinks Napoleon is losing control of France and that it will not be long before the Coalition forces overcome his army unless the Emperor is able to find new sources of both men and arms. He asked me to ride with him sometime soon. I had better practise my riding—poor Ginger has been sadly neglected of late, so I hope she does not take her revenge by throwing me in the mud in front of Mr. Walker!

She flipped a few pages.

12 August: Mr. Walker has been out of town on business, but he is now returned. He invited me to ride this afternoon but Mrs. Annesley said that it would not be proper, even if a groom went with us. Until I make my debut I must continue to be a child. It is quite irritating, and I think she is being over scrupulous, but I have already made one terrible mistake making my own decisions about propriety, so I will not argue with her about her decision!

She turned to the current day and wrote the following:

23 September: What a ghastly day! I was horrid to the dear colonel, but I am so tired of being watched and analysed! If only the colonel would realise that I am not six years old anymore, it would be easier for me. Patting me on the head and calling me "Little Cousin!" I am surprised that he did not look for plaits that he could pull to tease me as if I were a raw schoolgirl. It is beyond annoying. However, we are leaving in the morning for Netherfield and I will meet the Bennet family, so I cannot stay mad at my cousin—I have too many other things to think (and worry) about!

The post arrived before they were ready to leave the next morning. Georgiana looked at her two letters: the thicker letter directed in her brother's familiar handwriting and the other, thinner missive in a feminine hand, presumably from Miss Elizabeth Bennet. After a moment of consideration, she decided to open the shorter note first.

My dear Miss Darcy,—

I thank you for your kind letter of welcome to your family. I consider the opportunity to know you better as not the least of my sources of happiness upon my engagement to your brother, and I look forwards with pleasure to the time when we will all be together at Pemberley. As your brother will undoubtedly tell you in his letter, we are planning the wedding for the nineteenth of October, which will give us somewhat less than four more weeks to finish planning for the occasion. We will have a double wedding with my dear sister Jane and Mr. Bingley, whom I know you have met. I look forwards with great anticipation also to introducing you to Jane, as I believe you will find in her a true friend, as I always have. I must close now, as your brother is eyeing my pen and paper with

*impatience; his letter to you is already finished and he is
eager to post these.—With my best affection, your sister,*
Elizabeth Bennet

"So, Miss Darcy, was Miss Elizabeth angry and affronted at
your letter of congratulation?" Mrs. Annesley asked, gently teasing
her as she collected their final possessions upstairs.

Georgiana smiled, but relief flooded through her. "Of course
not. She writes a lovely note."

She picked up the other letter and opened it quickly. Her brother's letter consisted of several pages covered with his small, even
handwriting. After a quick perusal, she gave a sigh of satisfaction.

"Good news, my dear?" Mrs. Annesley enquired, looking up
from the embroidery she was packing.

"Indeed it is. My letter apparently arrived after he had seen
the colonel off, and he added a few lines at the end in acknowledgement before posting his. My brother and Mr. Bingley have
been discussing a trip to London to finalise their wedding plans,
and he believes that Mr. Bennet will approve his idea to include
the Misses Bennet in the party. Mr. and Mrs. Gardiner live in
London, and it will be more convenient for the young ladies
to be in town with their aunt to order their trousseaux." She
frowned slightly as she read further. "My brother has not told
Miss Elizabeth that I am coming. He thinks it will be a pleasant
surprise for her. I hope he is correct in that assumption." She
chewed her lower lip.

"My dear Miss Darcy, you must not chew your lip." Mrs.
Annesley patted her shoulder gently.

Georgiana stopped, her face flushed. "I am sorry; I know it is
childish. I will try to control myself."

Mrs. Annesley patted her hand. "Will your brother wish for you to have a new gown made for the wedding while you are in town?"

"I would suppose so, although he did not mention it. You know my brother; anything in the world I could possibly want is mine in an instant." She smiled softly and then darted a complacent look at her companion as she added, "However, I suspect he has more interesting things to think about now than a gown for me."

The carriage was finally loaded and the two ladies set off by nine o'clock, with the colonel following them on his horse. Georgiana sat back and made herself comfortable for the beginning of the three-day journey to Hertfordshire. Mrs. Annesley, dear woman, would most likely doze during much of the trip as the rhythm of the hoofbeats and the swaying of the coach frequently lulled her to slumber, and Georgiana would have many hours to prepare herself to meet all of her new friends and relations. This time was necessary, as the idea of adjusting her thoughts and manner to so many new personalities so she could converse easily and without embarrassment was daunting.

She and Mrs. Annesley had been alone together for much of the past year since her idiocy over Wickham. She thanked God that she had retained enough intelligence to confess their plans to elope to her brother when he had appeared unexpectedly at Ramsgate. When her brother had revealed to her the depths of Wickham's perfidy towards their family and his innumerable instances of misbehaviour (and she was sure that the tales of gambling and drunkenness were only the tiniest tip of a mountain of misdeeds that her dear brother had thought unsuitable for her ears), she had been shaken to the core of her being. The most upsetting aspect to

Georgiana's feelings was her brother's condemnation of his own actions in caring for her, accusing himself of the grossest neglect and irresponsibility in her upbringing. Colonel Fitzwilliam had shown a more reasonable concern; he was worried about her feelings towards the man who had insinuated himself into her heart to the point where she had considered defying the teachings of a lifetime to enter an unsanctioned marriage, but he had not wasted his breath in self-recriminations.

The thought of what she had nearly done still gave her gooseflesh. Romantic nonsense from an accomplished schemer—and one that she had known from childhood experience was untrustworthy—had nearly overthrown her sense completely. She was still astonished that he had been able to make her forget his practised falsehoods and schemes to put her brother wrong in his father's eyes during their youth. And their father had always fallen for his wide-eyed innocence, excusing his lies as mistakes or misunderstandings. It was only her father's knowledge of her brother's character which had saved the elder Mr. Darcy from punishing his innocent son. Georgiana, the much younger child who was barred by her age and sex from their activities, was always a silent observer, effacing herself and following the boys without their knowledge in order to be a part of their games, if only on the periphery. Wickham had not been able to hide his deceits from her sharp eyes then, yet the passage of years had temporarily erased those observations when he had appeared, tall and handsome, at Ramsgate. How easily he had convinced her of his change of heart and mind.

She shivered and drew her shawl around her shoulders. The carriage was cold, but the chill of her past errors was far more frigid. Her brother had not mentioned the affair in the year since Wickham had decamped from Ramsgate. She did not know if her brother had told anyone, other than the colonel, about the near disaster, but she thought not. He would, she knew, protect her person and her reputation with his life, if need be. Her dear brother. She hoped that Miss Elizabeth Bennet would cherish his noble heart and forgive him the stolid reticence and solemnity which marked his public face.

Her companion awoke, and the rest of the day was spent discussing the wedding and what Georgiana should wear to it.

As the dusk gathered over the autumnal landscape, the carriage slowed and turned into the courtyard of the inn where they usually stopped when travelling to town. Mrs. Annesley stirred from the quietude which had fallen over them in the last few minutes of the day, and they began gathering their wraps and accoutrements. While settling in and during their dinner, Georgiana was kept from her morbid preoccupation with the Wickham incident and her fears for the future by the colonel's lively conversation about London and family. Her preparations for the night then occupied her mind for a few minutes longer, but after the candle was snuffed she lay awake for several hours speculating about the Bennet family and how they would receive her.

Chapter 2

An unlessoned girl, unschooled, unpractisèd,
Happy in this, she is not yet so old
But she may learn.

—William Shakespeare, *The Merchant of Venice*

The next two days of travel went swiftly by and, too soon for Georgiana's peace of mind, the carriage pulled up on the gravel sweep before Netherfield Hall. Georgiana received her brother's embrace and kiss on the cheek as she always did, but she kept her arms around him for a moment longer than usual and, while the colonel was greeting Mr. Bingley, she whispered in his ear:

"I am so happy for you, my dear brother."

"Thank you, Georgiana."

He smiled down at her and kept his arm around her shoulders as they mounted the steps to Netherfield.

"We are dining here tonight, my sweet. Miss Bennet and Miss Elizabeth Bennet are joining us. I thought it would be easier for you to make Miss Bennet's acquaintance and renew that of Miss Elizabeth at an intimate dinner before you meet the rest of the Bennet family. They have a very lively household compared to the solitude of Pemberley and I did not want the experience to be overwhelming for you, as it was for me the first time I was a guest at Longbourn!" He gave her a crooked smile, and she was not sure if he was making a jest or trying to make her feel less of a mindless oaf. She could not imagine her mature and faultless brother overcome by a family dinner. He continued, not noticing her confusion, "We will be leaving in the morning for London as we have some pressing business to take care of before the wedding, so it may be a few days before you meet the rest of the Bennets."

She looked up at him and managed a smile. "Thank you for making things easier for me. I hope that Miss Elizabeth Bennet will be as pleased to see me as you anticipate."

"I have no doubts at all on that score, my angel." His smile was encouraging.

"Well, that is all right, then," she answered with more confidence than she felt. "What is Miss Bennet like?"

"She is very beautiful and gentle and kind."

Mr. Bingley finished giving instructions for the luggage and rejoined them as Mr. Darcy raised his voice slightly and said, "…and Bingley is the most amazingly lucky man on earth to have won her heart. I cannot imagine what Miss Bennet sees in him."

Georgiana smiled tentatively, although her brows raised in surprise at her brother's teasing of his friend, while Bingley roared with laughter and cuffed Darcy on the shoulder. "You will pay for that Darcy, my lad; you will pay." He turned to Georgiana and bowed. "However, Miss Darcy, he is quite right about my very good luck. Welcome to Netherfield. I hope you had an uneventful trip."

Georgiana twisted her gloves in her fingers as she answered, "It was quite uneventful, Mr. Bingley. I thank you."

Darcy stepped in and, looking at Mrs. Annesley and his sister in turn, said, "Are you ladies tired? There is time for a rest before we all dress for dinner, if you would like."

Mrs. Annesley smiled genially as she answered, "Miss Darcy can tell you that I have dozed for most of the past three days, but a rest still sounds delightful." She turned to Georgiana. "Do you want to lie down for a bit, or would you prefer a cup of tea?"

"I think a rest. I-I do not always sleep well while travelling."

Bingley added, "I would be happy to order tea upstairs for both of you and you can drink it while you relax a little."

Mrs. Annesley paused for a few seconds, looking expectantly at Georgiana before she turned to Mr. Bingley and said, "That would be lovely, Mr. Bingley, thank you."

Georgiana added a nearly inaudible "Thank you" as she fumbled with the fastenings of her bonnet and cloak and gave them to the waiting footman.

When the housekeeper showed them to their shared sitting-room, Georgiana went straight into her bedroom and threw herself down on her bed with a frown. Why could she not find the words for even the simplest of conversations? One would think she was mentally deficient the way she fumbled through the most routine words. Her brother must find her a terrible embarrassment, in spite of his obvious affection. "How in the world will you survive your presentation?" she asked herself scornfully. "And dinner tonight? The Misses Bennet will think I am the clumsiest dullard on earth." She blinked away a few tears of frustration and realised that she was very tired.

She would be better able to survive tonight's dinner if she could rest. She drew the coverlet up to her shoulders and closed her eyes.

Downstairs, the colonel found Darcy in the library, where he was putting away a book, and said:

"I thought I should share a few things with you, out of Georgiana's hearing."

Darcy raised his right brow in a wary look and sank into one of the leather reading chairs. "Is she having a problem of some sort?"

"Well… she seems to be very unequal in her spirits. She took me up quite sharply a couple of times while we were still at Pemberley, and I have never seen her like this. Mrs. Annesley says that she is very nervous about meeting the Bennets, but even more so about her presentation and coming-out. I am afraid that I was left with my mouth hanging open like a beached fish the first time it happened. Mrs. Annesley suggested that she have Georgiana apologise, but I did not wish to give the episode too much importance. She *will* have a great many demands upon her in the next year."

Darcy tapped his fingers upon the desk and mused for a moment.

"She seemed happy to be here when they arrived, and her letter to Elizabeth was welcoming and affectionate."

"Oh, I do not think she is upset about your marriage; in fact, that seems to be the only thing which pleases her at the moment. Her source of annoyance seems primarily to be me."

Darcy looked at his cousin in puzzlement. "You?"

"Yes. One of your neighbours from Lambton, Jonathan Walker, visited the afternoon I arrived and Georgiana seemed quite defensive about him. I do not believe I have met Walker before; he looks to be about twenty years old or so, much younger than we are."

"Yes, his father is the squire of Lambton. I do not know the son well, but his family is quite respectable."

"He also seems to be quite taken with Georgiana, although he showed appropriate restraint in his behaviour while he was visiting. Later, Mrs. Annesley mentioned to me that Walker had been very attentive during the summer and had, in fact, asked Georgiana to ride with him last month. Mrs. Annesley would not let her go without getting your explicit permission, and I reassured her that she had done right; it would not be proper for Miss Darcy to be riding with a young man when she is not yet out, no matter how well chaperoned. Georgiana apparently accepted Mrs. Annesley's stricture without protest."

Darcy nodded thoughtfully and leaned back in his chair. "Do you think that she has some affection for Walker?"

"I do not know." He raised his hands in defeat. "Possibly she just enjoys the company and the attention of a young man. She is, after all, almost seventeen years old. I simply do not know what she is thinking. I remember when she was a little girl, seeming hardly out of the nursery, and she would stoutly announce that she would play our games, whether it was racing our horses or playing cricket behind the stables."

Darcy laughed. "Yes, and only the sternest order from my father would dissuade her from following us. I had forgotten."

"Then, suddenly, her childish assurance seemed to fail her and the little lion became a terrified rabbit. I swear that sometimes I think she would turn and run if even I spoke abruptly to her." Fitzwilliam shrugged. "At any rate, I just wanted you to be aware of how unsettled her emotions have been of late."

Darcy wearily rubbed his hand over his face. "I do not feel up to this task of being a parent to my sister, Fitzwilliam. I thank God that I do not carry this burden alone."

"I hope Miss Elizabeth Bennet can help us understand what we should do for Georgiana. She, at least, has much experience with younger sisters."

"Indeed she does." Darcy finally grinned at his cousin and repeated, "Indeed she does."

❧

The Bennet sisters arrived a few minutes before dinner, and Darcy introduced the ladies.

"Georgiana, Mrs. Annesley, this is Miss Bennet. Miss Bennet, my sister Miss Darcy and her companion, Mrs. Annesley."

Georgiana was so nervous she almost forgot to curtsey, but remembered in time to make a short bob.

Miss Bennet said, "I am very happy to meet you, Miss Darcy. I have heard many lovely things about you." Her voice had a beautiful, light timbre which delighted the ear, and Georgiana suspected she would have an enchanting singing voice.

Georgiana blushed and stuttered, "Th-thank you. I am pleased to meet you, Miss Bennet."

Darcy continued, "And, of course, you have already met Miss Elizabeth Bennet."

This time Georgiana managed a creditable curtsey and murmured the phrases she had been forming during the drive from Pemberley, although she could not manage to bring her eyes up to Miss Elizabeth. "Of course. I am delighted to meet you again, Miss Elizabeth Bennet. I could not be more pleased, knowing that you are making my brother the happiest of men."

Her words tumbled out in a rush which clearly revealed their practised nature.

Elizabeth gently lifted her chin and smiled warmly at her. "Thank you, my dear. Your brother has made me very happy, too."

She put Georgiana's arm confidingly through hers and gave her fiancé an arch look as she said, "Now I understand all of your reticence regarding your plans this week." She turned back to Georgiana. "Your brother has been keeping secrets from me, Miss Darcy. In addition to concealing your visit, he refuses to reveal what business takes him to London, other than a visit to his tailor. Nonetheless, I am very happy that you will be here to help us with some of the preparations for our wedding."

They went to the drawing-room, and Elizabeth and Georgiana sat on the settee while Miss Bennet and Mrs. Annesley took chairs near them. The gentlemen looked on benignly as they made gentle conversation about the drive from Derbyshire.

The conversation flowed on through the evening until dinner passed quietly away, and Georgiana was relieved to find the Bennet sisters very easy to be with. They were attentive to her without making her feel pressured, quite unlike how she felt in the company of Mr. Bingley's sisters, whose fawning and excessive flattery over her very ordinary accomplishments felt like a heavy weight upon her shoulders.

When the ladies withdrew from the dinner table, Miss Elizabeth asked, "Will you play for us, Miss Darcy? I have heard of your love for music and it gave me much regret that I did not have the chance to hear you play when I was in Derbyshire last summer."

Georgiana blushed and looked down at her hands. "If you wish. I do love music, but I am certainly not a prodigy, just someone who has much time to practise."

Elizabeth's eyes twinkled as she said, "Well, that already puts you far above my ability. I am afraid I did not apply myself when I was young."

Georgiana went to the pianoforte and looked through the music. "Here are some arias that I have played before, although they are not the exact arrangements I have. I could try those, if you like."

Jane and Elizabeth smiled warmly at her and, even on such short acquaintance, Georgiana could see that Jane had a steady, serene temper which would smooth her way in life rather than pushing her headlong against obstacles. She was amused at the difference between Miss Bennet's temperament and Mr. Bingley's. Bingley's temper was equable, but his personality was effervescent and he was always the centre of attention and conversation in a gathering and always the first to laugh. She considered his temper to be much the reverse of her brother's; *his* preferred milieu was quiet conversation rather than the merriment of large, noisy parties. Miss Elizabeth was sweet and gentle, but she had a ready wit which suggested that she would hold her own in more lively entertainments. Georgiana liked both young ladies very much upon this first real meeting, but she hoped that her brother and Miss Elizabeth would suit each other after the excitement of the wedding had worn off. It was always so difficult to know if two people were really a good match for each other.

She had been playing the arias while these thoughts were churning through her mind and the distraction had allowed her to forget that she was playing for strangers. She finished the second piece, and Miss Bennet and Miss Elizabeth applauded, their faces showing genuine pleasure in her music.

"Will you play, Miss Elizabeth Bennet? My brother mentioned in his letter that you play and sing beautifully."

Elizabeth gave an ironic glance at Jane. "I fear that your brother is hearing my playing with the ears of affection, but I am quite willing to play. It is only fair that we take our turns and not force you to be responsible for all the entertainment."

Georgiana settled herself on the settee where she could see the performer and prepared to listen. Elizabeth played several traditional folk songs with simple melodies, but they were rendered very pleasing by the performer's clear, unaffected contralto and Georgiana could easily see how her brother might be charmed. When Miss Elizabeth finished she asked her sister to join her in a duet, which she did, and Elizabeth sang the harmony to her sister's melody. Georgiana had been correct; Miss Bennet had a very sweet natural soprano, and the two sisters' voices blended beautifully in a plaintive song which had been popular the previous spring.

By the time the two ladies had finished their duet, the gentlemen had joined them and Georgiana had lost her apprehension over her meeting with the two Bennet sisters and could see the possibility of real friendship with both women, even if she could not yet be herself in front of them.

The guests left early so the travellers could rest after their long carriage ride, but Miss Bennet invited the Netherfield party to breakfast with them at Longbourn the next morning before they left for London, and her offer was quickly accepted by the gentlemen.

"We will see you in the morning, then, Miss Darcy," Miss Elizabeth said with a squeeze of her hand.

Georgiana blushed, but said in a barely audible voice, "Please call me Georgiana. We will be sisters very soon, after all."

"I would be delighted, Georgiana; and please call me Elizabeth, or Lizzy, if you prefer. That is what my family usually call me."

Jane followed Elizabeth's lead in requesting that Georgiana call her by her first name and then the carriage pulled up to the door and Bingley and the Darcys saw their guests out. As they turned back to the house, Darcy put his arm around his sister and said,

"How did the evening go, my dear?"

"Very well, I think. Both of the Bennets are so thoughtful of my comfort that even I, 'Miss-afraid-of-her-own-shadow,' could not help but relax a little in their company."

Bingley, catching the end of their conversation, made a sound very like a snort and said, "Unlike my sister Caroline, who is so wrapped up in her own importance that she is never aware of the feelings of anyone else."

Georgiana flushed with shame. "I-I did not mean to disparage anyone else with my praise of the Bennets."

Bingley gave a brief grimace, embarrassed that he had made his guest feel awkward and then said quickly, "Oh, I know you would never think that, Miss Darcy. Pray excuse me for my abominable manners, but I received a letter today from my sister which was a masterpiece of insincerity and I am feeling a bit annoyed with her."

Georgiana managed to smile at them both before she excused herself and went upstairs. She lay awake for a while, reviewing the evening in her mind. Her final conclusion was that she had performed adequately; if her conversation was less than effortless in appearance, it was at least correct. She sighed with satisfaction and was able to drift off easily, as she had not done at the inns during the drive from Pemberley.

In the Bennet carriage, Elizabeth and Jane quietly talked about the evening. When they came to Georgiana's performance on the

pianoforte, Elizabeth said, "Georgiana's playing is really excellent technically. You can tell that she spends much time practising, but she did not seem to feel the meaning or emotion of those arias she was playing, and I am curious. Is she just nervous about playing in front of us, or is she too young really to feel the words yet? Or…is she, perhaps, hiding her deep feelings, unwilling to reveal too much of herself to the world? I will be interested to find out. In my experience, shyness is often a matter of too much feeling rather than too little. I think, at least, we were able to help her relax a little and enjoy herself this evening."

"She is a dear girl, but you may be right; she may be fearful of revealing too much of her soul to strangers. However, we will not be strangers long, and I agree with the assessment you made last summer that she is not at all proud and haughty, just very shy."

The next morning the residents of Netherfield Hall were up early to make sure they were packed and ready to leave for London. They arrived at Longbourn in good time to join the Bennet family at their breakfast, and Georgiana and the colonel were introduced to the rest of the family.

Mr. Bennet was a man of late middle age, with a slightly stooped but wiry frame and a small potbelly. His bald pate was surrounded by a fluffy fringe of grey hair and surmounted by a pair of spectacles. He greeted Georgiana with a bow and a kindly murmur but then faded into the background as the others were introduced. Mrs. Bennet was somewhat younger than her husband and dressed with an excess of ribbons and furbelows. She also possessed a shrill voice which overrode the quieter greetings of the others.

"Miss Darcy! It is so good to meet you at last!" she repeated several times as she curtseyed and pushed her other two daughters forward. "Is it not delightful to meet Miss Darcy, girls? And of course, Colonel Fitzwilliam! You are Mr. Darcy's cousin, are you not?"

The two younger girls agreed with their mother silently and Elizabeth interjected, "And this is my sister Mary and my sister Catherine, whom we call Kitty."

Georgiana curtseyed, but was unable to form the appropriate words of greeting, so she merely smiled while the colonel smoothly handled the matter. The youngest Bennet sister, Catherine, seemed quite unable to speak to the colonel, but her eyes were wide as she met him. Georgiana was amused. How could anyone be overawed by her cousin, who was so lacking in false dignity or arrogance…? Not that she should comment about the self-consciousness of others.

Her attention was diverted by a question from Mrs. Bennet, which she strove to answer sensibly while her thoughts continued to tumble with the myriad of impressions and sounds which surrounded her. She could not help but think to herself, "How could this woman be the mother of Jane and Elizabeth?" The voice alone was a shock, even though her hostess was clearly trying to be all politeness and was most definitely charmed by Colonel Fitzwilliam, particularly when she learnt he was unmarried. Her attitude towards Georgiana's brother was less clear. In fact, she seemed almost uneasy in Darcy's presence, but Georgiana could understand that. Her brother, kind and gentle as he was, possessed a formidable natural reserve, which even his own sister sometimes needed courage to breach.

Mrs. Bennet broke the awkward silence which had fallen during Georgiana's inattention with a flutter of her handkerchief:

"Shall we go into the breakfast-parlour?"

They all followed her, and Georgiana glimpsed a wary look which passed between Elizabeth and Jane, and she thought that she detected a lessening of the tension they had exhibited during the introductions now that the initial ordeal was over.

The breakfast was served upon the sideboard and each diner chose for themselves from among the eggs, kippers, and bacon. Mrs. Bennet invited Georgiana to sit next to her, and so her breakfast was peppered with numerous questions about her life and her accomplishments from her eager hostess. For Georgiana—seeing that Mrs. Bennet was not a lady of flawless refinement—her hostess evoked no awe or fear, and the questions, which were intrusive but friendly, she was able to answer without much difficulty. Mary and Kitty ate their breakfast silently but listened to her answers to their mother's questions with interest. Jane and Elizabeth did not say much, either, but their eyes were alert as they watched their mother, and they attempted to smooth the conversation with occasional comments and illustrations. Colonel Fitzwilliam and Darcy were absorbed in a discussion between Bingley and Mr. Bennet, and so Georgiana did not feel *their* expectations weighing upon her.

Nonetheless, she was relieved when breakfast was over and their hostess followed Elizabeth and Jane up the stairs with a simpered, "I had best make sure the girls have everything they need."

Georgiana smiled and curtseyed and began to move towards the door with the three younger gentlemen and Mr. Bennet. They paused to await the Bennet sisters, and the conversation languished until Mr. Bingley began to discuss hunting with Mr. Bennet and made a tentative engagement to meet at Netherfield again after their return from London. Georgiana watched her brother as he stationed himself at the edge of this conversation, listening but not participating in the discussion, and so she saw when he became aware of Miss Elizabeth descending the stairs.

The two young ladies glided elegantly and silently down the stairs, their mother fidgeting and fluttering behind them as she chivvied them under her breath. Before the group had taken more than two steps down the staircase, Darcy's head had turned, seemingly without his volition, towards Miss Elizabeth, and Georgiana saw a look upon his face which she had never before seen. His calm and dignified mask slipped for a moment and she saw his lips soften into a slight curve, his eyes kindling as he regarded his fiancée. Georgiana glanced surreptitiously at Miss Elizabeth to see her response to his burning look and saw her step falter briefly as her eyes locked with her fiancé's. It could not have been but a second's pause, but Georgiana felt a flush of heat from the almost visible connection between the two pairs of eyes. She dropped her gaze to her gloved hands, feeling that she had intruded upon the privacy of her brother and his bride.

The moment passed, and the Bennets continued their progress down the steps and joined their friends for the final farewells. Georgiana managed to thank Mr. Bennet and turned to his wife in time to catch a look of naked triumph on the older woman's face as she watched the two couples before the door. Mrs. Bennet pasted a complacent smile on her face when she saw Georgiana observing her, and said, "We thank you for joining us, Miss Darcy, and I hope we will see you again very soon."

Georgiana, disconcerted by Mrs. Bennet's sudden change in demeanour, stammered a few words, she hardly knew what, about her pleasure in meeting the Bennets, and turned quickly to follow the others to the carriage.

The ride was just noisy enough to make conversation inconvenient, so she looked out of the window at the countryside as they drove. The placid fields and hamlets soothed her, and she felt the tension in her body from the pressure of meeting so many people at one time disperse. The relaxation of her rigid muscles left her limp but with a mind which was still whirling; she had plenty to think about.

Chapter 3

For how do I hold thee but by thy granting,
And for that riches where is my deserving?

—William Shakespeare, Sonnet 97

With all the sights and sounds of the morning to review the drive went quickly, and it was not long after noon when the carriage pulled up in front of a neat brick house on Gracechurch Street. Georgiana had never been to the commercial areas of London and was pleasantly surprised at the elegance of the street on which the Gardiners lived, even though the house was only a few minutes from Mr. Gardiner's warehouses. They all went in to exchange courtesies with the Gardiners while the Bennet ladies' luggage was unloaded by the footmen, but they did not stay long. When Darcy rose to go, Elizabeth put on a severe expression and chided him:

"So, you are abandoning us to the mercies of seamstresses and milliners while you disappear on your mysterious business?"

He merely replied with dignity, "Do not worry, my dear Miss Elizabeth, your Aunt Gardiner's kind invitation to dine tonight will ensure that I return promptly to your door. I have not the least doubt of my future wife's ability to subdue any rampageous bolts of silk." With a solemn bow he left with Mr. Bingley, who, unlike his friend, was unable to control his mirth, and he burst into laughter as Georgiana and Mrs. Annesley climbed back into the carriage for the ride to Ashbourne House.

When they reached Audley Square and he was helping Georgiana out of the carriage, Darcy said, "I hope that you do not mind missing the first afternoon of shopping with the ladies, Georgiana. I know that the Misses Bennet will be ensconced with the seamstress at their aunt's house for most of the afternoon, but I would like your assistance with something."

Georgiana was surprised. "Of course, Brother, I will do whatever you wish."

"Bingley and I would like to purchase similar wedding gifts for our brides since they are as close as sisters can be and we are marrying on the same day, but we should like a young lady's opinion on our choice."

She smiled up at him, pleased that he thought her opinion had merit. "I would love to, Brother!"

"Excellent. We will stop here just long enough to have a cup of tea and then the colonel may return to his work and Mrs. Annesley may have a well-earned rest from her duties while we are shopping." He smiled at his sister's companion. "After we are finished at the jeweller's, Bingley and I will need to spend some time at our tailors and I need to interview several lady's maids Mrs. Burton has selected as suitable for Mrs. Darcy, so I will send you to Gracechurch Street when we are finished."

She nodded her agreement with this plan and they entered the house. They changed from their travel clothes and met in the drawing-room for their tea and cakes. Mr. Bingley ran upstairs while they were finishing, and the colonel was talking lightly about a party he was attending the next night as they waited for him.

"I am not very interested in the party—the family have a pretty, but exceptionally dull, daughter with whom they are trying to saddle me. However, their cellar is good and the other members of the family are entertaining enough."

In the brief pause which ensued, Georgiana abruptly asked, "So, Cousin, could you please answer a question for me?" The colonel nodded benignly and she continued. "Why did my father make you my guardian along with my brother? I am quite sure it was not that he thought my brother was irresponsible or incapable." She flushed with embarrassment when the words burst out of her mouth like daggers, but she sat up straight and looked her cousin in the eye.

"Georgiana!" Darcy said, his voice shocked.

"No, no Darcy! My little cousin has a legitimate question, even if not gracefully phrased, and deserves an answer." Fitzwilliam turned back to Georgiana, whose face was scarlet. "Of course your father had no concerns over your brother's capability as your guardian, but he probably wanted to lessen the fearful responsibility for the care of a young girl." He glanced at Darcy and his lips twitched irrepressibly. "He also undoubtedly wanted to leaven my cousin's rigid respectability and formidable dignity for fear that his daughter would end up a bluestocking of impeccable rectitude and scholarly habits instead of a lovely young lady ready to take her place in London society."

Georgiana stared at him, not sure whether to be angry or pleased. The colonel's countenance was perfectly bland and unreadable. She looked at her brother to see how he responded to this indictment. Darcy's face was calm, giving away nothing, but his eyes twinkled when he finally answered, "Perhaps my father thought that a ruler should have a jester to lighten the monotony of his days."

Fitzwilliam roared with laughter.

"Well said, Cousin, well said."

"If you will excuse me, I just remembered that my reticule is upstairs." Georgiana stood up and flounced out of the room.

When she returned to the drawing-room, Georgiana had reflected on the conversation and tried to put aside her bad temper. She realised that the colonel's assessment was probably close to the truth. Her father most likely had wanted two guardians for her to complement each other's strengths and weaknesses and her brother and cousin were well matched in that way, as well as being close friends. The two men looked at her warily when she came in the door, and she knew that they were trying to determine if her spate of ill temper had resolved. The colonel bowed to her good-naturedly and left to tend to his own business, and Georgiana was left to be ashamed of her churlish behaviour.

Mr. Bingley was finally ready and they returned to the coach; Darcy directed the coachman to Sheffield and Sons Jewellers in Bond Street. Georgiana had never been into a jeweller's before, and she was dazzled at the number and variety of beautiful pieces in gold and precious stones, her shame over her boorish behaviour quickly forgotten. After a survey of the room, she asked Darcy, "Do you have an idea of what you want, Brother?"

"We were thinking of, perhaps, bracelets." He looked at Bingley for confirmation and received a nod.

Georgiana thought Mr. Bingley looked as overwhelmed as she felt at the number of choices offered them in the shop. The shopkeeper, who had kept a respectful distance while they were conversing, now approached and bowed.

"How may I help you, Mr. Darcy?"

"My friend Mr. Bingley and I are both shopping for wedding gifts for our brides-to-be."

Mr. Sheffield's eyes sparkled, and he said, "Of course, Mr. Darcy, I would be delighted to serve you. Did I hear you say that you are shopping for bracelets?"

"Yes, as I was saying to my sister," he nodded towards Georgiana, "we would like the gifts to match as our brides are sisters and very close."

"Certainly, certainly, sir." The jeweller rubbed his hands together for a moment as he thought. "Come this way, please, sirs and miss, and I will show you what we have. If we do not have exactly what you want we can, of course, manufacture or obtain it for you. When is the wedding, if I may ask?"

Darcy told him and he said, "Yes, we should have plenty of time. Come this way, sirs, miss."

He led them to a small sitting area in the room next to the showroom and seated them then disappeared. In a moment a servant brought them tea, and the jeweller reappeared with a stack of wooden trays lined with velvet.

"I have selected a variety of styles for you to look at, sirs and miss," he bowed to Georgiana and the gentlemen, "so I can better judge what your taste is in this matter."

They all leaned forwards as he passed the trays one at a time so they could each see them. There were many bracelets, most with gemstones, of various weights. Many of them were very beautiful and would grace any ballroom in which they were worn, but Georgiana did not see any which seemed quite right. After looking through all of them, she glanced at her two companions and saw that they were also unsure. She said, "Ummm," and both men looked up.

"P-perhaps we could look at something a little different."

Darcy encouraged her with a smile and said, "What do you have in mind, my dear?"

"Well, I do not yet know the Misses Bennet well, and I know that it is customary to give impressive jewels for wedding gifts, but it seems to me that a wedding gift has a symbolic meaning far beyond other gifts and should be something that the recipients will see and use daily rather than something which will be locked away until a ball."

Darcy stared at her for a moment in surprise, and she blushed self-consciously and began to stammer, "B-but perhaps…"

"Do not be embarrassed, my dear sister, I am quite impressed with your insight. You have put your finger on exactly what was bothering me about these bracelets. They just did not feel right to me as a wedding gift."

She blushed even more and Darcy looked at Bingley for his approval, who said, "I think you are right, Miss Darcy. These are lovely and would make delightful birthday or Christmas gifts, but they don't quite suit my feelings in the matter of wedding gifts."

The jeweller, following the conversation, cleared his throat and said to Georgiana, "You are thinking, Miss Darcy, of a bracelet which could be worn every day?"

"Yes, exactly, sir."

"Aha. Give me another moment, if you please."

He handed the trays to an assistant and bustled back to the showroom. When he returned he held several more trays, which he presented to Georgiana first.

"Pray look at these, Miss Darcy. Are these more what you are wanting?"

The trays held numerous gold bracelets of various weights and designs. Some had a small jewel or gold charm. She looked them over carefully and finally chose a fine serpentine chain which had a delicate cross set with a ruby hanging from the clasp.

"I-I think that this is the one I prefer. What do you think, Brother?"

Darcy took the chain and tilted his head. "I think it is perfect, Georgiana. What do you think, Bingley?"

"I like it very much."

Georgiana boldly added, "I would have the cross set with a sapphire rather than a ruby for Miss Bennet, however. The colour will match her eyes. The ruby would be lovely for Miss Elizabeth."

Bingley nodded and smiled at her. "Yes, you are perfectly right, Miss Darcy." He turned to the jeweller and asked, "Could you obtain another, identical to this except with a sapphire on the cross?"

"Indeed, sir. The chain itself is a popular style and readily available, but the cross makes it distinctive. We can have the cross with the sapphire added in our workshop. There will be no difficulty at all."

While Darcy gave his final instructions on the bracelet for Elizabeth, Bingley asked the jeweller to show him some necklaces, as Miss Bennet would have a birthday less than a month after their wedding. After some deliberation, he chose a diamond collar and asked Georgiana for her opinion. When she approved they finished their transactions and left the shop, leaving Mr. Sheffield beaming behind them.

When they finished shopping, Darcy helped Georgiana into the carriage and asked her, "Do you wish to stop at Ashbourne House before you go to Gracechurch Street?"

Georgiana paused, unsure what to do, and Darcy added, "I believe the Bennet ladies are expecting you, and Mrs. Gardiner informed me that they would be in all afternoon with the seamstresses."

"If you do not mind, let us go to Ashbourne House and I will bring my evening clothes to Gracechurch Street, since we will be dining there."

Darcy smiled his approval and then gave the orders to the coachman.

When Georgiana arrived at the Gardiner residence, she found the ladies in the parlour surrounded by a blizzard of fabric samples, ribbons, and laces. When the maid announced her, Miss Elizabeth jumped up, saying, "Thank heavens you are here, Georgiana! My mind is spinning with all of these choices to make. Let us take a few minutes for a cup of tea before we plunge back into the maelstrom!"

Mrs. Gardiner nodded to the maid and the ladies moved to the drawing-room after the Bennets had set aside the patterns and plucked off the fabric swatches which were clinging to their gowns. When they sat down, Elizabeth turned to Georgiana and said, "My dear aunt wishes to give each of us a new ballgown for a wedding present, so we must select patterns for those as well as for all our other gowns. *Quelle horreur!*" She grinned at her aunt, with a twinkle in her eye.

Georgiana asked, "Have you decided on your wedding gowns?"

"I think I will have a white silk batiste gown with silver embroidery above the hem and on the bodice. I have a bonnet which I like very well and they are going to make another just like it, except white trimmed in silver ribbon, and with a short veil."

Jane added, "I am going to have a white gown with Valencienne lace trim, but I have not yet decided on my bonnet. Since it may be cold that late in October, I am going to have a lace spencer to match the gown, as well."

The conversation continued in a lively manner until they finished their tea then they adjourned again to the parlour, where the modiste had put the patterns and samples in order. The next two hours passed quickly as they looked at designs and material and Georgiana soon found herself making suggestions along with the others. It seemed like only a few minutes until it was time to dress for dinner. Mrs. Gardiner assigned one of the maids to help her dress and she soon returned and joined the others in the drawing-room.

When a footman announced dinner Mr. Gardiner offered Georgiana his arm and she was a little taken aback, but he said, "You are the guest of honour here, Miss Darcy." He smiled his merry smile at her and added, "Also, I believe my nieces have partners they prefer to their old uncle." She looked over at the two couples and said quietly, "And do they not look lovely together?"

"Indeed they do, Miss Darcy."

Mr. Gardiner patted her hand and led her into the dining-room. From her position at his right, Georgiana could observe both couples when she was not engaged in conversation with her dinner partner. Mr. Bingley could not keep his eyes off his beautiful fiancée and thereby neglected his hostess, who was on his other side. Jane showed more restraint in her admiration, but on one occasion when she glanced up Georgiana saw her give Mr. Bingley a long look which caused him to stumble and fall silent in the middle of the tale he was relating. Miss Elizabeth, to whom this story was directed, gave him a brief, amused smile and said, "You were saying, Mr. Bingley?"

Bingley looked blank for a moment as he tried to gather his wits together, but he finally took a deep breath and said, "Yes, well, the rest of the story was not terribly interesting." He quickly added, "Mr. Gardiner, have you had an opportunity to do any hunting this autumn?"

Georgiana felt a great urge to giggle but concentrated on cutting her meat. She knew that she would laugh out loud if her eyes met those of Miss Elizabeth, which she was sure would be dancing in merriment. She did finally glance at her brother, but a slight upturn at the corners of his mouth and a softening of his expression were the only signs that he had noted his friend's discomfiture.

To end the awkward moment, Miss Elizabeth asked Mr. Bingley what they had done in the afternoon.

"Oh, just errands, nothing terribly interesting," Bingley said blandly, his self-control reasserted.

"And you, Mr. Darcy?" she asked her fiancé.

"Oh, errands, as Bingley says."

"And it was necessary for Miss Darcy to accompany you on these errands?"

"I wanted to spend a little time with her as I have not seen much of her since our engagement."

"I see. A mystery, Mr. Darcy and Mr. Bingley? And abetted by my future sister?" she asked, her lips pursed in a delightful pout.

"My dear Miss Elizabeth," Mr. Bingley replied, an ingenuous look in his blue eyes, "gentlemen must sometimes have their secrets." He sketched a small bow towards Georgiana. "And sometimes young ladies are kind enough to indulge them."

Miss Elizabeth laughed and gave up her quizzing, contenting herself with giving an account of their day, making the most of the difficulties of choosing colours and fabrics and discussing concerns about style, while Georgiana sat silently listening and smiling over Miss Elizabeth's exaggerated saga. Finally, Elizabeth said, "So, Mr. Darcy, have we now given you more information than you ever thought possible about ladies' dress?"

"Not at all, I am finding it a fascinating glimpse into an arcane branch of knowledge. I had not realised all the profound subtleties of the subject." He smiled at her impudent grin and continued with his meal.

The ladies spoke of general topics when they withdrew from the table, and the gentlemen soon joined them in the drawing-room. Elizabeth sat next to Mr. Darcy and, while the others were involved in conversation, they discussed their plans for their honeymoon.

"I suggest that we spend a few days at the seaside before we return to London after the wedding, if that is agreeable to you," Darcy said. "I have a friend who has a house not far from Eastbourne. It looks over a private beach and has a delightful view of the sea. If we are lucky, the weather will continue pleasant. When we return we could then enjoy some of the amusements of town before travelling to Pemberley for the winter. There will not be many people in town during the hunting season, so it will be rather quiet, but we should still be able to find a play or a concert." There was a rueful note in his voice as he added, "I would prefer to give you a more elegant honeymoon in Paris or on the Riviera, but the war makes that plan a little too adventurous, I fear."

Elizabeth readily agreed with his suggestions.

"The seaside and London will be delightful. I confess that wondering whether an army would come marching through town might put a serious check upon my enjoyment of a trip to the Continent," she said with a twinkle in her eye but then added soberly, "Hopefully, it will not be many more years before that situation changes."

"The newspapers suggest that the Coalition armies have Napoleon on the run, but so they have said many times before. Perhaps they will be correct one of these days."

"We can only hope." Elizabeth smiled at him and added, "Will Georgiana return to Pemberley after the wedding?"

"No, she is going to visit our aunt and uncle, Lord and Lady Whitwell, for a few days. Their townhouse is only a few streets away from Ashbourne House, so she will actually be quite near. My aunt will be sponsoring Georgiana for her presentation and will be taking her in hand during the preparations. We may want to include Georgiana in some of our evenings out. The more experience she gains in society, the better."

He looked over at his sister, who was across the room talking to Jane by the fireplace, and his expression softened. Elizabeth's eyes followed his gaze. Georgiana's light brown hair glowed golden in the firelight and her eyes looked as green and limpid as water. They crinkled at the outer corners when she smiled, as she did now at something Jane was saying.

"Georgiana is such a sweet, affectionate girl! I am very much looking forwards to truly getting to know her before we are caught up in her coming-out," Elizabeth whispered then added after a quick glance at the group around the fireplace, "I hope that we can help her overcome her self-consciousness before that occurs."

Darcy nodded, his brow slightly furrowed, and Elizabeth quietly put her hand on his arm. They had talked a great deal about Georgiana during the long walks they had taken daily in the countryside around Longbourn after their engagement. Darcy had delayed Georgiana's debut in society because of her extreme shyness (as well as because of his own romantic preoccupations of the past year). Her lack of confidence made it likely that the ritual appearances of her presentation at court and coming-out Season would be a miserable trial for her and would be an impediment to her ability to attract an appropriate husband. Her guardians certainly did not want her to marry someone who was only interested in her fortune, but it would be very difficult for a stranger to break through her diffidence and find out what she was truly like. Her sheltered and parentless existence had probably been a rather lonely one, Elizabeth reflected to herself—quite unlike the tumult of the Bennet household.

The incident with Mr. Wickham more than a year and a half earlier had further eroded her confidence. Elizabeth had hopes that she could help her new sister emerge from her shell and become more comfortable in society but was unsure how she would accomplish this.

After a glance to make sure that the others had not noted their sudden quietness, Darcy cleared his throat and continued with his previous thought:

"We must have a ball at Pemberley after we arrive in the country so that our neighbours may meet you. We will follow it with one in the servants' hall so that all of our dependents may also celebrate our marriage. Perhaps we could have both balls around Christmas when your family will be visiting."

Elizabeth gave him a sceptical smile, and he responded to her unspoken comment: "Yes, I know what that look means, Miss Elizabeth. I have no greater love for balls now than I did a twelve-month ago, but I will do my duty for my lovely bride, no matter how difficult it may be. And, I must confess, performing my social duties will be much more pleasant with her at my side." He smiled down at her. "What say you to these plans?"

She returned his smile and answered, "I say that your proposals sound wonderful, so let us do as you suggest. Truthfully, the location of our honeymoon is not nearly as important to me as the company. Shall we join the others at the hearth?"

Georgiana had been surreptitiously observing her brother and Miss Elizabeth and she saw them both glance at her. She knew that they must have been talking about her, and she reddened as she tried to concentrate on what Miss Bennet was saying to her. She hoped that she had not merited their discussion by committing any egregious errors.

At the conclusion of the evening, as the others were talking over a plan to attend a play the following night, Elizabeth asked Georgiana, "Georgiana, my dear, you will join us for our shopping tomorrow, will you not?"

Georgiana glanced at her brother for approval.

"Of course you may go, dearest," he responded with an encouraging smile. "I will send you over in the carriage in the morning."

Elizabeth gently urged her, "Do come, Georgiana. We would love to have you with us."

Georgiana nodded her silent assent, and the ladies all agreed upon a time. Before they left, Darcy added, rather formally, "I hope that you will all join us at Ashbourne House in the evening for a light dinner before we attend the theatre."

They all agreed to this proposal, and the two Darcys and Bingley said their farewells.

Georgiana spent more than her usual time over her diary that night, trying to distil all the events of the day into a few lines.

29 September: Today has been a whirl of activity: meeting the Bennet family at breakfast, shopping with my brother and Mr. Bingley for wedding gifts for their brides and with the Misses Bennet for their trousseaux, meeting the

Gardiners again. The moment which stands out the most in my mind, however, is the look which passed between my brother and his fiancée when they thought no one was aware. It is very clear that my dear, reticent brother has a deep passion for his wife-to-be, and she for him. I trust that someday I will find a gentleman who gazes at me in that manner and who induces the same fire in my veins as seems to flow in my brother's.

The four ladies spent the next day at the seamstress's and shopping for shoes and bonnets and other feminine details. When they arrived back at Cheapside, Mrs. Gardiner urged her nieces to dress quickly for dinner, saying, "We are going to Audley Square a little early and our shopping took longer than I anticipated, so hurry and change girls. We will need to return Georgiana home in time to dress for dinner."

Surprised, Elizabeth and Jane willingly hurried with their toilettes and they all arrived at Ashbourne House at four o'clock. The butler, an elderly, grey-haired man of great dignity, admitted them with a deep bow and announced them as he preceded them into the drawing-room. Georgiana could see with amusement that Burton was burning with curiosity about the Misses Bennet, although she was sure the ladies would not notice his veiled glances. After greeting the others, Georgiana hurried upstairs to change. Her brother had asked her that morning to join him and Miss Elizabeth in the library when she was dressed; he was going to show his bride the Darcy jewels.

Chapter 4

Let me not to the marriage of true minds
Admit impediments.

—WILLIAM SHAKESPEARE, SONNET 116

WHEN THEY ALL REAPPEARED IN THE DRAWING-ROOM, THEY left Bingley to play host and Georgiana and Elizabeth followed Darcy into the adjoining room. A middle-aged gentleman in a sober suit of clothes was introduced to them as Mr. Bennington of the High Street Bank.

"I had Mr. Bennington bring over the Darcy jewels," Darcy said to Elizabeth. "Some of them have been in the family for generations and are in rather outdated settings. They have no historical significance or other importance except as family possessions and have not been worn in years; it is time that they were given new life. It has been years since Georgiana has seen them, so I thought she might join us."

Elizabeth smiled at her. "Of course."

Mr. Bennington removed the pieces one by one from the large

case in which he had brought them and Darcy gave them the history of each piece or set as it appeared.

"My grandfather gave these to my grandmother when our father was born," he said as he picked up a sapphire and diamond demiparure. "They had waited for many years to have a child, and my grandfather was very proud to have a son to carry on the family name."

"They are beautiful," Elizabeth said, touching one of the bracelets.

He picked up a heavy ruby choker.

"This one should be reset. The centre stone was brought back from India by a distant ancestor and the colour will look lovely on you, my dear, once they are in a better setting; this one is far too heavy for your slender neck."

Elizabeth nodded silently, and Georgiana saw her eyes getting larger by the moment as each piece of the jewellery appeared.

"I do not know why I should be surprised that the Darcys have so many wonderful jewels, but I confess that I am quite overcome with astonishment," she whispered to Georgiana, who gave her an amused smile.

Mr. Bennington brought out a splendid necklace and bracelet that particularly caught their eyes. A simple herring-bone chain of heavy gold formed the necklace. The clasp was a snarling dragon intricately carved of pale green imperial jade with delicate green flames flowing from his open mouth. The bracelet was a shorter length of gold fastened with a similar dragon clasp, but in the bracelet the dragon was sleeping, his head curled over his back.

"I remember these!" Georgiana exclaimed. "I remember my father showing me them once, and I was fascinated by the dragons. They somehow seem to have personalities."

"They are lovely," Elizabeth answered, carrying the necklace over to the light, "I have never seen anything like them."

The chains gleamed dully in the light, and the details of the dragons were somewhat obscured by the accretions of years of wear, but they were splendid still.

"One of our great-great uncles was an adventurer generations ago. He left his family and travelled for two years and brought the necklace and bracelet back from China for his wife—as a peace offering I would guess," Darcy said, glancing at them with a lifted brow as he removed the necklace from its case. "It is probably close to one hundred years old and looks as if it should have a good cleaning."

He nestled them back into the velvet case and picked up a beautiful diamond necklace and eardrops in a modern setting.

"These belonged to our mother. I remember her wearing them whenever there was a ball at Pemberley. My father gave them to her as a wedding present." He looked up at Elizabeth and added, "He left them to Georgiana, but I thought you might like to see them."

"They are beautiful. They will be lovely on you, Georgiana!"

Georgiana smiled and ducked her head. She was a little embarrassed that the diamonds would not belong to the mistress of Pemberley, but she was also relieved that Elizabeth seemed not at all put out that the jewels would not be hers.

While Georgiana examined her mother's jewels, Elizabeth turned to pick out another diamond necklace and eardrops and a rather ugly sapphire pendant which would be improved by a lighter, more modern look. When Mr. Bennington left to replace the remaining jewels in the bank's vault, Darcy locked the jewellery they had selected in a wall safe, saying to Elizabeth as he did so, "Tomorrow we shall take these to Sheffield's, and you may pick out the new settings." He turned to his sister. "Would you, perhaps, like to rejoin the others, Georgiana?"

She looked at him in confusion and saw his eyes flick towards the door.

"Oh, y-yes, of course. I would like to talk to Mrs. Gardiner before we sit down to dinner," she said weakly and then fled for the door.

❧

Darcy watched her until the door closed and then shook his head regretfully over his sister's lack of poise. After a moment he shrugged off his dismay, went to the desk, and brought out a small velvet jeweller's case from the drawer and presented it to Elizabeth, his smile a little shy as he handed it to her.

"This is an early wedding gift. Bingley and I picked these out yesterday with Georgiana's assistance. She felt, and I believe rightly, that a simple expression of affection would be more fitting than jewels and that it would be preferable to have something you could wear every day, not just at a ball."

"Your sister is a very perceptive young woman," Elizabeth said as she opened the case and smiled. Inside was the narrow serpentine chain of gold with its tiny cross. On each side of the clasp, on the inside, were engraved the initials EB and FD; when the bracelet was fastened their initials would be joined. He removed it from the case and started to clasp it around her right wrist but paused.

"Once I fasten this chain you cannot escape," he said gravely.

She blushed and answered quietly, "I'll try not to struggle too much."

He fastened it around her wrist and, his eyes locked on hers, raised her palm to his lips. Elizabeth impulsively threw her arms around him and kissed him. He drew her close for another, more lingering kiss then they reluctantly separated and rejoined the others in the drawing-room, Elizabeth hoping her flushed complexion was not too apparent.

A few minutes later, Elizabeth commented to the Gardiners and Georgiana, "I can see that a conspiracy has taken place in this house over the matter of these bracelets, but... I think Jane and I will probably try to forgive you."

She put her arm around Georgiana and whispered in her ear, "Thank you, my dear sister. The bracelet is perfect."

Georgiana searched her face. "Do you truly like it, Elizabeth?"

"Indeed I do. You could *not* have chosen better."

Georgiana let her breath out in a sigh of relief and smiled at Elizabeth. The more she knew about her sister-in-law, the happier she was. Her brother had chosen well.

After dinner they gathered their wraps and left for the theatre, an imposing building fronted with an arcade. The inside had been lavishly painted and decorated but was discoloured from the smoke of the many candles lighting the chandeliers, leaving to the elegantly dressed society gentlemen and ladies the task of providing colour and variety to the interior.

Georgiana was looking down as they made their way to the Darcy box, trying not to step on the hem of her companions' gowns, and it took her a moment to realise that the conversation in the foyer had dropped in volume to an intense murmur. She looked around her and noted that her brother was greeted with a slight nod by a few people, but most of those who took notice of their entrance merely stared and then turned to their neighbours to whisper excitedly in their ears.

She was uncomfortable under their blatant scrutiny, and she could feel the colour creep up into her face. She hurried after her brother, wondering if she had behaved improperly in some way and was relieved when they reached the box. She glanced at Elizabeth and saw that she was very stiff; her brother had a thunderous look on his face. Miss Elizabeth leaned over and said something to him and he forced his expression into more pleasant lines, but Georgiana was sure that he did not notice what was on the stage for the first fifteen minutes. She slumped in her seat and tried to attend to the singing, but the strange behaviour of the crowds and her brother's anger perplexed her.

The first half of the entertainment was a series of arias sung by Signora Catalani, the undisputed prima donna of London opera, and the audience was entranced until the last note died. Georgiana gradually forgot the odd behaviour of the theatregoers in the foyer as she was swept up into the music. When the interval came, Elizabeth needed to touch her arm gently to bring her back to earth so they could make their way to the refreshment room of the theatre.

The second half was to be a series of tableaux from the recent productions of the company, and the singer would be joined by her fellow cast members to present them. While they were discussing the programme, Georgiana glanced up and saw her cousin, Colonel Fitzwilliam, across the room; his curly, russet-brown hair was unmistakeable in the candlelight. She craned her neck and saw her aunt and uncle with him, their backs to the rest of the room.

"Brother, there are our aunt and uncle," she exclaimed to

Darcy. "We should say hello before the second part of the programme begins."

She started to turn away, but her brother surreptitiously caught her arm. She looked back at him in surprise.

"Please do not go, Georgiana," he said very quietly.

"Why not, Fitzwilliam?" she asked, confused, her voice lowered to match his.

She suddenly became aware of the silence of the crowd around her and flushed a brilliant red. It seemed as if everyone in the room was staring at her, and she wanted to sink into the floor in mortification. Elizabeth affectionately put her arm around Georgiana's shoulder and whispered in her ear:

"Do not be embarrassed, my dear; your aunt and uncle are upset with your brother because he is marrying me; it would simply be better not to bring attention to the relationship at the moment. Everything will be fine in time, so do not be concerned."

Georgiana nodded silently, her head hanging.

"I cannot believe that anyone could object to you, Elizabeth," she whispered. "Fitzwilliam should have told me."

"Thank you, my dear," Elizabeth returned with a smile. "You are right; you should have been told. You *could* do one thing to help me through this, if you would."

Georgiana's head came up at that.

"I will do anything that I can," she whispered fiercely.

"Then pretend that none of this has happened, and we will return to our seats with our heads held high and ignore the vulgar gossips."

Georgiana managed the ghost of a smile, put her shoulders back with a visible effort, and twined her arm through Elizabeth's. As they turned towards the entrance to their box, Lord Whitwell's group reached the doors to the auditorium. Just before they disappeared through the door, Colonel Fitzwilliam glanced at Darcy and his right eyelid drooped in a slow wink. The corner of Darcy's mouth twitched and he acknowledged his cousin with a minuscule nod, but Georgiana's smile was rigidly fixed. They returned to their seats and resolutely watched the remainder of the programme, but the joy had gone out of the evening for Georgiana and, she suspected, for Elizabeth as well. Elizabeth was sitting between Georgiana and her brother, so Georgiana could overhear some of her brother's discussion as he bent towards his fiancée:

"...his mother, my aunt, was very upset by Lady Catherine's letter about our... expects that you will be a fishmonger's daughter or some such ridiculous notion... Fitzwilliam says that he defended you as much as he could without, as he put it, 'imperilling his financially dependent status'... St. George has remained above the fray... in Scotland... gambling debts... calmed down somewhat."

Elizabeth's answer was clearer to Georgiana: "I am sorry that I am causing so much heartache in your family." She paused for a moment and then gave a mischievous smile. "Not sorry enough to refuse to marry you again but still sorry for the trouble you must go through."

"Actually," Darcy returned in a conversational tone, "I am rather enjoying the unusual sensation of being the family black sheep after years of stolid attention to the business of running an estate. Perhaps my taking over this role will be of material assistance to my scapegrace cousin St. George by drawing attention from his misdeeds to my own."

Georgiana barely prevented herself from a very unladylike snort at this commentary on her cousin Lord St. George, but her training prevailed and she turned her attention back to the stage. So, Miss

Elizabeth had refused her brother's hand before finally accepting it! She was astonished, but her speculation over the story of their courtship carried her through the second half of the programme and she was able to ignore the ill-mannered crowd staring at them.

When they arrived at Ashbourne House later that evening, Darcy caught Georgiana before she went upstairs.

"My dear sister, it just occurred to me—after a reminder by Miss Elizabeth, I confess—that you should have a new gown for the wedding also. I have been remiss in not having you order one while we are here."

"Dear brother," she said with affection, "I am not in the wedding party, but am just a guest. I have plenty of lovely gowns."

"Maybe, but I would still like to mark the occasion with a new gown for you, too." He paused for a moment, thinking. "Perhaps we should leave you and Mrs. Annesley here for a day or two. You could have the gown fitted and then return to Hertfordshire not long after us."

"Well, I guess that would be acceptable, although I hate to make the carriage come back for me."

He put his arm around her shoulder and kissed her on the top of her head.

"You leave that to me, little one."

That night she wrote in her diary,

1 October: Went to an evening of opera music—Signora Catalani is stupendous, but the audience seemed more interested in gaping at my brother and his fiancée—the jealous cats! My aunt and uncle Whitwell were there with the colonel, but they did not acknowledge our presence. The colonel winked at my brother—he seemed amused

*at the awkward situation—but I think he could have
done more than he has to help my brother, who is his best
friend as well as his cousin. I have no doubt that if my
aunt and uncle were to embrace Elizabeth into the family
there would be no difficulties with the rest of society. I am
going to ask my brother if I may stay at Ashbourne House
while they are gone on their honeymoon. I do not wish
to stay with my aunt and uncle while they are snubbing
my brother.*

The next day the lovers returned to Hertfordshire, leaving
Georgiana and Mrs. Annesley behind. Deep down, Georgiana felt
relieved to be alone with her companion again; the Bennet sisters
were lovely, but trying to make a good impression and converse
like an adult was causing her great strain. She hoped that someday
she would be able to join in a conversation easily and naturally
without needing to plan each comment like a general deploying
his army. The small delay before returning to Netherfield would be
salutary and allow her to overcome the headache which had been
nagging her since she witnessed the ill-mannered snubbing of her
brother and his fiancée at the opera.

With Mrs. Annesley's assistance, she chose the pattern and fabric
for her dress, but she was not really enthused about it. Her gowns all
had a high neck on the bodice, which was suitable for a girl not yet
out, but her upcoming presentation and Season would mark a time
when she could have more mature styles which flattered her figure,
and she felt that she was wasting her time on a dress which she
would only wear a few times. An idea occurred to her: perhaps she
could have some of her favourite gowns remade with lower bodices

before she came out. With this cheerful thought, she finished her dress order and they were back in Hertfordshire within three days.

The next fortnight passed quickly, punctuated by only one minor incident. A week or so before the wedding, the Netherfield residents were dining with the Bennets and the invitation had included Mr. and Mrs. Collins. Mr. Collins was Mr. Bennet's cousin, and his wife was Elizabeth's childhood friend Charlotte; they were visiting his in-laws at Lucas Lodge. The Collinses had been brought together with the Netherfield inhabitants several times since their return from London, and Georgiana had quickly realised that Mr. Collins was a fool. How could her aunt Lady Catherine de Bourgh tolerate his grovelling and scraping? Georgiana had always been terrified of her aunt, and her brother tried to spare her sensibilities by not taking her to Rosings Park when he made his yearly duty visit, but she had always thought her aunt an astute and clever woman (too astute and observant of the failings of others!). Her aunt's support of Mr. Collins, however, did not speak well of her judgement.

On this evening, while they were sitting in the drawing-room before dinner was announced, Mr. Collins casually said to Elizabeth and Jane, "I congratulate both of you again, my young cousins, on your excellent good fortune in your marriages. It will be most gratifying to me to do my part in assuring your future happiness."

Jane and Elizabeth glanced at each other, their faces unrevealing but their eyes wide. Elizabeth found her voice and said faintly, "I beg your pardon, Mr. Collins?"

"I said I shall be delighted to perform the marriage rites for my two dear cousins."

Georgiana knew that Elizabeth and Jane had arranged to have the service performed by Mr. Martin, who had been the vicar at

Longbourn Church for most of their lives, but the two young ladies were so taken aback by Mr. Collins's insistence that they seemed unable to marshal a protest. Fortunately, his wife saw her friends' dilemma and quickly stepped into the breach, saying in a shocked tone of voice, "My dear husband, do you really think that you should perform the service? Lady Catherine will be most upset if she learns that you have attended the wedding, let alone performed the service."

Mr. Collins's resistance was quickly overcome by this reminder of his noble patroness's fury over Darcy's marriage, and he immediately gave way.

"Well... perhaps you are right, my dear Mrs. Collins. I would not wish to offend my noble patroness. Yes, on further consideration I believe that it would be unwise to officiate at the service."

With a straight face, Elizabeth said earnestly, "Oh, Mr. Collins! You must certainly do nothing to upset Lady Catherine! Not after the kindness and condescension she has shown you and Mrs. Collins!"

"My dear cousin Elizabeth, you are so thoughtful of the well-being of others!"

Elizabeth gave him a humble smile and moved on to another topic of conversation. Georgiana described the scene in her diary that night, and concluded,

> ...As this small crisis passed before me, I was amused by Mrs. Collins's clever handling of her self-important husband. I cannot comprehend what my aunt sees in the gentleman. I should go mad being the object of his attention day after day.

The day before the wedding, Darcy and Bingley went off with Mr. Bennet to his solicitor to perform the last piece of business before the wedding itself: the signing of the marriage articles. Georgiana stayed at Longbourn with the ladies while they were gone. She was curious how much her brother was settling on Elizabeth but did not dare to ask him such a mercenary question. She had no doubt that he would be generous. The day was a sore trial as the elder Bennet sisters tried to keep their mother from gloating aloud over her daughters' imminent wealth, particularly in front of Georgiana. Mrs. Bennet was, of course, not present at the actual signing of the articles, but her avid interest was evident all afternoon until the exigencies of the wedding arrangements finally distracted her and the others could breathe a mutual sigh of relief at the respite.

The Netherfield party dined at Longbourn that evening but departed early, and Georgiana retired to her room as soon as they reached Netherfield. Her diary entry was brief:

> *18 October: The wedding preparations are all complete, and tomorrow is the day of reckoning! My cousin Fitzwilliam will arrive from London in the morning, but his parents are apparently not coming. I am going to bed now, but I do not anticipate sleeping much. There are too many changes and too many aggravations occurring tomorrow to allow me a restful sleep. Changes with my brother's marriage, and aggravation with my aunt and uncle for not accepting Elizabeth.*

The wedding day, when at last it arrived, went off beautifully. The day dawned cool and crisp, with a cloudless, pale blue autumn sky. Darcy and Bingley had stayed up after Georgiana had retired the night before, and she did not hear them come up until a quarter past twelve. At breakfast all were absorbed in their own thoughts until ten o'clock arrived and it was time to dress. The very last act of the gentlemen's valets was to offer their masters a small glass of wine with which to congratulate each other, and afterwards the gentlemen solemnly shook hands before they all climbed into the carriage for the drive to the church.

Eleven o'clock finally arrived, and the couples were married in the tiny Longbourn church with their families and a few close friends in attendance. Georgiana watched her brother standing before the altar, awaiting his bride, with a pang of painfully intense happiness. His face had its usual solemnity, but his eyes seemed to her to be glowing. She hoped that his marriage would be as fulfilling as he deserved. If only she could find a man of such heart and intelligence (if perhaps of somewhat less formidable composure!) as her brother. She also watched Mr. Bingley as he awaited his bride with a frank grin, obviously delighting in his good fortune. Perhaps she might find someone with Mr. Bingley's ease combined with her brother's intellectual attainments.

Colonel Fitzwilliam was sitting with Georgiana and her companion during the service, and he patted his cousin's hand as she dabbed her eyes with her handkerchief during her brother's vows. Georgiana was the first to embrace her brother and sister at Longbourn after the wedding, shedding a few more tears.

"This is supposed to be a happy occasion, little cousin," the colonel said in her ear.

"I *am* happy," Georgiana said with unconscious dignity. "I

apologise if my tears on the day of my only brother's marriage are an embarrassment to you, Colonel Fitzwilliam."

"I am sorry, Georgiana," he said with chagrin, although his eyes were still twinkling mischievously. "I should not tease you."

"Indeed you should not," she returned with asperity.

When the newlyweds had greeted all of their guests at the wedding breakfast, Colonel Fitzwilliam gave Darcy a brief letter from his father:

> *My dear Nephew and Niece,—*
>
> *I congratulate you upon your marriage and wish you great joy. I regret that we were not able to attend the ceremony, but hope that we may wait upon you this winter at Pemberley to give our compliments in person.—With our best wishes,*
>
> *Lord and Lady Whitwell*

"His lordship dared not risk the fury of Lady Catherine, it seems," the colonel commented to Darcy and Elizabeth. "Sad to have a father who is a coward," he added, shaking his head in mock sorrow.

"Would you face Lady Catherine's wrath?" Darcy queried with an ironic lift of his brows.

"I am a soldier, not an imbecile!" Fitzwilliam returned with a horror-stricken expression.

Darcy and Elizabeth laughed lightly, but Georgiana felt again a twinge of annoyance that some of their closest relatives would still not readily accept her brother's bride. She silently entwined an arm in Elizabeth's and her sister patted Georgiana's hand reassuringly.

Soon after the wedding breakfast, the two couples changed into their travel clothes and departed to the cheers of the guests. The Bingleys were to take a honeymoon in Cornwall, where he had rented a cottage. The Darcys left for their short seaside honeymoon, and Georgiana and Mrs. Annesley departed Netherfield for Ashbourne House soon after.

...for the mutual society, help, and comfort,
that the one ought to have of the other,
both in prosperity and adversity.

—BOOK OF COMMON PRAYER, "SOLEMNIZATION OF MARRIAGE"

D URING THE WEEK THAT HER BROTHER AND HIS WIFE WERE
gone, Georgiana was again prey to her nervous fears that
Elizabeth would be disappointed in her and that she would be
a dismal failure during her coming-out Season. The day of their
expected return found her chewing her lip pensively and staring out
of the drawing-room window into the private little walled garden
of Ashbourne House as she mulled over these thoughts during
the long hours she awaited their return from the south coast. Her
morbid imaginings were interrupted by Mrs. Annesley's entrance
and her soft, "You must not chew your lip, my dear."

She flushed and said, "I know, Mrs. Annesley. It is very
childish, but my nerves simply demand that I take out my fears in
some fashion!"

"What are you worried about, Miss Darcy?"

"Nothing, everything… I do not really know. I am just being foolish, I suppose," she said vaguely and steered the conversation in another direction. She tried the rest of the afternoon to appear her usual self, but it took all her effort.

Mr. and Mrs. Darcy returned from their honeymoon in a happy bustle which Georgiana thought, as she watched them from the stairs, covered an intense awareness of each other. It must be very difficult, she suddenly realised, to have the entire household be aware of your most intimate relations. She had never thought about it before; she was accustomed to having servants within hearing at all times, silently performing their duties. The housemaids could be ghosts for all the residents of the house would know, creeping into the bedrooms when the family was at breakfast lest they disturb the tranquillity of their masters and mistresses while they cleaned the grates and made the beds.

Her musings were disturbed when her brother looked up from giving instructions to the footmen and saw her balanced irresolutely on the bottom step.

"Georgiana! I wondered where you were! Are you not going to say hello?"

She blushed and smiled self-consciously as Elizabeth came over and embraced her before leading her over to kiss her brother.

"How is my girl?" He grinned at her like a schoolboy.

Elizabeth smiled and chided him, "The honeymoon is not even over and I have already been supplanted."

Georgiana, startled, glanced at her sister in alarm but then realised that she was teasing. Elizabeth saw her reaction and said,

"Do not mind me, dear Georgiana. I am a hopeless tease. What have you been doing, my dear?" she asked as they moved to the drawing-room.

"Oh, playing, reading, studying my French. The usual... Oh! I did visit my friend Catherine Freemont twice this week. Her father had some work to do before Parliament sits, so they returned early from the country."

Darcy added to Elizabeth, "Miss Freemont's father is a judge in the King's Court. Their town house is only a few steps away from here."

Elizabeth said, "It sounds from your voice as if you found most of your time dull. I am glad that you had a friend to visit. We must find more interesting activities now that we are back. I know that the little season is over, but there must be something going on in London."

"Mrs. Annesley told me that *Romeo and Juliet* will open tomorrow at Covent Garden." She paused, her brow furrowed. "I do not know how good the company will be. Would they not be playing during the main season if they were among the better performers?"

"Perhaps, but if that is the case we can enjoy it as a comedy instead of a tragedy," Elizabeth said with a grin, which Georgiana returned hesitantly.

"I am not altogether sure a romantic tragedy sets the proper tone for a new marriage anyway," Darcy said with a smile at his wife, "but I do enjoy Shakespeare."

Elizabeth agreed but commented, "I have never seen *Romeo and Juliet* on the stage, but I have always thought that the young lovers behaved extremely foolishly. If they had just waited long enough to make sure their messages were received, neither would have died... not that I should be quibbling with lack of proper communication in romantic affairs," she added in sudden embarrassment. Darcy chuckled over her blush while Georgiana stared at them in confusion.

Elizabeth reassured her, "Never mind, my dear. I am teasing again, except this time I am teasing myself."

A footman arrived with tea, and Mrs. Annesley joined them and welcomed the new couple home. They later had a quiet family dinner at home, and all retired early.

The next morning Georgiana came down to breakfast in a more resilient mood than that of the day before. She saw Burton's back as he disappeared down the stairs to the kitchen with the coffeepot in his hand, so she quietly opened the door to the breakfast-parlour herself. Her brother and sister were standing in front of the window which faced onto the garden, their bodies nearly touching. Before she could make her presence known, her brother leaned down and kissed his wife with a tenderness which made her heart ache.

With a deftness which surprised even her, she reversed her course and backed out of the room, closing the door as silently as she could. She wanted to run upstairs and hide her mortification at invading such a moment, but instead she went back to the staircase, walked part way up, and waited while the redness in her face subsided and her breathing calmed. When she caught the first glimpse of Burton returning with fresh coffee, she walked down the stairs again and crossed the hall. She noticed that Burton's usual catlike tread was absent and his heels clicked firmly on the tile floor; she smiled to herself. In the future, she too would make sure that her entries gave her brother and sister due warning of her approach.

"Good morning, Burton."

"Good morning, Miss Darcy. It is a lovely day outside."

"Indeed it is."

The butler opened the door and bowed her in to the breakfast-parlour where she found Mr. and Mrs. Darcy calmly eating their eggs and bacon.

Elizabeth looked up, a suspicious twinkle in her eye and blandly asked, "And how are you this morning, Georgiana?"

"I am fine, thank you." She blushed slightly again and looked down at her lap as Burton unfolded her serviette and offered it to her.

"Would you like coffee, Miss Darcy?"

"Please."

Darcy cleared his throat and said, "Georgiana, we were just discussing our plans for the day."

She raised her brows in a questioning look and said, "Yes?"

"We thought we would take a walk. Elizabeth has not really seen the neighbourhood or the park. Would you like to join us?"

She glanced from one to the other and decided that they were not just being polite in their invitation.

"I would love a walk. We may not have many more nice days before winter."

Elizabeth smiled at her. "Very true, my dear."

Georgiana ventured, "W-would you mind if I asked my friend Catherine to come with us?"

Her brother answered without hesitation, "Of course, Georgiana. If you will write a note to her I will send one of the footmen to Freemont House."

"I will do that, thank you... both of you."

She finished her breakfast, went upstairs to write the note to her friend, and received an acceptance by return messenger.

When they were ready to leave for their walk, the footman brought their coats. Darcy's was the same overcoat he had worn the day before, but, instead of Elizabeth's cloak, the footman brought her a beautiful, dark russet pelisse of fine cashmere trimmed with fur.

"I must not let my wife get too cold when she is walking," Darcy said as the footman opened the door for them. "I know, after all, that she is an avid walker."

"It is just beautiful. Thank you, my dear!" she said while raising her brows and glaring at him behind the footman's back for this sly reference to one of their early encounters.

She saw Georgiana's surprise at her ironic expression and as they left the house told the story of Jane's illness which had confined her to Netherfield for several days, and of Elizabeth's hike across the fields to visit her when her father's carriage was not available to take her.

"…and I arrived at Netherfield with my boots and petticoat covered with mud from the previous day's rain. The only circumstance which allayed my embarrassment was that the hem of my gown was still clean and I could cover at least some of the mud with it. I really thought that your brother would die of shock. I declare I was quite concerned for some thirty minutes that we would need to call the doctor for him."

Georgiana blinked and stared at the two of them. She was astonished to hear her stately brother made the subject of such pleasantries and half expected him to rise up in wrath. Instead, he gave a small smile to his wife and said, "Quite right. I have still not completely recovered from the experience."

They laughed, and Georgiana suddenly felt an outsider as their eyes locked for a long moment.

They were all distracted by the need to cross the street, and Georgiana had time to recover her poise. When they had negotiated the crossing, they turned and looked back the way they had come. The Darcy residence was a large stone edifice on a corner of Audley Square, the entrance facing the small, quiet, cobblestoned square and with a walled garden on the side facing noisier South Audley Street. The garden wall was high enough to muffle slightly the sounds of the traffic passing by outside and created an intimate little Eden into which the drawing-room and dining-parlour faced.

As they strolled around the neighbourhood, they showed Elizabeth many large homes along the streets and squares. The houses were all made of brick or stone, with three or more storeys and tiny flowerbeds along the slate-paved paths to the front doors. They were surrounded by low wrought iron fences, which enclosed the beds and the areas leading down into the kitchens. Similar fences surrounded the square itself: a small park with gravelled paths and benches for those who wished to sit and enjoy the sun or for nursemaids who would bring their charges out to play on the lawn.

After finishing a circuit of the area, they detoured north onto Hill Street and came to a brick house only a moment's walk from Ashbourne House. A small sign on the gate said, obscurely, "Mynydd Bwthyn." Elizabeth raised her brows and the Darcys both grinned at her. Darcy explained:

"Miss Freemont's mother is Welsh and her father amuses himself by using the Welsh language occasionally; usually for the mystification of his audience. Their friends and neighbours usually call this 'Freemont House.'"

"I cannot imagine why."

Georgiana tripped lightly up the stairs to the door, but it was opened by a footman before she could reach it, and her friend appeared immediately. Georgiana brought her down the stairs, took a deep breath, and said, "Elizabeth, this is my friend Miss Catherine Freemont. Catherine, my new sister-in-law, Mrs. Darcy."

The ladies curtseyed and Miss Freemont smiled gracefully and responded, "How do you do? I am very happy to meet you. Miss Darcy has been eloquent in your praise."

Catherine Freemont was a petite young woman with dark hair and bright blue eyes, and she had a low-pitched, musical voice with a very slight Welsh accent. Although not a classic beauty, her appearance was very striking and her manner was pleasant and elegant. Elizabeth returned her smile and answered, "It is my pleasure to meet one of Georgiana's friends. Have you known each other long?"

Georgiana answered, "For years. Catherine has two brothers much older than she, and we were the only little girls in the neighbourhood." She looked at her friend with a mischievous smile. "It is fortunate that we liked each other."

Catherine laughed. "Yes, it would have been very bad if we had loathed each other."

The two pairs of walkers turned and strolled on towards Hyde Park, the girls walking on ahead with arms linked. Elizabeth, when they were out of the girls' hearing, asked Darcy where Miss Freemont was from.

"The Freemonts have been neighbours of ours in London for generations, but they have a small country estate in Shropshire. Her father is the younger son of his family, hence the judgeship. Because of his place on the King's Court, they spend a great deal of time in London."

They found a path which wound under a grove of plane trees and turned onto it. There were very few riders out that day on

Rotten Row, and the chill in the air had discouraged the less hardy walkers on the footpaths. They wandered slowly along a neat gravelled path, and Darcy found a small bench about halfway down the length of it where he and Elizabeth could sit while the two girls walked to the end. The remaining autumn leaves, teased by the light gusts of a breeze freed from the enclosing buildings of the city, swirled around them like a golden and crimson blizzard. Elizabeth watched the dancing leaves, her hand through her husband's arm, and felt something rigid inside her relax. All of the tension of the past year melted in the cool autumn air and she was left feeling warm and light. She gave a small, contented sigh and Darcy turned his head towards her and smiled.

"Happy, my love?"

"Blissful—I suddenly feel as if I have been translated onto an entirely new Earth from the one on which I had been living, everything bright and new around me."

As he opened his lips to respond, a pair of urchins suddenly appeared with a ragged mongrel in tow to chase the squirrels around the trees before running off on some mysterious business of their own, but not before giving cheeky grins at the couple sitting, arms entwined, on the bench. Elizabeth laughed as the ungainly dog lolloped after the children.

"Well, perhaps not everything is bright and new!" she said, her thoughts involuntarily straying to the difficulties with various in-laws that disturbed her serenity like the urchins invading the park. She pulled her attention back to her husband. "However, I do feel that I have an entirely new outlook on life and on the people I know or meet. I remember a conversation I had with Jane not so many months ago, wherein I expressed to her my dissatisfaction with the human race and how inconsistent were the characters of so many of the people that I knew. This was after my friend Charlotte became engaged to Mr. Collins, an event which, as you know, shocked me greatly. I had not thought that she would disregard every better feeling merely to obtain a comfortable home."

"This was also, I presume, after Bingley had left Netherfield so suddenly."

She gave him a rueful smile and nodded. "Yes, indeed it was."

"And to what do you attribute your more charitable frame of mind?" he asked.

"I am not sure that I should say," she replied, raising one brow. "It could be detrimental to your character."

"I will try not to let it go to my head."

"Well then, it was finding a man who not only had a character that proved to be invariably honest and good in spite of all of my ungenerous acts and assumptions but also was willing to reassess all that he had believed in and to admit that he had been wrong. How could I do less? Even if you are, as I believe, unique among men, you still give me hope for the future of humanity."

Darcy bowed his head and stared at their linked fingers. After a minute he cleared his throat, glanced at her, and said softly, "You humble me, my dearest Elizabeth. I do not deserve you."

They sat silently, hand in hand, for a few moments. Then she roused herself and said teasingly, "Possibly not, but I am afraid that this ring has chained you to me forever." She added reluctantly, "It is getting a little cool—I suppose that we should walk home soon."

"If you wish—we would probably draw unwanted attention if we sat here until nightfall. And, it looks as if the girls are returning."

Darcy gave her a soft smile as he rose and turned towards home.

Before they reached Freemont House, Catherine invited Georgiana to spend the afternoon with her.

"I must be at home in case of callers, but most of our friends have not yet returned from the country, so we should have plenty of time to talk."

Georgiana turned to her brother. "May I spend the afternoon with Catherine and her mother?"

"Of course. I believe that we will do a little shopping. We have a few things we would like to get before leaving London. Shall we see you later for tea?"

"Yes, I will be home before dark."

Georgiana impulsively kissed her brother and sister before following Catherine into the house.

After a cup of coffee at Ashbourne House to warm them, the Darcys took the carriage to the shopping district and spent the remaining afternoon hours walking through the milling crowds, peering at the displays in shop windows and doing some desultory shopping. They stopped at a bookshop and looked over the new publications. Elizabeth picked up a volume of poetry and showed Darcy it.

"Here is the new poem by Lord Byron. Does Georgiana enjoy poetry?"

"She does. What is the title?"

"It is *The Giaour*," she said hesitantly. "I am not sure of the pronunciation of the title."

"Let us get it. She spent hours over *Childe Harold's Pilgrimage*, although I hope that she did not understand all of the allusions contained in it!"

They purchased the book and turned their steps towards Sheffield's Jewellery shop.

"This should let Georgiana know that we were thinking of her," Elizabeth said. "I want her to know that I care for her."

Darcy squeezed her hand, which rested lightly on his arm, and they entered the shop. Mr. Sheffield waited upon them himself and assured them respectfully that the jewels were ready for their inspection.

"Oh, they are lovely!" Elizabeth exclaimed when she saw them. "I cannot wait to wear them! They are simply works of art, Mr. Sheffield. And the Chinese dragons are truly wonderful now that they are cleaned. Thank you so much for your care."

The proprietor beamed at her.

"I thank you, Mrs. Darcy, for your kind words. I hope that you enjoy wearing them. If you would like, I will have them delivered to you this afternoon."

They agreed, but as they were leaving Elizabeth paused at a case near the door. In it was a single strand of small, perfectly matched seed pearls with a tiny amber cross hanging from it, a seed pearl embedded at the tip of each of the arms. She was entranced.

"Do you think that we could get this for Georgiana for Christmas?" she asked. "It would look wonderful on her."

Darcy had the jeweller remove the necklace from its case and carefully examined it with the jeweller's glass. After much discussion and further examination, he turned to Elizabeth.

"The pearls are lovely—are you sure that you do not want them for yourself?" he asked, smiling.

"Thank you, but I have a few jewels which need to be worn before I think about new ones—although I do love this, and so, I hope, will Georgiana."

"Then she shall have it," he replied.

At Freemont House, Georgiana and Catherine had a cup of tea with Mrs. Freemont and told her about their walk before going upstairs to Catherine's sitting-room. After some minutes, Georgiana interrupted her friend's chatter:

"Catherine?"

"Yes?" Miss Freemont turned away from the glass where she had been trying to replace a curl which had become dislodged during their walk and sighed. "I will just have to have Winthrop fix it if we have any callers." She focussed her attention on her friend. "What is it, Georgiana?"

"What was your first Season like?"

"Did I not write to you about it? I am sure I did."

Georgiana sighed. "Yes, you did, but it seemed so distant at the time. What was it really like?"

"Well, the balls were wonderful. My presentation was not as bad as I expected. Having a hundred girls waiting with me, all in the same state of agitation seemed to somehow… I do not know exactly… *dissipate* the emotion. I was presented late in the Season because my great-aunt, who was my sponsor, could not be here until then. I rather liked doing it later—although I had to worry about it longer—because I had already survived many balls and parties and was more confident that I could manage it."

Georgiana sighed again. Catherine plopped down on the pouffe at her feet, not bothering to lower herself gracefully. Georgiana could not help but laugh at her friend, who had always liked to run and play outdoors like a boy. It was astonishing how beautiful and graceful she could be when she tried. Catherine laughed with her then took her hand and said seriously, "What is really bothering you, Georgiana? Are you still petrified at the thought of your first

Season? Let me assure you that it is not nearly as gruesome as you fear. It was actually quite fun."

"I do not know, really. My brain tells me that there is no danger and that all the girls will be nervous, but the rest of me feels as if I am in mortal peril... I am terrified at the thought of appearing in public in front of so many people... I feel that I could quite easily gibber in terror when even *thinking* of my Presentation... What if I humiliate my family with some gaucherie...? That worry is too ghastly even to contemplate, even worse than my own embarrassment... I am worried that my brother's wife will not like me when she knows me better... I am worried that my brother will be disappointed in me and that I shall let my family down by being an awkward, dowdy wallflower, ignored by all of society as too unattractive to bother with." Her voice took on an acid tinge. "That fear I know, of course, is ridiculous because my dowry is enough to ensure that I will be courted by at least a few of the young men."

Catherine leaned over and put her arms around her friend and said, "I do not know why you consider yourself plain or unattractive, Miss Georgiana Darcy. You have a pretty face and beautiful eyes that a susceptible young man could drown in as well as intelligence and a gentle and refined manner. Your figure is womanly perfection, and you will have dozens of beautiful gowns to set off your looks to advantage. You must stop demeaning your good qualities."

Georgiana thought back to her childhood and recalled several embarrassing incidents.

"My cousin, Colonel Fitzwilliam, used to call me 'little frog' when I was about five years old. Not a very attractive description... although now that I think about it the name was likely because I enjoyed startling my brother and his friends by jumping out at them. I thought it was great fun." She smiled. "So, I suppose I can hardly blame the colonel for the nickname. However, his elder brother, Lord St. George, used to call me every sort of nasty name and pinch me when he did not want me around—which was most of the time. He was really quite disagreeable, and from the discussions I have overheard when the speakers thought I was not in hearing range—of his gambling and other unspecified carousing—he has not improved a great deal. I do not know why a young man who was almost grown should have been so intolerant of one lonely child, annoying though she may have been."

Catherine looked surprised. "What did your brother and the colonel do when he pinched you?"

"Oh, he never did it when they were near, except on one occasion when he did not keep track of the two of them well enough before he tormented me. My brother thrashed him soundly, with the colonel cheering him on. Lord St. George complained to his father, and my brother and cousin were sent to their rooms without supper."

"So they have been your protectors virtually your entire life."

"Yes… I suppose they have. I have wondered why my father chose to name two guardians for me and why he chose the colonel. I asked him a month or so ago—not very gracefully, I am afraid. His answer, stripped of the jests and drivel in which they were couched, was that my father chose two guardians to lighten the responsibilities of my upbringing. My cousin has always been… I suppose 'light-minded' would be a good description. He has never been very passionate about anything. He does his military duties and undoubtedly enjoys the benefits of wearing a handsome uniform. He never seems to be worried about anything or to have any doubts of his worth, but he does not seem to take life seriously." She paused for thought. "Let me put it this way: if I had a serious problem it would not occur to me to talk to the colonel about it, I would speak to my brother; but if I wanted to laugh and spend a lighthearted afternoon with a group of friends, the colonel would be on my guest list."

Catherine examined her hands intently. "You know, I met Lord St. George during the Season last year. He asked me to dance a few times"

Georgiana was surprised out of her misery. "Truly? You did not mention that in your letters!"

"No, it was not a significant enough flirtation to merit mention. We danced at a couple of balls and by then he had determined which girls had the highest rank and the richest dowries and he danced out of my life."

She said this last bit with every ounce of melodrama she could muster and placed the back of her hand against her forehead as she swooned onto Georgiana's lap. They both collapsed giggling but were brought up short when Georgiana saw the time. She jumped up.

"Oh dear! I must get home for tea. My brother is expecting me and we are going to the theatre this evening, so I mustn't be late."

She snatched up her reticule, which she had tossed onto a chair, and they both hurried out, pausing at the top of the stairs to smooth their gowns before descending. Catherine rang for the carriage and saw Georgiana off before she turned back to the house, her brow furrowed in concern for her friend.

The theatre was only partially filled that evening, in contrast to their previous visit the month before, but the turnout was good for the end of the little season. The Darcys were greeted coolly by several couples as they entered the lobby of the theatre and ignored by a number of mothers who were there with their as yet unmarried daughters, for Mr. Darcy was no longer the object of their schemes. Elizabeth kept Georgiana by her side and quietly returned the greetings of those few who deigned to acknowledge Darcy and were introduced to her. Georgiana could feel herself becoming rigid with indignation by the time they were halfway across the room. Finally, she could not stand silently by any longer, and she forced herself to smile and speak with syrupy warmth to a young woman she knew slightly, "Dear Harriet, how are you? It has been so long since I have seen you. How did your Season go last year?"

The confused girl glanced at her mother for guidance, and Georgiana greeted her as well.

"Mrs. Smythe-Barrington, how are you? Please allow me to introduce my sister-in-law, Mrs. Darcy." She stepped back and left the matron to speak to Elizabeth for a moment before they continued their promenade. When they reached the security of their box, Georgiana put her lips to Elizabeth's ear and said, "I heard that Harriet's fortune was not nearly enough to tempt any of the gentlemen to dare facing her dragon of a mother over the dinner table for the rest of their lives… There, I am as spiteful a cat as she is."

Elizabeth managed to keep her countenance, but Georgiana could see that her self-possession was severely tried, so she pasted a smile on her face and did not look at her sister again. She noticed that her brother looked grim by the time they were seated, so she touched Elizabeth's arm and nodded towards Darcy. Elizabeth leaned towards him and Georgiana heard her say, "Smile, my love; you do not want the gossips to think that we are fighting already, do you?"

He looked down at her with a half-smile as she affectionately put her arm through his and they all resolutely turned their attention to the stage as the curtain rose.

During the interval they stayed in their seats, but they again became the objects of interest of a number of members of the audience on the main floor, so Georgiana turned to Elizabeth and carried on a lively conversation about the play until the curtain rose again. In spite of the whispers and stares of the audience, Georgiana enjoyed it and even shed a few tears when the lovers breathed their last. She saw Elizabeth take out her handkerchief as well to dab surreptitiously at her eyes, both of them drawing an indulgent smile from their escort.

Their departure was a repetition of their entrance: a few nods and a brief introduction or two, but Georgiana noticed that the more contumelious matrons kept their backs turned and their daughters occupied with loud and determined conversation as they passed. They sailed through the crowd unhindered by further unpleasantness and then they were in the carriage and on their way home. After the footman closed the carriage door, Elizabeth leaned over and kissed her sister.

"You were brilliant, Georgiana. Thank you."

"For what?"

"You know very well what, my dear sister."

"For trying to teach London society courteous behaviour? I know that it is a hopeless cause; I could but try."

Her brother was watching her in mute astonishment, and she subsided with a blush.

"I-I hope I did not embarrass you, Brother."

"Indeed you did not. To quote my dear wife, 'you were brilliant' and I applaud you."

She blushed again and was silent for the rest of the ride.

Georgiana went upstairs immediately when they arrived at Ashbourne House, but the evening was pleasant, so she sat by her open window to cool off her warm cheeks and write in her diary before trying to sleep. Her window looked down into the garden, and she saw her brother and sister sitting on a bench with a bare-limbed lilac arched over them. She laid her head on her crossed arms and thought about the evening for a while and then sat up and wrote,

> *28 October: Romeo and Juliet was surprisingly enjoyable in spite of being presented by a lesser-known company. Unfortunately, the haughty matrons who control London society were out in force, eager to cut my dear brother and sister dead. I confess that I lost my temper and forced myself on one of the worst of the gossips, whose pallid and insipid daughter I know slightly, and introduced Elizabeth, allowing the gorgon no escape from acknowledging my sister. It was really quite delicious at the time, but I hope that my actions do not harm my sister's chances of acceptance in society. Oh well, the deed is done and cannot be undone, and I confess that I am unrepentant.*

As she gazed out of the window pensively, she saw her brother lightly trace the shape of his wife's cheek with his fingertips and Elizabeth reach up to run her fingers through his hair. Before

Georgiana could draw back, her restrained and reserved brother swept his wife into his arms and Georgiana could almost feel the heat of their passion. She jumped back from the window, feeling like a *voyeuse*, but she was smiling in spite of her burning cheeks when she climbed into bed.

Chapter 6

This having learnt, thou hast attained the sum
Of wisdom;

—JOHN MILTON, *PARADISE LOST*

THE NEXT MORNING, THE THREE DARCYS WERE FINISHING
their breakfast when the post came. Darcy paused over one
letter written on creamy hot-pressed notepaper as he sipped the
last of his tea. Elizabeth noticed his distraction and asked, "What
is it, my dear?"

"The note is from Lady Cranton inviting us to dine. She
includes you, Georgiana, in the invitation, by the way. Cranton
was at Cambridge at the same time as I, but he was a few years
older and we were not close friends. I ran into him at my club
yesterday and spoke with him briefly. He was always insatiably
curious about other people's affairs, so I suspect that he wants to
be among the first to meet you, Elizabeth. I also seem to recall that
he and my cousin St. George had a bit of a falling-out last year
over an affair of honour, so he may want to spite St. George a little

by welcoming me, the family outcast, as well." His final remark was a trifle acid.

"Well, we do not need to go in that case, do we?" Elizabeth queried as she refilled his cup.

"Well, it is not required, certainly, but Cranton was not a bad sort—at least he was not when we were at university. I do not really know if he has changed," Darcy mused. "He was always rather like a puppy who was eager to be friends with everyone; like Bingley in some ways, now that I come to think of it. That wasn't a quality I appreciated at the time, but I think that I might be more tolerant of it now." He smiled down at her. "He and his wife are known for their frequent dinner parties, which are small but select... They try to put together an assortment of interesting people, not just those who are socially prominent, but people who are accomplished in their fields.

"I think, on consideration, that we should go; I want you to be accepted wherever you choose to go in society, so I would not wish to reject the hand of friendship if it is offered. Also, the Cranton's parties have the reputation of being stimulating without pandering to the dissipated element of the *haut ton*, so I would not be concerned taking Georgiana with us." He smiled at his sister and then gave Elizabeth a sly glance. "In addition, I could probably use the experience to further my transformation into a full-fledged human being, a process which was started a year ago by a young lady in Hertfordshire."

"All right, if you wish, dear," Elizabeth said with a slight smile. "However, I think that you are fairly human already—of course, one can never practise too much, as Lady Catherine kindly pointed out to me *several* times while I was playing the pianoforte at Rosings Park."

Georgiana stifled a giggle as a footman entered to replenish the platters on the sideboard. Her sister certainly had Lady Catherine's character down.

When they finished and were leaving the table, Georgiana, thinking ahead to the evening, asked her, "Elizabeth? Could you help me decide what would be appropriate to wear tonight?"

"I would be delighted, my dear, but to tell you the truth, I am going to consult Lambert about my toilette. We will ask her advice about yours as well."

They went upstairs and found the maid organizing her new mistress's dressing-room.

"Lambert? Miss Darcy and I need your advice. We are going to a dinner party tonight, and it will be my first appearance at a private party since my marriage. I wish to appear reasonably à la mode, but I do not wish to stand out from the other ladies. This will also be Miss Darcy's first formal dinner outside of the family circle."

Lambert considered for a moment as she scanned the gowns in the wardrobe. "*Oui*, Madame Darcy. I would suggest the cream silk with the Pomona sash. It is au courant but not too assertive and will make a lovely background for your jade necklace and bracelet, if you should wish to wear them."

"Very good, Lambert. That sounds perfect, and I would love to wear the jade first. They are quite unique. Shall we see what Miss Darcy has to choose from?"

They went down the hall to Georgiana's room and Lambert looked over each of her evening gowns, finally selecting a cream silk with a satin stripe.

"I would suggest this, Miss Darcy. You will blend with Mrs. Darcy, and I can arrange some pearls in your hair. Mademoiselle will be *très élégante*."

"Thank you, Miss Lambert."

"My pleasure, Miss Darcy." The maid curtseyed and left. Georgiana sighed with relief and commented to Elizabeth, "I am glad I will not need to worry about that all day."

"Yes. It will not be long before you have your own maid, you know. In fact, I think your brother is interviewing one tomorrow. He trusts he can find someone suitable before we leave for Pemberley so she can return with us. She will have several months to learn your tastes and wishes, and Lambert can train her before your first Season."

Georgiana winced. "I would prefer not to look that far ahead in time, if you please."

Elizabeth chuckled at her expression but gave her a reassuring embrace.

"Do not worry; you will be fine, my dear."

"I hope you are correct. If you will excuse me, I think I will practise the pianoforte."

"Of course."

Georgiana spent the next two hours playing mournful largos and adagios, until she had played herself out of her morbid fears, but she still felt a nervous flutter in her stomach when she went upstairs to change. She came tentatively down the stairs when it was time to leave and gasped when she saw Elizabeth.

"Oh my. You look wonderful, Elizabeth! The Chinese pieces are even more beautiful than I realised."

Elizabeth kissed her cheek and said, "Thank you, my dear. You look lovely too."

Georgiana glanced down at her gown. "I suppose I look well enough for a little girl." She sighed and they left the house for their dinner at Lord Cranton's.

When their carriage pulled up in front of Brentwood House, the Darcys alighted and were admitted by a footman. Lord Cranton was a heavyset man in his early thirties with thinning dark hair and a bit of a paunch who greeted them enthusiastically and introduced his wife. Lady Cranton, in contrast to her husband, was a tall, elegant woman dressed in the height of fashion. She greeted them politely, but rather coolly and then examined Elizabeth speculatively.

"I am pleased to meet you, Mrs. Darcy; your fame precedes you," she said courteously.

"And how is that Lady Cranton? I did not realise that my activities were of sufficient note to constitute fame," Elizabeth returned irrepressibly.

Lord Cranton interjected with a guffaw, "Darcy's cousin, Colonel Fitzwilliam, has been singing your praises for weeks, I assure you."

"Our cousin does me too much honour," Elizabeth returned politely.

"If you will enter the salon you may thank him yourself, as he is one of our guests tonight," Lady Cranton said with a flicker of amusement in her eyes. "He must be commended for his judgement," she added as she slipped her arm through Elizabeth's and led her into the salon to meet the other guests. Georgiana was pleased that her cousin Fitzwilliam had made the effort to praise Elizabeth.

Most of the men seemed to be "Lords" or "Sirs" and were generally known to Darcy, and they seemed uniformly eager to make Elizabeth's acquaintance. Georgiana tried to remain unnoticed, but her brother and sister made sure that she was introduced. The ladies in the room were, at least superficially, courteous to Elizabeth, but there were a few that Georgiana thought looked rather rapacious, watching her sister with jealous, predatory eyes as the gentlemen gathered round to be introduced. Colonel Fitzwilliam excused himself from the group he was in and greeted his cousins warmly.

"It is good to see the three of you," he said. "I trust everyone is well at the Darcy household."

Elizabeth assured him that they were quite well and he asked how her family was coping with the loss of two daughters at once.

"My father finds it very difficult to have us out of the home circle," Elizabeth said, "but the Bingleys reside only a few miles from Longbourn, which must be of some consolation to him."

Darcy interjected smoothly, "How is your family, Fitzwilliam?"

"My parents are very well and are back at Whitwell Abbey," he said, his eyes twinkling. "I am sure you will be hearing from them soon. It is such a shame that they were unable to join me at your wedding."

"Indeed it was," Georgiana said under her breath.

The colonel gave her a piercing glance before turning back to Darcy, and she felt herself flush with embarrassment.

"I trust that we will see them soon," Darcy said, with dryness that only his family would detect.

When dinner was announced Elizabeth, to Georgiana's surprise, was expected to lead the way into the dining-parlour with Lord Cranton. She could see the jealous looks of the other women boring into her sister's back like daggers, and she wondered briefly whether Lord Cranton was purposely trying to make Elizabeth unpopular. A glance at his face assured her that his straightforwards nature was unfeigned and he was simply unaware of their looks as he paid the honour due to the new bride. Georgiana heard her name.

"Miss Darcy?"

A slightly built but boldly handsome and dissolute-appearing young man with dark auburn hair and intense grey-blue eyes was offering her his arm. He had been briefly introduced to their group as Lord Byron. She had been struck dumb on meeting the notorious poet, whose unsavoury reputation had reached even into her sheltered life, but finding herself his partner was a shock. She managed to curtsey and take his arm. Fortunately, it was only a moment before they were seated, with Lord Byron between Georgiana and Elizabeth. Georgiana listened unabashedly to his conversation with Elizabeth, as, she noticed, did a number of the guests at their end of the table.

"I am delighted to meet you Mrs. Darcy. I understand that you and Darcy were married only a few days ago."

"Yes, my lord, only about a week ago."

"I congratulate you. I am desolated, however, that I have never met you in the years that I have been in London. I thought that I had met all of the beautiful young ladies here, and now I find that I have missed two of the loveliest." His glance included Georgiana in his compliment.

"My family lives very retired in Hertfordshire, my lord," Elizabeth answered him simply.

"A shame, but I am very pleased that I am now able to make your acquaintance. How did you and Darcy meet?"

She gave him a very short version of their courtship, which seemed to amuse the poet.

"I do not know Darcy well, but I can see that I have underestimated his fire and audacity, Mrs. Darcy. I would have guessed that he would make a much more—shall we say?—*conventional* alliance with one of the belles of the *haut ton*."

"I think perhaps, my lord, that many people underestimate the depth and breadth of my husband's mind," Elizabeth said firmly.

"I certainly did!" Lord Cranton interjected with a laugh. "And I have known Darcy since we were at Cambridge! He always took top honours, but no imagination at all!"

Elizabeth answered, with a knowing look at her host, "From what I have heard of undergraduates, my lord, perhaps imagination is something that should be discouraged at a university."

The gentlemen both laughed good-naturedly as the soup was served, and Georgiana had a moment to gather her thoughts and glance around the table before Lord Byron turned to her.

Her brother was seated across from her and part way down the table with an attractive young woman in a very low-cut sapphire gown to his right and an older woman dressed in elaborate purple satin to his left. The older woman had introduced herself before dinner as Mrs. Hatfield. She was polite enough to her dinner partners but seemed to have only partial attention to give them, spending most of her time attempting to watch an older gentleman down the table who was talking animatedly with the young woman seated between him and Darcy. The young woman, on the other hand, seemed far more interested in Georgiana's brother, turning often from her more loquacious partner to ask his opinion, gazing into his face while he answered politely but with a touch of the sardonic in his smile.

Lord Byron claimed Georgiana's attention, but his remarks to her were in a very different tone than those to Elizabeth. His face was open and friendly and his conversation gentle and undemanding, allowing Georgiana to listen and nod mutely. He told one little anecdote of his school days, and she could not help but smile at his humorous manner. He seemed pleased with her response but did not question or pressure her. When the fish course arrived, Georgiana turned to her right-hand partner, as courtesy dictated, but the elderly man was absorbed with his dinner and only made the minimum of conversation required for politeness. She was thus able to keep an eye on Lord Byron out of the corner of her eye. He had an almost magnetic gaze, which he now turned eagerly back upon Elizabeth.

"I must ask you, Mrs. Darcy, whence your jewels came. I have never seen anything like them."

"They have been in the Darcy family for generations, my lord, and came originally from China."

"They are magnificent."

"I thank you, my lord."

"And so, Mrs. Darcy, how do you find London? Have you been here before?"

"Yes, my lord, but only to visit my aunt and uncle and take in the occasional concert or play. I have not spent any great amount of time here."

He was eager to hear what she had seen and, as she told him, his eyes seemed to bore into her. Elizabeth seemed unaware of the intensity of his gaze and calmly mentioned that they had attended *Romeo and Juliet* that week.

"It is not one of my favourites among Shakespeare's works," he said. "I would recommend *Hamlet* for the person of discriminating taste. Shakespeare's portrayal of the edge of madness rings very true to my ear. Have you seen it?"

"No, my lord, but I have read it. I found that *Romeo and Juliet* seemed much more credible on the stage than it had in my reading. It is difficult to really appreciate the passions driving the characters when you are merely reading dialogue, particularly dialogue in archaic English." He leaned towards her and appeared to be even more intent on her words as she spoke of passions. She glanced at Georgiana and hurried on. "I prefer his comedies; *Much Ado About Nothing* is my favourite, I believe. I am of rather a cynical temperament, I confess, but I nonetheless prefer my entertainment to have a happy ending. Perhaps also I identify myself overmuch with Beatrice." She smiled, and Lord Byron seemed charmed.

"I am positive that you could have very little in common with Beatrice, Mrs. Darcy," he said gallantly. "Besides having no resemblance to 'my Lady Disdain,' I have difficulty picturing you threatening one who had done a family member wrong to 'eat his heart in the marketplace.'"

Elizabeth smiled again, this time a little thinly, and Lord Byron adroitly interpreted her look, asking, "But perhaps I am wrong and *Mrs.* Darcy also has more fire in her temperament than is visible to the eye." He looked at her questioningly with a slight, expectant smile on his face.

Elizabeth drew back a little and answered noncommittally, "Who does not have someone in their past who sparks their ire?"

"Very true. You are a wise woman, Mrs. Darcy," he said with an intimate smile.

Elizabeth gave him a vague nod and turned readily when Lord Cranton claimed her attention. Georgiana tensed a little, knowing that she would be the object of Byron's attention again, but he was joining in the conversation with his host and his dinner partner. When he did turn back to her, she managed to be listening intently to the partner on her right until Byron's attention was diverted by Elizabeth again.

Lord Byron was certainly most interesting to listen to, and his intensity made it seem that the woman he was talking to was the most fascinating woman in the world, but his eager conversation teetered upon the edges of propriety, and Georgiana was happy that she had not needed to manoeuvre further through the hazards of speaking with him. Elizabeth seemed immune to Lord Byron's charms, and she had an amused smile on her face as she caught her husband's eye.

All in all, Georgiana found her first foray into society to be rather an unsettling experience, although she had managed to survive the dinner table conversation without resorting to much more than smiles and nods at her partners.

As they drove home, Darcy was able to explain some of the undercurrents that Georgiana and Elizabeth had noted in the room.

"Mrs. Hatfield was watching her husband, who was two places to the left of me. He has a reputation as a lady's man, and, well, let me just say that I would not want my wife or my sister to be left alone in his company. Poor Fitzwilliam was seated between two mothers who are notoriously eager to part with their unattractive single daughters. He probably considers himself fortunate at this moment *not* to have an inheritance or he would have had an uncomfortable evening—rather like a nice plump cow swimming in a school of piranhas."

Georgiana laughed aloud at this picture of her cousin, and her brother smiled at her and went on:

"Cranton told me, when we had a moment alone tonight, that he was amazed at how much I had changed since university. He was happy to see that I had the sense to recognise a woman of quality, even if she did not have an inheritance to sweeten the pot, and he expressed the sentiment that the coming Season would be improved by your presence. So you have obviously made a conquest. I assured him that I fully appreciated my good fortune."

He smiled smugly down at his wife. "By the way, you have not yet said how you got on with the notorious Lord Byron."

Elizabeth described her discomfiture at being his dinner partner, adding, "He is a talented poet, but he would be very uncomfortable to be around very much. Those gimlet eyes of his are quite disconcerting. I was rather surprised at how small he is—I somehow expected a reputed roué such as him to have a more impressive figure." Georgiana nodded her agreement.

"The man is a menace to society in spite of his small stature and clubfoot—or, possibly, it is *because* of those characteristics. I am not surprised that you found him dismaying."

Elizabeth glanced at Georgiana. "I have met other menaces to society; in fact I am now related to one, as you know. The main difference between the two of them is that Lord Byron has a title and money to buy his way out of trouble, while Wickham has nothing but his looks and his lying tongue," she said with a sniff, which caused Darcy to chuckle as they climbed the stairs to their room.

Georgiana went stiff at the mention of Wickham. Elizabeth was related to Wickham? Why had she not heard of this before? She suddenly remembered that Elizabeth had another sister; one who was no longer at home and had barely been mentioned while she was in Hertfordshire. After a moment's thought she realised that her brother had probably not wanted to remind her of Wickham and Elizabeth undoubtedly assumed that she knew. She spent a sleepless night wondering what Elizabeth would think of her when she found out.

The next morning she appeared at breakfast with pale cheeks and smudged eyes. Elizabeth was alone in the breakfast-parlour and Georgiana asked, "Where is my brother?"

"He had some business to take care of before we leave for Pemberley."

"Oh… Elizabeth, there is something I want to tell you. The conversation last night made me think of it. I-I do not wish for there to be secrets between us." She took a deep breath and then continued, fingering and repositioning her cutlery as she spoke. "I do not know what my brother has told you, but about a year and a half ago I was convinced by a young man of our acquaintance to elope. I thought that he loved me, but he was only trying to punish my brother for not giving him money, and he wanted my fortune. Fortunately, my brother discovered the plan and saved me from a terrible mistake, but… but since that time I feel that I cannot trust others. I feel that all of the young men that I meet are interested only in my fortune and I cannot believe their protestations of regard. I cannot believe that they are truly interested in a girl without beauty or grace, whose only charm is a large fortune and that is part of the reason I feel so uncomfortable in society."

Elizabeth gently embraced her sister and said, "You are very wrong if you think that you are either of those things, my dear sister. You are very attractive, and although I have not seen you dance, I can see that you move elegantly and well; so do not tell me that you are graceless. Your beauty, though, is a quiet beauty; not the bold sort which stops conversation when its possessor enters the room. Frankly, there are very few women who can do that, and those that do are not necessarily the women with the most handsome features in the room, but they feel beautiful and confident of themselves and that confidence affects their smile, their walk, and their conversation. The most important part of a woman's beauty is in her mind. I suspect that when you realise your powers you will be a woman to contend with; you have the brain, the talent, and the education to fascinate any gentleman you wish to. It all depends on you and whether you choose to be a lady's slipper hiding under the woodland foliage and only revealing your exquisite beauty to those who search for you or you decide to be a rose in the garden, intoxicatingly fragrant and impossible to overlook."

Georgiana giggled nervously at this picture, and Elizabeth laughed with her.

"Enough, I do not want to swell your head—I prefer it as it is. And… as far as Mr. Wickham goes, I know far more about him than you can possibly imagine, since he is married to my youngest sister."

"I-I did not know, but I wondered last night. I do not want to criticise your brother-in-law…"

"Do not be concerned about my feelings in this matter." Elizabeth flicked her fingers, as if waving Wickham away. "I have no great love for him. During the early months of our acquaintance he told innumerable lies about the entire Darcy family, which I believed implicitly until I became better acquainted with your brother and learnt the truth. It was humiliating to learn how easily I could be taken in about someone's character. I thought that I was so clever at assessing people's true nature. I know too, dear Georgiana, that *you* were the one who told your brother what Wickham was planning, so you saved yourself by your honesty with him.

"You need not be ashamed that you could not detect the insincerity of such a practised rogue, and you also need not be reticent about discussing him with me, if you have something you wish to say. I know that your brother does not like to remind you of that time and he is very backwards about advertising his own good qualities, so perhaps you do not realise that my sister eloped with

Wickham, but he had no intention of marrying a girl without a dowry. Only your brother's intervention saved my sister's reputation and, at the same time, my entire family's good name. No, no, you need not be concerned about blackening Wickham's name with me. I am only too happy to be relieved of his company."

Georgiana embraced her and sighed. "I feel much better now that we have this understanding between us. I did not like feeling that I was hiding something from you that might make you think less of me."

They had invited the Gardiners to dine the last evening they were in town, and Georgiana was pleased to see them again. The elder Gardiners had such courteous manners that even she was not intimidated by their attention. At least not much. All of the Gardiners would be coming to Pemberley for Christmas, and Georgiana had heard Elizabeth and Jane making complicated plans so that they could both see the most congenial of their relations, without subjecting their husbands and Georgiana to the peculiarities of the others. Georgiana was pleased to realise that Mr. and Mrs. Collins were not included in their plans. She had seen quite enough of her aunt's pet rector while in Hertfordshire.

Chapter 7

Where'er I roam, whatever realms to see,
My heart untravelled fondly turns to thee.

—OLIVER GOLDSMITH, "THE TRAVELLER"

As they rode in the carriage on the long highway that curved northwards towards Derbyshire, bundled into cloaks and gloves with their feet warmed by heated bricks, the travellers discussed Pemberley. Once they had settled in, Elizabeth would have to begin learning to be the Lady of the Manor (Georgiana could not avoid thinking of it with capital letters). Elizabeth picked up the thread of a previous conversation and said, "My sister Jane and I both have some experience managing a household, because my mother's frequent ill health required that we sometimes take up her responsibilities, but up until now I have never had the super-intendence of a large household of servants. I admit that I find the prospect rather daunting."

"You will have many things to learn, I grant you," Darcy replied, "but I think Mrs. Reynolds will turn out to be your greatest friend in that process. I have a suspicion that Burton has been sending Smithfield reports all along, and it is clear that you have won him over. If it were not for his high regard for the dignity of his office, I am sure he would have been clucking like a proud hen over her chicks this entire week."

Georgiana agreed. "Mrs. Reynolds has longed for a mistress for many years. I do not believe that she will try to usurp your authority, and *I* certainly will not. I am quite happy to leave the duties to you, my dear sister."

The two young women smiled at each other.

When they finally reached Pemberley after three days of driving, they were all ready to remove from the carriage. Even with the unhurried pace and the almost voluptuous comfort of the Darcy carriage, the journey began to take a toll after those three days. When Georgiana had last driven through Derbyshire, there had still been leaves on the trees, but now they were barren skeletons and the chill of coming winter was in the air. Still, it was wonderful to see the beautiful, rugged country that was her home.

As the carriage began to slow and turn past the lodge and onto the drive into Pemberley, Georgiana began watching for the moment when the manor house would appear. The demesne was ten miles around and forested over much of its extent, and the road wandered through the trees for nearly a mile before they reached the top of a ridge and a vista opened, revealing the enormous Palladian edifice of Pemberley House. Georgiana sighed in contentment when it appeared.

They pulled up on the gravel sweep and Smithfield and Mrs. Reynolds appeared to greet them with a crowd of servants behind them, all smiling in welcome of their master and mistress. Mr. Darcy's lips curved upwards as his eyes met Elizabeth's and he whispered, "Welcome home, Mrs. Darcy," as he handed her out of the coach. When Georgiana had also alighted, a little girl came shyly forwards with a bouquet of asters and chrysanthemums for each of the ladies, and the housekeeper curtseyed and said, "May we wish you joy upon your marriage, Mr. and Mrs. Darcy? And welcome home, Miss Darcy."

Smithfield bowed and said a few words of his own, which were almost drowned by the clapping of the other servants after they had curtseyed or tugged their forelocks. The Darcys all smiled upon them before ascending the steps to the main hall, where they were met by a huge black dog with a massive head who was seated near the staircase. He rose to his feet and waved his plumed tail when they entered, and Georgiana immediately went over to pat his head affectionately.

Elizabeth looked shocked and said, "My goodness; that is the largest dog I have ever seen!"

Darcy answered her. "This is Pilot; he was my father's dog and as you can see is beginning to get a bit grey around the muzzle. He is, fortunately, of a very placid disposition."

"I would hope so! I did not meet Pilot last summer," she added while gingerly patting Pilot on the head.

"No, we keep him in his kennel when there are visitors touring. We don't want to cause swooning or apoplexy when he appears." Darcy scratched Pilot behind the ears as he talked about him, the dog accepting the attention with dignity.

After changing out of their travel clothes they all met in the drawing-room, where tea was waiting.

"I thought you might need some refreshment after the long drive, so I ordered tea as soon as we arrived," said Georgiana diffidently, suddenly concerned that she might have overstepped her proper boundaries giving orders in what was now Elizabeth's home.

"Bless you, my child," said Elizabeth with a warm smile. "You may have saved my life, for I am indeed ready for tea!"

Georgiana gave a nervous smile and then blushed awkwardly.

Elizabeth poured out the tea and changed the subject. "Georgiana, dear, would you be willing to show me around Pemberley tomorrow morning? Mr. Darcy needs to meet his steward, and I am much too impatient to wait for him." She gave him an impish grin and turned back to Georgiana.

Georgiana looked down at her hands but nodded with a smile.

They all retired early that evening after the long drive, and Georgiana settled into her room again. She felt very odd being here in her familiar home with Elizabeth part of the family. She liked her new sister very much, but she still felt off balance as she adjusted to the great changes which had occurred. She sat down at her desk with her diary and thought for a few minutes before she dipped the pen in the ink bottle.

> *7 November: We are finally returned from London and Pemberley is unchanged, yet somehow different. I am to give Elizabeth a tour of the house tomorrow, but I am already seeing my home through the eyes of a stranger and it is rather disconcerting. I hope she loves it as much as I do.*

When Georgiana sought out Elizabeth after dressing the next morning, she found her in the room which had been her mother's morning-room when Georgiana had been an infant. The room was small and intimate and was very comfortably furnished in a feminine style. It contained a finely carved walnut desk of beautiful proportions, perfect for a lady's correspondence and other business. Elizabeth had rearranged the items on the desk to suit her taste and had taken out paper to write a letter when Georgiana arrived.

"Are you ready for a tour of the house, Elizabeth?" Georgiana ventured, hesitating in the doorway.

"I will be in a moment, my dear. I am expecting Mrs. Reynolds so we can go over the menus and accounts. Do you mind waiting? I would be happy to have you listen in so you can add any comments you have and I can ask you questions later if I need to."

Georgiana sat down. "I am not sure that I know enough to help you, Elizabeth. My brother has always run the house as well as the rest of the estate. I probably should know more than I do." She stared down at her hands.

Mrs. Reynolds arrived at her door and Elizabeth invited her in. They reviewed the menus for the week and Elizabeth approved them. Mrs. Reynolds also gave her a list of all the household and outdoor servants and reviewed it with her as well. As they finished Elizabeth said, "Thank you Mrs. Reynolds, I believe that will be everything, except that I would like to ask you to show me the picture gallery one day and tell me the history of the paintings. I know little of the art of painting, but I am interested in the family history.

"I will do so with pleasure, Mrs. Darcy, whenever you wish. As Mr. Darcy has perhaps mentioned, I have a great interest in the family history."

"He has indeed, Mrs. Reynolds."

Mrs. Reynolds curtseyed and departed, and Elizabeth turned to her sister.

"I am ready now, Georgiana. I am sorry to delay you for so long."

"Not at all, Elizabeth," she said, a little breathless in her eagerness to be obliging.

"Shall we go down and start in the entry hall and then work our way upstairs?"

Georgiana nodded and they went downstairs. They started at the front door and saw all the rooms on the ground floor, most of which Elizabeth had seen the previous summer, but which she wanted to see again so that she could orient herself. The rooms were arranged around the four sides of a pleasant courtyard with a formal garden that provided an attractive view from the inside rooms. Georgiana started the tour tentatively, not sure how much detail she should give. She merely named the rooms and opened the doors so that Elizabeth could see them. After Elizabeth had asked her a few questions, she began to lose some of her self-consciousness and her sister's interest soon had her adding comments on the history of the manor house and the family:

"This is the ballroom. We have not had a ball here within my memory. My brother, as I am sure you know, does not like balls." She risked a brief smile at Elizabeth.

Elizabeth laughed and said, "Indeed, I do know. The ballroom will be used next month, however, as we are planning to have a ball when the Bingleys are visiting after Christmas. It is a beautiful room—we could probably fit a hundred couples in here without crowding."

Georgiana smiled again and walked on to the next door. It opened on a chapel, which made a small wing off the back of the house; the windows were of stained glass and filtered multicoloured light over the Darcy tombs in the back. Gold chrysanthemums decorated the altar and it was very quiet, separated as it was from the routine bustle of the rest of the house. After a moment's silence, Georgiana whispered, "My parents are in that tomb in the near corner."

Elizabeth took her hand and they walked over to it. It merely said "Darcy" over the stone lintel, but there were small plaques on the wall beside the tomb listing the Darcys who were interred there and their dates of birth and death, including "George Alexander Richard Darcy" and "Lady Anne Winslow Darcy."

"My father used to come here every morning and sit for a few minutes, and Mrs. Reynolds still makes sure that there are fresh flowers on the altar every day. The chapel has not been used for regular services in years, only the occasional funeral."

Georgiana could not keep the sadness out of her voice, and Elizabeth put a reassuring arm around her. She silently led her back to the main hallway of the house and they continued their circuit of the house, a little more subdued than before. When they reached the picture gallery along the back of the house they merely walked through, stopping only at the portraits of Darcy and Georgiana and one of their parents.

They eventually returned to the entry hall and ascended the main staircase, a large, gracefully curved sweep of white marble, to reach the family quarters on the first floor. In addition to the master suite, which consisted of a corner sitting-room with one bedroom and dressing-room along each side of the northwest corner of the house, there were twenty bedrooms on this floor. Georgiana and Mrs. Annesley had rooms on the opposite front corner, all of them facing the tree-covered ridge that filled the view from the east side of the manor.

The other sixteen rooms on the first floor were furnished as guest rooms, providing plenty of space for large parties. All of the rooms were elegantly appointed, although the furniture in the less-used bedrooms at the back of the house was covered with dust cloths, giving it a ghostly appearance that was at odds with the morning sunlight streaming around the edges of the draperies. As they toured the bedrooms they passed several housemaids who curtseyed to them before continuing their morning work, peeking at them from the corners of their eyes as they did so.

The second floor held the servants' quarters—small, simple, but comfortable rooms—and the nursery and schoolroom, as well as quarters for a governess, which were all empty now. Elizabeth seemed interested to see the schoolroom where generations of Darcys had learnt their lessons and they lingered there for a few minutes. There were well-worn schoolbooks neatly arranged on the bookshelves and appearing rather forlorn. She pulled out a tattered copy of *Gulliver's Travels.*

"This was one of my favourite books when I was young. Of course, I thought that Lilliput and Brobdingnag and all of the other countries in the book were real places."

"I did too. I actually enjoyed it more before I understood that it is a satire."

"So did I."

They smiled at each other rather shamefacedly and Elizabeth moved on to a lone drawing that was hanging forsaken upon the wall, signed by Georgiana in a childish hand.

"I drew that when I was seven," she said with a nervous laugh.

"It is quite good for a seven-year-old, but I am sure that you can do better now." Elizabeth gave her a gentle smile. "Do you have a portfolio of your drawings?"

Georgiana nodded.

"You must show me them sometime, Georgiana."

She blushed and nodded. "If you like."

They returned to the ground floor and Georgiana took her into the conservatory at the back of the house, which they had skipped earlier. It was a large glass addition filled with beds of ornamental trees arranged with flowering plants at their feet. A few of the trees were covered with shiny dark green leaves and had fruit on them—oranges and lemons. In the centre of the conservatory was an open space with a slate floor, furnished with wicker chairs and chaises longues and scattered with small tables. It was the most informal room they had yet visited, and the fragrance of the fruit scented the air, which gave it the feel of a summer's day in the midst of autumn's cold winds. Elizabeth was delighted with it.

"This is lovely, Georgiana! Shall we have a cup of coffee in here?"

"I would like that. I am glad you like the conservatory—it is one of my favourite places at Pemberley," she said with a smile.

Over their coffee Elizabeth delicately drew out her sister-in-law about herself, her likes and dislikes and her passions.

"I know that you are very fond of music, my dear. How long have you been studying the pianoforte?"

"I started when I was five or six; I do not recall exactly. I had a governess who was very interested in the arts; she could play, and draw, and paint beautifully, and it was her influence that made me also love them."

"I believe I heard mention that you are also learning to play the harp?"

"Yes, but I am just a beginner. I have a master who comes once a week from Lambton to teach me, when I am at Pemberley."

"You are fortunate to have a teacher available so far from the city."

"Yes. He is a retired schoolmaster, but he is willing to teach me. He also helps me with the pianoforte. He is very fond of études and scales." She rolled her eyes and Elizabeth laughed.

"I am sure that I will meet him one day. What else do you do with your days?"

"Well, I do some needlework, but I am not very fond of it. I like to read and Fitzwilliam's library has an endless supply of books. Thank you again, by the way, for *The Giaour*; I have wanted to read it since I heard of its publication. I wish that Lord Byron could have given it an easier title, however."

"I would certainly agree with that! What do you like to read besides poetry?"

"Oh, everything. I suppose that I enjoy history the most."

Pilot appeared at the French doors that led back into the house, and Georgiana rose to let him in. He flopped at their feet, his forepaws crossed and his head up, gazing at them.

"He is a beautiful beast—quite a noble brow," Elizabeth commented.

"Yes, he is. I adore him, but he is such a monster—I have learnt to step aside when he walks by so that I am not covered with drool."

They smiled at each other, and Elizabeth added, "I suppose a huge, slavering Newfoundland dog, no matter how benign, is not the most appropriate pet for a lady."

"Perhaps not," Georgiana said, looking at Pilot wistfully.

Later that afternoon, Darcy found Elizabeth reading in the library and she told him about the tour. When she finished she hesitated for a moment then asked, "My love, what was your mother like? I have heard much about your father, but I do not feel that I know your mother at all, excepting, of course, her appearance in her portrait."

"Well, I will see if I can capture her personality for you. I have given much thought to my parents and who they were in the past twelve months of my life, so I can probably sketch her more adequately than I would have been able to before you and I met." He paused to smile down at her and then continued, "She was very much like my aunt, Lady Whitwell, in looks, as you will see when you meet her and can compare her to my mother's portrait. They were very close in age, only eleven months apart, while Lady Catherine was almost ten years older. Their father was the Earl of Winslow. The family was very small and he had no male relatives, so the title would die with him—to his great distress.

"I remember my mother as very cool and elegant. She had a calm demeanour like your sister Jane, but without Jane's warmth of personality. My father loved her very much and put her on a pedestal like a goddess, and she seemed happy to remain there. I feel, thinking back with the advantage of maturity, that she was rather—I suppose 'detached' would be the best word—from life. I do not remember ever seeing her passionate about anything, but then she died when I was thirteen years old, so my memories are quite possibly imperfect.

"As you would guess from the difference in our ages, Georgiana was born when my mother was past her youth and the birth was apparently a very difficult one. My mother was never in good health after that, and she died when Georgiana was less than two years old.

"My father carried on his duties after her death, as he had always done, but his heart was not quite with us. One of the penalties of being in love with your wife, I suppose." He smiled at her again, this time a little sadly. "Like most children of our background, we were both raised by nurses and governesses, but I cannot help but feel that Georgiana would have benefited by having parents to serve as an example, advise her, and oversee her upbringing, as I did for most of my youth."

Elizabeth frowned down at her hands. "I see—Poor Georgiana. It is not surprising that she does not have confidence in herself when she really never knew her mother, and her father was grieving for most of her life." After a few moments she added, "I will be interested to meet Lady Whitwell. She sounds quite different from Lady Catherine, which, I must add, is a blessing."

Darcy laughed. "Indeed it is!"

As the days passed, Georgiana became more relaxed around Elizabeth, and Mrs. Darcy found her sister-in-law a sweet and thoughtful companion. Georgiana confided to her one sunny day, as they took a walk on the grounds accompanied by Pilot, that she had never felt comfortable around Mr. Bingley's sisters, with their criticisms behind the backs of their so-called friends.

"I confess that I was fearful that my brother would marry Miss Bingley since she expended a great deal of time and attention on him and my brother's intimate friendship with Mr. Bingley gave her considerable access to him. I was not quite sure what his thoughts were about *her*, since he was invariably courteous, so I was very happy when I found out about his high regard for you, even before I met you! I should have known that he would not be led to make a mistake… he never is."

Elizabeth gave her an enigmatic smile and then patted her sister's hand and thanked her for her regard as they continued their walk.

Chapter 8

Still in thy right hand carry gentle peace…

—William Shakespeare, *Henry VII*

The three Darcys gradually made the rounds of their neighbours, introducing Elizabeth to the local gentry. Darcy had, without question, the largest estate in the neighbourhood, but there were a number of pleasant manors nearby and they visited them all.

First they made an early afternoon call on Sir Andrew Ffoulkes, whose manor, Kympton Hall, was a mile from the village of the same name and about four miles from Pemberley. The Ffoulkeses had a daughter just two years younger than Georgiana, but she did not know them well. They were an old Derbyshire family and had lived at Kympton Hall for about ten years, having previously lived in the south of the county on a smaller manor. Sir Andrew was a bluff, gregarious man, somewhat stout and pompous, with the look of the stereotypical English country gentleman: blue eyed, ruddy cheeked, and in his mid-forties. His looks suggested that he spent a great deal of time out-of-doors, and his conversation was mainly concerned with the state of his pheasants and whether the weather would be fine enough to hunt in December.

When Georgiana had first met the Ffoulkeses, she thought they were an oddly matched couple. Lady Ffoulkes appeared to be much younger than her husband, had dark, Gallic good looks, and spoke English with a distinct French accent. She was slender and elegant and appeared as if she would be quite comfortable in a Paris salon. Georgiana wondered how she came to be married to this most English of country gentlemen. The Ffoulkeses had seven children, and Sir Andrew also had two unmarried sisters who lived with them, both in their early thirties and in appearance much like their brother. Both sisters spent the visit fussing over their nieces and nephews and scrutinizing their visitors in a way that Georgiana found rather unnerving, especially with the sisters' too prominent eyes and pale lashes.

During the visit, Sir Andrew mentioned that Lady Ffoulkes's widowed brother, the Comte de Tournay, was expected for Christmas and would stay a fortnight, and he expressed his hope that the three Darcys would join them for dinner while the count was visiting. They indicated their willingness and made their fare-wells. On the way home, Elizabeth asked, a little hesitantly, "Do Sir Andrew's sisters always stare in that way?"

Darcy laughed and answered, "Not always. Perhaps they find you an interesting study, or maybe they have not seen the latest London fashions."

Georgiana interjected suddenly, "I have always thought that they looked rather like a pair of geese flanking a swan when they sit on either side of Lady Ffoulkes, as they did today." She faded into silence and a flush crept up her neck as she neared the end of her comment, but she joined Darcy and Elizabeth weakly when they chuckled at her apt description.

Lady Ffoulkes and her sisters-in-law returned their call very soon and the Darcy ladies found Joanna and Augusta Ffoulkes a little more personable when their nieces and nephews were not distracting their attention, but neither had much to say. Lady Ffoulkes was very pleasant and, while Georgiana was struggling through a conversation with the two odd sisters, she quietly told Elizabeth a bit more of her history, which Elizabeth related to Georgiana and Darcy after they left.

"Her father, the late Comte de Tournay, had a large estate in the south of France, but was well known at court and advised the king to be more moderate in his dealings with his subjects. When the Revolution came and the Bastille was breached, her father took all of them back to their chateau for safety, but the Terror did not leave any of the aristocracy untouched, and eventually they were arrested and imprisoned. They were saved on the very brink of death from the guillotine by a courageous group of English gentlemen who spirited them across the English Channel to safety. Her husband was one of those gentlemen, and that is how they first met."

Georgiana's eyes were wide with astonishment. "And when did they marry?"

"They waited about two years. She was only fifteen when they met, but her husband was twenty-four and had already inherited his estate. So, although the terrible events in France delayed their marriage, when she reached age seventeen she insisted that her parents agree to their engagement. She loved Sir Andrew and saw much more clearly than her parents did that they would not be returning to their previous life in France." Elizabeth paused for a moment and then continued, "I saw her spirits were depressed by her story, so I changed the subject. They have a daughter who will be coming out next year. They do not come to town for the Season, ordinarily, as it is too expensive to lease a house large enough for their entire family."

When she had related this history, Elizabeth asked Darcy, "Did you know of Sir Andrew's past—that he helped rescue Lady Ffoulkes's family from the guillotine and brought her to England?"

"I heard something about it when I was a boy, but it was long after the event and the gentlemen involved kept their identities very secret. I was not really aware that it involved people that I knew."

Elizabeth looked at Georgiana and shook her head in amazement.

"I think that I would remember if my neighbour had been a swashbuckling hero, would you not Georgiana?"

"Indeed I would. I had no idea that Sir Andrew had a secret past."

Elizabeth tilted her head, considering her husband. "I wonder if you would have joined a small, secret band of saviours in their rescue of the French aristocracy if you had been old enough. What do you think, Georgiana?"

She smiled and said, "I could easily picture my brother being a hero."

Georgiana was amused when her brother actually blushed at their speculations and chuckled to herself about the conversation all afternoon.

The afternoon post brought Elizabeth a letter from her sister Lydia, the first she had received since their wedding:

My dearest Sister and Brother,—

Congratulations on your marriage. I hope that you are as happy as are my dear Wickham and I, and I wish that I could have been at the wedding, but we are very lively here in Newcastle and I could not be spared. I hope that Pemberley suits you very well, Lizzy, and that you find Miss Darcy very agreeable. We are currently searching for new living quarters as the ones we are now in are far too expensive to leave us money for food and clothes at the end of the month. I assume that you will be spending the Season in London at Mr. Darcy's town house. If you find yourself in need of company, write to me and I would be happy to join you.—Yours, etc.

She showed Georgiana the letter and said, "I have told you a little about my sister Lydia and the incident with Wickham."

Georgiana nodded.

"I shudder to think of her uncontrolled behaviour being associated with the Darcy name and tainting your first Season. Lady Catherine's predictions of social ostracism would be swiftly validated."

Georgiana hesitated for a moment and then finally asked, "Why is your youngest sister's temper so different from your own and your sister Jane's?"

"I am afraid that my younger sisters did not have the supervision they needed while growing up." A crimson spot appeared on each of Elizabeth's cheeks. "You have met my mother. She has never seen the impropriety of her two youngest daughters' behaviour, I am afraid, and has encouraged both of them to do nothing but think of young men and flirtation. I admit that a great deal of my concern over the effects of having Lydia visit are my desire to prevent you from seeing all of the weaknesses of my family, at least until you know some of us better. My amour propre demands it, I am afraid."

"So what will you do about her letter?"

"I must write to her and make it politely but firmly clear that an invitation will not be forthcoming. Diplomacy is wasted on Lydia, I am afraid. She never hears anything she does not wish to. Anyway, as we obviously will not invite Wickham to visit we will probably not be importuned too often. Fortunately, I can assuage my guilty feelings by sending my sister a few pounds of my pin money. I have no difficulty at all believing that the finances of two such heedless people are in a shambles."

Soon after they had returned to Derbyshire, Darcy had called upon a new neighbour, Sir Robert Blake, at Coldstream Manor, which was about six miles from Pemberley. Sir Robert had turned out to be a young man of around Darcy's age who had inherited a large fortune two years previously, and who had recently fulfilled his father's dying wish by purchasing the estate. He had taken posses-sion while Darcy and Elizabeth were preparing for their wedding in Hertfordshire, so Darcy had not previously had an opportunity to call upon him, but he had been favourably impressed at his first visit and returned home with an invitation to dinner.

After telling Elizabeth and Georgiana of his visit while they awaited tea in the drawing-room, he added, "I think that we will find the Blakes most agreeable neighbours." He turned to Elizabeth. "I suppose that I will be considered a traitor to my class, but I must say that since I have tried to moderate my prejudices and choose my friends for their merit rather than just their birth, I have collected a much more interesting group of friends. I blush to think that a year ago I would not have called upon the Blakes because of their association with trade. I must count the pleasure of Sir Robert's acquaintance as one more benefit of meeting you, my dearest Elizabeth."

"I am glad that there *are* benefits, my love," she answered with a smile.

"There are many, I assure you," he said quietly, his eyes locked on hers.

They did not notice Georgiana's embarrassed blush as she occupied herself with selecting a biscuit from the tea tray.

During the ride to Coldstream Manor a few days later, Darcy told them what he knew of the Blakes:

"From what I have heard, Sir Robert's father was a mercer and accumulated a great fortune providing uniforms for the military in the wars with both Napoleon and the Americans. Lord knows we have had plenty of wars in the past twenty or thirty years! He was elevated to the baronetcy after giving some sort of assistance to the Crown and had intended to purchase an estate consonant with his wealth and importance but died suddenly of a fever before fulfilling his ambitions. Sir Robert inherited the family business as well as the family fortune, with instructions in his father's will to provide for his brothers and sister. His middle brother serves as his agent and factotum in the family business in Leeds, where their factories are located. The youngest brother and sister live at home and Miss Blake keeps house for Sir Robert at the manor. I believe that you will find

Sir Robert very pleasant, and I have hopes that his brothers and sister will be likewise agreeable."

Sir Robert retained no traces of his modest lineage, and was very much the gentleman in appearance. He was above average height, although not as tall as Mr. Darcy, and fair haired, his eyes the colour of cornflowers but with dark lashes and brows surrounding them. He greeted them cordially:

"I am most delighted to meet you Mrs. Darcy and Miss Darcy," he said, bowing to each of them in turn. "May I please introduce my sister, Miss Emily Blake, and my youngest brother, Mr. Edward Blake?"

Miss Blake was fair in colouring like her brother but had eyes of an unusual tawny golden brown. She was pretty and her gentle manners were pleasing, but her voice was at odds with her appearance: high pitched and childish sounding. She was gracious to her guests, and Elizabeth and Georgiana made an effort to make their new acquaintance feel welcome to the neighbourhood. Their discussion, when the ladies withdrew to the salon, was pleasant but of the most banal type: Miss Blake talking about what she had done while in Leeds on a recent visit to her other brother, a subject which might have had some interest but which the speaker did not imbue with any vivacity or piquancy.

When the gentlemen finally rejoined them, the Darcy ladies had more of an opportunity to assess the youngest of the Blake brothers than had been possible earlier in the evening. Edward Blake was a young man of middle height, modest good looks, and somewhat shy manners who greeted them quietly and spent most of the evening listening to the conversation, only joining in when asked a question. Elizabeth enquired what his plans were for the future.

"Are you going into the family business as well, Mr. Blake, or do you have other plans?" she enquired.

"I am not really interested in business, I am afraid," he replied with a brief laugh. "Rather than helping my brothers, I am hoping for a military career. My eldest brother has kindly offered to purchase a lieutenant's commission for me once I determine the regiment that I would prefer."

Elizabeth smiled at him. "Well, not everyone is the same, and with the war going on the military offers many opportunities for advancement, I would guess."

"I believe that it does, Mrs. Darcy," he answered. "I confess that my dreams are more of the heroic stamp than could be answered for by a career in trade, although I *am* hoping to obtain a discounted price on my uniforms from my brothers."

Elizabeth laughed with him and the conversation moved on to other topics.

In the quiet of the carriage on the way home, the Darcys discussed the evening. During his interval with the gentlemen after dinner, Darcy had found the two Blake men to be well informed about the state of the war and other current affairs, and he had had a very lively discussion with them about the current prospects for the conflict. The Blakes' business interests had given them some insights into the conduct of the war and had stimulated them to follow the news closely. He had enjoyed himself very much, sparring pleasantly with them over their port about what the future would hold against Napoleon.

"I find myself looking forwards to our next engagement," he said, "if you will forgive the play on words."

"I am not sure we should associate with them if they are going to have such an unfortunate effect on your vocabulary," Elizabeth teased him.

Georgiana watched them with eyes wide in surprise as their badinage went back and forth. Elizabeth seemed to note her sister's surprise at her saucy repartee and smiled reassuringly at her in the dim light as they drew up to the front entrance of Pemberley House.

The next morning Elizabeth was alone at the breakfast table when Georgiana came down. After greeting her, Elizabeth delicately cleared her throat and said, "Georgiana, I wanted to talk to you about something."

"Yes?" she said absently as she sat down with her plate.

"I have noticed you looking rather shocked when I tease your brother."

"Yes, I was rather surprised, at first," she said indistinctly, looking down at her hands.

Elizabeth gently continued, "I do not want you to be uncomfortable, but I want you to realise that it is much different being married to a man than it is being his much younger sister. A wife may tease her husband though he might not tolerate such freedom from someone to whom he stands as a father."

Georgiana looked up briefly and said slowly, "Yes, I did realise that after I thought about it for a while. I suppose that it had never occurred to me before. My mother died when I was so young that I have no recollection of my parents together, and I have no young relatives who are married. My brother, for all his affection for me, has always been rather serious and dignified. I believe it is because our father's untimely death put him in a position where he was required to take up all of the family responsibilities at an early age, including the responsibility for an eleven-year-old sister." She glanced at Elizabeth with a shy smile. "I am happy that he has married someone who is able to help him take off the yoke of duty for a while. He has changed a great deal since he met you, Elizabeth; his heart seems much lighter." She took Elizabeth's hand and gave it a quick squeeze. "So, do not worry about me, my dear sister. I am pleased and delighted to see the two of you together."

Elizabeth grinned and said, "You are a very wise young woman, Miss Georgiana," just as the footman came in to check the serving dishes, and they continued their breakfast.

That afternoon, they called on the squire of Lambton, who was an elderly gentleman named William Walker. He was rather portly in appearance but had an open countenance and blunt, friendly, but unrefined manners. His manor, The Yews, was located at the edge of the village and was of a moderate size: a brick, half-timbered manor house of Tudor ancestry which almost disappeared behind mounds of musty, ancient yews. Squire Walker welcomed them heartily to his parlour and introduced Elizabeth to his wife Beatrice, a little, cheerful woman some years younger than her husband who reminded Georgiana of a wren as she tilted her head alertly while she followed the conversation.

While they drank tea, Mrs. Walker told Elizabeth about their two daughters and their families, who lived near Derby, and about their son, who ran the estate while his father devoted himself to his duties as justice of the peace.

The son, Jonathan Walker, entered the parlour while they were visiting and he greeted them courteously, seating himself between Georgiana and Elizabeth and making himself agreeable during the proffered tea. Georgiana glanced at him surreptitiously as he talked, viewing him with new eyes since her argument with the colonel. He was slightly built and dark complexioned, almost swarthy, with dark hair and hazel eyes and attractive features, although with a mouth and chin somewhat softer than could be considered the ideal of masculine beauty.

During the visit he asked Georgiana questions about her recent activities and she willingly told him about her stay in London, although she felt very conspicuous with her brother watching them and, for the most part, kept her eyes on her hands folded in her lap as she spoke.

When she glanced up, he gave her an intimate smile and she reddened and immediately turned her gaze back down at her hands. It was mortifying to have their conversation overheard; she could not be herself with an audience.

Elizabeth diverted Jonathan with a few comments about the opera night they had attended, and Georgiana was relieved. They did not stay long and left with protestations of friendship and invitations to return from Squire Walker. As they drove home, Darcy said to his sister, "Mr. Walker seems to like you very much, Georgiana."

Her face flamed and she compressed her lips and silently glared at him, half afraid that he would be angry at what she knew was gross insolence.

He raised his brows at her response and then held up his hands and said, "All right. If you do not wish to talk about him we will not."

Biting off her words, she answered, "I am tired of everyone analysing every word that I say to any single young man I meet! I just wish the entire next year was over."

They lapsed into a silence, and Georgiana slumped miserably into the corner of the carriage. What possessed her to behave so churlishly towards both of her guardians when they were only concerned for her future welfare? She just could not seem to help herself.

When they pulled up in front of Pemberley, she went directly upstairs to her room and threw herself on her bed.

Downstairs, Darcy stared up at Georgiana's fleeing back. Elizabeth slipped her arm through his and led him to the drawing-room, where they could shut the door on the servants.

After a long silence, Darcy finally spoke, his voice harsh with concern, "What is wrong with Georgiana? I have never seen her like this. Fitzwilliam told me that Walker was showing an interest in her, and when he tried to talk to her to find out her feelings towards him she snapped at him, too."

Elizabeth gave him a crooked smile. "This is not at all surprising, my dear. Georgiana is under a great deal of strain and will be dealing with many changes in her life over the next year. Sometimes young women do not want to talk about their feelings, particularly when they do not yet know what those feelings are. Also, it is my experience that it is often the girls who have been the most proper and restrained who have the most difficulties expressing their innermost feelings about the young men they meet. I will try to give her an opportunity to speak tomorrow, when she has calmed down, but we cannot force her to speak if she does not wish to. If we push her too hard she may not tell us anything, even if there is something worrisome which we should know. We must wait until she is ready."

Darcy covered her hands with his. "God help us."

"Amen."

In the middle of the night, after lying awake for several hours, Georgiana got up and lit a candle. Elizabeth had come to her door when they were ready to sit down to dinner and Georgiana had managed to tell her she was not hungry without biting her head off. She could not face the looks from her family and did not want the servants discussing her below stairs. She pulled her diary from her bedside table and took it to her desk. She calmly took out a pen and dipped it in the inkwell.

> *21 November: What is it about Mr. Walker that makes me turn into a raving lunatic whenever any of my family mentions his name? Sometimes I think I am going mad with frustration. I constantly feel the weight of their expectations on my shoulders, crushing me. I like Mr. Walker well enough, but I hardly know him and my overreaction to their every question or comment is going to make them think I care more for him than I do. I must try to behave properly and answer their questions calmly if I am to deflect their interest. After my behaviour with Wickham I cannot blame my brother and the colonel for being suspicious of any interest shown me by any young man. Tomorrow I resolve to begin again and try to behave like the lady my mother would have wanted me to be. Pax.*

The next morning, Georgiana forced herself to glide smoothly down the stairs and into the breakfast-parlour. She filled her plate from the sideboard and accepted a cup of coffee from one of the footmen. When the servants left, she lifted her eyes to her brother and sister and said calmly, "I apologise for my behaviour yesterday. It was uncalled for and I am sorry. It will not happen again."

In the thundering silence which greeted this proclamation she began eating her breakfast. Darcy cleared his throat and looked at Elizabeth beseechingly. She spoke up and said, "Thank you, my dear. We are happy that you are feeling better today."

"I thank you, I am. Do you think the weather will be mild enough for a walk today?"

"I do not know."

Darcy ventured tentatively, "Lester came in earlier with a question about the dogs, and he said it was not too bad."

"Perhaps we could walk in the afternoon, then, if the weather is suitable."

"An excellent idea."

They all went back to their breakfast with relief.

After Georgiana had retired to the music-room and they could hear a molto vivace rendition of "Le Coucou" pouring from the piano-forte, Darcy spoke softly to Elizabeth:

"I know that we must tread carefully with Georgiana's feelings, but I felt that I must make some effort to know Mr. Walker's character, since he is so clearly interested in her. So, after we came home yesterday I had a confidential talk with Johnston, my steward. He says that the local gossip is that Mr. Walker is a gambler and is rapidly going through the assets of his father's estate."

Elizabeth was shocked. "His father and mother are so pleasant. Do you think that they know what he is doing?"

"It would seem not. The squire seems to be interested only in his public duties and trusts his son completely."

Elizabeth thought about his words. "I do not think we should tell Georgiana about this when she is already so annoyed with any questioning or interference."

"I agree, but I wanted you to know my suspicions so that you may discourage the connection if the opportunity comes up. I think we must handle this very delicately, especially since they are old family connections and we can only exclude young Walker from Pemberley by breaking with his parents, and I do not have anything but rumour upon which to base my reservations about him."

"It is worrisome that he seems so interested in Georgiana, however, when he is known to be in need of money."

"Indeed. Her fortune enables her to marry without regard to the fortunes of her husband, but it does make me turn a jaundiced eye upon any man who begins courting my sister while in acute financial distress."

She nodded grimly and they went upstairs to dress.

Chapter 9

Heap on more wood!—the wind is chill;
But let it whistle as it will,
We'll keep our Christmas merry still.

—Sir Walter Scott, *Marmion*

Within a fortnight, the Gardiners arrived for the Christmas holiday. They came on a cloudy, gusty day just before the Darcys were to sit down for a cup of tea, and Elizabeth greeted them with embraces and kisses, Darcy with smiles and handshakes. Georgiana curtseyed and smiled silently during the confusion of the unloading of the children and luggage. Since her emotional outburst a fortnight before, she had been uniformly thoughtful and demure, but Elizabeth, in her heart, felt that her sister was fighting to keep her spirits up for their sakes. She did not tell Darcy of her concern over Georgiana's forced placidity because she was not sure if she understood her sister's feelings and did not want to worry him when he was so relieved about her improved spirits. Now, Georgiana turned to the little ones with a kind smile and spoke to them for several minutes, learning their names and ages again and laughing when one of the younger boys did a little caper of excitement. While Georgiana was thus occupied, Mrs. Gardiner, her eyes twinkling, whispered to Elizabeth and Darcy that she had brought the package that they had requested.

"Where is he?" Elizabeth asked quietly.

"In a basket on the floor of the carriage," she replied. "The children will be wild to see him. We thought it best that they not play with him during the journey, as I feared the enthusiastic attentions of four children would be overwhelming for the poor little creature."

"You are probably right about that," Elizabeth returned with a conspiratorial smile.

Mrs. Reynolds arrived at that moment to take the Gardiners upstairs to change out of their travel clothes and to refresh themselves before rejoining the Darcys in the drawing-room for tea. Georgiana went upstairs with them, holding the hands of the two youngest children, who were boys aged four and five years, respectively. When they were gone, Elizabeth and Darcy went to the footmen who were unloading the carriage and had them bring in the basket. They opened the lid and peeked in. Curled up on a scrap of blanket was a tiny white puppy, small enough to fit in the palm of a hand. He opened his eyes sleepily and wagged his whip-like little tail, which curled in a near circle over his back.

"He is adorable—Georgiana will love him!" Elizabeth said excitedly. "When shall we give him to her?

"We won't be able to hide him, so I would suggest that we do it immediately when she comes downstairs," Darcy said.

At that moment Georgiana came down the sweeping staircase, pausing in the middle of the flight and looking perplexed when she saw them bending over the basket.

"Come down, Georgiana, dear, we need to give you your Christmas present a little early!" Elizabeth exclaimed.

Georgiana tripped lightly down the remaining stairs and hurried over. When she saw the puppy, she exclaimed, "A puppy! He is just adorable! Is he really for me?"

"Of course he is, my dear," Darcy said fondly.

She reached gently into the basket and picked him up, cradled him against her and stroked him, and then burst into tears.

"I am sorry," she said thickly, wiping her eyes. "I have wanted a puppy since I was a little girl. You are so good to me." Her eyes welled up again.

The puppy wagged his tail and licked the tears from her face then started whimpering. Darcy gently took him from her with a smile and gave him to one of the footmen, saying, "He probably needs to go outside for a moment; he has had rather a long ride today."

While this was taking place Georgiana embraced her brother tightly and laid her head on his shoulder, the tears still sparkling in her lashes.

"Thank you, my dear brother. You are too, too good to me."

"You should thank Elizabeth," Darcy said, kissing her affectionately on the forehead. "It was her idea and she arranged it with the Gardiners."

She embraced Elizabeth and whispered, "Thank you, my dear, dear sister. I do not deserve either of you."

She released them and took out her handkerchief and dabbed at her eyes.

"What kind of dog is he?" she asked, trying to make her voice sound matter-of-fact.

Elizabeth answered, "He is a Maltese. I knew someone once who had one and he was very sweet—the dog, I mean." They all laughed and then she added, "Do you know what you want to name him?"

"I must think about it—this is such a surprise that I am quite overwhelmed."

The Gardiners came down the stairs and Georgiana ran to them, embracing them and sweetly thanking them for their part in bringing her gift. The children, meanwhile, were crowding around the footman who had returned with the puppy. Georgiana took the little dog and held out her hand to the smallest of the children, saying,

"Let us take him into the drawing-room, shall we?"

They trailed after her happily, and they all sat on the floor in a circle while the now wide-awake puppy gambolled around them. The older adults sat outside the circle and had their tea, amused by the antics of the puppy and the children. The elder of the two boys said suddenly, "You are so lucky to have a puppy!"

Georgiana's eyes widened, and she said, "That is a perfect name for him! I shall call him Lucky!"

That night she recorded in her diary,

15 December: My wonderful brother and sister gave me a puppy for Christmas! I am going to call him Lucky, and he is an adorable little ball of white fluff. Elizabeth says that he will only weigh about seven pounds when he is full grown, and he will have long, silky hair. I insisted that he stay in my room tonight, and he has a neat little basket made up for his bed. I have wanted a puppy for years, but their kindness makes me feel even worse about my disgusting behaviour of the past months. I am even more determined to keep my spirits calm and cheerful to repay their patience.

The next day, Georgiana appeared a little wan in her glass as her maid, Durand, dressed her hair; she had been kept awake much of the night by Lucky's whimpering, but she tenderly held him and petted him in spite of her fatigue.

"I'm sure he will be better soon," Elizabeth reassured her when they met in the parlour after breakfast. "After all, this is the first time he has been away from his mamma."

The children all looked very sad at that idea but started laughing when Lucky stuck his head over Georgiana's arm, where he was nestled comfortably, and looked at them with his black button eyes. The tiny tip of his tail was visible, curled over his back and vibrating furiously in excitement.

That afternoon Georgiana introduced Lucky to Pilot, who generally spent his day sleeping in the library near his master's desk. They all watched Pilot warily as Lucky waddled up to him, alert for any signs of aggression towards the tiny dog who was invading his territory. Pilot, however, waved his tail majestically while he sniffed the newcomer thoroughly, his muzzle as large as the entire puppy. When he was done with his examination he licked him with his huge tongue, knocking him off his unsteady little paws. Lucky returned the compliment, giving the great nose in front of him two quick licks and then rolling over on his back with his tail wagging.

"It seems that Pilot is going to accept him," Darcy said with relief, and Georgiana picked up Lucky and went back into the parlour, patting Pilot affectionately as she went by.

The day passed quickly, but by dinnertime Georgiana was exhausted, tired out by the incessant motion of a house full of children and by her lack of sleep the night before. Bessie, one of the younger housemaids, had been given the task of entertaining the children while they had their dinners upstairs in the nursery and the adults ate theirs in the quiet of the dining-room. Georgiana was too tired to be self-conscious and she was able to converse with Mrs. Gardiner without hesitation during dinner and afterwards in the drawing-room while they had tea and coffee, but it was a struggle to stay awake and she went upstairs early.

The next morning, Elizabeth received a letter from Jane, which she read upstairs before she and Darcy went down for breakfast.

"Oh, dear. Jane wishes us a Happy Christmas and then she continues,

> *…I must tell you, dearest Lizzy, that Caroline has joined us unexpectedly for Christmas. She was to spend it with the Hursts, but she and Louisa had a disagreement (which Bingley attributes to bad temper resulting from Darcy's marrying you, but which I would not like to think of my sister-in-law) and she left town and came to Netherfield. If it is not convenient for you to have an additional and unexpected guest, I fear that we must stay here, for I do not feel that it would be correct to leave her. I will say that she has been very courteous to me since our marriage and has been a charming guest since her arrival. Please write to me as soon as possible and let me know what you wish me to do.—With our dearest love, etc…"*

Darcy agreed with Elizabeth that they were obligated to invite Miss Bingley, and she wrote back immediately to invite her cordially to come with Charles and Jane to Pemberley, but she commented as she finished the letter, "I can think of few people whom I would not prefer to Miss Bingley as a guest, knowing that she tried so hard to capture your heart, and her jealousy added to our mutual dislike to make her insufferable to be around in all of our previous encounters. She is the epitome, in my view, of the worst of society—snobbish, disdainful, and deeply engrossed in her own importance." She sighed and, with a chagrined smile, added, "I suppose that I should try to repress my feelings about her. I have erred in the past in my evaluation of character. Perhaps I will be proven wrong in her case as well."

Darcy gave her a sly smile and returned, "You must take consolation, at least, in the fact that you were the victor in the contest for my heart—even though you did not know at the time that you were competing for it—and realise that it must be even more trying for her to be your guest than for you to be her hostess."

Elizabeth agreed but warned Georgiana that Miss Bingley was coming, much to Georgiana's dismay.

"Oh dear," she exclaimed, "I hope her manners have improved since the last time I saw her! I was quite disgusted with her nasty comments about you after your visit here last summer, and it gave me great pleasure when my brother was finally driven to set her down about it."

"Was he now?" Elizabeth commented, surprised by Georgiana's vehemence after her fortnight of almost unnatural calm. "Well, we must try to forgive her for her past jealousy. She will probably be more amiable now, since she will want to continue to visit Pemberley."

"No doubt," she replied tartly.

The rest of the week before Christmas passed quickly away, and Christmas Day arrived with just a dusting of snow to make everything sparkle in the pale sunlight. When Georgiana entered the breakfast-parlour, she found her sister-in-law sitting flushed-faced at her usual place. When Elizabeth saw her she jumped up and ran to her and kissed her on the cheek.

"I understand that you are partially to thank for my lovely gift, my dear girl!"

"Only partially," said Georgiana with a grin. "So… I am guessing that you liked it."

"It it lovely! I never thought to own a Shakespeare first edition, and I adore his sonnets! I will treasure it. However did the two of you manage in the short time we were in London?"

"Perseverance and an exceptional bookseller," Georgiana said laughingly. "And, you forget that I was in London without you for two short periods of time!"

Elizabeth gave her a final squeeze, and they turned to smile at the Gardiners as they arrived en masse to breakfast. The children could hardly eat between their excitement over the presents and the unusual treat of joining the adults at the table. When they had finally finished their breakfasts, they were allowed to open their packages and then Bessie took them off to the schoolroom to play with their toys and the adults finished eating in peace. Afterwards, they opened their presents and Georgiana's eyes widened when she opened her pearl necklace.

"This must surely be the most beautiful present I have ever received," she said then looked down at her lap where Lucky was sitting. "Other than you, Lucky!"

She once again hugged and kissed her brother and sister for their kindness, as well as the Gardiners for the beautiful embroidered Indian shawl they had given her.

The cook outdid herself and Christmas dinner was a sumptuous feast of roast goose and venison, Yorkshire pudding and buttery roast potatoes, with plum pudding at the end. The children were again allowed to join the adults in the dining-parlour for this special occasion, seated at a small table just for them with Bessie supervising and helping the littlest ones cut their food. They were overawed by the sparkling chandeliers and the footmen silently attending the table but managed to eat some of their meal. Georgiana sat at the main table with the adults, and her eyes sparkled in the candlelight as she ate and talked and watched the children solemnly doing their best to behave correctly. By the time dinner was over, the littlest ones were drooping from exhaustion and Bessie took them up to bed, their feet dragging even as they protested that they were not at all tired.

The rest of the family retired early, worn out from the excitement of Christmas Day. Georgiana dragged herself upstairs and took out her diary before she flopped on the bed, unheeding of her silk gown. She opened to where the ribbon marked her place and read through the previous fortnight's entries. Those bitter thoughts seemed so long ago that they hardly seemed written by the same person. She had kept her word to herself and kept her temper under control; it had been easier with the children and the puppy to entertain and keep her occupied. There had not been time for more than token visits by neighbours to wish them Happy Christmas, so there had not been any discussions of young men or her feelings. However, the colonel would be arriving on the morrow after spending the holiday with his family at Whitwell Abbey, and his visit would be the true test of her resolve. At least Lucky gave her a distraction if she was tempted to needle her flippant cousin Fitzwilliam.

The next day was Boxing Day and the Darcys were up early to supervise the distribution of the Christmas boxes to the Pemberley dependents. When they were finished, the family had a quiet breakfast and enjoyed their last day together, for tomorrow the Gardiners would leave for Hertfordshire.

The colonel arrived in good time on the lightly snowing afternoon, and the Gardiners were interested to meet him, for Elizabeth had told them how pleasant the colonel was after she had first met him in Kent the previous spring. Georgiana and Elizabeth welcomed him to Pemberley, and he bowed over their hands gallantly before Elizabeth introduced him to the Gardiners. He greeted them and they talked easily as they moved into the drawing-room. He was a welcome addition to the dinner table that evening, entertaining them with (hopefully embellished) stories about his life since they had last seen him. He finished a tale involving some new recruits and some errant buckshot and Georgiana commented sardonically, "I hope that this story is not entirely true, Colonel. I would hate to think the safety of the royal family in such inept hands."

"I swear to you, little cousin, that the tale is entirely—or at least mostly—true."

His audience laughed and Georgiana rolled her eyes. After they finished eating, Georgiana went upstairs and brought Lucky down to meet her cousin.

"This is Lucky, our new watchdog, Cousin," she said sternly. "Beware if you decide to sneak downstairs for a glass of ale or a bite of cheese during the night. He is especially fierce about cheese thieves."

"I am sure he will be a welcome addition to the pack when we go hunting tomorrow as well, my dear little cousin," he teased. "He will likely be the first to flush the birds, although those short legs may have some difficulty getting over the stiles."

"Lucky is far too intelligent to spend his morning running around in the mud and the cold as you will be doing, dear cousin," she replied, giving him an impudent grin.

The Darcys and the colonel excused themselves after dinner and made their required appearance at the servants' party. Elizabeth and Darcy led the first dance, followed by Georgiana and the colonel. When they finished the dance the colonel bowed to his partner and said, "You are a charming dancer, little cousin."

Georgiana gave him a sly look. "I was going to say the same about you, Cousin. You have improved much since you tripped over your feet at the New Year's ball when I was eight years old."

The colonel gave a thunderous look at Darcy. "Did your brother tell you about that?"

"Oh no, I saw it. After my governess sent me to bed, I got up and watched the dancing from upstairs through the balusters. I laughed so hard that I had to run back to my bedroom so as not to be caught spying. Of course, the next day I had to pretend ignorance or give myself away."

Colonel Fitzwilliam rolled his eyes at Darcy. "The sins of our youth will never be forgotten will they?"

Later, Georgiana sat on her bed, chewing her lower lip, before writing,

26 December: It was wonderful to be back on my former terms with my cousin Fitzwilliam tonight and he seems to have forgotten my previous ill-humour. However, I was jolted when I teased the colonel about something which happened when I was eight and he commented that "the sins of our youth will never be forgotten." I was doing the same thing to him that I have accused him of, i.e., never forgetting my past errors! I am sure that he knows I was only teasing him, but I feel badly about my saucy attempt to embarrass my easygoing guardian. I should be more forgiving of others' mistakes, but, more importantly, I should be more forgetful of them. Sensitive as I am of my egregious and humiliating behaviour with Wickham, I should not poke fun at others about their trivial indiscretions and errors. Fortunately, the colonel's innate good humour brushed off my faux pas with a joke. I hope that he was not hurt by my callous comment.

She sighed, closed the book, and blew out her candle.

The adults stayed up rather later than usual talking that last evening of their visit, but the Gardiners were up and ready to leave by nine o'clock the next morning. After the bustle of packing and loading the carriage they all said farewell, and Georgiana saw tears glittering in Elizabeth's eyes. She walked over and put her arms around her sister, and they clung to each other in the chilly air as they watched the carriage disappear into the woods.

Chapter 10

All the world's a stage,
And all the men and women merely players.

—William Shakespeare, *As You Like It*

Pemberley was quiet that day after the loss of their friends, but Georgiana felt an air of expectancy in the house as they waited for the Bingleys and Mr. Bennet and Kitty, who were to arrive in a few days. She was eager for the next round of guests, for avoiding too much intimacy within the family circle was her object. If there was no time for questioning and speculation about her marriage prospects, there would be no opportunity for her to lose her temper. Also, the less chance she had to speak, the less likely it was that she would embarrass herself with an awkward attempt at pertness.

In the meantime, Mrs. Reynolds was bustling about, making sure that everything in the house was perfect for their visitors. Her brother and the colonel spent the mornings out with their dogs and the kennel master when the weather permitted, hoping to flush a few pheasants but mostly attempting to train a couple of young dogs. Georgiana went up to the music room and played her harp for two hours to make up for her negligence over the holidays and to avoid a tête-à-tête with Elizabeth and her too observant eyes. She felt like a tightrope walker, carefully balancing her emotions and reactions to avoid both biting sarcasm and ill-timed jocularity.

When she left the music room she encountered Elizabeth in the hall.

"Are you done playing, Georgiana?"

"Yes, my fingertips are sore. I have not been playing enough to toughen them to the strings."

"I am just on my way to find Mrs. Reynolds so we can work in the picture gallery."

"I will join you, if you do not mind. I always enjoy hearing about the history of my ancestors, particularly some of those who made rather bad ends. It is interesting to see if you can see their history painted into their portrait faces."

"I had not thought of looking at it that way. I have heard of occasions, although I do not know if the stories are true, when subjects were unhappy with their portraits because the artist revealed too much about their true character in the work. Apparently, in some of these cases at least, the sitter actually paid extra to compensate the artist for not allowing him to display his work at the Academy, took the painting, and it was never seen again."

"It would be very interesting to see those paintings, would it not?"

Elizabeth agreed and sent a footman for Mrs. Reynolds, and they spent about an hour in the gallery. Elizabeth had decided after her first session trying to learn the family names and history that she would record the histories of the paintings; so, after this day's session, Georgiana sat down with her and prompted her while she wrote as much information as they could recall in a journal.

"Well, my dear, I think that we had better quit for today. My brain is full of as many facts as it will safely hold. Thank you for your patience, Georgiana."

"It was my pleasure, my dear sister."

They busied themselves later in the afternoon with making preparations for the ball that they would hold to coincide with the Bingleys' and the Bennets' visit. After they had decided on the many details with Mrs. Reynolds (or, rather, Elizabeth had decided while Georgiana listened with dismay at all the details involved), Elizabeth suggested a walk to her since the day was fine, although cold. She accepted and they bundled up in their warmest pelisses and gloves, setting out along one of the paths beside the trout stream with Lucky on his lead and Pilot accompanying them.

They meandered along the paths, keeping fairly close to the house since it was too cold to walk far, and Georgiana kept the conversation on the subject of the ball. All of the local gentry had been invited as well as some from farther away who were old acquaintances of the Darcy family and who would stay the night at Pemberley afterwards. They would have ten of their guest rooms filled, and Georgiana was both excited and apprehensive because she had never been to a ball nor seen so many guests at Pemberley.

"I am always so fearful of saying the wrong thing or not doing what I am supposed to, Elizabeth. I don't know how to stop feeling so nervous," she admitted, as she fidgeted with Lucky's lead.

"Experience will help, my dear. With music, practise allows you to know instantly where to put your fingers while reading a piece. Practise making introductions and small talk are the same; the more you work at it, the easier it is."

Georgiana frowned. "But there are so many possible variations in human intercourse, Elizabeth. You cannot write down a single version of a conversation and rehearse it until you are perfect."

There was a long pause while the two ladies considered the difficulties.

"Perhaps I could help you," Elizabeth finally said. "We could pretend various situations and you could practise your responses so that they will eventually come naturally to your lips." She gave the girl a wry look. "I know that I hate it when I think of something witty to say after the opportunity to speak has passed!"

Georgiana laughed in spite of herself and said, "I doubt if I will ever be witty, my dear sister, but it would be nice to not feel a fool every time I meet someone."

They agreed to try Elizabeth's plan when they could be alone and made their way slowly back to the house, Georgiana laughing sardonically to herself about the results of her efforts to avoid situations which could develop into discussions of her thoughts and feelings about single young men. Hoist with her own petard.

In the meantime, the gentlemen were watching the kennel master put the dogs through their paces.

"Darcy," started the colonel, hesitantly, "I want to congratulate you again on your marriage. Mrs. Darcy is a wonderful woman and I am quite jealous of your good fortune in marrying her." He smiled, looking a little chagrined. "If I had been an eldest son, I might have been tempted to woo her myself."

Darcy regarded him quizzically, for it was not like his easygoing cousin to be dissatisfied with his lot in life.

"I know that I am very fortunate, Fitzwilliam, and I cannot believe it myself," he said quietly. He then added in a lighter tone, "I will just have to annoy you as I did when we were lads and quote the Bard to you: 'Get thee a wife,' Cousin."

"I would like to marry," the colonel returned soberly. "I am ready to settle down, but finding the right woman is the obstacle. After so many years at court, I am afraid that I have developed rather a jaundiced eye for society women—they all seem to be rather shrill and brainless, not to mention the moral standards of those who gather round the Prince Regent. That, of course, includes the exceedingly small number among that set who would even consider marrying a penniless younger son." He paused for a moment, slapping his gloves against his hands absently, and then continued, his eyes on the line of trees which marked the end of the field.

"Did I tell you that Lady Catherine has been very attentive, writing to me weekly and hoping that I will return for a visit again soon? I think that I am the next sacrificial victim selected to marry our poor cousin Anne." He grimaced. "I need a wife with a good fortune, but I am not willing to sacrifice every other comfort to marry for it. My father has been gently hinting to me that I should marry Anne; I think he feels that he will have done his duty by his younger son if he can marry him to the de Bourgh money and keep it in the family. To give him his due, I do not believe that he has seen Anne in several years since he is not fond of his sister-in-law's domineering nature and prefers to be amiable from a distance. He probably does not realise how ill Anne truly is. I know that Lady Catherine always sends glowing reports of how much better some new treatment is working." He shrugged off his unaccustomed seriousness, pulling his gloves on briskly and adding, "Still, there is always hope! Thank you for listening to my whingeing, Cousin."

"I am happy to give you a shoulder to cry on, Fitzwilliam," Darcy said, clapping him on the back. "Perhaps we can find some pleasant ladies at the ball next week who have not been jaded by too much time at court."

Fitzwilliam smiled vaguely and abruptly changed the subject. "How has Georgiana been?"

Darcy glanced across the field to locate the kennel master and then said in a low voice, "She has been very pleasant over the past fortnight, but before the Gardiners arrived we had a major set-to. It was after we had called on Squire Walker and his wife so I could introduce them to Elizabeth. Jonathan Walker came in during our visit and was very attentive to Georgiana, so afterwards I commented that he seemed to like her very much and she positively turned to ice. She then proceeded to tell me that she was sick of having her every move and every word minutely examined. She apologised the next day and has been very even tempered since, but I do not believe her equanimity is because the problem is resolved. Until the Gardiners arrived and provided an easy distraction, she seemed as taut as one of the strings on her harp." He suddenly looked at his cousin. "Have you ever seen what happens when a harp string breaks?"

The colonel stared at him in surprise at this seeming non sequitur. "No, I do not believe I have."

"When the string weakens and breaks it gives off a report like a gun, and the change in tension causes all the other strings to lose their tuning."

"Ah, I see your point. I, too, am concerned that the pressure that society and family put on her coming-out, at least in her perception, will cause Georgiana to break down. It pains me to see how little regard she has for her own worth. When she was a child she was lively and spirited and had no shyness around others. When she became a young woman she seemed to lose all sense of confidence. I am sure it did not help that your father died around that time."

They both stood silent, lost in the past, until the dogs and the gamekeeper returned from the end of the field.

The gentlemen rejoined the ladies for tea in the afternoon and Darcy asked, "How was your morning, ladies?"

Elizabeth and Georgiana told of their plans for the ball and about their walk (excluding only their plans for Georgiana's "lessons") while they poured the tea.

Fitzwilliam turned to Georgiana. "I hope, little cousin, that you are planning to give your old guardian the first dance at the ball."

Georgiana looked at her hands, suddenly shy, but said calmly enough, "Of course, Cousin."

"Good, it is settled then. We must show the local youths how it is done," he said, just a little too heartily.

Georgiana sat silently and the conversation flowed around her. Soon afterwards, the gentlemen retired to the billiard-room and the two ladies went upstairs to Georgiana's room. Mrs. Annesley was visiting her family for the holidays, so they would be undisturbed while they practised the social graces. Elizabeth played various parts and coached Georgiana when she was at a loss, which was frequently.

"Let us try, again, my dear. Let us try a situation that will soon occur. I will be my sister Jane and I am arriving at Pemberley with my husband, my sister, and my father. You must greet them and then introduce them to Colonel Fitzwilliam. I will play all the other parts as well. All right?"

Georgiana nodded, her face grimly intent.

"My dear Miss Darcy, it is delightful to see you again." Elizabeth embraced her and then stepped to the side and said in a deep voice, "It is good to see you again, Miss Darcy."

Georgiana covered her mouth and giggled nervously.

"I am sorry; it is too funny watching you."

Elizabeth chuckled. "Yes, it probably is, but let us keep our focus on your responses!"

Georgiana took a deep breath and put a pleasant smile on her face as she held out her hand and shook "Bingley's." "Thank you, Mr. Bingley. Welcome to Pemberley. I believe you know my cousin, Colonel Fitzwilliam?"

Elizabeth answered, trying a voice that was just a little lower than her own, "Delighted, Colonel. Yes, we met in London, quite some time ago."

Elizabeth said, "And now my papa and my sister Kitty come in."

Georgiana smiled and curtseyed. "Hello, Mr. Bennet, Miss Catherine Bennet. It is good to see you again." She stopped, frozen, as she desperately searched for the next phrase.

Elizabeth looked at her expectantly until finally Georgiana threw up her hands in despair.

"Now what should I do?"

"You could invite them to follow Mrs. Reynolds upstairs to change and refresh themselves. If they had come just a short way, you could invite them into the drawing-room or wherever you were planning to entertain them and then order tea."

Georgiana sighed.

"I just seem to freeze. I wish you would instead ask me to conjugate a French verb or recite a passage from a history text, as long as I did not need to do it in front of anyone else. I wish I could be witty and playful like you are, Elizabeth."

"My dear sister," Elizabeth said gently, "please, please do not try to be someone else—you want to be yourself. The main purpose of this playacting is not to make you into someone you are not but to make you able to show your lovely, true self without being uncomfortable and shy."

"How can someone like me compete with all the beautiful, charming young ladies like you?"

"I thank you, Georgiana, for the compliment, but you are an attractive and intelligent young woman, so do not wish to trade places with someone else," Elizabeth said bracingly. "Now, let us try to go back to the beginning and go step by step through greetings; perhaps we are going too fast."

They struggled on for another quarter hour, and Georgiana sighed, "I do not think that I am a good actress."

Elizabeth laughed. "Your brother would probably be happy to know that; think of his horror if you really *were* an actress…! I believe you need to think of this a little differently, Georgiana. You must realise, dearest, that we are all actors, every moment that we are in the society of another person. Every time we are courteous to someone we do not like, or feign an interest in the conversation of someone who is a bore, we are acting. Even with those we love we are acting when we cover up a bad mood or pretend more interest in our friends' activities than we actually feel in order to avoid hurting their feelings. Our entire existence outside of the circle of our intimate friends and family is only appearance, a masque if you will, which covers and protects our true selves."

"I never thought of it that way," Georgiana said slowly, remembering her attempts to keep her equanimity over the past month.

"The other thing that you must realise," Elizabeth added," is that you have the felicity to be able to choose your marriage partner without having to worry about fortune causing difficulties. When you are in society you will often have the superior status, so you need not be embarrassed or worried about what others will think of you; they will be more concerned with gaining your favour than in criticising your behaviour." She gave Georgiana a sidelong glance. "Anyway, those who are your superior in rank will also want your favour because of your dowry and impeccable family background."

"I know that," Georgiana said, hanging her head, "I sometimes feel like a prize heifer at auction…"

Elizabeth gave a rueful laugh. "Sometimes the interactions between single men and women *are* not much different from a livestock sale, Georgiana. Just be sure *you* are the one making the purchase, dear girl."

They embraced and then went to their rooms to change for dinner, each meditating upon the conversation.

And tune thy jolly voice to my fresh pipe,
And all the daughters of the year shall dance!

—WILLIAM BLAKE, *POETICAL SKETCHES*, "TO AUTUMN"

THE BINGLEYS AND THE BENNETS ARRIVED THE NEXT AFTERNOON. The footman announced the appearance of the carriage to the ladies as they sat in the music room, Georgiana playing the harp while Elizabeth listened and fitfully worked on her needlepoint. They went downstairs and met Darcy and the colonel in the hall as they came from the library. Georgiana had hesitantly agreed to Elizabeth's suggestion that morning that she introduce the colonel to everyone, but, in spite of their practise, her hands were shaking and her palms damp.

Miss Bingley entered first and greeted them, her face wreathed in smiles.

"Mrs. Darcy, Mr. Darcy," she said effusively to Elizabeth and Darcy as she curtseyed. Then she embraced Georgiana fervently and exclaimed, "And of course, my dear Georgiana! How wonderful it is to see you!"

"Welcome to Pemberley, Miss Bingley," Georgiana replied with a stiff smile. "May I please introduce you to my cousin, Colonel Fitzwilliam?"

Miss Bingley's eyes had already found the colonel, and she curtseyed gracefully. "I am very happy to meet any relation of the Darcys, Colonel. I was desolated that I did not have the chance to be introduced at my brother's wedding."

The colonel bowed and murmured, "*Enchanté*, Mademoiselle."

Georgiana looked sharply at him, but his face was a picture of unexceptional courtesy and Miss Bingley did not seem to notice the dryness in his tone. Jane and Bingley appeared and Elizabeth embraced and kissed them both.

"Welcome, my dear sister and brother. And of course you know Georgiana." Jane embraced Georgiana and Bingley shook her hand cordially.

"Georgiana, it is so good to see you again," Jane said to her and smiled her gentle and irresistible smile. Georgiana felt her stiff posture relax, and after a moment she recalled herself, saying smoothly, "Mr. and Mrs. Bingley, you are, of course, acquainted with my cousin, Colonel Fitzwilliam."

Jane offered the colonel her hand. "I am delighted to see you again, Colonel."

Bingley shook the colonel's hand and the two men fell into conversation.

Mr. Bennet and Kitty had come in behind the others. Mr. Bennet embraced Elizabeth tenderly before he greeted the others and then Kitty kissed Elizabeth on the cheek and shyly curtseyed to Darcy and the colonel. Georgiana was relieved when the colonel picked up the conversation and she could listen from the background.

After the visitors had changed out of their travel clothes and refreshed themselves upstairs, they all met in the drawing-room. Georgiana wanted to hide at the edge of the group, but she saw that Kitty was more than a little awed by her surroundings, so she exerted herself to go over to her new sister. After they had talked awkwardly for a few minutes about the drive to Derbyshire, Georgiana said, "Would you like to see my puppy? My brother and sister gave him to me for Christmas. Your Aunt and Uncle Gardiner kindly brought him…" She chattered on as they went upstairs and then brought Lucky down to the salon to meet everyone. Kitty was enraptured by the puppy and soon the two young women were at ease, playing with Lucky and talking without embarrassment to each other while the rest of the conversation ranged freely around the room.

"Darcy, I would like to discuss a couple of things about Netherfield with you when we have a chance," Bingley said. "I would like to increase the bird population, but I do not want to take too much of the land out of production."

"Perhaps we could sit down and talk about it tomorrow morning?"

"Splendid. I brought the maps so you can see more clearly what I am talking about, but you are already familiar with the Netherfield lands."

Elizabeth was sitting with Jane and Mr. Bennet and catching up on all the news of Longbourn and Meryton. When they had covered everything in Hertfordshire, Elizabeth told her sister about the ball she and Georgiana had planned. Miss Bingley had managed to seat herself next to Colonel Fitzwilliam and appeared, to Georgiana at least, to be quite satisfied with her companion as she demanded his attention with as much determination as she ever had Mr. Darcy's a year ago.

After dinner, when the gentlemen had rejoined them, Elizabeth, at the colonel's request, played the pianoforte and sang and then she and Georgiana played a duet they had been practising for the occasion while their guests enjoyed their coffee and tea. Colonel Fitzwilliam sat next to Kitty during the performance, but Kitty looked down at her hands during most of their conversation, her cheeks pink.

After they had finished playing, as the guests circulated around the room, Elizabeth found herself standing next to the colonel, a little apart from the others.

"I have not had the chance to speak to you much since my arrival," the colonel said quietly. "I wanted to thank you for all that you have done for Georgiana. I can see that she is already a little more comfortable in company, and Darcy tells me that you have taken her under your wing as a true sister. She is still very young, even for her age, and it is reassuring that she will have you to advise and guide her—it is very difficult for two old men like Darcy and me to care for the needs of a sixteen-year-old girl without a woman's advice. Mrs. Annesley, of course, has been very good to her, but a sister just a little older than she will understand her far better than we can."

"You don't need to thank me, Colonel," Elizabeth said in some embarrassment. "Georgiana is a sweet girl and I love her dearly already."

"Well, I won't mention it again, but I just wanted you to know that I appreciate your efforts," the colonel murmured absently as he looked over at his ward, who was giggling with Kitty at some of Lucky's antics.

The days passed quickly. The Friday of the ball soon arrived and the house was filled with the bustle of preparations. Elizabeth and Georgiana met with Mrs. Reynolds immediately after breakfast, but dealing with the many details of the ball took them most of the morning. When they were finished they returned to their guests and found that the younger gentlemen had gone for a ride, while Mr. Bennet was reading in the library. The ladies spent the rest of the morning talking and working on their needlework as it was too cold for a walk.

Georgiana had shown Kitty the conservatory earlier in the week, and they enjoyed playing with Lucky among the tropical foliage. He was already learning to fetch a rubber ball on command, although he was still clumsy and often tumbled head over heels trying to chase it, landing on his nose with a very surprised look on his face, to the amusement of the girls.

The morning of the ball, Georgiana asked casually, "Have you been to many balls, Kitty?"

"Oh, yes. When the militia were quartered in Meryton last winter there were several private balls. Mr. Bingley gave one at Netherfield Hall and the militia gave one as well. Most of the time, though, we had smaller dances, parties, and teas, as well as the balls at the Assembly Hall. It was really lovely having all of the officers available for dancing, although not all of them could dance well." She giggled, remembering a couple of ensigns who had been hopeless, and then shrugged. "Then, in the summer they moved to Brighton and life in Meryton was very dull in comparison."

"Your youngest sister is married to an officer, is she not?"

"Yes, Lydia is married to Mr. Wickham. He was a lieutenant in Colonel Forster's regiment, but he changed to the regulars when he and Lydia married, and they are stationed in Newcastle."

"Do you miss seeing your sister?"

Kitty considered a while and then slowly said, "Lydia and I spent all our time together as the two youngest of five daughters. We were not interested in anything but the officers from the moment they came, and they absorbed all our thoughts. But they left for their summer quarters, and Lydia was invited to go with them as the guest of Colonel Forster's wife... I was mad with jealousy. Why should she be allowed to go when I was not, particularly since I was two years older? Then she eloped with Wickham. My father was furious, and my mother swooned and took to her bed while he went off to look for them. When she had first written and hinted that this might happen, I thought it just a lark; she told me that they were eloping to Gretna Green to marry. Their actions almost destroyed my family. After the news came out we heard all sorts of bad things about Wickham and about his gaming debts.

"When Wickham was finally induced to marry Lydia, with the assistance of my Uncle Gardiner, they came to stay for a fortnight before leaving for Newcastle. When they arrived you would think that nothing had ever been done wrong by them. They did not have an ounce of shame between them. I do not want to do that to my family. I know that I will not find a husband such as Mr. Bingley or your brother. I have no fortune, no family name, no particular qualities of intelligence or grace, and I do not have enough beauty to tempt a gentleman to overlook those deficits. I am just an ordinary girl whose father is a gentleman, and the men who are in a similar situation cannot afford to marry without money." There was a note of despair in her voice.

Georgiana took her hand and squeezed it. "I think you do not give yourself enough credit, Kitty, but you must consider one thing. When you do find a young man who wishes to marry you, it will be because he loves you, not because he wants to enhance his social standing with your fortune or your family name."

Kitty looked at her friend and sighed.

"And, my dear, since your sisters have married well, you will at least have a chance of meeting some gentlemen."

"I know, I know; Lord knows that's all my mother talks about. I wonder if Elizabeth will invite me to come to London when you go."

"We will just have to make sure that she does." Georgiana gave her a grin which finally caused an answering smile on Kitty's face. After a moment, Georgiana leaned over and wrapped her arms around her and patted her gently on the back. Kitty whispered, "Thank you, Georgiana."

They had an earlier and larger repast than usual that afternoon, not quite dinner but more than tea, for they would need time to prepare for the ball and supper would not be until midnight. Georgiana and Kitty sat side by side on the settee and sipped their tea and whispered nervously to each other. Elizabeth saw that they were not eating and said, "You must try to eat, my dears. It will be a long evening before supper is served."

Georgiana swallowed, her face pale, and nodded. Jane passed them each a cucumber sandwich.

"Please try, my dears."

They obediently bit into their sandwiches and slowly ate them, but neither was able to eat any of the cakes or scones offered on the tray, and eventually the gong sounded that it was time to dress.

Upstairs, everything was in a state of hushed pandemonium as the ladies' maids and valets rushed to and from their masters' and mistresses' rooms on urgent errands—to touch up the ironing of a cravat or find a needle and thread for a repair. Georgiana's lady's maid, Durand, had come to Pemberley with them but she was young and still learning, so Elizabeth's maid was to do Georgiana's and Kitty's hair. When they knocked on Elizabeth's door Durand admitted them. Lambert was in the middle of telling her mistress, with a somewhat malicious twinkle in her eye, that she and Oliver had agreed that the master and mistress should be especially dazzling tonight.

"I have been planning a new hairstyle for you, Madame Darcy, which I saw while we were in London and have been waiting for an occasion to try. I think it will be *très chic*, Madame, and will be *magnifique* with your new gown. Oliver has selected, pending monsieur's approval *naturellement,* a black waistcoat which has a very thin, pale yellow stripe in ze pattern, which will thus pick up ze *couleur* of Madame's gown. Nothing blatant *vous comprenez*, but just a leetle hint to ze other ladies that Monsieur Darcy belongs with Madame."

"Very well, Lambert," Elizabeth said, as Lambert's accent became more and more pronounced in her excitement. "I put myself entirely in your hands."

With an air of supreme satisfaction, Lambert began her work. When she finished Elizabeth twirled around so the girls could see her.

"You look wonderful, Elizabeth!" Georgiana applauded, and Kitty nodded her agreement, her face beaming.

"Thank you, ladies. Lambert, you should do Miss Darcy next because she will need to be ready early to greet the visitors."

"*Oui*, Madame Darcy." The maid tested the heat remaining in the curling tongs and turned to Georgiana.

When she looked down over the balustrade and saw everyone gathered downstairs for the ball, Georgiana was dazzled by the rainbow of colours. Jane's pastel pink gown competed with Miss Bingley's vibrant russet. Elizabeth's lemon-coloured gown shimmered with iridescence in the candlelight and the newly set diamonds in her ears and around her neck reflected a million points of light around the hall. Georgiana felt a little musty and worn compared to their splendour, in spite of her pale satin gown and the strands of pearls Lambert had woven into her hair.

Georgiana had just begun to look around for Kitty when she appeared behind her, gowned in blue-grey silk, her hair a confection of curls and ribbons.

"Georgiana, you look lovely!"

Georgiana smiled ruefully. "Thank you. I just wish that my gown was a trifle more stylish. The one part of my official debut that I am looking forwards to is that I will be allowed to wear lower-cut bodices on my gowns."

"Well, you look very well anyway." Kitty took her arm and they walked down the stairs together.

"You ladies look splendid," Elizabeth said as she kissed Georgiana and Kitty and smiled at Miss Bingley.

The gentlemen soon joined them, and the guests began arriving for the ball. The Darcys were kept busy greeting their guests and introducing them to the Bingleys and the Bennets. Georgiana was relieved to find herself between Elizabeth and her brother in the reception line. She had merely to say "good evening" and curtsey, and the responsibilities of greeting and introducing would be left to her brother and sister. When Jonathan Walker arrived with his parents, he greeted Darcy and Elizabeth and bowed over

Georgiana's hand. Georgiana was embarrassed at this public display of peculiar regard and felt her cheeks burn. To divert his attention, she gestured to Elizabeth's other side and said, "Mr. Walker, this is Miss Catherine Bennet."

Walker purred, "Delighted, Miss Bennet" then turned back to Georgiana. "Could I possibly engage you for the first two dances, Miss Darcy?"

Georgiana, her eyes staring at her toes, mumbled, "I am sorry, I am already engaged for the first two."

"Perhaps the second pair then?"

"Yes, thank you."

"Miss Bennet, would you, perhaps, give me the pleasure of the first two dances?"

"Why yes, Mr. Walker, I would be delighted." Kitty swept into a curtsey which Georgiana could only envy.

Georgiana breathed a sigh of relief when Walker had passed and she had only some elderly friends of the family to greet.

The orchestra had begun playing as soon as the first carriage rolled up to the door, and when the guests had all arrived Elizabeth and Darcy led the first dance. They were followed down the line by Georgiana and Colonel Fitzwilliam and Jane and Bingley. Kitty followed the Bingleys with Jonathan Walker, her face showing her pleasure in being asked for the first pair of dances.

Elizabeth was kept busy by her husband making the acquaintance of all their guests. Georgiana found herself the centre of attention around the dance floor, with several young men vying for her attention every moment she was not dancing. Kitty stayed by her side and when they had a moment's peace, whispered, "I am staying with you, Georgiana, so I can catch a few of the disappointed cast-offs from among your admirers."

Georgiana lifted her brow at her sister and they both giggled, but she could not maintain her good humour when there were so many demands upon her attention. One of the gentlemen in her coterie was Sir Robert Blake, who asked her to dance early in the evening and then gave Kitty equal time. Sir Robert's handsome looks and genial temper struck Georgiana. She had thought of him as being in the same generation as her brother and too old and experienced for her, but he was quite good looking. He was very kind, his conversation light and undemanding. She enjoyed their two dances and gave him as much encouragement as she was capable of, hoping for another pair of dances after supper. Georgiana, while she was waiting to go down the line, watched Kitty dance with an awkward young man of about eighteen who had crooked teeth and ears like a jug. She had already forgotten his name, but he was most likely a not unpleasing partner as his parents had made sure that he knew how to dance properly.

As the first part of the evening wore on, Georgiana could feel herself tiring from the pressure of all her dance partners. She was relieved when Elizabeth rescued her and made sure that she was seated with her sister and brother for supper, leaving Kitty to sit with Jonathan Walker and Sir Robert Blake's middle brother, James.

At the supper table, Georgiana studied the Comte de Tournay, who was across from her. He had arrived at his sister's for Christmas, as expected, and tonight was the first time she had met him. The Darcys had been invited to Kympton Hall for dinner two days hence, so they would all have a better opportunity to learn his tastes and temper then, but this, her first glimpse of him, was intriguing. He was somewhat over forty years old and handsome in a dark, brooding way but looked rather dissipated; his lower lids were pouched, and deep creases marked the line between his nose and mouth. In spite of having lived in England for more than twenty years he was consciously French, with Continental manners. He had tried to make himself agreeable to Georgiana during the first half of the ball, but she had not known what to say to him. Elizabeth must have seen her dilemma, because she had swept him up and introduced him to Miss Bingley. He had seemed to be quite pleased to dance with her and Caroline had appeared entranced to meet a count, even one whose fortune had disappeared into the churning maw of the French Revolution.

Georgiana was not so well satisfied, however, with Jonathan Walker, who seemed to be always hovering near her. When he talked to her, he leaned towards her in an intimate manner which made her want to step back away from him, and only the most stringent effort prevented her from fleeing. Elizabeth had been keeping an eye on them and she again rescued Georgiana when Mr. Walker was pressing her to allow him to escort her to church.

"Please say you will, Miss Darcy. I am counting on you."

Elizabeth appeared at his side and interjected mildly, "Counting on her for what Mr. Walker?"

He started but quickly recovered himself.

"I am trying to convince Miss Darcy to allow me to escort her to church this Sunday, Mrs. Darcy."

"I am sorry, but I am afraid that Georgiana will have responsibilities with our guests on Sunday, Mr. Walker." She managed to infuse the refusal with a creditable counterfeit of real regret, but Georgiana could hear the chill in her voice.

"Ah. Perhaps another time then. Miss Darcy, Mrs. Darcy." He bowed and moved off.

Elizabeth watched him for a moment as he asked Miss Blake to dance and then turned to Georgiana, who sighed in relief.

"Are you all right, my dear?" Elizabeth whispered.

"I am now. Thank you, Elizabeth. You are my friend forever. I did not know what to do with him," she said with a brief smile.

Elizabeth grinned at her and went back to Darcy's side, relieved that Georgiana still had a spark of spirit remaining. Darcy had noticed her defection from his side.

"How is Georgiana doing?"

"She seems to be fine, but I thought I needed to give her a little assistance in detaching young Mr. Walker. I think she is beginning to find him too persistent. He rather reminds me of a limpet."

Darcy chuckled but had a wary look in his eye as he watched Mr. Walker dance with Miss Blake. "A very apt comparison, but if necessary we will forcibly disengage him and throw him back into the sea."

"Indeed we will," she murmured and turned to talk to some guests who were approaching. Colonel Fitzwilliam stopped at her side after finishing a set on the dance floor and commented on the change in his cousin.

"I have never before seen Darcy so relaxed and happy at a ball," he said. "You are a miracle worker, Mrs. Darcy." He gave her a courtly bow.

She smiled archly at him and thanked him but commented, "You just keep your eye on Georgiana, my dear cousin. I do not want her to be overwhelmed with all these young men. They are insistent enough to give her, as the Scottish would say, a '*cauld grue*.'"

He looked over at his ward and said, "You are right, my dear Mrs. Darcy, and Jonathan Walker is the most importunate of them all. I believe that I will go break up the group and ask her to dance again; I think an old cousin can have a second dance without causing undue comment."

Georgiana was beginning to feel very limp when her cousin strolled over and neatly captured her from the mass of gentlemen in a manoeuvre that did credit to his military training. She felt her tension dissipate as they danced the set, and she revived enough to notice the other young women watching them. She looked at her cousin speculatively and noted for the first time his soldierly carriage and his pleasant countenance. She could, perhaps, see why (annoying as he could sometimes be) he always had plenty of invitations to parties when he was in London.

She scanned the room. Kitty was dancing every dance and had partnered with Edward Blake, the youngest of the Blakes, at least twice that Georgiana had seen. They made a pleasing couple as they went through the figures of the dance and Kitty's face was flushed with heat and gratification. Her new friend seemed to be enjoying herself now that she had overcome her awe at being at Pemberley.

She saw Elizabeth go to the door and speak to her father, who had appeared from his refuge in the library. Georgiana was sure that her brother would also prefer to spend the evening in the library; she well knew his dislike of balls and dancing. He, however, was doing his best to be a good host and seemed actually to be enjoying himself. She noted these things while she and Colonel Fitzwilliam were engaged in a conversation with Miss Blake. Georgiana reflected to herself that Miss Blake, pleasant as she was, was rather insipid and silly. Still, her manners were excellent, and it was nice to have another young woman to talk to occasionally. She saw that Miss Blake seemed to be rather taken with the colonel, smiling at him attentively whenever he entered the conversation, which was often, with his easy manners. She coolly examined the two of them while they talked to each other, her face, she hoped, impassive. Miss Blake was attractive and her fortune was suitable for her cousin, but she hoped that he could find someone who was more than just a pretty face for a wife.

She suddenly felt very tired and she went to her sister-in-law and whispered, "It is almost two o'clock, Elizabeth, and I am exhausted. Would it be discourteous for me to go upstairs now?"

"No, of course not, my dear. It is very late for you, and you do look ready to collapse. I am sorry that I did not notice earlier." She put her arm around the girl.

"It came upon me rather suddenly," Georgiana said with an attempt at a smile. "I think the war between fear and excitement kept me going far beyond my strength."

With a pat on the hand, Elizabeth sent her up to her room. Kitty was apparently still full of energy, for she was dancing, but Georgiana could barely drag herself up the stairs. The ball continued until almost three o'clock, and she was still lying awake when the orchestra finished with "Sir Roger de Coverley." She heard the murmur of the guests who were leaving saying good night to their host and hostess and the guests who were staying the night straggling up the stairs to their rooms. By half past three, the house was quiet and she finally slept.

The remaining guests from the ball made their departures in the early afternoon the next day, and the Darcys spent the rest of the day with their family. Everyone was tired from the ball and the Bingleys and the Bennets would be leaving on the morrow, so they were all a little subdued that last day. After the late night Georgiana felt as if her eyes were filled with sand. She spent an hour in the music room playing some of her easier music to try to wake up, but even the "Rondo Alla Turca" did not arouse her. She was still at the pianoforte when Elizabeth came looking for her.

"Georgiana, I am concerned about Kitty," Elizabeth said. "Miss Bingley seems to be with my sister Jane indefinitely and she barely tolerates poor Kitty."

Georgiana said, "Yes, I have heard her make unkind comments to her several times and then turn around and praise me to the skies in front of her. Miss Bingley is very foolish if she thinks that I do not see through her attempts to humiliate Kitty. I do not like being used as a tool to spite my friends."

"I thought I would ask Mr. Darcy if Kitty could stay with us when my family leaves, but I wanted to talk to you first. Having Kitty here will affect you more than anyone."

Georgiana, without hesitation, said, "I would like to have Kitty stay, Elizabeth." She slid off the piano bench. "Let me ask my brother for permission for her to stay."

"If you like. Thank you, Georgiana, that is very kind of you."

She found her brother alone in his library that afternoon looking for a book he and Mr. Bennet had been discussing and broached the subject of Kitty staying with them. He immediately agreed, saying, "Of course, my dear, if you like. I think it an excellent idea."

When she thanked him, he kissed her affectionately on the top of her head and she hurried off to find Elizabeth; the two of them then went to Kitty's room to ask her if she would like to stay.

After searching the house, they finally found her sitting silently in the conservatory, watching the snowflakes fall against the glass. When Elizabeth made her proposal to her, Kitty jumped up from her chair and clapped her hands, dancing around the two ladies and saying, "I would love to stay here, Lizzy, Georgiana, thank you *so* much!"

After Kitty's elation had died down, they spent the remainder of the day quietly and Georgiana, after struggling to stay awake, finally went upstairs in the afternoon to rest. When she rejoined the family for tea, she noted that Miss Bingley was exceedingly attentive to both her brother and the colonel until Sir Andrew Ffoulkes and the Comte de Tournay rode over so the count could make his farewells to his new acquaintances.

"And where is your estate, Monsieur le Comte?" Miss Bingley asked casually as they all drank tea in the drawing-room.

"It is about twenty miles from Windsor, Mademoiselle," he replied. "It is a small estate but, unfortunately, virtually all of our land was lost during the Terror and the current régime is impervious to the demands of the former aristocracy to be reinstated to their lands. I am resigned." He shrugged eloquently.

"It must be very difficult to be living in exile from your homeland, Monsieur le Comte," she purred.

He eyed Miss Bingley speculatively for a moment then put on a sad but noble face and put his hand over his heart. "*Oui,* Mademoiselle, it is a very sad thing, but we must make the best of it. We are fortunate to have had the assistance of our English friends to help us escape from the Terror with our lives."

Georgiana was tempted to applaud this performance, but Miss Bingley gave a melancholy sigh and said, "Will you be visiting London during the upcoming Season, Monsieur le Comte?"

"*Bien sûr.* I always try to spend part of the Season with friends in London. You understand that I am unable to afford an establishment of my own in town; however, I have friends who are willing to oblige with an invitation."

"Possibly we will see you there then, my lord, as my brother and his wife are spending the Season in town and have kindly invited me to join them. My elder sister and her husband also live in London and have extended an invitation as well."

"That would be delightful, Mademoiselle Bingley."

Both the count and Miss Bingley seemed gratified by this conversation and Georgiana was very well entertained, especially as she noted the sardonic glint in the count's eye when Miss Bingley turned her attention to his brother-in-law, Sir Andrew.

While Sir Andrew and the count were still visiting, the Blakes arrived on the same errand: to say farewell to the Darcys' guests. Miss Blake seemed charmed to see all of the gentlemen together but spent most of her time vying for the colonel's attention, which he seemed happy enough to give. Georgiana watched Miss Bingley and Miss Blake dancing attendance on the single gentlemen with amusement.

Kitty Bennet seemed to prefer Mr. Edward Blake, and she sat next to him the entire visit. In half an hour both sets of visitors left, after bidding farewell to the Bingleys and the Bennets.

Early the next morning all of their friends departed; the Bingleys and Mr. Bennet to return to Hertfordshire and the colonel to return to his duties at the Court of St. James.

After they were gone Georgiana went up to her room to write in her diary, which she had neglected of late.

3 January: All our guests have gone and the house has returned to its somnolent quiet. Kitty has remained and will stay with us until we all leave for London. Now I cannot avoid the thought of my presentation and coming-out; they are what will consume my time and mind until summer. I shudder at the thought of being examined and judged for all those months, but it cannot be avoided. Aut vincere aut mori.

Chapter 12

Behold, I shew you a mystery;
we shall not all sleep, but we shall all be changed,
In a moment, in the twinkling of an eye…

—I Corinthians 15:51–52

O NE RAINY DAY IN EARLY MARCH, GEORGIANA AND KITTY WERE in the drawing-room with Lucky trying to concentrate on their needlework when they heard a horse ride up. When Smithfield opened the door Georgiana heard Elizabeth say, "Colonel! I did not expect to see you again so soon. You are most welcome! Have you come for Georgiana's birthday today?"

"Mrs. Darcy, I am, unfortunately, here on business and it is very important that I speak to Darcy immediately. However, I did bring Georgiana her present," he said in a grave voice quite unlike his usual tones.

"Of course, Colonel, I believe he is in his library. Smithfield, would you please announce the colonel?"

"Yes, madam."

When Georgiana, drawn by this enigmatic interchange, arrived in the hall, Elizabeth stood with the gift in her hands, looking after the colonel quizzically as the heavy mahogany door of the library closed behind him. The two ladies stared at each other for a moment then Georgiana shrugged away her perplexity and returned to the drawing-room.

Later, her brother came to find her as she was absently playing with Lucky, part of her mind in the library and her heart beating faster with anxiety. She had never heard her cousin sound so grim.

"Come to the library, Georgiana my dear, I need to talk to you," he said quietly. His mouth was compressed in a thin line as he led her into the library, where Elizabeth was waiting for them, and carefully shut the door.

"Where is the colonel?" she asked as she sat down, watching her brother pace in front of his desk for a moment before he spoke.

"He is on his way back to London, as I will be tomorrow morning; and then most likely I will travel to the Continent."

"The Continent!" Elizabeth exclaimed. "What do you mean?"

Darcy clasped his hands behind his back and stopped in front of them. "The colonel came here with the express purpose of giving me a message. It is of an extremely sensitive nature, but I do not feel that I can leave without giving both of you some explanation for you will have to cover my absence while I am gone. I am 'requested,'" he said in a voice heavy with sarcasm, "to go to London and meet the Prince Regent, who has a task that he has 'requested' that I do and that may involve travelling out of the country."

"The Prince Regent!" Elizabeth said with astonishment.

"Yes. As you both know, I do not associate with the fast set that makes London its home and of which the prince is the leader. His behaviour is scandalous and irresponsible in many ways and, as you might guess, I do not approve of it. It has always been my impression that the Prince Regent does not approve of me either, considering me, I am sure, to be rather like Banquo's ghost at the feast," he said dryly. "Be that as it may, he apparently wants me to do something which he feels, and which, just as importantly to me, the colonel feels, only I can do. I do not yet know what that errand is and it does not matter. I would prefer that you know as little as possible so that you do not have to guard your tongues constantly for fear of letting too much slip.

"You know that the colonel is a member of the Horse Guards, which are charged with protecting the royal family, but what you may not know is that our cousin's primary charge is to protect the safety of the Prince Regent himself. How Fitzwilliam can spend so much time working intimately around the prince and his cronies and avoid the corruption that springs up around them, I do not know, but he seems to be able to manage it, and the Prince Regent places a great deal of trust in him.

"In spite of his glib tongue and easy manner, Fitzwilliam can be extremely reticent when it is necessary. In fact, much of this information on his role at St. James I have gradually accumulated over the twelve years he has been in the Horse Guards, mostly from what other people have told me. At any rate, I will be leaving in the morning and I must be finished with this 'errand,' whatever it may be, by the time Georgiana is presented at court. It would not be discreet to miss it, as anyone who knows me will be sure that I would not miss your presentation, Georgiana, for anything but a dire catastrophe. If I am not back in time there will be talk."

"I see," Elizabeth said, a worried look on her face. "…At least, I do not see, but I understand what you have told me so far. What am I to do about Georgiana's presentation?"

He sat down next to her and took her hand. "Well, the one bit of good news Fitzwilliam brought is that his parents will be coming to Pemberley—they will probably arrive within a few days—and my aunt will take responsibility for all of the details of Georgiana's presentation. Unfortunately, I will be gone when they arrive, so you will have to meet them for the first time with Georgiana alone to support you. I do not know what they think of our marriage by now, but at least Georgiana's need for my aunt's experience and social standing during her first Season will give them an excuse to meet you that even Lady Catherine would not gainsay.

"Actually," he added, "I think that you will like them, Elizabeth. They think rather too much of their position in society—a charge which I am hardly in a position to criticise, considering past events—but they are not bad sorts, and I think they will approve of you when they know you. I suspect that they have only stayed away thus far because they did not want to deal with the carrying on of Lady Catherine over our marriage, but I am not surprised that their sense of family responsibility for Georgiana has overcome their hesitation in that matter. You must both tell anyone who asks that I was called away to London on business and that you will be joining me there soon."

"And what if you have not returned by the time we arrive in London?" Georgiana asked, her voice wavering.

"Then you must tell enquirers that I had to return to Pemberley unexpectedly to finish some business so that I will be free for the Season and that I will rejoin you in London before your presentation."

Elizabeth spoke up. "What do I tell your aunt and uncle?"

"Apparently, they have been told enough by the colonel to let them know that I will not be here and that they are not to ask the reasons."

They left the library, but Georgiana's thoughts were in a confused whirl. She tried to exert herself to behave normally when she returned to the drawing-room, but it was not long before she pled a headache and went to her room. At least there she did not need to put on a front to deceive Kitty.

That evening they celebrated Georgiana's birthday with a family party. Cook made Georgiana's favourite dinner and outdid herself on a lovely cake filled with raisins and nuts. She managed to smile and exclaim when she opened her presents, and she hoped that her distraction would not be too obvious to Kitty. Her brother gave her a pair of pearl earrings to match her necklace and some new music, and Kitty had sewn a slightly lopsided reticule that matched her best pelisse. Elizabeth had purchased a new spring bonnet for her to wear during the Season and knitted a warm scarf and mittens for her, with a matching coat for Lucky. Georgiana had to laugh when she saw the coat and told Lucky, who was sitting on her lap, that they would wear them for their walk the next day. The colonel's offering was the last to be opened and she gave a brief smile when she saw the delicate gold bracelet cradled in the velvet-lined box and then put it aside to cut her cake. Kitty examined the bracelet and exclaimed, "It is beautiful, Georgiana! How lucky you are to have two guardians to buy you presents!"

Georgiana smiled at her brother and replied, "Indeed I am."

Afterwards they withdrew to the music room and she played a few songs before they all retired.

9 March: Today Colonel Fitzwilliam came with some business for my brother. I am chagrined to find that I have been misjudging my cousin for years, thinking him pleasant and entertaining but shallow. I am having

*difficulty changing my picture of him in my mind, but I
am determined to do him justice. I must try not to equate
light-heartedness with light-mindedness. I wonder how
many other people I have unconsciously misjudged. I
remember now my cousin's kindness when I was little and
his endless patience with my oddities. I also remember
his anger when he found his brother tormenting me. His
reaction was exactly the same as my brother's. They were
both quite willing to fight Lord St. George, but their sense
of fair play prevented them from both attacking him at
once, and the colonel gave in to my brother's greater right
to avenge the wrong done his sister. I am sounding quite
mediaeval here, the age of chivalry reborn!*

She closed her book and put it in the drawer of her bedside
table, still contemplating what she had heard that day.

When Georgiana came down to breakfast the next morning,
her brother was gone and Elizabeth was sitting with her teacup
in her hands, staring out of the window. She turned when she
heard the door open and exclaimed, "Georgiana, why are you up
so early!"

"I could not sleep, so I thought that maybe we could put in
some extra practise time today."

"Kitty is not up yet, I assume?"

"I have not seen her."

"Let us eat then, and we will start our practise."

By the end of two hours, they were both ready to rest for a
while. Georgiana felt exhausted; even her hair was hanging limply

around her face. She collapsed onto a chair and took a sip of the cold tea sitting before her.

"I am just not able to do it, Elizabeth. I cannot spontaneously carry on the sort of witty repartee that I see others do. I guess that I have a pedantic, pedestrian mind. Maybe I have no sense of humour, although I used to think I did. I can laugh and talk and tease those few people whom I know intimately, but the thought of the next few months and the fact that my entire future turns upon attracting a husband whom I can love and trust for the rest of my life turns me into marble."

"Hmmm." Elizabeth patted her warm forehead with her handkerchief and thought for a few moments. "I think that we need to change your thinking. It is true that the search for the proper husband is important, but you do not need to decide this year. I know that society puts on a great deal of pressure during a young woman's coming-out year to find a husband or be thought a failure and an eternal spinster, but that thinking is ridiculous. A year ago, when I was twenty, I had resigned myself to never marrying because I did not have a dowry and I was not willing to marry just for financial security. That is what my friend Charlotte did when she married Mr. Collins."

Georgiana smiled at her. "I always wondered why she married him. I also wonder how my aunt can tolerate him."

"I wondered that myself the entire time I was in Hunsford last spring... At any rate, my point is that it is not necessary to find a husband before you are eighteen, or even twenty. Particularly you, Georgiana. You have everything a woman needs to attract a husband but a husband is not necessary to ensure your comfort in life. You are not a woman who will have a few good years and then fade away into insignificance. More likely, you will find that maturity will allow you to recognise what you want and who you want to spend your life with. Do not be in a hurry, my dear, and do not let anyone pressure you into making a decision you are not ready for."

Georgiana examined her teacup while she thought about Elizabeth's words.

"I still do not know how not to be intimidated by my Presentation and all the balls and parties. I do not know how to form a sense of someone's mind from trivial conversation immediately. I would rather meet new people one at a time and get to know them in a natural fashion, as I did with my friend Catherine Freemont."

Elizabeth smiled at her. "You sound very much like your brother, my dear." After a few sips of tea she finally added, "I think what you need to do is avoid trying to chatter with people. It is not your style of intercourse. Instead, imagine yourself a princess. You are dignified but gracious. When you do not know what to say, you just smile enigmatically and nod intelligently while the other person talks. If they are interesting you will soon have something you want to say. If they are not, you can use the time to muse about something more engaging. Conjugate your irregular verbs if you must. Most gentlemen, in my experience, prefer to do all the talking themselves anyway. You must not use your brother as an example of the typical man; he is quite unique."

Georgiana laughed at the picture she had conjured. "All right. Perhaps I can do that."

Her performances soon began to improve and by working intensively over the next day they made some little progress.

On the morning of the second day after Darcy's departure, the day was sunny and windless after several days of rain, and Georgiana was ready for a break from her incessant practising, so she convinced Elizabeth and Kitty to join her in a short walk with Lucky and Pilot. They bundled up in their heaviest cloaks and warm bonnets and gloves and put Lucky in his new sweater then walked quickly down to the stream, where they turned up a path that was partially sheltered from the brisk air by rocks and shrubbery. They had walked about a half mile and were just ready to turn back when Lucky tugged on his leash, stiffening and growling as he stared towards the woods. At the same time, they were hailed.

"Mrs. Darcy, Miss Darcy, Miss Bennet, I am very glad to see you," Jonathan Walker called cheerfully as he broke out of the trees and swaggered casually towards them. Behind him appeared two retainers carrying shotguns. Seeing their startled faces he added, "I apologise for surprising you, but we were hunting and lost our way. We evidently wandered onto Pemberley land inadvertently and I am happy to know now where we are. I saw Mr. Darcy drive by several days ago, apparently on his way to town, so I was afraid that we would not find succour in our distress." He smiled ingratiatingly.

Georgiana felt a cold trickle of ice down her spine when she saw the guns and Walker's arrogant attitude but kept silent as Elizabeth answered, "Indeed, sir, you must have wandered a great way."

"Yes, I am afraid we have," he said engagingly.

Georgiana, observing him from the edge of this conversation, noted that his smile did not reach his eyes, which studied them with chilly composure. He paused, and Georgiana could hear the wind rustling the dead leaves in the profound silence of the woods. He continued, and she could almost see him calculating his response, "May I escort you ladies back to the house, or were you going to walk further?" He looked meaningfully at Georgiana.

Elizabeth answered him, her face rigidly controlled, "I am afraid we must turn back. We have already walked farther than we should and it would be very rude to be late for our guests."

"Oh, you have guests? I will not intrude, then, but will go only as far as the drive, where we can cross to the main road." He offered Georgiana his arm and Pilot, who had been sitting quietly behind Elizabeth with his eyes glued upon the unwanted guests, growled deep in his throat, like the rumble of thunder.

"You are too kind, sir," Georgiana responded. Ignoring his proffered arm to pat Pilot on the head, she managed to put the dog between herself and Walker.

After the three men left them at the drive, Kitty whispered to Elizabeth, "What is going on?"

Elizabeth touched a finger to her lips and shook her head slightly, hurrying them towards the house. Georgiana picked up Lucky, who continued growling softly as he peeked at the men from over her shoulder. They went quickly up the stairs and into the house while Pilot stayed behind on the terrace, silently watching the intruders walk down the drive. The ladies stared at each other while they caught their breath in the hall and a footman assisted them in removing their wraps.

"I think, perhaps, that we would all like some hot tea to warm us up. What do you think, ladies?" Elizabeth said, in an obvious attempt to behave as usual.

The others nodded silently and went to the drawing-room while Elizabeth gave the orders for their tea.

"Well?" Georgiana said when she had closed the door of the drawing-room.

"I don't know exactly what Mr. Walker's game is, but he is beginning to make me very uneasy," Elizabeth said slowly. "His claim to have accidentally wandered onto Pemberley land is patently false. It is a full six miles to the Walker property, and they would have crossed several roads on the way by which he could have oriented himself. He also knew that Mr. Darcy was gone." She paused and then said carefully, "I am afraid that Mr. Darcy has heard that Mr. Walker is in some financial difficulties. He might feel that Georgiana's fortune could be the solution to his problems and wishes to press his suit however he can. At any rate, I strongly recommend that we do not walk out alone, even near the house, and we will take a couple of footmen with us when we walk together."

She attempted to smile reassuringly, but Georgiana felt lightheaded with the shock and she saw that Kitty pressed her hand to her lips as she nodded. Elizabeth added, with a weak simulation of her usual pertness, "Georgiana, you did very well, my dear. An empress could not have been more deadly courteous."

Georgiana smiled tightly, her confusion and dismay turning to anger at the audacity of Walker's invasion.

Elizabeth, mistaking the pale set of her face for fear, said reassuringly, "I hope that your aunt and uncle will be here very soon, my dear—I expect them in the next day or two. I will feel much safer with their support."

At that moment the tea tray arrived and broke their tense conclave. Elizabeth changed the subject, but they were all rather thoughtful as they drank their tea.

The three ladies were very relieved when, at a few minutes before five o'clock, a fine carriage with four horses and liveried coachman and footmen pulled up the gravel drive. Lord and Lady Whitwell had arrived.

The three women rose when the visitors were announced, and Georgiana advanced to greet her aunt and uncle.

"It is lovely to see you my lord and lady," she said smoothly, giving them each a curtsey. "I would like to introduce you to my sister-in-law, Mrs. Darcy, and her sister, Miss Catherine Bennet."

Their visitors smiled and kissed Georgiana and greeted Elizabeth and Kitty courteously, if a little warily. George Fitzwilliam, Earl of Whitwell, was a slim, grizzled man of about fifty years, of medium height, and with blue eyes and a weathered complexion. Lady Whitwell was tall and slender, almost as tall as her husband, and had light brown hair liberally mixed with silver and with streaks of pure silver in front. She wore her hair in a simple style that enhanced its beautiful colour and her gown of blue emphasised the pale blue of her eyes. Although both had rather reserved faces at rest, the lines around their eyes indicated that they were not without good humour and were more accustomed to smiling than frowning. Elizabeth and Kitty returned their courtesies, Kitty somewhat hesitantly.

"I have heard so much about you," Lord Whitwell said, his face flushing briefly, "and I am happy to finally meet you."

Elizabeth returned the compliments calmly, but Georgiana could not repress a smile as her sister responded to his common-place greeting: she was quite sure that he had heard a *great* deal about Elizabeth from Lady Catherine. She ordered tea for her guests and the familiar ritual of pouring and serving allowed everyone to recover from the awkwardness of the introductions. Once the greetings were over and Lord and Lady Whitwell had told Georgiana the family news and given her the birthday present which they had brought for her (a pair of fine doeskin gloves), the atmosphere became somewhat more relaxed and the time passed quickly until dinner.

The next morning Elizabeth rose early, in the hope that she could speak to Lord Whitwell about Jonathan Walker before the others arose. She was fortunate and found him breakfasting alone in the small breakfast-parlour.

"My lord, may I speak to you for a few moments before the others join us?" she asked.

"Of course, Mrs. Darcy," he answered, his brows tilted quizzically. "How may I serve you?"

"I wanted you to be aware of a situation which has arisen since my husband left for London and to ask for your advice, but I do not wish to further alarm my sisters," she said diffidently. "One of the young gentlemen of the neighbourhood has been rather importunate towards Georgiana, and my husband has heard some things which have given him cause for concern about the young man's character. We do not feel that we can avoid his society entirely as his father's ancestors have been the squires of Lambton for many generations and are long family acquaintances." She then proceeded to tell him of the incident of the previous day and the measures she had adopted.

"You feel that the young man is a threat to Georgiana?" Lord Whitwell asked, a little scepticism in his voice.

"I feel, at least, that we should be excessively cautious to ensure Georgiana's safety," Elizabeth returned, suppressing the little sting of irritation she felt at his doubt. "The young man is deeply in debt and might feel that a forced marriage to Georgiana might answer where his charm did not. At the very least, he has accosted us on Pemberley property and lied about his reasons for being here."

"You are certainly correct about Georgiana's safety being paramount," he said, tapping his fingers nervously on the table. "Well, we will adopt your measures and possibly we should leave for London a little sooner than we had originally planned."

"Thank you, my lord."

They decided to leave in two days and, as Lady Whitwell had brought her favourite seamstress with her to sew the gowns Georgiana would need for her debut, the ladies spent the morning looking at patterns and fabric samples while the maids began readying their trunks. While they were discussing gowns with Lady Whitwell, Georgiana earnestly insisted to her aunt that her ball-gowns be cut lower in the bodice than what Lady Whitwell was suggesting she wear.

"My dear aunt, I am an adult now, and you do not want me to look like a child for my first Season, do you? I am not asking to appear in an unseemly way, but I would like to be as fashionable as is consistent with propriety."

Lady Whitwell seemed surprised at Georgiana's firmness of will but finally agreed that a lower neckline would be acceptable:

"I suppose we must show you off to best advantage, my dear, and you do have a lovely figure," she said as she eyed Georgiana appraisingly. "I am sorry, Georgiana. I am having difficulty remembering that you are all grown up. I do not have any daughters, so I am not sure what the other young women are wearing during the Season, but you are correct: the current fashion is for a lower-cut bodice."

Georgiana merely smiled.

Their time with the seamstress was interrupted in the early after-noon when Jonathan Walker came to call. Elizabeth introduced him to Lord and Lady Whitwell in the hall and ordered refresh-ments for their guest as they accompanied him to the drawing-room. His avowed reason for calling was to apologise again for disturbing their walk the day before and to ask if the ladies would consider taking one with his escort later. He did so while keeping an eye on Pilot, who was standing at the foot of the stairs watching him in an intent silence that Mr. Walker seemed to find more intimidating than the previous day's growling, as evidenced by the glances he repeatedly flicked between the dog and Lord and Lady Whitwell. Georgiana reflected to herself in amusement that it would take a strong constitution to face the entire Darcy clan if Mr. Walker did not behave properly.

"I am so sorry, Mr. Walker," Elizabeth said, answering his ques-tion without much warmth, "we are just now preparing to go to London with Lord and Lady Whitwell. We will be gone for the Season, so we are simply overwhelmed with business that must be concluded before we can leave. I doubt that we will have time for walks, even if the weather is conducive."

"Of course," he said politely, looking coolly into her eyes. "In that case I would, naturally, not want to take up any more of your time." He turned to Georgiana as they said their goodbyes and made a deep bow. "I trust that you will find the Season delightful, Miss Darcy, and hope that you will not forget your friends in the north."

"I never forget my friends, Mr. Walker," Georgiana replied, her eyes meeting his with chilly courtesy. "Good day to you, sir."

Georgiana and her aunt went back upstairs to the schoolroom, where the seamstress was holding court, but Lord Whitwell detained Elizabeth for a moment with a touch on her arm as she turned to follow them.

"I apologise for my doubts earlier this morning, Mrs. Darcy. I agree with you that Mr. Walker is a man of whom to beware. He has a cold eye that belies the courtesies that come from his mouth. I think I will have the forester and some of his men check the woods occasionally during the day and make sure that he does not become 'lost' again."

"Thank you, my lord; I appreciate your assistance," Elizabeth answered. "I am sure Georgiana will feel better knowing that Mr. Walker cannot disturb us."

He returned her warm smile and went back to the library, where he had been reading before Mr. Walker had arrived, while she followed the others upstairs.

Chapter 13

Utrum que enim vitium est, et omnibus credere et nulli.
(It is equally unsound to trust everyone and to trust no one.)

—Seneca, *Epistulae*

WHILE ELIZABETH WAS RETURNING UPSTAIRS TO REJOIN HER sisters and Lady Whitwell, Darcy was recovering from a brutal ride to London. They had changed carriage horses at posting inns along the way and ridden from dawn to dusk to dawn, arriving at Ashbourne House on the morning of the second day. Burton had received the letter informing him that Darcy was coming to do some business, and he greeted his master without surprise at the unorthodox time of his arrival. Darcy ordered that breakfast be served in an hour and hurried upstairs, where his valet had already arranged a hot bath and clean clothes.

He tried to relax and enjoy the hot water as it soaked away the aches and stiffness from the trip, but without much success. As he was dressing, Burton brought a message from Colonel Fitzwilliam that he would pick him up at nine pm to take him to Carlton

House. The Prince Regent would be preparing to go out for the evening, and there would be a minimum of hangers-on to note their meeting. Darcy sent an acknowledgement and an invitation to dine at seven.

He was dressed in his finest evening clothes when the colonel arrived, and they left as soon as he and the colonel had finished dining. On the ride to Carlton House, the colonel told him that they would enter by the main entrance to avoid any suspicions; it would not do to have them seen sneaking around the back entrance like conspirators.

"The Prince Regent chose this time," the colonel explained, "because there is enough moving about to make our presence inconspicuous, but his usual sycophants (my word, not his) are dressing for whatever amusement they have planned. He is most insistent that this be handled confidentially."

"Have you any idea yet why he wants to see me?" Darcy asked.

The colonel shook his head. "No, he has not dropped a syllable beyond what I told you at Pemberley. All I know is that he needs a gentleman who is completely discreet to perform some service for him. You, Darcy, are the most discreet person I know." He gave his cousin a brief grin.

The carriage pulled up at the entrance of Carlton House and they alighted and walked up to the door, which had opened to reveal the majordomo by the time they had reached the top step.

"Good evening, Colonel Fitzwilliam, how may I serve you?"

"My cousin, Mr. Fitzwilliam Darcy, has an engagement with His Majesty the Prince Regent, Childes."

"Yes, sir, I will ascertain if His Majesty is ready to see you. Please wait here."

"Thank you, Childes."

Childes returned immediately (causing Darcy to lift a brow in surprise), bowed them into an adjoining chamber dominated by a massive mahogany desk, and then left, shutting the door behind himself.

The Prince Regent entered quietly through an inner door. "Well, Darcy," he said coldly, "I see that you are punctual, as usual."

"Yes, Your Majesty. I pray, Your Majesty, tell me how I may serve you." Darcy returned his slight bow with one frigidly correct and stared levelly at his monarch.

The Prince Regent was a large man and his features were not unhandsome, but his looks were marred by his obesity and now, in his late middle age, he had a debauched look, with bloodshot eyes and sagging jowls.

"I have an errand that needs to be performed, of a most confidential nature," the prince said as he paced the carpet, his hands clasped behind his back. "This errand requires someone who speaks French fluently and who is familiar with the Court; characteristics which are available in abundance among my courtiers. However, it also requires someone who can think quickly and keep his own counsel when he needs to; these characteristics are *not* found in great measure at the Court. The person performing this errand should also be someone whose absence will not be immediately commented upon, and so must be someone who is not a regular in court circles. The colonel has suggested that you would be the best man for this errand."

"The colonel does me too much honour," Darcy said, unsmiling.

"Darcy," the prince said impatiently, "as you know, I have always considered you to be a prig, always disapproving of the enjoyments of others and too unimaginative to step out of the mould your father formed for you. I hear, however, that you were recently married and that your bride is a gentlewoman of no family name or pretensions, nor of any fortune."

Darcy glanced at the colonel, his brows furrowed.

"No, no, I did not hear it from the ever-discreet colonel; it is a matter that I heard mentioned briefly in court gossip. Frankly, it was the cause of some chagrin to a number of predacious mammas." He smiled slightly and flicked his fingers dismissively. "Now that you are married they have gone on to other, juicier topics of conversation. The incident has, however, made me wonder if I have misjudged you over the years. I wonder if, perhaps, there is more to you than meets the eye if you have the audacity to risk the displeasure of your formidable aunt Lady Catherine de Bourgh in order to marry as you wish." The Prince Regent eyed Darcy speculatively. "I would prefer to turn this problem over to Colonel Fitzwilliam, whose reticence I trust implicitly; however, he has his own work here and I cannot spare him."

"If you have decided that I am the one who must perform this act, perhaps you will give me more details of what it is," Darcy said, careful not to let his impatience show.

The prince sighed, rubbing his well-shaven chin uncomfortably. "I would prefer to avoid the entire topic, but ignoring it will not make the problem easier. So… about two months ago a new ambassador from the Austrian court arrived with his wife and household. His wife is French, a ravishing little creature who is about twenty years younger than her husband. We became friendly, and one thing led to another, but after a couple of weeks I tired of her attentions and wished to move on to… greener pastures, shall we say?" He looked at the ceiling and clasped his hands behind his back again, his movements uncharacteristically awkward, as Darcy gazed at him stonily. "She, however, with Gallic passion and tenacity, was not ready to fade into obscurity with the gifts and favours of a prince to remember, but had taken, as insurance against such an eventuality, something from my room. I need to have that item back."

"What is the item, Your Majesty," Darcy asked, his jaws clenching, "that is so important that you are willing to risk a scandal to obtain its return?"

The Prince Regent sat behind the desk and irritably turned a paper knife over in his hands. "It is a packet of letters. The letters are from a lady who has been a friend for many years. They are quite indiscreet. I do not know how Frau Klein found them and spirited them from my room, but they are gone."

"How can you be sure that they were stolen by the ambassador's wife?" Darcy asked.

"She left London not long before I discovered the loss—sent home by the ambassador because of her scandalous behaviour, presumably." He added in an aside, "He is one of those horrible, rigidly upright Germanic types who could not see that it was an honour to have his wife singled out by a monarch. In any case, I received a letter from her a few days after, written from Paris, demanding what was, literally, a king's ransom for the letters and threatening to send them to my wife if I did not pay her, a consequence that I need not say would be most undesirable." He shivered slightly in horror, dabbing his lips with his lace-edged handkerchief. "The difficulty is that I do not have that kind of money, my income being totally inadequate to cover my expenses, as you are probably aware—which is why Parliament must peri-odically, and most grudgingly, give me grants to pay my debts," he added irritably. "I most certainly do not have the money to pay off blackmailing females."

Darcy suppressed a sigh. "Just how sensitive are these letters, Your Majesty?"

"Sensitive enough to affect the succession to the throne," the prince said simply, finally looking Darcy in the eye.

"Good Lord, Your Majesty," Darcy said weakly, "how many letters are there, all told?"

"There are about twenty of them; I do not know the exact number, but they were tied in a packet with a pink ribbon when they were stolen. Of course, I cannot know whether they have been separated since the theft."

"Are there any other political concerns at stake that you know of, Your Majesty," Darcy asked, "such as a foreign head of state who wishes to embarrass you or something of that sort?"

"Not that I know of," replied the prince hesitantly. "I have not heard any murmurs of that kind since this started, but it would certainly be to Napoleon's advantage if the British monarchy was in jeopardy and the country in turmoil; and the lady is undeniably in Paris, not in her husband's native country."

"If we could summarise the problem, then, Your Majesty: you wish me to travel to Paris while Napoleon is crouching near there with his army, baring his teeth at the armies of the Sixth Coalition, find these letters, and return without allowing them to fall into the hands of either Napoleon *or* the Coalition on the way. Is this correct?"

"Quite correct, Mr. Darcy," said the Prince Regent, lifting his fat chin pugnaciously.

"How do you propose that I get the letters from the lady, and how can I be sure that I have them all, Your Majesty?"

"You could get them back the same way she obtained them in the first place," the prince said, a smug smile crossing his face.

"I am sorry, Your Majesty, I am not willing to go that far to assist you."

"No, Darcy, I assumed you would not be," he returned with disgust.

"Where can I find this femme fatale, Your Majesty?" Darcy asked pointedly.

"I have the particulars here." He took an envelope from his inside jacket pocket and handed it to Darcy. "You must be ready to leave in the morning; the lady is expecting an answer within the next few days. I am sure you can find a ship willing to take you to Calais, for a consideration," the prince said briskly, standing up and starting towards the door. "The colonel tells me that your sister is to be presented at the Drawing-room in four weeks, so you must be back before that day. He looked back as he reached the door and paused, his hand on the knob. "You will present your wife at the same time; I am eager to see what type of woman was able to capture the well-regulated heart of Mr. Fitzwilliam Darcy."

"Yes, Your Majesty," Darcy said in resignation, bowing as the door clicked shut. He had hoped to avoid putting Elizabeth through the ordeal of the formal presentation at court, since he had no intention of attending any court functions with either his wife or his sister, but there would now be no alternative. He and the colonel made their way back out to the entrance in silence, where his carriage appeared, summoned by some unseen lackey.

"Well, this is a delightful situation that you have dropped me into, Fitzwilliam," Darcy whispered bitterly. "I have not the first idea of how to accomplish this 'errand,' and the fate of the Crown may hang upon its success. Thank you so much, my dear cousin."

"I am sorry, Darcy," the colonel said, shifting uncomfortably in his seat, "but I could not think of anyone more capable than yourself to do this discreetly. I would have undertaken it myself if I could have absented myself, but I am in the middle of an important investigation. We have received several reports suggesting that there is an arms smuggling ring operating between here and France. These reports are not through official channels and are more in the nature of rumours than actual confirmed reports, but there are some suggestions that these same men may find it to their benefit to assassinate the Prince Regent and keep the war going, which is how I became involved. I think you will agree that the Prince Regent's safety is more important than his love letters, and on the positive side, this is an opportunity for you to improve your standing with the prince, which may be of benefit to both Mrs. Darcy and Georgiana."

"Well, it is done now, and I have agreed to attempt the thing. I will contact you when I return, as it is unlikely that I will be able to do so safely until I am back on English soil. What do you think the Coalition is planning over the next few weeks?"

"I know, as do you, that Napoleon is in France, where he has been driven by the Coalition forces from Eastern Europe. The British forces are moving up from the south towards Paris. Napoleon could conceivably be in Paris by the time you arrive there. If you must escape quickly, it would be better to try to leave from the south of Paris and meet up with the English forces or, better yet, from the west and avoid the armies entirely. Darcy," the colonel added seriously, "be careful, Cousin, I am not ready to lose you and I had no idea what this errand was going to involve."

"Believe me, I will be as careful as I can. I have a good many reasons to want to return unscathed."

The two men shook hands solemnly before the colonel alighted and Darcy saw his cousin staring after the carriage before it rounded the corner and he was blocked from view.

At ten minutes past midnight, Darcy left the house in a hackney chaise, and he instructed the jarvey to drive to an inn on the Dover highway where the post chaise stopped. Burton had been given instructions to tell any callers that he was out of town but would be back within three weeks. As he drove away from Ashbourne House, Darcy suddenly realised the date and grimaced to himself. It was the Ides of March. He hoped they were more fortunate for him than they had been for Caesar.

Lord and Lady Whitwell and the rest of the Pemberley party arrived in London several days after Darcy's departure. They had taken a leisurely four days to travel and Lady Whitwell had instructed Georgiana on court protocol during the drive; they had practised the court curtsey in the evening after they dined. By bedtime each night, Georgiana was trembling with nerves and sore muscles, sure that she would not survive her presentation without at least one major solecism. Her life would be ruined and she would be a laughing stock. Each night she would lie in bed, Lucky tucked comfortingly in next to her, and her stomach would churn as she tried to block out the instructions still repeating in her head. When she finally slept she would have only two or three hours rest before it was time to rise and dress for the day of travel. She was greatly relieved when she finally felt the cobblestones of the London streets under the carriage wheels.

The coach stopped first at Ashbourne House to drop the young ladies and Mrs. Annesley; then Lord and Lady Whitwell had gone on to their own town house, Longford House.

The subsequent week was a confusion of dress fittings for Elizabeth and Kitty, as well as Georgiana, as they would all need a well-stocked wardrobe for the many parties and balls. Lady Whitwell continued Georgiana's lessons, and Elizabeth and Kitty joined her so she would not feel so singled out. Mrs. Annesley was put to work listing all the orders which had been placed and performing errands for Lady Whitwell. When the week ended and the fittings were finished, Kitty accepted an invitation to stay with her Aunt Gardiner for a week or two and Georgiana thought she looked relieved to be leaving the incessant activity behind as she drove off in Mr. Gardiner's carriage.

As the week finished, Georgiana felt she had improved her curtsey and learnt many of the court rules, although she still quailed when she thought of her presentation, and her aunt's detailed instructions and warnings had not relieved her anxiety. More importantly, she was also terribly worried about Elizabeth. She was sure that Elizabeth was as uneasy about Mr. Darcy and his strange command appearance with the Prince Regent as she was, but her sister-in-law looked more than worried. She looked pale and ill, and she was not eating well. Georgiana was almost more concerned about her than about her presentation. Almost. Lady Whitwell's crisp voice broke through her reverie:

"Let us try again, ladies. You must place your train over your arm and when you are called by the lord chamberlain you will walk to the door and into the Presence Chamber. You will gracefully put down your train, one of the lords-in-waiting will spread it out behind you, and then you will move forwards until you are facing the throne. You will then curtsey to the Prince Regent and to any other members of the royal family who are present—and you must not let the feathers fall out of your hair! Let us again practise your curtseys, my dears, and how to back out of the chamber afterwards; you must not turn your back on your monarch!"

The deep, court curtsey was very difficult; to perform it, rise gracefully (without wobbling) and then back out while controlling the three-yard-long train had seemed almost impossible at first. Under Lady Whitwell's strict tutelage they had all pinned table-cloths to their shoulders to practise and they had repeated their curtseys and retreats over and over, until Georgiana had to exert all her self-control to not collapse in a screaming fit on the floor. When, finally, Lady Whitwell declared that they were doing well the Darcy ladies took the carriage back to Ashbourne House and flopped on the chairs in Elizabeth's sitting-room, too tired to even ring for tea.

After sitting and staring into space for fifteen minutes, Georgiana jumped up and said, "I need some fresh air. Are either of you interested in a walk?"

Elizabeth sighed and said, "I am sorry, Georgiana, but I am exhausted. I think I had better drag myself to my room and rest until it is time to dress for dinner."

Mrs. Annesley said, "I should like a walk, Miss Darcy. I have not been working as hard as the rest of you and some fresh air would be very welcome."

"I will just need to change my shoes to something more suitable for walking."

"I will meet you downstairs in, say, fifteen minutes. Does that suit you?"

"Perfectly."

There was a hesitant tap on Elizabeth's door at five o'clock while Lambert was fixing her hair, which was mussed after her nap. When the maid went into the bedroom and opened the door Elizabeth heard a throat clear and then Burton's voice, unsure and embarrassed to be invading the mistress's private rooms.

"I'm sorry, Miss Lambert, but I need to speak to the mistress."

Elizabeth, alarmed at his tone, jumped up and ran to the door, afraid that he had received bad news about her husband.

"What is it, Burton?"

He cleared his throat again. "I'm sorry to bother you, Mrs. Darcy, but Miss Durand is in quite a taking. Miss Darcy and Mrs. Annesley have not returned from their walk and it is almost dark."

She was speechless for a moment, her head spinning. "What? When did they go out? Miss Darcy was speaking with Mrs. Annesley about a walk just as I came upstairs to rest at, oh, about three o'clock I believe it was. Has no one seen them since then?"

"No, madam. Miss Darcy and Mrs. Annesley went out just after that, with a footman to accompany them. John it was."

"And John is reliable?"

"Yes, madam. He has been with us for fifteen years and has always given satisfaction. This is his first time in London; he came with us from Derbyshire."

Elizabeth tried to think what to do. She did not want to overreact, but this was a decidedly ominous occurrence and her stomach clenched with fear for her sister. Hyde Park was safe enough during the day, if one was careful, but the large expanse of woods would be a frightening place after dark. After a moment's thought she said to Burton, "Send Durand to me immediately."

His face looked relieved at her decisive voice. If only she could feel as calm as she apparently appeared.

Burton returned within minutes with Durand.

Elizabeth looked at the maid's pale face, her hands convulsively clenching the skirt of her gown, wrinkling the fabric. She spoke softly but firmly. "Durand, when did Miss Darcy go out?"

Durand sniffed, trying to control herself. "It was not long after three, madam. She and Mrs. Annesley and one of the footmen."

"Did Miss Darcy say anything to indicate in which direction they would be walking or which path they would take?"

"Not that I recall, madam." She paused to think for a moment. "I do remember that Miss Darcy mentioned yesterday that she would like to take one of the short walks which go through the woods. She expressed a desire to see if the trees were beginning to leaf out." She sniffed again and her face collapsed, her refined accent slipping. "Oh, what could have 'appened to 'em, mum? I be so worried! I did not know what to do and I kept thinkin' they would be back any minute!"

Elizabeth patted the maid's shoulder briefly and then, when her snivelling did not abate, shoved her unceremoniously into Lambert's arms. She turned to Burton, who was still hovering in the doorway.

"Burton, order the carriage. I will drive down towards the park and see if they are there. It is possible that one of them has turned an ankle or something and they are having difficulty getting home. I should like a couple of reliable footmen to go with me."

Burton stood up straight.

"Yes, madam. Right away."

He disappeared down the servants' staircase.

Elizabeth turned to Lambert, who was still comforting the weeping Durand.

"Tsk, Durand! Stop your crying this instant! You are making a spectacle of both yourself and Miss Darcy."

Durand gulped and swallowed her sobs. She managed to mumble, "Yes, mum."

Elizabeth added in a softer tone. "I am sure Miss Darcy and the others will be perfectly fine. It does not do to anticipate trouble."

"Yes, mum."

"Good. Lambert, my cloak please."

"Yes, Madame."

Suddenly Durand cried out, "Madam! I just remembered! A few days ago I heard Miss Darcy talking to Mrs. Annesley about walking from the Stanhope Gate to the Serpentine! They decided not to go as the weather looked like it might rain, but maybe that's the way they went!"

Elizabeth smiled at the maid. "Very good thinking, Durand. We will start there."

Within ten minutes, Elizabeth was down the stairs and out the front door, where she found Burton climbing up onto the box with the coachman.

"Burton! What are you doing?" He started and stepped down, looking embarrassed.

"I am going with you, madam, with your permission. I know I will not be of much help if one of them has turned an ankle, but there are also two footmen on the back." He lowered his voice. "I thought that the fewer servants who know about this the less gossip there would be, so I thought I should go myself."

Elizabeth looked at him for a moment and saw with pity his distress. Burton had made serving the Darcy family his entire life and would have known Georgiana since her birth. She turned to enter the coach.

"Very well. You are probably correct, Burton. Start at the Stanhope Gate."

The elderly man climbed stiffly back up onto the box and sat next to the coachman and they departed. Elizabeth searched the streets, trying to peer through the deepening dusk thickened by a smoky haze from the coal fires, but she did not see any movement.

They reached the park quickly and drove up and down Park Lane, staring into the clumps of leafless trees and shrubs. When they reached the corner, the coachman stopped and Burton climbed down and opened the door.

"Which way should we look, madam?"

Elizabeth considered.

"Let us go back to the Stanhope Gate and we will send the footmen down the path that goes directly to the Serpentine. It was late enough in the day that I do not think Miss Darcy would have taken a circuitous route."

"Yes, madam." He went around to the back of the carriage to talk to the footmen. When he had clambered stiffly back up onto the box, the coachman turned the carriage around and they went back up Park Lane to the Stanhope Gate. The two footmen jumped off the back as soon as the coach stopped moving and trotted into the park. Elizabeth drummed her fingers on the window ledge as she peered after them, her sense of unease expanding in the silence. She suppressed her desire to rush after them; they were old retainers of the Darcy family and they would do their best to find Georgiana, but each moment sitting there in the dark seemed like an eternity.

Fifteen minutes passed and she suddenly saw a movement out of the corner of her eye. When she looked out again she saw three men; the two outer ones seemed to support the middle one. As they approached she felt her heart sink into her toes. All three men wore the Darcy livery. The carriage rocked as Burton jumped hastily down from the box and rushed to the footmen. After a short conversation he jogged awkwardly back to the carriage door and spoke between pants for breath.

"Mrs. Darcy. John says they were set upon while walking back on the path from the Serpentine. Two men. One of them coshed John with something heavy—some lead shot in a sock, maybe."

"And Miss Darcy and Mrs. Annesley?"

"He doesn't know. When he awoke a few minutes ago with a splitting head it was almost dark and he was lying alone under a large yew. He was off the side of the path, he says, and an entire army could have marched by without seeing him. We are just lucky he awoke and called out or they would not have found him."

Elizabeth stared at him grimly.

"Put John inside the coach, Burton."

His eyes widened with surprise.

Elizabeth made an impatient gesture. "He is not fit to ride outside. Drive directly back to Ashbourne House. The footmen will take John inside and send for the apothecary. He must have that head seen to. Then, you will come with me and we will drive to Longford House. I need to talk to Lord Whitwell."

Burton bowed his head, but she could see his satisfaction at not being excluded from the hunt for Georgiana. It was only a matter of minutes before they were on the way to Longford House. When they pulled up to the door, Elizabeth alighted and marched to the door, followed by Burton. She rang the bell and a look of astonishment ran over the face of the Longford House butler when he opened the door. His eyes flicked to Burton and back to Elizabeth before he ushered them in with a semblance of his usual dignity.

"How may I serve you, Mrs. Darcy?"

"I wish to see Lord Whitwell on a matter of some urgency."

The butler glanced again at her face and said hastily, "I will ascertain if his lordship is in, madam."

He walked with unceremonious haste towards the dining-room and disappeared, to reappear within seconds with Lord Whitwell on his heels, serviette still in his hand.

"Mrs. Darcy!" He paused, taken aback at the expression on her face. "Hanford said that you are here on an urgent matter. Come into the library; there is a good fire in there. Hanford, bring wine."

"Yes, your lordship."

Elizabeth glanced back at Burton, who was standing awkwardly in the hall.

"I would like Burton to come, too, Lord Whitwell. He knows all the particulars of why I am here."

"As you wish."

Elizabeth was soon divested of her cloak by a waiting footman and it was but a few steps to the library. As soon as the door closed out the Longford House servants, Elizabeth said succinctly, "Lord Whitwell, Georgiana has been kidnapped."

Chapter 14

Ah Fear! Ah frantic Fear!
I see, I see thee near.

—WILLIAM COLLINS, "ODE TO FEAR"

GEORGIANA PACED THE LENGTH OF THE SMALL BEDROOM, AS she had many times since they had been locked in after their abduction, and reviewed the incidents of the day. The afternoon had been crisp, necessitating a brisk pace to keep warm, but there was no wind and she had enjoyed the fresh air in the park after the exertions of the day. They had walked all the way to the Serpentine and had just turned back when a carriage had drawn up on the road which intersected the path in the middle of the park. As soon as the carriage had come to a halt, two men had jumped out. It had taken but a moment to see the scarves wrapped around their lower faces and their hats drawn down over their brows, and she had known that they were trouble. She had tried to scream, but her throat closed convulsively and the only cry she had managed had been a feeble croak.

With a strength born of fear, she had clutched Mrs. Annesley's hand and swung her around, picked up her skirts and turned to run, almost dragging the older woman before she could respond and start running. They had taken only a few steps before one of the men had grabbed her. Out of the corner of her eye, she had seen the other raise his arm up and bring it down. The resulting ripe-melon thud had not boded well for John, the footman who had accompanied them. Before she could speak, she and the protesting Mrs. Annesley had been bundled into the waiting carriage.

The windows had been covered with black cloth, tacked down so that they could not see out. One of the men had climbed in with them and settled onto the opposite seat with his arms crossed over his chest, while the other had climbed onto the box, and the carriage had jerked into motion. Except for Georgiana reaching over and taking Mrs. Annesley's hand, they had sat, frozen, on the hard seat while the carriage drove quickly through town. She had tried to keep track of the turns, but had inevitably lost her bearings.

Finally, after what seemed to be hours, they had arrived at a house. It seemed to be in the country; it was quiet except for the sounds of a few birds which had not yet settled down for the night, and one frog peeping in the distance. The men did not touch them but blocked either side of the door when it opened so they had no choice but to go straight into the house.

When they entered the small front room, Georgiana finally found her voice.

"Just what is going on here? You had better release us immedi-ately or my brother…"

One of the men, the shorter of the two, laughed. "You mean your brother who is in France? It will be a long trip for him to get back tonight to rescue you, Miss Darcy."

Georgiana was shocked back into silence and Mrs. Annesley spoke up, stepping in front of Georgiana as she did so:

"Just what are your intentions? If you try to lay even a finger on this young lady I will…"

The same man who had spoken before interrupted her with a coarse laugh.

"Don't worry about your little chick, old woman. We do not want to hurt her; her uncle might not pay as well for damaged goods. As long as you behave and her family comes across with the money, you are safe enough."

Georgiana felt the blood in her veins turn to ice at what the man was crudely implying, and she was afraid her limbs would not support her. Mrs. Annesley, noticing her weakness, put her arm firmly around her waist and faced the men with a grim expression.

Just then, an old woman shuffled into the room, holding a twig broom and sucking her lips in and out of her toothless mouth. The man who had been speaking, whom Georgiana had mentally dubbed "Shorty" because of his lesser height, made an impatient movement and said harshly, "You two get into that room. If you behave yourselves like ladies you will have no trouble. The shutters are all sealed shut, so you needn't think you will escape."

The two women, still holding onto each other, walked in the direction the man indicated and soon found themselves locked into a small bedroom. The room was sparsely furnished, and the dresser top was dusty. Georgiana sat slowly down on the bed, her eyes staring at her companion, and whispered, "What is happening? Why are they doing this?"

Mrs. Annesley sat down next to her and whispered in her ear, "I do not know. Is your brother really in France?"

"I am not sure; he thought he might have to go to the Continent, but he did not say where. I don't believe he knew at the time he left Pemberley."

"These people must have an informant close to the family to know so much about your brother."

Georgiana nodded silently and then got up and checked the windows. They were indeed sealed shut, as the short man had said. She did not bother to try the door; she had heard the lock snick as the key had turned in the keyhole and, even had it not been locked, she would not want to face the two men who would be just outside the door. She settled onto the bed again and clasped her hands in her lap to stop their shaking. Mrs. Annesley put her arms around her charge and drew her head onto her shoulder, rocking her like a baby. Georgiana relaxed in her arms and covered her face with her hands, trying not to burst into tears.

They stayed that way for more than an hour as the dusk faded into a darkness unrelieved by candle or fire, until they heard a commotion in the outer room. The kidnappers were yelling and there were several loud crashes; then silence fell. The two women stared at each other. What was going on? It could not be a rescue attempt, for there was no way that Georgiana's family could have found where they were so soon. They listened intently and heard the sound of something heavy being dragged down the hallway outside their door then the metallic rattle of a key in a lock.

After another two hours, Georgiana's fear was becoming displaced by her hunger. Except for a cup of tea in the early afternoon, they had not eaten since breakfast.

"I hope they are not going to starve us," she whispered to her companion.

"I doubt they will. It will not help them if we are nothing but bags of bones when we are released." She smiled encouragingly at her charge.

As if in response to their words, the key sounded in the lock and the door swung open. Georgiana was astonished to see Jonathan Walker stumble inside, his hands and feet shackled. She gave a cry and stood up and he smiled ruefully at her, his right eye swollen shut.

"I am sorry; the rescue did not quite come off the way I had planned, Miss Darcy."

"Rescue?"

He paused until the toothless old woman had shoved a tray onto the small table in the corner under the watchful eyes of the two gaolers, who then shut and locked the door again, before he answered in a whisper:

"Yes, Miss Darcy. I was riding in Hyde Park in the dusk—I prefer Rotten Row when it is not completely engorged with people—and I saw those two men accost you and knock out your man—a footman, I presume?"

Georgiana nodded silently.

"I did not at first realise who you were, I only knew that two ladies had been attacked. I turned my horse to follow their carriage and managed to keep it in sight without them seeing me... At least I thought they had not seen me. Unfortunately, they were waiting for me after I left my horse down the road and crept up to the house. It is the only one along this stretch of road, so I knew it had to be the place where they had disappeared, and when I crept through the yard I saw a bit of the carriage through the open door of the barn. This is not the kind of place that would have a carriage and horses. At any rate, they jumped on me and here we are."

Georgiana suddenly noticed a smudge of red on his cheek and said, "You are bleeding, Mr. Walker!"

He reached up his shackled hands to touch the right side of his scalp, where a large bruise oozed blood. "It is nothing. Just a little scrape, Miss Darcy."

"You must let me clean it… if we can find some water to dampen my handkerchief."

She went over to the table and looked in the cracked pitcher on the tray. "Here is some water." She dampened the handkerchief and came back, her face flushed in embarrassment at the intimacy of the process as she gently wiped the blood off his face and head. "There. Now just hold that on the wound for a while and it should stop bleeding. I suppose we should try to eat. I do not know whether I am hungry or ill, I feel so peculiar."

Mrs. Annesley said, "We should all try to eat something or we *will* be ill."

Jonathan Walker stood up and, with his shackled arms, tried to help Mrs. Annesley pull the table over to the bed, since there were no chairs in the room. Walker gestured to Georgiana.

"Miss Darcy, you must sit down and eat first."

She protested briefly at being first, but soon gave in to their importunities and managed to swallow a small portion of the lumpy porridge and bread on the tray. Once she had eaten a few bites she realised that she was starving, and so she fought to eat her share of the food, and no more. After about an hour they heard the jangle of the gaoler's keys and he opened the door, roughly gesturing to Mr. Walker to come with him. The door was locked after him and the two ladies were again alone. It was now completely dark and they still had no candle to light the room, so after sitting silently in the dark for some time Mrs. Annesley said, "Well, I suppose we might as well try to get some sleep. Our captors do not seem to mean us any immediate harm."

Georgiana nodded and added, "Yes, I suppose so. I feel ill thinking of how worried Elizabeth and my aunt and uncle must be right now. I hope that John was not hurt too badly."

"He probably just has a sore head and is being cosseted by Mrs. Burton in front of the kitchen fire."

Georgiana gave her a wan smile. She knew that her companion was trying to keep her spirits up and she appreciated her efforts, but she could not empty the vision of Elizabeth's frantic search for them from her head. They drew back the thin covers of the bed and climbed in, huddling together for warmth as the chill of night crept into their fireless prison.

"Kidnapped!" Lord Whitwell said, shocked.

Elizabeth nodded. "Yes, impossible as it sounds." She proceeded to tell him of the afternoon's events.

"The footman was injured?"

"Yes, but not badly. He has a lump on the back of his head the size of a hen's egg but no broken bones, as far as I could tell. The apothecary is with him now."

Lord Whitwell reached back and rang the bell and Hanford appeared in the doorway.

"Hanford, I am writing a note to Colonel Fitzwilliam and you are to deliver it into his hand as soon as possible. You are not to speak of this to anyone but the colonel." He looked over his reading spectacles at the butler. "Have I made myself clear?"

Hanford bowed. "Yes, your lordship. If you will just ring when you are ready, I will go as soon as you finish the note."

Before the man left the room Lord Whitwell was scribbling a note then folding and sealing it. He rang and Hanford took the note and left.

During this interval, Elizabeth sat back in her chair, relieved to share her burden with two men as capable as Lord Whitwell and the colonel. After Hanford had disappeared, Lord Whitwell said to Elizabeth, "Now, Mrs. Darcy, please repeat everything again from the beginning. I must know every detail if we are to find Georgiana."

She went slowly over all, from the conversation between Georgiana and Mrs. Annesley before she retired to rest until she appeared at the door of Longford House. When she finally stopped talking, he said, "Do you have any suspicions of anyone in the matter?"

She thought a moment. "This morning I would have said that it was impossible for anyone we know to do something such as this. The only man that I was ever concerned about in the past was Jonathan Walker."

"Do you know if he is he in town?"

"He is. We saw him not two days ago when he called. He had a cup of tea and conversed with all three of us very pleasantly. He did not seem different or unusual in any way. He is staying with another neighbour from Derbyshire, Sir Robert Blake, who seems a man of great probity. We also had dinner at Sir Robert's last week when he first arrived in town. I did not see anything to concern me that evening. Mr. Walker was attentive to Georgiana, but so he also was to Miss Blake. Mrs. Annesley mentioned to my husband several months ago that Mr. Walker seemed quite interested in Georgiana and has occasionally asked her to join him for a walk or to go riding, which she has declined to allow Georgiana to do, even with a chaperone. She felt that since Georgiana was not yet out she could not sanction such an intimate relationship with a young man without consulting Georgiana's guardians. She said that Mr. Walker had accepted her strictures graciously and merely expressed the thought that Georgiana's coming-out could not be too soon for his satisfaction."

As she reached the end of this speculation, they heard the front door open and the murmur of voices. Elizabeth rose and faced the door, and she noticed that the others did the same. In a brief moment, the colonel burst in and looked around at those in the room, not missing the presence of Burton.

"What in the devil is going on, Father? Hanford caught me as I was leaving my lodgings for the evening and gave me your note. What did you mean 'a matter of the utmost urgency'?"

Lord Whitwell held up his hand to stop the impetuous flow of words and said curtly, "I would, after further consideration, describe it more as a matter of life and death. Your cousin Georgiana has been abducted."

"Abducted! You must be joking. How could someone kidnap her in the middle of London? Surely she was not out alone."

"She was not. Please give Mrs. Darcy the courtesy of your attention. Mrs. Darcy, will you please repeat the story once more?"

"I will repeat it a thousand times, your lordship, if it will shed some light on this ghastly mess."

He smiled encouragingly at her and she started again, leaving nothing out. At the conclusion, the colonel was standing in front of the fireplace staring into the fire, his hands clasped behind his back. He continued that way for several minutes after she finished then looked up.

"Do we have any idea who might have done this and why?"

Lord Whitwell said dryly, "Is her fortune not enough to explain the why? There are very few young ladies even among the nobility who possess such a rich dowry."

"Yes, but there are several possibilities which we must consider, and they each require a different course of action. The first, and most obvious, possibility is that Georgiana was abducted to extort a ransom from my cousin. The neatness of her capture in the park—away from the Darcy household, most of whom would have given their lives to protect her—suggests a familiarity with the family and the household routines which a complete outsider would be unlikely to have. Georgiana is not a person whose life is scheduled during every moment of the day, and this confrontation in the park was obviously well planned; it was not an impulsive crime. If this is the case we will soon be receiving a random demand.

"The second possibility, which I place somewhat higher than the first, is abduction to force her to marry someone so he can obtain her dowry. This person would have to have information on Georgiana's fortune, but such information is easily obtained; everyone in the upper levels of society knows her net worth to the penny, I have no doubt. The fact that Mrs. Annesley was not also injured and left behind would tend to support the idea of a forced marriage if the perpetrator of this crime is a member of the gentry or nobility who wants her money desperately but also wishes to keep his place in society. He will keep Georgiana with her chaperone to try to minimize the damage to her reputation and, thus, our motivation to seek revenge.

"The first thing we should do is send riders to Gretna Green. They will not be able to force her into a quick marriage in England but would have no difficulty finding someone happy to marry a clearly unwilling bride across the border in Scotland. In both cases, the villain is counting upon our desire to avoid a scandal to force us to keep quiet once the deed is done. There may be other possibilities which will come to us later, so keep your minds open to other ideas.

"I am going back to the officer's mess now. I have a couple of men whose discretion I know I can rely upon. I will send them posthaste to Scotland to try to cut the kidnappers off if they headed that way. Did the injured footman know at what time they were attacked?" He looked at Elizabeth.

"He was light-headed and confused so I do not know how reliable his testimony is, but he thought that they had been in the park about one hour, which would put it at around four o'clock. They had reached the Serpentine and were returning when it happened. He said that dusk was falling, but they could still see clearly."

"I am assuming that this man's history would suggest he is trustworthy?"

Burton cleared his throat and spoke up, "Yes, sir, I am quite confident he is not involved in this, except as a victim. He has served at Pemberley for about fifteen years and this is his first trip to London in that time. We brought him because we needed a larger household staff during Miss Darcy's Season. He is very upset and trying to insist on going out with the others to search for her."

Elizabeth surreptitiously wiped the tears welling in her eyes.

Both gentlemen were immediately on their feet, offering her their handkerchiefs. She gave them a weak smile. "Thank you, both of you. If you don't mind I will accept both handkerchiefs. I think I may need them."

She sat up and tried to control her tears. "Is there nothing else we can do, Colonel? It is unbearable to just sit and wait."

He gave her a sad smile. "I wish I could think of more. I am not good at sitting and waiting for others to do the work either, but a few trustworthy men can be more discreet than I can running madly about on my own. If I suddenly disappeared it would be all over the court, and it is possible that our kidnapper may be a member of the *ton*.

Elizabeth had been staring at her hands, clasped tightly in her lap, while he had been speaking; but she now looked up. "Do you think that this could be related to my husband's reasons for travelling to the Continent?"

Fitzwilliam paused and thought. "I have no reason to believe that his business there involves more than the one person he is meeting, so I do not think so, but I really do not know. I think we should keep it in mind. I have also considered the possibility that this is related to my own activities in some way, although I do not have any specific suspicions. It would be of great benefit to an assassin to have me distracted from my duty to the Prince Regent by concern for my cousin."

Elizabeth, staring at her clenched hands, said softly, "And what should I tell the servants? It is obviously impossible to prevent all of them from knowing the entire story, thus far."

The colonel considered. "If you would like, I will return to Ashbourne House with you and Burton. Most of Darcy's servants have been with the family for many years and I hope with the efforts of myself, Burton, and Mrs. Burton we can limit how much of this spreads outside of the house."

"I would be most grateful if you would, Colonel. I do not feel at all capable of dealing with this on my own."

Lord Whitwell interjected, "And there is no reason that you should be required to, my dear lady, when you have a family to assist you."

The colonel offered her his arm and they left for Ashbourne House immediately.

⁕

As the pale light of dawn gradually lessened the darkness in their room, Georgiana awoke from a brief and troubled sleep with a start. She felt the warmth of Mrs. Annesley stir next to her and she was grateful not to be alone.

"Are you awake, Georgiana my dear?"

"Yes."

"Did you sleep at all?"

"Very little, but I did drift off for a bit."

Soon they could hear stirring in the house, and the old woman, who did not seem to speak, silently brought in a ewer of water and a towel. They tried to wash and make themselves as presentable as possible with only cold water, but it was difficult. Mrs. Annesley tried to smooth her charge's hair with her fingers and repin it neatly, but Georgiana was sure she looked a fright in her rumpled gown and flattened curls.

"I hope Mr. Walker was not too uncomfortable last night."

Mrs. Annesley nodded, her lips occupied with holding her hairpins while she tried to redo her own hair. Finally she patted the resulting chignon.

"I suppose that is the best I can do under the circumstances. I also hope that Mr. Walker is safe. He probably had a sore head to keep him awake."

They suddenly heard the key in the lock, and Walker was pushed roughly into the room before the old woman brought them another tray of food. Apparently, they were to have their meals together.

After the door was locked again, Mrs. Annesley said softly, "I hope that your night was not too uncomfortable, Mr. Walker."

"I had a bed to lie on and my head stopped throbbing after a while. I cannot complain, except to chastise myself for my ineptitude at rescuing you, Miss Darcy. I should have gone to your uncle or to your cousin, Colonel Fitzwilliam."

Georgiana gave him a tremulous smile. "Do not be stupid, Mr. Walker. If you had, you would not have known where to take them. We are both most grateful for your efforts, and, truthfully, your presence increases my hope that we will escape this peril safely."

He smiled at her and bowed. "I thank you for your confidence in me, Miss Darcy. I have hopes that I can find some way to escape my dungeon, and my first task is to try to convince our gaolers to take off my shackles. They must know that I cannot escape—they have kept me in the cellar where there is only a tiny grate to admit light, not large enough for a body to go through. If I can get loose I must creep up the stairs and go out the door or through an unbarred window, if there is one."

"I will pray for your success, Mr. Walker."

"Thank you, Miss Darcy." He smiled warmly at her, and she flushed and looked down at her hands.

"Perhaps if you ladies could lend me a hairpin, I could fashion a picklock of some sort to open the shackles. I cannot say that I have any previous training in such, but I will have plenty of hours to work on them."

Georgiana smiled eagerly. "Yes, of course. Mrs. Annesley, could you find a pin in my hair that we could remove without all of it falling down?"

"I am sure you could spare one."

Mrs. Annesley found a pin and was going to hand it to Mr. Walker when they heard the key in the lock again. She quickly put the pin in his hand and sat down next to Georgiana and looked towards the door. The taller of their captors stuck his head in and bared his rotting teeth in a feral grin.

"Well, young sir, it is time for you to retire to your quarters. I hopes you found them comfortable last night?"

"Quite luxurious, thank you, my good man," Walker said calmly as he walked to the door, the hairpin concealed in his palm.

The rest of the day, Georgiana fidgeted around the room, hoping to hear some sound that would tell her that Mr. Walker had been able to escape, but the farmhouse was silent. She wondered if the kidnappers were gone during the day. It seemed unlikely that they could keep such silence if they were present.

As the light began to fade in the afternoon, she received the answer to her questions when she heard someone moving about the front room, and their companion was returned to them for the evening meal; another dish of porridge and some more, increasingly stale, bread. Her heart plummeted when he appeared, but she hid her disappointment and commented dryly, "The cook's repertoire of dishes seems rather limited, does it not? Perhaps we should see if she could take some lessons from our cook."

Walker laughed, almost choking on the lumpy porridge he was eating. "Miss Darcy, you will be the death of me! I hope that I can keep my wit functioning as well as you do under these circumstances; your courage is an inspiration to me."

Georgiana flushed a deep red and concentrated on her food. "I do not think that I am particularly brave. I feel as if my throat is closing tighter with each moment."

Walker smiled and said, "Miss Darcy?"

She glanced up briefly.

"You are one of the bravest people I know."

He reached out and took her hand. When she looked up again he raised her hand to his lips, the shackles making his movements awkward. Mrs. Annesley cleared her throat and he dropped Georgiana's hand and turned to her.

"Mr. Walker, do you think that there is any chance that you may be able to escape?"

"I have not yet had the opportunity to tell you my news. Our friends have moved me upstairs—I think they were tired of coming down to get me—so there may be a chance of removing one of the shutters if I can get these leg irons loose. I could probably steal one of their horses with my arms shackled, but I would have difficulty with my legs bound."

Georgiana smiled to herself.

Walker was quick to see her expression.

"And what are you smiling about?"

She paused, embarrassed. "I was just thinking that a woman would not have that problem since we must always ride sidesaddle." Her voice trailed off.

Mrs. Annesley asked, "Do you think that they have sent a ransom demand to Mrs. Darcy?"

"I do not know. I haven't heard a sound all day."

The sound of the key was at the door again, and the shorter kidnapper ordered Walker roughly out of the room. Georgiana heard the key grate in the lock of the nearby room where Walker was now being held. She sighed, obscurely reassured again by the knowledge that a friend was near, even if he was also a prisoner. The two ladies retired early again as they were still left without candle or fire to see by.

At Ashbourne House, Elizabeth had paced her bedroom most of the night of Georgiana's disappearance, until exhaustion forced her to recline on her settee and she had dozed off for an hour or so.

She was up early and fidgeted nervously about her sitting-room, trying to keep a calm countenance for the sake of the servants, without much success. The colonel finally called at nine o'clock while she was toying with her food in the breakfast-parlour. She jumped to her feet when he entered, but sank back while the footman quickly set him a place at the table. When they were finally alone, the colonel looked into her eyes and she saw that, in spite of his outwards calm, his eyes were dark and furious and his teeth were clenched so tightly that his jaw muscles stood out. After a moment's struggle, he controlled himself and said, very quietly, "I sent two men to Scotland last night. We will, hopefully, hear something definite from them soon. This morning I would like to take the injured footman with me and go over the ground that they covered in the park to see if I can find any sign of the passage of their abductors."

Elizabeth nodded silently, her throat dry and aching with the tears she held back. He saw her hands clenched on her handkerchief and said kindly, "Pray try to keep your spirits up, Mrs. Darcy… Elizabeth. We will find Georgiana, and her abductors will pay for their crimes."

Tears began to flow in earnest from Elizabeth's eyes.

"I just hope Georgiana need not pay also."

His lips compressed.

"I also hope that her life is not blighted by the actions of these men. We will do what we can for her. All I can think about is the satisfaction I would receive from running these men through for her sake. A pistol would not be nearly as satisfying a way to punish them."

"We must find them first."

"Indeed."

The colonel gulped down a cup of coffee and rose, bowing perfunctorily to her before he left to find John, the footman who had accompanied the two ladies to the park.

Chapter 15

Oh what a tangled web we weave,
When first we practise to deceive!

—SIR WALTER SCOTT, *MARMION*

AFTER THREE DAYS OF CAPTIVITY, GEORGIANA AWOKE BEFORE dawn from another troubled sleep. They had seen Mr. Walker for short periods at each of the two meals they were served daily, and as she lay quietly, trying not to disturb Mrs. Annesley, she wondered now that their captors had allowed them to know that Walker was also a prisoner. She also wondered that she had not seen before how curious this was. Surely it would have been better, whatever their plans were, to deny their prisoners the knowledge that someone had already found them, even though his rescue had been unsuccessful. If I were a kidnapper, she thought, I would be very nervous that someone had found my location. What guarantee was there that Mr. Walker had not sent a friend or servant for help before trailing their carriage? Would it not be sensible to move their prisoners to another location? It might be difficult to set up another secure house, but surely it would be worth a great deal to make sure that their hostages would not be rescued.

Their self-assurance bothered her obscurely, but she could not find an explanation, so she determined to put those thoughts away for the moment. She did not want to think about her family, frantic with worry for her sake, searching vainly for her, so she blocked those thoughts from her mind as well and decided to think about something else entirely. After a moment, she settled on her music as a safe topic and closed her eyes and mentally played the sonata she had been working on, concentrating all of her restless energy and frustration into seeing the music in front of her and feeling the keys under her fingers.

It was, as far as she could tell from the changes in the faint light which penetrated the shutters, nearly an hour before Mrs. Annesley stirred.

"Georgiana?"

"Yes, I am awake."

"Did you sleep at all, my dear girl?"

"A little," she whispered. "As each hour goes by and I think of the terrible pain and worry my family must be experiencing I find myself becoming more and more angry. I am so furious that I feel I must spontaneously combust and the thought of doing violence to our captors has firmly taken root in my mind, and I cannot remove it. What my sister must be going through! The ability of evil men to terrorise and ruin the lives of innocent women cannot be God's will. It cannot."

"I am sure you are right, my dear, but what can be done about it? Women are not as strong as men and cannot fight them by physical means."

"No, but they should not have the power to control us with the threat of scandal and public ruin. These men know very well that if we escape we will not want to bring them to justice for fear of sullying my reputation and standing in society, so they are safe from retribution by legal means."

Mrs. Annesley embraced her reassuringly and they turned to their usual attempts to fix their hair and wash, their conversation lagging. As she tried to untangle her hair with her fingers, Georgiana was repulsed by the greasy, stringy feel of the unwashed mass tumbling to her waist.

"My hair is positively disgusting. What I would give for a bath!"

Mrs. Annesley agreed, "Yes, I am feeling very dirty, and sleeping in our clothes has not helped their appearance."

They finished their tasks and sat on the edge of the bed to await their breakfast, which was not long in coming. Again, Mr. Walker was shoved unceremoniously into the room in front of the wizened old woman who brought the food. Walker's shackles were off his ankles, but his hands were still bound. When the door had slammed and the lock clicked shut behind the old woman, Walker greeted the two ladies:

"Good morning, ladies. As you can see, I am still a guest in this fine establishment." He bowed over Georgiana's hand and she could smell the clean scent of French-milled soap coming from his hair, which was tousled but did not appear greasy. She jerked involuntarily and then tried to smile to cover her confusion. Walker noted her start.

"Are you well, Miss Darcy? You look pale."

"Y-yes, I am fine. I am not surprised that my looks have suffered during my ordeal."

"It would take a great deal to damage your looks, Miss Darcy."

She flushed with embarrassment and looked down at her hands. As she did so, she noticed Walker's boots. They were not the same boots he had worn the day before. Both pairs were black, but these had a more rounded toe than the ones he had worn previously. She had particularly noticed the toes because she had been staring down in embarrassment while he was complimenting her courage, but she also noticed that there were no scrapes or gouges in the leather, as there would have been after many hours in shackles.

She gently took back the hand he was still holding and went to get Mrs. Annesley some porridge. While her back was turned and the others were chatting about inconsequential matters, she reviewed the events over the past few days frantically in her mind, her shaking hands automatically spooning the porridge into bowls. She could think of several circumstances which struck her now as incongruous, and she felt as if the scales had dropped from her eyes. What were the chances that an acquaintance would have witnessed their abduction? Why would the kidnappers allow him to follow them to the isolated house when they evidently knew he was there, judging by his immediate capture? Why would the gaolers be so kind as to rid Walker of his leg irons, other than to make it easier for him to "escape?" She had no answers to her questions, but when she turned back to Mrs. Annesley with her companion's breakfast, she had succeeded in controlling her visage, and she was able to converse normally, she thought, with Walker.

Mr. Walker was dragged out of the room after the meal, and Georgiana stood at the window, trying to see through the slats of the shutters. She decided not to tell her companion about her suspicions; the elderly Mrs. Annesley was far too artless to keep up the pretence of ignorance. Frankly, Georgiana was even less adept at subterfuge, but she could not return to the previous day's innocence, so she must mask her knowledge for both their sakes.

Elizabeth awoke at dawn on the third day after the kidnapping and stared bleakly at the hangings which covered her bed. The colonel had been unable to find any witnesses to the abduction, and his efforts to confirm Walker's innocence had been unavailing. He had called in the afternoon of the day after Georgiana's disappearance and told her abruptly, "I did not find anything in the park that helped in our search and I can prove neither Walker's innocence nor his guilt. He is supposedly visiting friends in the country, but Sir Robert does not know their name."

He had rubbed his hand over his face, and she had noticed the dark circles around his eyes.

"May I get you a drink, Colonel? Or perhaps a cup of tea?"

"Thank you, tea would be fine—if I can swallow it. I feel as if I am choking on my anger and guilt."

"Guilt?" she had said, her brows lifted.

"Yes. The first time I have had sole responsibility for my ward and I have lost her. I do not know what I am going to tell Darcy." He had stared up at the ceiling and blinked several times. "And poor, sweet Georgiana. What she must be feeling now, abandoned by those she trusts."

Elizabeth had set down her teacup with a crash. "Colonel, there is no purpose in blaming yourself; I am the one who was most responsible for Georgiana's well-being. If there is any fault, it is mine. In any case, blaming ourselves will not return Georgiana to us."

The drawing-room door had opened and Burton had entered with his silver salver and offered it to the colonel.

"A message just arrived for you, Colonel Fitzwilliam, sent from Lord Whitwell."

He had picked up the missive and thanked Burton. After the butler had returned to the hall, he had unfolded the earl's fine notepaper and examined the enclosed note folded inside, and Elizabeth had joined him. There had been nothing distinctive about the notepaper, which appeared to be of the cheapest sort, but he seemed reluctant to open it. She had looked up at him curiously, and he hurriedly opened the seal, which had been pressed with a large thumb to hold the folded paper closed.

Colonel Fitzwilliam,—

We have your ward, Miss Darcy. We will return her unharmed as soon as you pay us £10,000. You have two days to gather the money. We will contact you then. Do not attempt to find us or you will be sorry, and so will she.

The letter was unsigned and the writing was crude in appearance, in contrast to the educated spelling and grammar.

Elizabeth had felt the blood drain from her face.

"How will we obtain that much money, especially with my husband gone?"

"I will go to my father immediately. Perhaps he can convince the bank to lend him the money, but two days is not long."

"I suppose the longer they hold Georgiana, the more chance there is that they will be discovered." She had felt her stomach lurch and had quickly sat down, covering her face with her hands.

"Should I call your maid, Mrs. Darcy?"

Elizabeth had shaken her head. "No, I will be fine. Go quickly to your father. He is undoubtedly as undone as we are; I do not wish to keep him in suspense."

He had looked at her for a moment with concern then turned

and left. She had remained sitting for several minutes, she then forced herself to drink her tea and return to the needlework he had interrupted, but her hands were shaking too much for her to control the needle and she soon gave up.

The remainder of the afternoon and the next two days had crept by with agonising slowness, without news of either Georgiana or Walker. Lord Whitwell was negotiating with his bank for a loan, secured by the deed to Longford House, which was not bound in the entail on his estate, and the colonel was still trying to gather information from his agents. Those who had gone to Gretna Green had come back empty-handed. There was no sign of anyone fitting Georgiana's or Mrs. Annesley's description, and their watch on the roads had failed to bring any further sightings.

Elizabeth, without an active part to undertake in the rescue of Georgiana, spent her days pretending to attend to her usual duties while she went over the details of her sister's abduction again and again. She needed to suppress her natural irritability over her lack of any useful task to assist the men and pretend to be calm and unperturbed. Lady Whitwell, also without a role in this crisis, visited her and they talked about Georgiana and her ordeal frequently. Her support was a great comfort for Elizabeth and made the maddening hours pass more quickly.

On the fifth morning, Elizabeth rang early for Lambert and dressed in a morning robe. She stared at her face in the glass while Lambert tidied her hair, her eyes dark-circled and haunted and her cheeks pale, and then turned away from the sight. While she was picking at her breakfast, Burton entered with his salver.

"A letter, Mrs. Darcy."

She picked up the familiar coarse envelope and nodded to

Burton, who bowed and left after one long, backwards glance. She opened the letter and read:

> *Miss Darcy is eager to return to her home. Mrs. Darcy will carry the money to St. Paul's Cathedral in a satchel at one pm today and wait to be contacted. She will come alone. If there is any sign that she is accompanied you will never see Miss Darcy again.*

Elizabeth felt a cold chill and wrapped her shawl more tightly around her. She must find the colonel, and quickly. She hurried out to the hall and said, "Burton, the carriage. I must go to Longford House immediately."

"Yes, madam."

The carriage raced through the early morning streets and she stepped down in front of Longford House within minutes. It was the work of seconds to acquaint Lord and Lady Whitwell of the most recent letter, and Lord Whitwell sent upstairs for the colonel, who had been staying with his parents during this threat to the family. When he came downstairs, his eyes still puffy with sleep (or more likely lack of it, Elizabeth thought), he read the letter through twice.

"There is no way on earth that you are going to put yourself in the power of these criminals."

Lord Whitwell nodded in agreement.

"No indeed. We will not risk you, Mrs. Darcy."

"But why do they want me to deliver the money?"

The colonel chewed on his lower lip, a mannerism startlingly like that of his ward, Elizabeth thought with surprise as she waited for him to speak.

"They probably feel that Mrs. Darcy is less likely to be a threat, which is undoubtedly true, because of my feelings at the moment."

Elizabeth looked up at him and saw the barely contained flicker of fury in his eyes again. She spoke up, "I will deliver the money. We have no choice."

They continued to argue over the details of the payment in Lord Whitwell's library, while they awaited the arrival of the money from the bank, until Lady Whitwell, who had maintained a shocked silence during the entire conversation, said, "Do not argue about it any more. Mrs. Darcy is willing to risk her life for Georgiana, as we all are. She will do what needs to be done to obtain Georgiana's return. Instead of arguing whether she should be allowed to do it, we should be trying to determine how to protect her safety as much as we can under the circumstances."

The two men stared at her then tacitly gave in and began discussing whether they could place several men inside St. Paul's vast interior while awaiting the arrival of the bank officer with the money in the late morning.

The banker had just departed from Longford House after delivering the £10,000 when there was a peal from the doorbell, and seconds later the library door burst open to reveal Jonathan Walker, dishevelled and dirt smeared, his hands bound with shackles. Hanford fluttered behind him, looking shocked.

"Please. I know where Miss Darcy is."

They all stared narrowly at him as he gasped out, "They captured me after I followed their carriage from the park. I had been riding just before dark. I did not know it was Miss Darcy until later, I just saw two women pulled into a carriage. It was only today that I was able to escape from the house. You must come with me. They will know that I am free and we must get there before they can move their hostages."

The colonel called for the carriage. Lord Whitwell hurried after him, saying, "I will go with you." Fitzwilliam stopped abruptly and said quietly to his father, "No, I will go alone. You must get the ransom money ready and take Mrs. Darcy to St. Paul's if I do not return before the time. If the man who is to pick up the ransom has already left the house where they are holding Georgiana we will miss him there, and he must think everything is going as planned if we are to capture him. It is also possible that he may have someone watching the house."

His father nodded his reluctant agreement and returned to the library and the two ladies as the hooves of the horses and the carriage wheels thundered over the cobblestone streets.

In their prison, Georgiana and Mrs. Annesley were well aware of Walker's escape. Their gaolers had "discovered" his absence first thing in the morning and burst into the ladies' room to check on them. The door was relocked and their breakfast had been forgotten in the noise and confusion in the yard outside. Georgiana sat carefully on the bed, turning this latest event over in her mind as the minutes and hours ticked by silently. Mrs. Annesley tried to distract her with inconsequential chatter, but Georgiana did not even hear her.

The afternoon arrived with the abrupt entrance of the taller gaoler, his face contorted in what Georgiana thought was supposed to be a grin, his yellow teeth horrible in his unshaven face.

"'eres your breakfusses, ladies. Don't you be thinkin' that your young man's escape is going to help ye. We be pickin' up the ransom today then we'll be gone before he can get to town and back."

Georgiana plucked up her courage and asked, "And what will happen to us?"

He smiled more broadly. "Oh, you don't need to worry, miss. You'll be taken care of."

She repressed the shudder she felt at his words and stared him in the eye until he turned and left them, carefully locking the door again. They ignored the inevitable bowl of tasteless porridge, and Georgiana spent the next hours pacing the tiny room. Suddenly, in the mid-afternoon, she heard the sound of racing hoofbeats on the road outside. There was an explosion of sound in the outer room and then sudden silence. A brief sound of harsh voices ended with the sound of boot-clad footsteps, and in a moment the door to their room burst open, revealing Colonel Fitzwilliam, a pistol in his right hand. He wavered a moment when he saw her then his lips formed the name "Georgiana."

She ran to him and he clasped her roughly to his left side and looked at his cousin's companion.

"Are you all right, Mrs. Annesley?" His voice was quiet and calm, but Georgiana, looking up at him, saw the steel in his normally placid blue eyes.

"We are both very well, Colonel, but quite ready to return home," said Mrs. Annesley.

He gave her a brief smile and said, "Let us go then."

They had started towards the door when several shots rang out. Colonel Fitzwilliam shoved Georgiana behind him. He called out, "Walker?"

"Yes, Colonel. You may come out. Do not bring the ladies out yet."

The colonel released Georgiana from the painful grip he had on her and motioned them to stay in the bedroom. He disappeared through the door and they heard a brief murmur of voices before the colonel reappeared.

"The kidnappers are dead. They tried to attack Walker."

He swung Georgiana up in his arms and said, "Keep your eyes closed. You should not see this."

Georgiana pushed her face into the breast of his coat and felt his hand on the back of her head, crushing her face to his chest. She felt him turn and heard his voice as he spoke to Mrs. Annesley, "If you will wait in the bedroom, I will return for you."

Mrs. Annesley said, "Thank you, Colonel, I prefer to risk the horrors of that room than stay in this bedroom a moment longer."

"Then put your hand on my shoulder and look straight ahead as we go out."

The colonel walked quickly down the hall, through the outer room and out of the door. Georgiana could feel the fresh air on her face before he loosed his hold and put her gently on her feet. Walker was standing in front of the outer door, his arms hanging loosely at his side, his fingers barely gripping the two pistols in his hands. Fitzwilliam said curtly, "Get a grip on yourself, Walker; we need to get the ladies out of here."

His voice seemed to rouse Walker, who looked up at Georgiana in shock and said abruptly, "Yes, we must get them out of here. This is no place for a lady."

They entered the carriage and in minutes were racing for town.

After a few minutes the colonel broke into Georgiana's thoughts, "Are you sure you are unhurt, Georgiana?"

"Oh… oh, yes, I am fine." She smiled awkwardly at him. "But I would dearly love a bath. You may want to sit on the other side of the carriage until I have had one."

He laughed, a short bark of surprise.

"I believe that I can tolerate you even unwashed, little cousin. I am not letting you more than arm's distance away until we are safely home." He managed a twinkle in his eyes. "I thank God that I did not have to tell your brother that you were snatched away on my watch and I was unable to find you."

She smiled at him, a hint of mischief returning to her pale face.

"No, that *would* be frightening would it not?"

"Indeed. We must be very grateful to Mr. Walker. He came to us as soon as he could after his escape so we could rescue you."

"Did he?"

He looked a little surprised at her cool answer, and she forced a smile at Walker.

"We are most thankful for our safety and your part in ensuring it, Mr. Walker."

He gave her a humble smile and said, "It was my pleasure to be of assistance to you and Mrs. Annesley." He bowed to both of them, and Georgiana closed her eyes and leaned against the colonel's supporting arm until the wheels rattled onto the cobblestones of town. She opened her lids to a narrow slit and observed Jonathan Walker. He was staring out of the window, the picture of stunned grief, his dishevelled hair and smudged face a tragic mask of regret.

When the carriage pulled into the mews behind Ashbourne House they hurried into the house through the back, the darkness hiding their arrival from prying eyes. Elizabeth greeted them with relieved astonishment and enveloped Georgiana in a crushing embrace.

"My dear girl. Thank God… thank God."

Georgiana disengaged herself and whispered, "Let us go upstairs."

Elizabeth gave a tiny, puzzled frown but said, "Of course. Durand will have a nice hot bath for you."

Georgiana turned to Jonathan Walker and held out her hand. "Thank you, Mr. Walker."

"You are most welcome, Miss Darcy." He glanced at the colonel and said, "May I call tomorrow and make sure that you are quite recovered, Miss Darcy."

She smiled at that.

"Please do, Mr. Walker."

The colonel saw him to the door while the ladies climbed the stairs.

Later, after soaking in hot water for nearly half an hour and washing her hair repeatedly, Georgiana came downstairs to the drawing-room in a morning robe with her hair hanging damply around her face. The colonel was talking quietly with Elizabeth and Mrs. Annesley.

"Are you ready for some tea, Georgiana, my dear?" Elizabeth asked her.

"Yes, please."

She thought she had never tasted anything so refreshing, and she drank the hot tea thirstily while the colonel took up where he had left off.

"So Walker held them at gunpoint while I broke open the door to the bedroom where they were held." He rubbed his shoulder and made a rueful face. "Perhaps I should have taken the time to find the key. My elderly bones are not accustomed to such rigors." His face suddenly became serious. "But I needed to make sure Georgiana was unhurt. Unfortunately, the scoundrels tried to over-power him while I was releasing the ladies, and he had to defend himself. They are both dead. I would have liked to talk to them and find out who they were working for. We have much to thank Walker for."

Georgiana abruptly set her cup on the tray.

"I am afraid I do not agree with you there, Cousin."

Three shocked faces turned towards her.

"Jonathan Walker was involved in our kidnapping. I think it most likely that he planned the entire affair."

There was a jumble of voices as her audience exclaimed, but she held up her hand.

"At first I was taken in when he pretended to have been captured and imprisoned, but after a couple of days there were a few things which niggled at my mind. Why would our captors so obligingly allow him to share meals with us? It allowed him to play the injured hero to perfection, but what benefit would *they* get from it? Each time they released him from his 'prison' they risked his escape. Then after the first day or so, they kindly took off his leg shackles so it would be easier for him to make a credible escape. It would have been more believable if he had pretended to use my hairpin to open it just before his 'escape,' but he must have become impatient with the restrictions of the shackles. What finally opened my eyes, however, was when he kissed my hand upon joining us on the third morning and I could smell the perfume from the fine soap he had washed with. I assure you that we were not given soap, let alone fine French-milled soap. Also, that day he had on a different pair of boots. He must have thought I was too stupid to notice, and they were black, as the previous pair had been, but they were not the same boots and there were no marks of the shackles on the leather."

The three others stared at her in horror. Finally, the colonel asked, "What was his purpose, then, in kidnapping you? When he brought us in he lost all chance of obtaining the ransom.

Mrs. Darcy was at St. Paul's with the ransom all afternoon and no one ever came for it."

"I believe that his plan was to ingratiate himself with me and with my family with his heroism and obtain my hand with your blessings."

"And the ransom demand? It was just a blind to put us off the scent?" Elizabeth asked.

Georgiana nodded. "*Sans doute.* He probably realised that I would not consent to marry him before my first Season, if at all, and there was the risk that I would meet someone I preferred to him over the next few months. How could I, or my family, turn him down when he had been instrumental in saving me, and, moreover, when he knew enough to ruin my reputation forever and destroy any chance of a good marriage? It was a subtle and clever plan and might have worked if his vanity or his low regard for my intellect had not caused him to put his personal comforts above the success of his plan."

They all sat in silence, digesting her words and fitting them into what information they had. After a few minutes, Elizabeth looked from Georgiana to the colonel.

"What are we going to do?"

The colonel reluctantly opened his mouth, but before he could speak Georgiana cut in, startling them both, "There is nothing we can do. This is precisely why he thought he could get away with our kidnapping. In the absolute worst circumstance he could avoid arrest and imprisonment by promising to hold his tongue. He might even be able to extort some money from my family to ensure his co-operation. At best he could succeed and marry a woman with a large fortune and live off her money. At least until it ran out. I should hate to be bound to him when the money ran out."

Elizabeth shuddered in horror, but the colonel just stared at Georgiana's face, his jaw working. She smiled at him.

"Do not worry about it, dear cousin. I am sure that he will meet a bad end which will pay him back for what he has done, which included murder as well as kidnapping" She paused and looked at her cousin, whose expression showed his shocked awareness of the significance of her statement.

"He could not allow those men to be questioned," he said flatly.

"No… Colonel, I would like to allow him to call tomorrow, as he requested."

The colonel leapt to his feet. "Are you mad? You have just said that he is a kidnapper and murderer!"

"I am not mad. I wish to have a few words with Mr. Walker. I do not want him to be in any doubt about my understanding of the situation."

The colonel stared at her in astonishment and then, finally, nodded.

"If that is what you wish, Cousin. I will make sure I am here when he calls."

"Why do you not come to breakfast and then stay the afternoon? I would not want you to miss him." She looked at him levelly and then smiled.

The colonel appeared to be rather nonplussed at Georgiana's calm demeanour after her terrifying experiences, but he worked to recover his self-control and then bid them goodbye and left for his parents' house. He had sent a message when they had returned, informing them of Georgiana's rescue, but they did not yet know all the details.

Chapter 16

The best-laid plans of Mice and Men
Gang aft a-gley.

—Robert Burns, "To a Mouse"

WALKER CALLED AS EARLY AS PROPRIETY ALLOWED THE NEXT afternoon and looked sleek and handsome since ridding himself of his shackles. Elizabeth was the only member of the household downstairs when he arrived, but she sent a message up for Georgiana and the colonel, who were ensconced in the music-room, awaiting Walker's arrival. They arrived simultaneously and Georgiana still wore the determined aspect with which she had stated her observations the night before. Walker jumped up and met Georgiana in two strides, leaning to kiss her hand as she bobbed a curtsey but was circumvented when she pretended not to see his outstretched hand and turned towards the colonel, "Is Mrs. Annesley down? Perhaps I should call her."

The colonel answered her, "She said she would be down in a moment."

"Well, perhaps I will go ahead and pour then. Mr. Walker?"

She handed him a cup of tea with a steady hand and poured for the others.

"Well, Mr. Walker, I thank you for coming so that I can express my feelings about your role in my rescue."

"You do not need to thank me, Miss Darcy," he demurred.

"Oh, but indeed I do. I want you to understand my feelings fully in this matter. I have already informed my cousin and my sister of the truth: that you were not only involved in the kidnapping but were most likely the organiser and leader of the entire episode."

Walker's mouth hung open for a moment in shock before he pulled himself together and said, "Miss Darcy, how can you say that? I was as much a prisoner as you and your companion!"

"It is quite interesting that you were a prisoner and yet you were allowed to bathe with fine perfumed soap, and in spite of being snatched off your horse and shackled you had more than one pair of boots with you."

Walker glanced at Elizabeth and then the colonel. His eyes widened briefly when he saw the expression in the colonel's eyes and the grim set of his mouth and he turned quickly back to Georgiana.

"Miss Darcy, I am sorry if I have inadvertently offended you, but I have no idea what you are talking about. My only thought was to save you from your attackers."

He stood and the others rose.

Georgiana smiled blandly and said, "I just want to make sure that I am rightly understood, sir. You will never see a penny of Darcy money so you need not waste your time feigning bonhomie and affection. Good day, sir."

She turned towards the door with Elizabeth, and Walker made to follow and escape with his air of offended dignity intact, but the colonel said quietly, "A moment, Mr. Walker?"

Walker paused in indecision, but the door closed behind Georgiana before he could escape. The colonel began speaking as soon as the others were gone, his eyes examining the empty teacup he still held in his hand.

"My cousin wished to express her feelings and I indulged her because I thought that she deserved to have her say, but I would also like to say a few words. I know as well as you that we cannot call down the force of the law upon you because of the risk to my cousin's reputation should you make the affair public, as I have no doubt you would do to get your petty revenge. However, I should like you to consider a point or two." He lifted his eyes to Walker's and the younger man flinched. Fitzwilliam continued in an offhand, even disinterested, tone. "If I hear the slightest rumour impugning my cousin's honour, even the smallest vague hint that she is not the innocent that we both know she is, then I will kill you. I do not care who actually starts the rumour; you are the one who will pay with his life. Also consider that I have friends in power and no known connection with you. Who would suspect me if you should suddenly disappear? Do you understand?" He raised his eyes and stared directly into Walker's.

Walker stared at him for a moment and then nodded slowly.

"Yes, I understand. If I keep silent then I am safe?"

"Only as long as Georgiana's reputation is safe. Not quite the same thing."

"Agreed."

Walker offered his hand, but Fitzwilliam looked at it with distaste and Walker flushed, seeming more embarrassed by the snub than by the enumeration of his crimes. He started to turn towards the door, but the colonel spoke again, "One more thing, Walker."

"Yes?"

"Lord and Lady Whitwell are expected at any moment so I would suggest that you depart forthwith. My father tends to have old-fashioned notions about men who victimise young women, and his temper is not as well controlled as mine."

Walker left without another word.

Lord and Lady Whitwell arrived a half hour after Walker's departure and were shown into the drawing-room, where the colonel awaited them. As soon as Burton closed the door, Lady Whitwell demanded, "How is Georgiana? Is she hurt? Is Mrs. Annesley injured? Where is she?"

Fitzwilliam held up his hand to stop the flow of words:

"Peace, Mother. Georgiana and Mrs. Annesley are quite unharmed. I will send upstairs for her if you will give me a moment." He looked at his father. "I told you last night what Georgiana had noticed about Walker during their captivity."

Lord Whitwell nodded.

"He called a short while ago, as he had said he would, and Georgiana stood up and threw his perfidy in his face." A smile flickered briefly over his face. "You should have seen her, Mother. She was magnificent! After she swept out with Mrs. Darcy I had a few more words with Walker about the consequences should he impugn Georgiana's reputation in any way."

His father raised his brows. "And the consequences were?"

Fitzwilliam's lips thinned. "Perhaps it is best that you not know."

"I see."

His mother broke in:

"Could I see Georgiana now? I must see her with my own eyes and make sure she is safe."

Fitzwilliam smiled genially at her. "Yes, Mother." He rang for a footman and sent word upstairs to Georgiana and Mrs. Darcy that Lord and Lady Whitwell had arrived.

After she was embraced and examined and Lady Whitwell had shed a few natural tears over her ordeal, Georgiana comforted and calmed both her aunt and uncle enough that they could turn to other subjects. The first to speak was the colonel, who reluctantly stood and said, "I am sorry to abandon this reunion, but I have several items which I must resolve after my absence from the palace the past few days." He turned to Georgiana. "I am more pleased than I can say to see you safe at home, little cousin. I am also glad that I will not need to tell your brother when he returns that I lost his precious little sister but can mention it as a past event."

Georgiana smiled at him with no trace of irony and said, "I thank you for rescuing me, Cousin. I am much obliged."

"Only doing my duty, Miss Darcy. There is no particular merit in that."

A week ago she might have bristled at his patronising tone, but she was far too pleased with him to take umbrage.

When he had departed, Georgiana turned to her aunt and said, "How many days until my presentation? I have rather lost count."

"Nine days only, my dear. As soon as you are recovered I am afraid we must go back to our practises."

"I am quite recovered now, my dear aunt. Shall we start again tomorrow?"

Lady Whitwell looked at her dubiously, but she saw that her niece's colour was high and she seemed in good spirits.

"If you are sure, my dear. Come to Longford House tomorrow morning and we will finish the fittings. Mrs. Darcy's and Miss Bennet's gowns are finished—we told the seamstress that you were ill, so she worked on theirs first."

"Oh!" Elizabeth exclaimed, "I almost forgot. Your friend Catherine Freemont has called twice. We told her you were too ill for visitors, so you should let her know that you are well. She was quite concerned."

"Dear Catherine! I will send her a note immediately and invite her to tea."

Lady Whitwell spoke up, "Georgiana, there is a ball two nights from now, on Monday; it is the first of the debutante balls and is being put on by my friend, Lady Morton. Will you be up to attending, my dear?"

"Oh yes. I hope the seamstress can finish one of my ball-gowns in time! I do not want to wear my little girl clothes to the first ball."

"I will hurry her on. If we work very hard in our remaining time you should be quite ready on your presentation day."

"I am sure I will be."

They all looked at her in astonishment at this surprising comment, and she laughed at their expressions.

"Do not look so surprised, all of you! After what I have been through this week, I cannot find it in my heart to be nervous about something as insignificant as a presentation at court. Or a ball, for that matter."

The next day they were all involved in the bustle of readying Georgiana for the ball and the continued practises in courtly graces, but Georgiana did not forget her brother. That evening, when Colonel Fitzwilliam arrived to dine with them at Longford House, she drew him aside and asked him, "Cousin, when is my brother to return? I am worried about Elizabeth; she is looking very ill and I am sure it is over her unease regarding him. She was not looking well even before my abduction."

Fitzwilliam glanced over at his cousin's wife and answered quietly, "Yes, she does look ill; I noticed it before. I am sorry, Georgiana, I do not know exactly when he will return. I am sure, however, that even if his business is unfinished he will return for your presentation."

"I hope so," she said, watching Elizabeth. "I do not believe she is sleeping at all, and the terrible worry over me certainly did not do her any good.

Elizabeth was, indeed, very worried about Darcy. When the exquisite relief of Georgiana's recovery had faded, she was more distrait than ever over her husband's absence. She exerted herself mightily during the day to keep Georgiana's renewed spirits up, but she was unable to dissemble to herself when she was alone in her room, and sleep seemed further away each night. When she could not avoid a glass, she could see that her face was still strained and white—an appearance that she hoped would be attributed by those outside the family to the stress of Georgiana's presentation. When she finally fell asleep at night, it was to be visited by fantastic dreams filled with unseen perils and vague fears, which left her more exhausted when she awoke than she had been before retiring.

She found herself a little irritated that the colonel continued to treat Georgiana as he would a child, even after her queenly performance when she faced down Walker, but she suppressed her feelings, knowing that her prickly mood was a reflection of her worries and not the colonel's fault. Georgiana, she was pleased to see, appeared quite collected, listening to her uncle and her cousin courteously and occasionally speaking herself. Elizabeth was quite sure that, with her keen perception, her sister felt all of the tensions in the room, and her composure encouraged Elizabeth to make a greater effort to take part in the conversation and keep it flowing smoothly.

The next day was Sunday, and the entire family went to church together, sitting in the Darcy and Whitwell pews. Elizabeth heard hardly a word of the sermon, occupied as she was with saying several prayers: for Darcy's return, for the success of Georgiana's presentation, and for her new sister's safety and future happiness. By the time the hour-long service ended, Elizabeth felt as if her legs were leaden and she was afraid that she would not be able to rise in her exhausted state. The colonel noticed her pallor as he passed up the aisle and offered her his arm.

"Are you well, Mrs. Darcy?" he asked quietly, his face a polite mask, but his eyes worried. "Do you need to sit down again for a moment, or should I bring the carriage up?"

"No, I am well, I thank you, Colonel," she replied, barely above a whisper. "I am merely a little tired. The strain of the last few weeks is beginning to catch up with me." She tried to smile reassuringly, but the effort was weak.

"I will escort you and Georgiana home," he said. "Perhaps you are too tired to come to Longford House for dinner again tonight?" He looked at her questioningly.

"I will rest a little this afternoon and then I am sure I will be fine by evening. Do not worry about me, Colonel."

They caught up with the others and Elizabeth made a supreme effort to appear as usual, but she was very relieved to arrive at Ashbourne House. They were met at the door by Burton, who smiled happily and said, "You will be pleased, madam, to know that the master arrived not thirty minutes ago. He is upstairs in his room, changing."

Elizabeth thanked him breathlessly, left Georgiana to make her farewells to the colonel, and hurried upstairs. She arrived at their sitting-room just as Darcy, hearing her footsteps, came out of his dressing-room, fastening the cuffs of a fresh shirt, his hair tousled and damp.

"Elizabeth!"

He caught her up and clutched her tightly against his breast, his face buried in her hair, completely disregarding the presence of his valet, who quietly let himself out the other door. She felt tears of relief stinging her eyes as she clung to him. Then, suddenly, the room began spinning and she heard, from a long way off, Darcy's voice say again, "Elizabeth!"—this time in concern and agitation.

When she opened her eyes, she was lying on the settee in the sitting-room and Darcy was holding her hand. "Elizabeth," he said in a worried voice, "are you ill, my darling? Should I have Burton call the doctor?" He glanced over to the door where Burton was peeking in, a worried look on his face.

She struggled to a sitting position, saying, "No! I am well; I am just—rather tired. I am sorry to worry you. What happened?"

Darcy nodded to Burton, who silently closed the door.

"When I was holding you, you went limp in my arms," he said with relief. "I did not know what to think... you were so pale and thin. I am afraid that the last few weeks have been too much for you."

"I cannot believe it—I have never fainted in my life! Of course, I have never had so much reason to be out of countenance." She smiled wanly up at him, tears welling up in her eyes, to her great embarrassment. "You do not look well, yourself, my love. You look as if you have not eaten or slept in days." She gently touched his cheek.

"Yes, I am tired, but I will be fine now that I am home to stay." He smiled and looked at her tenderly.

After a few minutes, Elizabeth remembered Colonel Fitzwilliam and Georgiana.

"You must call Georgiana and the colonel upstairs. There is something we need to tell you."

"Can it not wait?" he said in surprise.

"I am afraid it cannot."

Darcy went slowly downstairs and found his sister and his cousin in the drawing-room.

"Fitzwilliam," she cried when she saw him, "I am so glad you are home! Is Elizabeth all right? She looked very pale after church today." She kissed him affectionately and Darcy embraced her and said, "She seems very weak, but she insists that the two of you come up."

Georgiana and the colonel glanced at each other and then she said, "Perhaps we should get it over with."

The colonel nodded his agreement. "Yes. Darcy we have a tale to tell you and the sooner the better."

Looking perplexed, Darcy followed them upstairs to the sitting-room, where Elizabeth was still lying down.

They all sat down, and Darcy looked at each of them, waiting for them to start. After a wordless consultation, Colonel Fitzwilliam nodded to Georgiana and began:

"While you were gone, Darcy, we had a frightening occurrence."

At his cousin's look he quickly said, "Everything is resolved now, but at the time it was… a terrible disaster."

He went on, with Georgiana's assistance, to tell him the story of her kidnapping. In spite of her reassurances that she was completely unhurt, her brother looked like the wrath of God when they finished.

"And what has been done about Walker?" Darcy snapped.

Fitzwilliam glanced at Georgiana and Elizabeth and said, "I will explain later, Cousin."

Darcy did not press for further details, but changed the subject.

"Fitzwilliam, could you arrange a meeting with your employer as soon as possible? I should like to finish this business and forget about it."

"As soon as I can."

Chapter 17

Love looks not with the eyes, but with the mind.

—William Shakespeare, *A Midsummer Night's Dream*

T HE NEXT MORNING AT BREAKFAST, DARCY WENT THROUGH THE large stack of mail which had accumulated while he was gone, much of it invitations to various social events.

"It is brought home to me while reading the mail how much has changed in my life in the last year," he commented to Georgiana.

"Why is that, my dear brother? Are there fewer invitations than in the past?" she asked in surprise.

"Not at all, in fact there might possibly be more; however, last year most of the invitations were from families who had unmarried daughters while this year they are from families with unmarried sons."

Georgiana blushed and Elizabeth laughed at her. When Darcy had nearly finished his last cup of coffee, Burton came into the breakfast-parlour and announced that Colonel Fitzwilliam was awaiting him in the entry hall.

During their ride to the palace, the colonel said uneasily, "Darcy, you are as thin as a rake. Did you eat at all while you were gone?"

"Fear not, Cousin, I am well enough; and I will be more so when I finish my report today."

"So, you were successful?"

"In more ways than one."

"Meaning what, Darcy?"

Darcy held up his hand. "Wait just a few minutes, Cousin, and you will hear part of the tale when I tell it to His Highness and the rest afterwards."

"All right, all right, I will be patient."

They rode the rest of the way in silence, Darcy with his eyes closed and the colonel watching him in concern. A few minutes from their destination, Darcy roused himself to say, "Oh… I will tell you one thing, Cousin, which might amuse you. His Majesty's nubile young French woman is at least thirty-five years old and of rather—shall we say—ample proportions?"

The colonel laughed heartily and commented, "I am not at all surprised!"

When they reached the palace they were ushered into the Prince Regent's presence immediately. When the door had closed behind the majordomo, the prince eyed Darcy with some apprehension and said, "Well?"

"Well, Your Majesty, I can report some success with my errand."

"What the devil does that mean, Darcy?"

"I will give you a précis of the tale, Your Majesty, if you will give me leave." He paused briefly for the prince's nod of assent.

"My man and I left London the morning of the fifteenth and hired a ship to take us from Dover to Calais. The weather was a little stormy, but we found a captain who was planning to make the passage anyway and convinced him to earn a little extra money transporting us. We took the post chaise to Paris and found lodgings near Frau Klein's *auberge*. Over the next week we watched her *appartement* and I met with her almost every evening to discuss the ransom, but she was just playing cat and mouse with me; I could see she had no intention of giving up the letters without the money. My man made friends with the lady's maid and convinced her to obtain the letters for us if she could get them. She thought that her mistress kept them in her dressing case, which mademoiselle was not permitted to touch, but she was finally able to break into the case while Frau Klein was entertaining a gentleman. The man who was visiting apparently is English and visits her occasionally for some type of business. When the Frau expects him the maid is sent on an errand, always something which takes an hour or more to perform. On this occasion, the resourceful girl pretended to go out then quietly returned and crept into her mistress's bedchamber. She was prepared to use a hairpin to open the lock, but she found the case unlocked and there were no letters inside.

"On March the twenty-ninth, the English batteries south of the city began a desultory firing upon the city. They did not seem to be very serious about the bombardment, but there was some minor damage to a few buildings in the area. The populace, however, was panicking and pouring out of the buildings to flee, and I suspected that the Frau would use the disorder to try to flee with the letters now that she was undoubtedly convinced that she was not going to receive the money she was seeking. I stationed my man at the rear door of the *auberge*, and I took the front. My man caught her leaving through the rear, shrouded in an enveloping cloak. Her maid obliged by searching her person, and she found the packet of letters in the pocket of her petticoat. There were two bundles, the thicker of which was tied in pink ribbon and directed on the outside to you, Your Majesty."

Darcy pulled the packet out of his breast pocket and handed them to the Prince Regent, who rifled through them quickly.

"There are twenty-two letters in the packet. I trust that is all of them, Your Majesty?"

"I believe so. It looks about the right thickness."

"Then, if you will give us permission to withdraw, we will leave you in peace, Your Majesty. I would give you one piece of advice, however, Your Majesty. Burn the letters or they will give another blackmailer another chance in the future."

The prince was engrossed in reading the letters and merely waved his hand in dismissal, so the two men bowed and left St. James Palace.

When they had regained the carriage, Darcy spoke, "Cousin, I did not tell His Majesty the entire truth in there."

"What do you mean?" the colonel said in surprise.

"I did not just look at the directions on the letters. I felt that I needed to truly confirm that they were the letters we needed, so I read one of them."

Colonel Fitzwilliam merely looked at him enquiringly, one brow raised.

"It was from Mrs. Fitzherbert and addressed His Majesty as 'My Dearest Husband.'"

"Good Lord," the colonel exclaimed quietly. "So he really did marry her. Were the letters dated before his marriage to the Princess of Wales?"

"Oh, yes."

"Then it was no exaggeration to say that they could affect the succession, was it?"

"No. Although the marriage was not legitimate in the eyes of the law since it was not legally sanctioned by the king, it could be legitimate in the eyes of the Church, which would make the Prince Regent a bigamist. I hope he destroys the letters. He was a fool to keep them in the first place."

"I am appalled," the colonel said in a resigned tone. "I cannot believe that His Majesty would be so blind as to think that it was safe to keep them. It is an open invitation to blackmail at the very least, as we have already seen. Imagine if she had succeeded in delivering them to Napoleon." He shook his head in dismay.

"Well, it is over now. I pray God he has no other incriminating items that he is keeping secreted in his rooms."

"Amen, Cousin."

"Now, I have one other piece of business for you, which I think you will find interesting."

The colonel raised his brows. "More business?"

"Yes. I mentioned that when I obtained the prince's letters from Frau Klein, there were two additional letters in a separate packet. Both were directed to her. He drew two envelopes from his breast pocket and handed them to his cousin. They were on thin, poor quality paper and were written with a leaky quill. The first said,

> *Frau Klein,—*
> *I have all the merchandise your employer requested and will deliver on April the twentieth. W. is becoming nervous and does not trust me. He insists on accompanying*

me. We may need to deal with him. I will meet you in
Calais at the usual place and time.—

Schwartzmann

The second letter was in a similar hand and simply said,

It is too dangerous to wait until the twentieth. I must
deliver earlier. Meet me on the fourteenth.—

Schwartzmann

The colonel looked at them, a frown on his face.

"These are written in English in what looks like an English hand, yet the writer has a German name or nickname. What does Schwartzmann mean in English?"

"Did you not learn German?"

"You know I despised my German master," he said with a grin.

Darcy sighed and shook his head. "It could be a description or an attempt to hide his identity as well as a name. It means Black Man."

The colonel's eyes narrowed. "Or could it be Blackman?"

"Possibly."

"Darcy, this is in strictest confidence. Horace Blackman is a sea captain who has been an informant for the Crown for many years. Only a handful of men at the palace know of his identity. It sounds from the letter as if the correspondent is smuggling something. If he is meeting the lady in Calais on the fourteenth, he must be leaving Dover on the thirteenth at the very latest, and today is the eleventh. If he is the one who is smuggling the arms to Napoleon then…" He paused for a moment in thought and then said sharply, "Take me back to the palace, Darcy. I must speak to someone immediately."

Darcy obligingly ordered the coachman to turn around and head back towards St. James Palace, where he dropped his cousin.

The colonel did not reappear at Longford House, where Georgiana was having the finishing touches put on her ballgown. She examined herself in the glass critically. The creamy, sheer silk with the fine lace emphasised her clear complexion and fit beautifully, the bodice delightfully décolleté. Her gloves came above her elbows and fit like a second skin. Her silk fan had a delicate floral design which added a touch of colour to her ensemble as she opened it and practised giving it a slight flutter as she peeked over the top of it. A little coy, but not bad, she thought. She put her shoulders back and turned to see the side view. Very nice. Thank heavens she had a good figure! She went into the sitting-room where her aunt and Elizabeth were waiting and rotated with her arms out so they could see the gown and then opened the fan so they could envision the entire effect at the ball.

Lady Whitwell gave her a pleased smile. "Lovely, Georgiana, dear."

Georgiana looked at Elizabeth for her opinion.

"You look positively delicious, Georgiana," Elizabeth said with a smile.

"Take off the gown, dear girl. Do you wish to take it to Ashbourne House, or would you prefer to dress here before we go?"

"Since we are going together I may as well come here to dress. Can Hatfield do my hair, or should I bring Durand?"

Her aunt considered. "Durand has not done your hair for a ball and she is still a little inexperienced. Bring her with you and she can assist and learn from Hatfield."

"That sounds like a splendid idea. Shall we go, Elizabeth? We both should rest before the big night and Kitty will return from the Gardiner's in a few hours."

"I am ready whenever you are."

"It will only take me a moment to change."

On the way home in the carriage, Georgiana cleared her throat and hesitantly said, "Elizabeth… I think that after tonight's ball I will move to Longford House until my presentation, if that is all right with you."

"Why of course, if you want, my dear."

"I thought that I would take Kitty with me so that you and my brother may have some time alone." She blushed slightly in embarrassment.

Elizabeth squeezed her hand and thanked her with a quiet smile:

"You are very sweet, Miss Georgiana Darcy."

"Just promise me that you will come to Longford House every day to help me, my dear sister," she added in an anxious tone. "I am relying on you."

"An easy promise to make—I would not miss it for the world."

That evening, Elizabeth and Kitty dressed early and escorted Georgiana to her aunt's house. Kitty's eyes sparkled in excitement over the prospect of being the guest of an earl, and she was occupied with her own thoughts in the carriage. On the way to Longford House Elizabeth said, "Georgiana, I understand from your aunt that your cousin Lord St. George will be at the ball tonight."

Georgiana answered indifferently, "Yes, I heard something of the sort."

"I have heard very little about the colonel's brother," Elizabeth said. "What is he like?"

"In looks he is rather similar to the colonel—fairly tall with curly brown hair and blue eyes—but in temper he is quite different." Her voice became tart. "His name is George Lewis Winslow Fitzwilliam, Viscount St. George, and he is aware of that title *and* of the fact that he will inherit the earldom from his father, every minute of the day, I do assure you."

"It doesn't sound as if you like him very much, Georgiana," Elizabeth said in surprise.

"I do not and have not liked him since I was a little girl, and neither does my brother, truth be told, which is probably why you have heard virtually nothing about him. My brother would not malign his relations to you, but he treats St. George with deadly courtesy to his face and ignores his existence when he is out of sight. St. George has been in Scotland for the past six months in exile at one of my uncle's estates as punishment for his gambling and carousing and running up of large debts." She paused and sighed. "From all that I have seen and heard, particularly from my friend Catherine, most of the young men in London are the same: gambling and racing and boxing are all they think about. They sound like very dull company."

Elizabeth laughed. "Many girls would find those characteristics exciting, my dear, but I am glad that you do not! But then, you have always been a Darcy, and the Darcys do not waste their time on such foolish things." She added dryly, "Which is probably why the Darcys continue to have a healthy estate to pass on to their heirs." She smiled at Georgiana and tilted her head. "How do you know all this about your cousin? I am sure your brother never told you these things."

"I have my sources of information, Mrs. Darcy," she said primly.

Lady Whitwell had a cold collation for them to eat before it was time to dress. In spite of her comments to the contrary, Georgiana was so excited and nervous that she could hardly swallow, but she forced herself to eat two finger sandwiches and a small piece of cake. Kitty cleared her plate without difficulty, and Georgiana was steadied by her calm by the time she needed to go upstairs and dress.

Darcy joined them when it was time for the ball, and they required two carriages to carry everyone to the dance. When they arrived they were introduced to the young man of the house, a gangly youth who appeared younger than his twenty-five years and, unfortunately, had no chin to speak of. Georgiana was relieved to find that he was not at all intimidating; he was not going to frighten her into immobility. She gracefully accepted his hand for the second pair of dances, although she could not avoid a flicker of amusement during their introduction. She curtseyed and moved into the ballroom with her family.

Just before the first pair of dances began, she saw Lord St. George speaking with his mother. They were evidently talking about her because St. George glanced up and then began making his way through the crowd of bystanders.

He greeted Darcy, gave Elizabeth the briefest of nods when he was introduced, and bowed over Georgiana's hand.

"My dear cousin Georgiana, how grown up you look! Have you a partner for the first dances?"

"No, Cousin, we just arrived."

"Perhaps you will honour me with your hand for the first then?"

She gravely accepted his offer with a curtsey, took his proffered arm, and they made their way onto the dance floor. Although she had never liked her elder cousin, she had to admit that he was an excellent dancer and could be quite entertaining when he bothered to exert himself. At least a dance with her unloved cousin allowed her to metaphorically dip her toe into the society pond that was the ballroom, and also put her nerves in order. The conversation lagged a little during the middle of the set, and Georgiana asked Lord St. George, "Is your brother attending tonight? I have not seen him since church yesterday, but I thought from something your mother said that he would be here."

"I have not the slightest idea if he is coming or not. He has been quite the will-o'-the-wisp since I arrived yesterday evening."

Georgiana nodded and their turn came to go down the line.

When they finished their dances, St. George thanked her smoothly and she was claimed by the young man of the house for his two dances. She found that this gentleman was quite intelligent and interesting to talk to, in spite of his unpromising appearance, and she enjoyed their conversation as much as the dance.

After her second set, she was asked to dance by a handsome young man, this one, according to her aunt's whisper in her ear, the eldest son of a viscount.

She smiled at him over her fan and said, "Thank you, Lord Wilshire, but I am very thirsty. Could we postpone our dance until I have had a glass of punch? If you like I will hold the next set for you."

"I would be delighted to bring you a glass of punch, if you will allow me. I do not at all mind catching my breath for a few minutes."

Georgiana smiled again and he left to do her bidding.

While she was waiting for Lord Wilshire to return, Georgiana looked around the room. She was astonished at the number of debutantes at the ball; there appeared to be almost fifty girls in all. She saw Catherine Freemont on the dance floor, and she nodded to her friend and went back to observing the crowd filling the room. She wanted to watch and see how many people spoke with her brother and sister, and she was pleased to see that there were several who greeted her brother and were introduced to Elizabeth. The cynical imp in the back of her mind told her that their friendliness was most likely because they had sons who needed wealthy wives, but she did not care what the reason was, as long as her sister was acknowledged.

Her partner returned with her punch and after she had finished sipping it they danced. Lord Wilshire was a good dancer and very polite but did not have much to say about anything but the ball. She mentally categorised him as "nice manners, but boring."

Georgiana was in high spirits when they went home. She chattered about everyone with whom she had danced and with whom her friend Catherine had danced and was very pleased with the evening. Her pleasure was very much tinged with relief at the success of her first ball, but it was pleasure nonetheless. Kitty had also danced, but Georgiana finally noted that she did not say anything on the way home and eventually her silence dampened Georgiana's effervescence. When they arrived at Ashbourne House, Georgiana retired to her room ahead of the others and to her bed but heard Elizabeth say to Kitty, "Come in here for a minute, please, Kitty."

Kitty nodded and they disappeared into the drawing-room.

After closing the door, Elizabeth asked, "What is the matter, Kitty? Are you upset about something?"

"I was asked to dance only four times the entire evening!" Kitty said, her lower lip trembling.

"Dearest," she said very gently, "you must realise that you are moving in a very different society than that in Hertfordshire. The parents of these young men probably know to a penny how much our father is worth, and they are not going to allow their sons to dance with someone who cannot bring them a dowry for fear that they will fall for you—and those with daughters do not want the competition.

"In addition, they are most likely surprised—if not shocked—at Mr. Darcy's marriage to me, a woman of no standing in society, and are waiting to see if I will be accepted or if I will be branded a shameless fortune huntress who will drag my husband's good name in the mud with my behaviour. I am sorry, my dear sister, but those are the facts of life. You must just be pleasant and enjoy the dances that you get, and when people know both of us better they may allow their sons to dance with you more. I think that you already know that if you were not with Georgiana, you would not have been asked to the ball at all, nor would I if I was not married to Mr. Darcy."

Kitty's eyes filled with tears at this recital of facts, but she hung her head and said, "I am sorry, Lizzy, I did not quite realise the position you are in. I will try to enjoy myself, but I must say that the militia in Hertfordshire was much more pleasant than London society."

Elizabeth embraced her sister and they walked slowly upstairs together. She related this conversation to Darcy, who shook his head.

"I am sorry that she has had to face this. I had hoped that by attending with us Kitty would be accepted, in spite of the difficulties you have had. I will talk to Georgiana now that she has survived her first ball of the Season, and I am sure that she will be able to assist in some way."

"Thank you, my love. That will probably help. I do not want to push that responsibility onto Georgiana when she has so many other things to think about, but if she realises how Kitty is feeling I have no doubt that she will do what she can. She is an unselfish girl."

Upstairs, Georgiana was finishing her entry in her diary.

10 April: The ball was very enjoyable tonight, although I was disappointed that I did not see the colonel. I had to make do with his brother as a dancing partner (and I must confess he is an excellent dancer), but I know him too well to be charmed by his pretty lies. Since my rescue by my cousin Fitzwilliam I cannot but feel that I should make up for the way I misjudged him for so many years and, most particularly, for my nasty and spiteful tongue during the past few months. He truly does feel strongly about some things, including his duties towards his ward.

She tapped the end of the pen on her lower lip, thinking about her entry. Finally, she dipped her pen in the inkwell and quickly scrawled,

I wonder how he feels about the girl herself.

She tossed down her pen and sanded the page before she slammed the book shut. After she had climbed into bed, she tried to sleep, but she could not stop thinking about that last comment.

You might as well admit to yourself that you love him, Georgiana. Even if you tell no one else, you should be honest with yourself. She thought back to the day of her rescue and the shock she received when her easygoing cousin burst into her prison to save her. He had looked like a hero of old, ready to battle dragons to save his lady-love. Except, of course, that she was not his lady-love. She was his ward—a backwards and ill-humoured child whom he loved only as a sister. She turned irritably onto her back and stared up into the darkness, pondering whether she truly loved him or if she was merely showing the effects of her gratitude and a strong case of hero-worship over the man who had figured in that dramatic rescue scene. Of one thing she was certain, hero-worship or not, she certainly did not feel for him now as a sister should.

Chapter 18

Lord what fools these mortals be!

—WILLIAM SHAKESPEARE, *A MIDSUMMER NIGHT'S DREAM*

THE DAY CAME FOR THE BINGLEYS' ARRIVAL, AND THEY CALLED on the Darcy household after settling into the house they had leased near Berkeley Square for the Season. Elizabeth had confided to Georgiana that morning that she wondered where Miss Bingley would stay during the Season: with her sister, Mrs. Hurst, or with her brother Charles and Jane. Caroline and Mrs. Hurst had made up after the differences which had separated them at Christmas, and they both enjoyed the pleasures of ridiculing all of their "friends" in private after meeting them at social events. But on the other hand, their brother had a much better fortune than Mr. Hurst and so could afford more of the expensive pleasures of London.

"I hope she chooses to stay with the Hursts so Jane will not have to listen to Caroline's unkind chatter," she confided to Georgiana.

Georgiana emphatically agreed.

Elizabeth and Jane met affectionately at Ashbourne House, and Georgiana and Kitty were almost as delighted to see Jane as was Elizabeth. They had planned an enjoyable afternoon visiting together while Darcy and Bingley went out to their club, and Jane looked in as excellent health as she had at Christmas, in spite of looking a little tired after the move of their household. She seemed a trifle flustered as they caught up on the news from Hertfordshire, fidgeting with her handkerchief and teacup. Georgiana was surprised at Jane's lack of composure, which was quite unlike her usual demeanour. When they had caught up on the London news, Jane glanced around at her sisters and Georgiana, her cheeks slightly flushed, and said, "My dears, I have something that I want to tell you. I have known for several weeks, but I wanted to tell you in person, so I did not mention it in my letters. I am going to have a child."

They all gasped in surprise and embraced her. Elizabeth was the last to embrace her and she held her for a long time, exclaiming, "I am so happy for you, my dearest sister! I should have known from just looking at you; you look even more lovely than usual! I cannot believe that you could keep this a secret! Do our parents know?"

"I have not told them yet. I wanted you to be the first among our relations to know…" She hesitated for a moment and then added to Elizabeth with a sigh, "I have one other piece of family news to relate, Lizzy. Our mother received a letter from our sister Lydia before our departure from Netherfield. She, too, is expecting a child. Our mother's transports of delight were quite overwhelming, so Bingley and I decided to tell them about our happy news in a letter while we are here."

Elizabeth laughed at the expression of chagrin on Jane's face as she said this and agreed that her plan was sound but shook her head over their sister Lydia's condition.

"This is most unfortunate. Lydia is in no way mature enough to care for a child, and the Wickhams will fall even further into debt with the additional expenses. But let us put aside these distressing thoughts. We cannot change the situation and we have happy subjects to talk about."

They spent the afternoon in chatter about the baby linens Jane was having made and about how soon the baby was due to arrive. Jane expected her confinement to be around mid-September, and now that she had told them she relaxed and enjoyed the visit.

That evening the Bingleys dined with them and the Darcys had avoided any outside social engagements this one night so that they could spend the evening with the Bingleys before they continued the round of parties. The evening was one of quiet pleasure, and Georgiana tried to just relax and enjoy this rare respite.

A few days later, Georgiana had the final fitting of her court dress. When Lady Whitwell went downstairs for a moment and she had a few moments alone with Elizabeth, she confided to her that she was less nervous about her presentation than about Lady Whitwell's ball.

"My aunt is planning to invite a great number of people, and everyone of importance will be there. Both of my cousins will attend, of course, as well as all of the other eligible young men that she can find." She paused and then changed the subject abruptly. "You *will* help me dress for my aunt's ball, won't you, Elizabeth?"

"Of course, dearest. Lady Whitwell will be busy with the ball, and Lambert and I will help Durand dress you. Your gown is lovely; they delivered it this morning. I had forgotten about it until this moment, but I have it at the house, ready for you."

"My gown for the ball will, I hope, be much better than this presentation gown," she said as she looked down in dismay. The wide hoops of the skirt, so eighteenth century, did indeed look rather silly, but the seamstress had done her job well and it fitted perfectly. The gown was white and the bodice was low cut and off the shoulder, as required for court dress. The sleeves were a mere suggestion of a wisp of gauzy silk and the long train, fastened to the gown just behind the shoulders with silk rosettes, was of soft white silk that flowed behind her like cream when she moved. The rest of her gown was encrusted with seed pearls and embroidery, all in white, and just the tip of her satin slippers peeped out from under the stiff hem. The tall white ostrich plume for her head was tightly sewn onto a small brooch, which they would pin securely to the back of her upswept hair. Georgiana sank into her deep curtsey and rose in one fluid motion and then Elizabeth lifted her train and spread it gracefully over her left arm so that she could back out of the room. She was ready.

The next morning Darcy and Elizabeth were at Longford House very early. They had a leisurely breakfast, which Georgiana could barely touch. Lady Whitwell encouraged her to eat something.

"We would not want you to faint from hunger while you are awaiting your turn, my dear," Lady Whitwell said gently. "We may have to wait hours at the palace."

"I know," Georgiana sighed. "Perhaps I can get a piece of toast down. Where is Colonel Fitzwilliam? I thought he was going to come over this morning so he could see my gown."

"I am sure he will be here soon," her aunt reassured her. "Now eat your breakfast, dear girl."

Georgiana was sure she appeared as wan and lifeless as she felt, but she forced herself to sit up straighter and to eat the toast and drink a cup of chocolate. When she had finished, the ladies retired to Georgiana's room upstairs to help her dress while the gentlemen tried to relax over their tea and read the morning newspapers.

The footman had just poured them each a second cup of tea when Lord Whitwell choked on a sip and put down his paper, coughing.

"Are you all right, Uncle?" Darcy asked with concern.

His uncle shook his head and pointed to a notice in the paper. Darcy took it and read aloud:

> *"Sir Robert Blake announces the engagement of his sister, Miss Emily Blake, to Mr. Jonathan Walker. The couple plan a quiet wedding in the country."*

Darcy dropped the paper and stared in shock at his uncle. When he could speak, he said hoarsely, "The man has no shame. Does he think he is so invulnerable that we will stand by and allow him to marry a young lady of our acquaintance?"

"Apparently he does."

A footman entered to announce the arrival of Colonel Fitzwilliam, who came in with his eyes flashing in excitement. He was slightly out of breath and threw himself down in a chair without ceremony, barely managing to keep the scabbard of his sword from hitting the chair as he did so.

"Have you heard the news?"

"Yes. I cannot believe that he thinks he can get away with this."

The colonel gave his cousin an odd look.

"What are you talking about, Darcy? I am referring to the news that Napoleon has finally abdicated. He is to go into exile on Elba and the entire palace is in an uproar."

Darcy silently pointed to the engagement announcements in the paper. Fitzwilliam stood to lean over the table so he could read the item above his cousin's finger. As he read the short article, his face blanched and he glared at his cousin before throwing the paper onto the table.

"The scoundrel thinks he has us by the b—," he glanced quickly at his father and finished, "throat and that we will not dare call him out."

Darcy nodded grimly. "He apparently has an endless supply of gall."

"What are we going to do?"

"I would say the first thing is to talk to Sir Robert in confidence. I think that we can safely trust his discretion, and I am sure he would wish to know this about his sister's fiancé."

"Yes, do that." Fitzwilliam stood up abruptly. "Apologise to Georgiana for me, and give her my best wishes for her presentation, will you? I cannot sit here and make cheerful conversation while that blackguard tries to victimise another young lady. I have work to do, and it may help take the bitter taste out of my mouth while I consider our options in the matter."

Both agreed and he left. A moment later, Elizabeth came into the breakfast-parlour.

"I saw the colonel rushing off. Is there something the matter?" she asked in confusion.

They explained Napoleon's exile and the colonel's duty at the palace, and her eyes grew very large.

"So the war with Napoleon is definitely over. I can hardly believe it is true. I will tell Lady Whitwell and Georgiana."

Before she could leave, Lord Whitwell interjected, "Are you sure that you should tell Georgiana? I would not want her composure to be overstrained on such an important day."

Elizabeth smiled and gently said, "My lord, Georgiana is not a child and she is not a simpleton. You cannot hide a piece of news such as this, and she will not thank you if you try."

"I suppose that you are right, my dear; I am being an old fool. She must know sometime and will wonder why there is so much activity at the palace."

Elizabeth walked over and patted his hand, her eyes twinkling. "'Old' and 'fool' are the last words that I would think of associating with you, my lord."

He lifted her hand and kissed it and she ran back upstairs, her errand downstairs forgotten for the moment. Darcy stared at his uncle in surprise at his gallantry, and his lordship cleared his throat and turned back to his newspaper. Darcy picked up his paper and hid a smile behind its pages, Walker forgotten for a brief moment.

Georgiana was disappointed that the colonel could not stay but said, "He was, of course, needed more at the palace! So the war is finally over." Her eyes sparkled as she continued to dress. "My presentation is hardly of the magnitude of importance of Napoleon's final defeat, although it will be an interesting story to tell my children someday." She grinned at Elizabeth and her aunt.

They finished their preparations and she swept downstairs to show her uncle and her brother her costume, curtseying to them both. Then she and her aunt left for the palace, Georgiana's hoop skirt barely fitting into the carriage. The day was, fortunately, sunny and fairly warm, so she would not be too chilly after leaving her cloak in the carriage and entering the palace.

Elizabeth and Darcy returned to Ashbourne House and spent the rest of the day discussing the news about Napoleon and awaiting Georgiana's return. Kitty sat with them for a while but Darcy's tension made her nervous, and eventually she excused herself and escaped upstairs to entertain Lucky while his mistress was gone. Darcy was ultimately reduced to pacing the floor of the drawing-room after abandoning all attempts to divert himself. Georgiana finally arrived home at about four o'clock, looking exhausted and relieved. Elizabeth and Darcy both kissed her affectionately when they met her in the hall.

"I don't need to ask how it went," Elizabeth said. "I can see that it went well."

Georgiana sighed and sat carefully down on the sofa in her hooped skirt. "It went perfectly fine, but I feel like a limp piece of rag. What a day! There were more than a hundred women and girls to be presented and they kept interrupting the line when messengers came for the Prince Regent... Well, it is done and I survived without tripping on my hem or falling over during my curtsey or having my plume fall out of my hair. And, I need never do it again!" She smiled in exhausted contentment.

"Why don't you go and find Kitty and tell her about it," Elizabeth suggested. "She has been waiting eagerly for your return."

Georgiana nodded and took herself upstairs. Elizabeth heard Kitty meet her on the way through the hall and smiled at their laughter as they went up together. Darcy sat on the sofa with his head resting on the back, gave a sigh of relief, and commented, "I feel as though I have been through a battle—and lost!"

Elizabeth smiled and said, "My poor, dear husband! Now that Georgiana's presentation is over you can relax. I have no doubt now that her first Season will be a success."

"I thank heaven for that…! Elizabeth?"

"Yes?" She looked at him in surprise at his grim tone.

"I need to talk to both you and Georgiana about something when she has changed and rested a little from her ordeal."

She stared at him for a brief moment. "I thought there was something else worrying you. I will go up and see what Georgiana is doing."

The two ladies were back downstairs within fifteen minutes. Darcy took them into his library where they would not be disturbed and they all sat down, Elizabeth and Georgiana staring at him with large eyes. As he paused to choose his words, Georgiana finally said, "What is it, Brother?"

"I suppose there is no gentle or easy way to say this. This morning's paper had an engagement announcement for Mr. Jonathan Walker and Miss Emily Blake."

"No!" Georgiana put her hand to her mouth.

"I am afraid so."

"We cannot allow him to marry her!" she said in agitation.

"We will not, but we want to proceed carefully so Walker does not realise we are moving against him. We do not want him to spread the story of your kidnapping in revenge."

"If it is a choice of damaging my reputation versus letting a young woman we know marry that evil man, I will risk my reputation," she returned grimly. "I will not let that man ruin a friend's life—not if I can prevent it."

"I am hoping it will not come to that choice. The colonel and Lord Whitwell know about this, but say nothing to anyone else. I am going out to my club. Sir Robert is a member and I am hoping that I will see him. I do not want to risk going to him at his home since Walker is staying with them."

They both nodded in agreement.

When Darcy returned later he told them that he had not met Sir Robert, but he assured his wife and his sister that he would try again the next day.

"If I do not casually run into him, I will risk sending an invitation asking Sir Robert to dine with me at the club. Now let us forget Walker and ready ourselves for dinner. We do not want Kitty to know that we are upset."

The next evening, they attended a large ball given by another acquaintance of Lady Whitwell's, Mrs. Dalrymple, for her daughter Justina.

Justina Dalrymple was a small, pretty, and vivacious girl of twenty years who was entering her third Season and who possessed a tart wit that amused the gentlemen, and she had rather a good opinion of herself. She had many admirers but had not deigned to accept the hand of any one of them, declaring to one and all that she would enjoy herself before tying herself to a husband. Her parents were anxious to have their daughter married before she was much older for fear that she would end up a spinster and made sure that every eligible gentleman in town received an invitation to the ball. Georgiana was slightly acquainted with Justina, and she whispered to Elizabeth that Justina was very pretty but her tongue was rather sharp.

"In fact, she reminds me a little of Miss Bingley, who, by the bye, has just arrived," she said in a dry tone.

Elizabeth looked up and saw Caroline Bingley posed in the doorway, Bingley and Jane standing unobtrusively behind her. One of the gentlemen separated himself from the group that was milling around the debutantes and approached the arriving trio; Georgiana suddenly realised that it was the Comte de Tournay. He was dressed in the latest fashion and was really a fine figure of a man in spite of his forty-plus years. He must be making the rounds of the parties to find another wealthy wife, she thought cynically. One would think that he would look for a wealthy widow closer to his own age rather than a woman young enough to be his daughter, but perhaps a widow would not be youthful enough for his discerning tastes—and might come with additional encumbrances, such as children. Georgiana could not picture the suave aristocrat as a doting father to someone else's child.

Georgiana greeted the Bingleys and then was claimed for the next dance by the eldest Dalrymple son, a handsome young man, if overly taken to preening like a peacock. She had told him that she would only dance with him if he danced with Kitty the next pair of dances, and he had agreed, perplexed that a debutante would want to help a competitor find dancing partners. When there was a break in the dancing, Elizabeth thanked Georgiana quietly for her kindness to Kitty and asked her if she had arranged the exchange of partners. Georgiana blushed and admitted that she had, saying, "I did not realise that you would notice. You are far too acute, Elizabeth! Do not tell Kitty, please."

"That was very kind of you, dearest."

"Not at all. I have no interest in a man who thinks he is prettier than I am, so why should I not direct him towards Kitty as a dancing partner?"

Elizabeth smiled and shooed Georgiana back to the debutantes.

The evening passed uneventfully, and Georgiana was satisfied with the number and quality of her dancing partners. She could feel her brother's eyes watching her every move as she progressed around the room, and she could tell that he was a little nervous for her still, so she gave him a smile as she moved to the head of the set.

About an hour after the ball began, Colonel Fitzwilliam arrived, handsomely outfitted in a beautifully cut black coat and breeches and snowy stockings. Elizabeth was standing by Georgiana when he greeted his cousin.

"I am pleased to see you, my dear little cousin. I am sorry that I missed you yesterday morning, but I hear that your curtsey was flawless," he said, bowing to her.

Georgiana flicked a glance at Elizabeth and then returned the colonel's courtesies. She moved off when her next partner, an impeccably dressed young gentleman with a pleasantly ugly face, came to claim his dances with her.

The colonel turned to Elizabeth and asked her if she would like to dance.

"I know that my cousin does not enjoy dancing and I would not want a handsome young lady such as you to be unable to enjoy the ball." He smirked at Darcy, who just shook his head and rolled his eyes.

As they danced, Elizabeth could not resist teasing the colonel about his own matrimonial ambitions.

"You will never find a wife, Colonel, if you spend your time dancing with the married women."

"Very true, but I like to do a tactical analysis before plunging into the maelstrom of battle," he said, his eyes alight with mischief. "It is a very difficult problem when the loveliest ladies are already taken," he added with a courtly bow.

"I thank you, sir, for the compliment; however, I suspect that there are probably plenty of pretty young ladies who would be happy to dance with you and with whom you could find ample consolation."

"It is not the dancing, but the predatory mammas that frighten me," he said with a straight face.

Elizabeth laughed and they continued their dance. After a moment the colonel added, still with a light tone, "Seriously, however, the mammas who are interested in the younger son of an earl seem to be those with no breeding and plenty of lucre; they wish to get their foot in the door of the nobility and their daughters have not the beauty or charms to attract an eldest son. It is quite frustrating."

"Perhaps you should not confine your search for a wife to the ladies of London, Colonel."

He smiled. "Perhaps you are right."

They finished their dance in silence, and when the colonel went off to ask the daughter of the house to dance, Elizabeth stood again with Darcy and watched the dancers. Elizabeth noticed that Georgiana gravely observed her cousin as he made the rounds of the room while at the same time trying to listen attentively to her various partners' conversation.

On the way home in the carriage, however, Georgiana threw off her serious mood and chattered about the ball with Kitty, who seemed to have had a better time than at the previous one, and the two girls went upstairs giggling together. Darcy and Elizabeth made their way sedately up in their wake, and Elizabeth sighed in relief at the success of the beginning of Georgiana's Season.

The next morning, Darcy left for his club, where he was still trying to catch Sir Robert Blake, leaving Elizabeth and Georgiana to eat alone. Kitty was a late riser and usually missed breakfast. Georgiana was lightly discussing the previous night's ball with Elizabeth, when her sister decided to ask, "So tell me, my dear, what do you think of the young men in London? Have any caught your eye?"

Elizabeth's eyes widened in shock as a sudden flare of red rushed up Georgiana's face and she averted her eyes.

"I am sorry, Georgiana. I did not mean to embarrass you!"

"No, no… I-I should like to tell you," Georgiana whispered, as her eyes filled and a teardrop fell on her clenched hands.

"If you are finished, let us go up to my sitting-room where we can be private," Elizabeth said quickly.

When they were settled in front of the fire, Georgiana paused to gather her thoughts then said, "I like the gentlemen I have met well enough, excepting only Mr. Walker, of course. Sir Robert is especially nice and very handsome, and I like his brothers and sister, too. The problem is that… well," she paused for a moment, her throat constricted. She took a deep breath to calm herself and plunged on, "My heart is already taken."

Georgiana could see that Elizabeth's thoughts went instantly to Wickham, and she quickly said, "Do not worry, Elizabeth; I am not in love with a married man!"

She turned her eyes down and stared at her hands as they twisted her handkerchief and whispered, "I am in love with Colonel Fitzwilliam. Until my brother told us of his actual role at the palace I thought my cousin a dilettante, funny and entertaining but lacking any serious purpose in life. When I heard about his responsibilities and the respect in which he is held by the Prince Regent I struggled to change my opinion of the man I thought I knew but clearly did not. I finally understood why my father made him one of my guardians. Then I was abducted and when the colonel burst into my room to rescue me like a knight in shining armour…"

She stopped and laughed once, harshly. "I sound like some dewy-eyed lack-wit. What I realised was that he was not a man lacking passion. He was quite ready to kill someone to protect me. I have tried to decide if I am suffering from an understandable case of hero-worship or whether I love him as I should love the man I marry. I have thought back over my entire relationship with the colonel and realise now that I have loved him since I was a little girl.

"I remember when I was six years old and I was afraid to ride my pony. He spent the entire fortnight of his holiday teaching me to ride. He was so patient, and he never made fun of me for being frightened in spite of his being a grown twenty-year-old who was afraid of nothing. I did not see at the time that his care for and patience with a lonely little girl was far beyond what most men would show a young girl who was only a cousin and not his responsibility. He quietly goes through life doing his job without any fanfare. He does not try to impress everyone or put on an act. He is just himself, and that is a fine man who any woman could love and respect."

Elizabeth took her hand gently.

"Well, dearest, there is no reason that you cannot marry Colonel Fitzwilliam. I will speak to your brother…"

"No!" she cried, clutching Elizabeth's hand until her sister winced. She released it immediately and said, "I am so sorry, Elizabeth, but please promise me you will not talk to my brother about this!"

"But, why not, Georgiana? He could talk to the colonel…"

"No! That is exactly what I do *not* want!"

"But, dearest…" Elizabeth said insistently.

Georgiana riveted her eyes upon Elizabeth's and said, "Do you not see? I do not want the colonel to feel *obligated* to marry me. I do not want him to marry me only for duty to his family—I want him to marry me because he loves me... I want the kind of love and respect that you and my brother have for each other, not a cool, logical arrangement for the benefit of the family. Oh, it would solve so many problems! The colonel would have a wife with money, Georgiana would have a husband, and we would not have to worry about the threat of Walker revealing the kidnapping scheme because the colonel already knows," she finished bitterly.

"I begin to see the problem, my dear," Elizabeth said rather helplessly. "But what can we do about it?"

"He thinks I am a child; when he visits he kisses me dutifully and pats me on the head like he does Pilot. He rescues me at the ball if the young men get too importunate, but he does it as a duty to a child towards whom he has a responsibility. He even calls me 'little cousin'—sometimes I could just slap him for that!" she said passionately.

"Yes, I noticed him doing that," Elizabeth said absently. "So... what do you want me to do, Georgiana?"

"I do not know. I just do not know how to even begin to get his attention," she sobbed. "I am seventeen years old and am no longer a child, but how do I make him see that, and how do I find out if he cares for me without risking awkwardness and humiliation for both of us? It would be mortifying if he found out that I love him and he does not feel the same towards me. And how could he? He thinks I am still six years old."

Elizabeth embraced her and Georgiana clung to her. She stroked her sister's hair and said, "Well, Georgiana, my dear, the only answer I can give you now is that I will give this problem some thought and we will see what we can do. As far as I know, the colonel does not have a particular young woman he is interested in, so I think he is safe for the moment—although he might have a dozen young women courting him and I would not know!"

"Heaven forbid!" Georgiana said, smiling wanly through her tears.

"Now dry your eyes, my dear, and we will see what we can do."

She carefully blotted her eyes, and, after sitting quietly for a few minutes with their arms around each other to compose themselves, they each went to their own room to think about the problem.

Chapter 19

When you have done all you can in the interest of prudence,
Leave the rest to the gods and take the plunge.

—Horace, *Odes*

THE NEXT MORNING, ELIZABETH CAME TO GEORGIANA'S ROOM after breakfast.

"Georgiana, my dear. I have been thinking. I believe that we should talk to Lambert and see what she suggests to catch the colonel's eye."

Georgiana looked dubious. "Do you think she could help?"

"I am quite sure she can."

"Can we trust her to keep a secret?"

"She is most discreet."

They walked down the hall to Elizabeth's room and found Lambert touching up some of Elizabeth's dresses with an iron. Elizabeth explained the problem in general terms: that Georgiana was trying to attract the attention of someone she had known for many years and who treats her like a child.

"How can we convince him that she is an adult?"

Lambert considered for a moment, tapping her chin with her finger.

"I would suggest that we try to make a complete change in appearance. Mademoiselle Darcy is very attractive so we do not want to make her less attractive—*quelle horreur!*—but a style and colour of dress and a hairstyle which are completely different and make her appear older may do ze job. Because, Madame *et* Mademoiselle, ze gentlemen, they do not respond to subtlety; while Cupid's little arrows sound lovely and romantic, he would be much more effective with ze truncheon."

Elizabeth laughed and Georgiana collapsed onto a chair giggling. When she recovered herself, Georgiana said, "But what would you specifically suggest?"

Lambert looked at Georgiana and said, "If you would come here, please, Mademoiselle Darcy."

Georgiana stood up in front of the maid and Lambert looked her over from head to toe, felt the texture of her hair, and examined the colour of her eyes and the dimensions of her figure.

"Mademoiselle Darcy, you usually wear ze white or ze cream gowns, *oui?*"

Georgiana nodded, fascinated by this evaluation.

"I would suggest that we try to find ze silk in ze sea-green colour; a light green with ze grey tone. Mademoiselle has beautiful eyes of a changeable colour; they will look more green or blue depending upon what she wears. Let us emphasise ze less common colour. We will also use just ze most subtle touch of rouge, and I have something to darken ze lashes a bit. She also has a beautiful long, white neck which we want to feature. Here is ze gown I would recommend."

She took a piece of paper and sketched a detailed gown, with colours marked for the various parts.

Elizabeth asked, "What about her hair?"

"You usually wear ze simple style, so I would suggest several tiny braids looped from the front to the back, a cascade of curls at the crown and a few wisps of curl around ze face to bring attention to your smooth, white forehead. To finish it off, three long ringlets to hang over your shoulder. Very enticing!" She kissed the tips of her fingers. "Now, about ze jewellery. I have seen you wear ze pearls with ze tiny cross?" Georgiana nodded. "Zay are very nice, but he has undoubtedly seen them. What else do you have?"

Georgiana looked at Elizabeth, who immediately said, "Your mother's diamonds, Georgiana."

Lambert was pleased. "Ze diamonds will be ze perfect finish. What could be more elegant and sophisticated? When are we to make this transformation, Madame?"

"Do you think we could have the dress finished by this weekend? The Elliots are giving a very large ball and I think all the single men in London have been invited."

"*Oui*, I will send for the seamstress and we will start immediately."

She bustled off to begin preparations and Georgiana tried to stifle another nervous giggle with her fingertips.

"Do you really think it will work, Elizabeth?" she whispered.

Elizabeth put her arms around her. "I think that we have nothing to lose. I think it will take an earthquake to bring the colonel out of his complacence, and I, for one, am willing to do my best to bring about that earthquake, if that is what you want."

Georgiana's faced turned grim. "I will do my part, too, if it kills me."

The next five days flew by. They continued to have engagements every night and although Georgiana tried to be sparkling and friendly to her cousin, she did not see any signs of awareness of her existence by him beyond the indulgent notice he had always given her. She was becoming increasingly frustrated with him and complained (with a petulance that was very unusual for her) to Elizabeth when they were alone.

"The colonel is oblivious to me. How can men be so unaware of what is going on around them? I wonder if I must knock him over or do other violence to him before he notices that I am alive."

Elizabeth laughed a little. "You must forgive him, my dear sister, for men do not like change any more than the rest of us and ignore it for as long as possible."

"He has been paying a lot of attention to Justina Dalrymple lately; he has danced with her more than once at several of the balls. You don't suppose that he is considering making her an offer, do you?" she said with a frown.

"I certainly hope not; I have seen her speak rather sharply to her mother a couple of times in public—I would not be easy about his chances of happiness with her, even were there no other consid-erations. However, I agree that he is spending far too much time with her, but tomorrow night is the Elliots' ball and you are ready to make your 'appearance' there."

Georgiana put her hand to her throat nervously, but she nodded in agreement. That night, she wrote,

23 May: All of the plans have been made and my costume prepared for the ball tomorrow night. I have been distracting myself and trying to calm my nerves

with Horace, figuring that reading ancient works would be either boring or soothing enough to help me sleep. I came upon a line in his "Odes" which I found quite apt: "When you have done all you can in the interest of prudence, leave the rest to the gods and take the plunge." That is strong: permitte divis cetera.

The next evening, the ladies went upstairs earlier than usual to prepare for the ball. Elizabeth hurried through her toilette with Lambert, quickly donning her cream silk dress with the green sash and her Chinese jewellery and then they went to Georgiana's room where Durand had all of the clothing ready. Georgiana had continued wearing white and cream-coloured dresses while the new gown was being sewn, so the new gown would be a splash of colour to contrast vividly with the others, as well as being the last word in decorous sophistication.

Lambert swept up Georgiana's light brown hair into three shining braids on either side of her head and into a confection of curls on her crown, emphasising her height, and the three ringlets hung tantalizingly over her left shoulder. Durand then helped her into her stays, tightening them to enhance her bust line. Next, Lambert and Durand helped her into white silk stockings and a white cotton batiste petticoat that ended just above her ankles. The gown was next, a sea-foam green satin bodice and skirt, which was reflected in the colour of her eyes. The skirt of the gown was split from the waist to the hem to show an underskirt of finely pleated white silk that swept almost to the floor, peeping out below the green skirt. At the shoulder began the barest suggestion of a puffed sleeve, in green satin to match the bodice, and the low, scooped neckline was enhanced with a sweep of stiff, finely pleated white silk that stood up from the front of the shoulders and around the back, gently cupping the back of her long, slender neck and framing her face.

Durand helped her mistress don her white satin dancing slippers and then Elizabeth stepped in. She brought out the jeweller's case she had been holding and opened it. She fastened the diamonds that had belonged to Lady Anne, obtained from the bank that afternoon, around Georgiana's neck and the eardrops onto her earlobes. She stepped back, and she and the two maids examined their charge. The diamonds sparkled in the candlelight, the central pendant just reaching the top of her décolleté, and the dress picked up the colour of her eyes beautifully. After a moment of intense consideration as they walked around Georgiana, looking at all sides of her costume, Lambert smiled and nodded, and Elizabeth said, "Yes, you are ready, Georgiana."

Georgiana examined herself in the glass and smiled slowly at Elizabeth.

"Yes, my dear sister, I believe I am."

They covered her gown with a white satin cloak, careful not to crush the pleats around the neckline of her dress. By the time Darcy had appeared from the drawing-room Elizabeth had her cloak on as well, and they left as soon as Kitty appeared a moment later. Darcy commented in the carriage that the ladies looked very well. Georgiana and Elizabeth smiled at each other and at Kitty as they thanked him.

When they arrived at the ball, which was given in a large ball-room at the rear of their host's home, Elizabeth took Georgiana and Kitty to a dressing-room to make sure that their costumes were perfect before they went into the ballroom. Darcy had gone ahead and was standing with Colonel Fitzwilliam and Lord St. George. They all three turned when the ladies entered, and both Georgiana's cousins and her brother stared for a moment in surprise at Georgiana. She wanted to laugh at the astonishment on their faces. The viscount recovered first and stepped forward to take Georgiana's hand, bowing over it and saying, "My dear cousin Georgiana, how lovely you look tonight! I hope you will give me the pleasure of your hand for the first dances."

"Of course, Cousin," she answered gravely.

The colonel watched them as his brother led her to the dance floor and joined the lines facing each other then walked over to Justina Dalrymple and asked her to dance. Darcy looked quizzically at Elizabeth and she said brightly, "Doesn't Georgiana look well tonight, Mr. Darcy?"

"She does indeed," he answered, turning his gaze to follow his sister speculatively as she danced. "She looks like a queen. Is there some reason for this dramatic change in hair style and ornamentation?"

"We are merely increasing the stakes in the matrimonial game—sometimes men need to be hit over the head before they notice the obvious."

He looked at her in perplexity. "And who might she be trying to 'hit over the head' tonight?" he asked as he watched Georgiana dance, her eyes glancing over at Colonel Fitzwilliam several times. He looked at the colonel, who was watching Georgiana rather to the neglect of his own partner, who looked piqued. Before Elizabeth could form an answer which would not give away Georgiana's confidences, Darcy's face took on a look of surprised awareness, "Surely not Fitzwilliam?"

Elizabeth smiled briefly. "Would you have any objections if it *were* the colonel?"

"None at all; my cousin is a fine man. I am just—surprised—I did not expect it. The last I heard she was sniping at him. How long has this been going on?"

Elizabeth temporised, since Georgiana had not yet given her permission to tell Darcy. "Georgiana finds it very frustrating that he treats her like a child. She is not a child any more."

"No, much as I hate to admit it, she is definitely no longer a child," he replied, lifting one brow at Elizabeth's avoidance of his question. She watched the dancers and pretended not to see.

They watched as the pair of dances ended and a crowd of young men surrounded Georgiana. The colonel observed them from across the room until his cousin accepted a partner then approached an unattached young lady and obtained her hand for the next dances. After they finished, Georgiana was again besieged by several young men, and Colonel Fitzwilliam joined Darcy at the side of the room. While Elizabeth was talking to Jane, who had arrived not long before, she overheard the colonel comment to Darcy,

"I hope that all these young bucks don't overwhelm Georgiana, Darcy. Perhaps I should rescue her from them."

Elizabeth, watching them from the corner of her eye, was surprised when Darcy looked his cousin in the eye, his face expressionless, and said very quietly, "Oh, I don't think she needs to be rescued any more. She's not a child, Fitzwilliam." The colonel stared at him for a long, frozen moment, his brows raised in surprise and then he looked back towards Georgiana.

"I believe you may be right, Darcy," he said slowly, "but I think I will ask her to dance anyway."

Without another word he walked towards his cousin as she stood with a couple of other girls in the cluster of admirers.

Lord St. George appeared on the opposite side of the group but, before he could catch Georgiana's eye, Colonel Fitzwilliam neatly manoeuvred himself between the others, as he had done at the Pemberley ball, and took Georgiana's hand, cutting off one of the young men before he could finish his awkward attempt at asking her to dance. Georgiana nodded to her cousin and took his arm, her eyes downcast as he led her to the floor, acutely aware of the warmth and strength of his arm through her gloves. As she rose from her first curtsey to start the figure she brought her eyes up to meet his, and she saw him stiffen. He covered his discomposure quickly and began the dance, but he appeared rather bemused as he danced the figures, his neck flushing slightly each time the dance returned him to his partner. Georgiana, for her part, kept her eyes modestly downcast as she moved down the line but raised them to meet his briefly each time they faced each other, the challenge in hers offering a counterpoint to the small, serene smile on her lips.

When they finished their dances, the colonel led Georgiana back to her friends and made his way to the refreshment table, where he slowly drank a cup of punch while he watched his cousin dance the next dances.

Later in the evening, Viscount St. George again asked for her hand for a pair of dances, and Georgiana accepted him, but she was distracted during the dance because the colonel was watching them with a serious intensity that was quite uncharacteristic. She hoped that he would ask her to dance again, but he kept his distance, maintaining his observation post and ignoring the other young women.

Georgiana was exhausted as they rode home from the ball and she noticed that Elizabeth looked very tired also. They both had entertained such intense hopes for the evening and she did not know quite what to think of the results.

When they arrived home, Georgiana and Kitty went immediately upstairs, but Darcy held Elizabeth back and gestured towards the drawing-room, closing the door behind them after they entered.

"Did you know that Georgiana was interested in the colonel before tonight?"

Elizabeth paused but could see no way to avoid the direct question, "Yes, I have known for a few days."

"Why did you not tell me?"

"Georgiana told me in confidence and asked me not to tell you, so I felt I could not betray her trust."

"Why did she not want me to know? I could have spoken to Fitzwilliam…" His brows knitted in irritation.

Elizabeth glared at him. "That is exactly what she does *not* want!"

"I don't understand; why would my sister not want me to know her feelings when it concerns her entire future?" he exclaimed, his voice momentarily rising before he forced it back down to a whisper.

"She is in love with him and wants him to marry her because he loves her, not because he feels a family obligation," she said crisply. "If you talk to him about her feelings for him, it is tantamount to asking him to marry her. He probably will agree because he feels a responsibility towards her and the match is very eligible for the both of them as far as fortune and background. She, however, does not want to spend the rest of her life with a guardian; she wants to spend it with a husband—and it is entirely your fault that she feels that way!" She stopped, shocked at her own vehemence.

"My fault! What do you mean?" he asked with asperity.

"Your sister, my dear husband, wants a marriage with the love, affection, and, I hope, trust," she said dryly, "between husband and wife that you have achieved." Then she added hurriedly, with a slight blush, "...albeit through months of agony and uncertainty beforehand, of which she has probably only the slightest comprehension."

They stared at each other.

"I am sorry, my love," Darcy said finally and slumped down onto the sofa, rubbing his brow. "I am being a mutton-headed dolt. I, of all people, cannot blame Georgiana for not wanting a neat and polite marriage arranged by family members when she could have a 'marriage of true minds' as her brother and sister have." He finally smiled at her and took her hand and she felt a rush of relief that he was not annoyed because she had not shared Georgiana's confessions with him earlier.

She returned, quietly, "*Comprends-tu la situation maintenant, mon amour?*"

"*Oui, je la comprends parfaitement. Mais, mon Dieu, quel problème!*"
"*Oui, c'est vrai.*"

They slowly mounted the stairs, both musing over what she had told him. As Elizabeth turned to go to her room, Darcy stopped her again and whispered, "Is there nothing we can do to help this situation?"

"I think that we have done everything we can do; it is up to Georgiana now," she said, her confidence returning.

He nodded in reluctant agreement then turned to his dressing-room, shaking his head as he went.

Later, when Elizabeth was asleep, Darcy stared up into the darkness and reviewed the discussion in the drawing-room without satisfaction. The question of his sister's feelings for her cousin, and his for her, was of only peripheral importance to his current reflections.

His thoughts and actions in the beginning of that conversation struck him as unpleasantly similar to those of the person that he had been eighteen months ago—the ghost of an affronted, arrogant man rising like the miasma from a crypt to assault his intellect and emotions. He had managed to suppress that old Darcy this evening, but it was disconcerting to know that he still lurked in a dim corner of his mind, waiting to appear at the slightest provocation. Elizabeth's ironic comment about trust had struck home, bringing him abruptly to his senses.

He had always wanted Elizabeth to be Georgiana's sister and it was only fair that she should keep her sister's confidences, just as he knew she would keep his. The insufferable pride which had caused all of the emotional pain he had endured during their courtship was clearly not excised, merely dormant. He must make sure to keep that phantom of the past in the deepest dungeons of his mind. He smiled to himself. No doubt Elizabeth would point out his error, as she had tonight, should he stray towards overweening arrogance again.

Another question rose in his mind. What should he do about Georgiana and Fitzwilliam? He had already taken a small step towards enlightening his cousin about Georgiana's regard for him when he opened Fitzwilliam's eyes to the fact that she was no longer the gangly little girl who had followed them adoringly, barred from joining their pursuits by both her youth and her gender. Even he, who had provided her with all of the accoutrements of a young lady for the past five years, had been rattled tonight when he had seen her in the ballroom. He had, for a fraction of a second, not recognised the elegant woman before him as the same young lady, barely out of girlhood, who had kissed him on the cheek this morning when she came down to breakfast. He had felt a sense of loss as she glided off for her dances with her cousin St. George, the foreshadow of her inevitable loss to adulthood and marriage. That Georgiana was ready for the change was unarguable after tonight, and the answer to his question was clear. She did not want him to influence the colonel's decision. As Elizabeth had said, it was up to Georgiana now.

Georgiana was still lying awake and staring up into the darkness when her brother drifted off to sleep. She had gone immediately to bed when they arrived at Ashbourne House, with nothing more than a faint "goodnight" to anyone. She had hoped to drown her uncertainty in the arms of Morpheus, but she could not. With a sigh, she finally rose and lit a single candle before pulling out her diary. She scanned the last few pages and sighed again before dipping her pen into the ink.

> *24 May: The ball went well tonight with regard to my costume and I was able to throw myself wholeheartedly into my performance, but I am confused and unsure as to the results. The colonel seemed stunned by my appearance, but I could not detect whether he was overcome with love at my mature appearance or simply shocked at my bold glances when we finally danced. He certainly looked more ill than in love. Lord St. George, on the other hand, seemed quite impressed with his newly adult cousin and danced attendance along with the other single men. What an ironic twist of fate that is! For my part, every time I look at the colonel I see something new. Every feature is somehow more defined: the solidity of bone and muscle, the quirk of a brow, the curl of hair above a collar. It is*

as if he is changing before my eyes, except that I know that the changes are not in him, they are in me; it is my sensitivity to his looks, his actions, and his words which mark a revolution in my thinking. He is the same man he always was. Perhaps I will talk to Elizabeth in the morning and ask her opinion of the evening. I hope she has some counsel or comfort for me.

She carefully placed the pen in the holder and her diary in the drawer of her bedside table and climbed back in bed, but it was long before she dozed off.

The next morning, Georgiana was waiting in the breakfast-parlour when Elizabeth and Darcy came down.

"Why are you up so early, my love? You need your sleep if you are going to attend all of the parties for which you are engaged," she exclaimed.

"I awakened early and could not fall back to sleep," she said with a serious countenance.

Darcy glanced at Elizabeth and said, "Well, I had better go; I am expecting to meet with Bingley at the club for breakfast soon and I would not want to keep him waiting."

He quickly left the room.

Elizabeth turned back to Georgiana, who was picking at her food, the corners of her mouth drooping.

"What is bothering you, dearest?"

Georgiana sighed, her lip quivering slightly.

"I was disappointed that the colonel did not dance with me again last night. I am probably being unreasonable, but I hoped that after all of the preparations we did before the ball he would respond more." She stopped and smiled ruefully. "I guess that I expected him to fall at my feet in a swoon when I appeared in the room."

Elizabeth quickly reassured her. "You must give him a little time. I believe from my observations last night that he now realises that you are a woman, not a little girl. That alone was a great step for him to make. You must now make him also realise that he loves you. You must conquer one difficulty at a time."

Georgiana sighed and said, "You are correct, of course, but it is difficult to be patient. I am so afraid that he will make an offer to someone else before I can convince him to look at me, especially since you and my brother have given him such a model of domestic felicity to strive for." She managed a brief smile before resuming, "While my brother was still unwed and I was not yet out in society I felt I had all the time in the world and did not want this year to arrive. Now I feel as if time is rushing away like a runaway horse while I am plodding behind in the dust. I hope that I have not grown up too late. Last night it was all I could do to keep myself from throwing my diary, my pen, and everything on my dressing table across the room in my frustration. If you will excuse me, I think I will play the pianoforte; it will probably 'soothe my fevered brow.'" She made a determined effort to smile and left the room.

When Darcy returned in the early afternoon he sought out Elizabeth in the drawing-room while the two girls were upstairs playing with Lucky and asked her how Georgiana was.

"I thought it best that I leave this morning so that she could talk to you confidentially, but I am concerned about her."

She reassured him again. "Trust me, I have lived with three younger sisters, and this is not abnormal. She is a bit overwrought about the Season and the prospect of marriage and everything that is changing in her life. She will be herself again when the suspense of this year is over—whether she is engaged by that time or not—unless of course the colonel becomes engaged to someone else during that time."

"I hope you are right, my love. I feel as if I have aged several years in the last few months." He rubbed his hands wearily over his face.

"I feel the same. I am afraid that I am going to collapse before the Season is over. Between watching over Georgiana and Kitty both, I think that I am wearing down to a mere shadow of my former self."

"You do look tired, my love," he said with a worried frown. "Why don't you rest this afternoon?"

"I believe I will, if I can."

She took his advice and rested for two hours in her room that afternoon. She felt much better afterwards and decided to ask Jane if she would invite Kitty to stay with her for a few weeks. Jane called in the afternoon, soon after she rose from her rest, saying, "I sent a note earlier, but Mr. Darcy said that you were resting. Are you feeling quite well?"

"I am well—just a little tired after all the parties and balls for Georgiana."

"Perhaps I should ask Kitty to stay with us until you are feeling better," Jane said immediately.

Elizabeth laughed, shaking her head in astonishment. "I was going to ask you if you would invite her, but you have anticipated me, as you usually do."

It was soon settled that Kitty would spend the next fortnight with the Bingleys and help Jane with a party she was planning. She went happily to Berkeley Square the next day, and the Darcys were left to their own devices.

Chapter 20

The course of true love never did run smooth.

—WILLIAM SHAKESPEARE, *A MIDSUMMER NIGHT'S DREAM*

GEORGIANA HAD EXPECTED TO SEE THE COLONEL IN THEIR drawing-room very soon, but three days went by and they saw nothing of him, not even at the parties they attended. Viscount St. George, on the other hand, was a daily visitor, stopping for short visits each late afternoon to talk to Elizabeth and to be charming to Georgiana. His social graces were formidable, and he was able to converse on a variety of topics in an interesting fashion. His easy manners rivalled those of his brother, but Georgiana always found him rather too interested in his own self. She noticed that when he passed a glass he always checked his appearance in it and stopped to rearrange a fold of his cravat or the curl tumbling artfully over one brow. He was courteous to Elizabeth in a condescending way, which clearly demonstrated that he knew of her rather humble origins.

Georgiana tried to be gracious and to appear to be happy to see him, considering it good practise for her social skills, but she forgot him when he was not preening himself in front of her. She was, however, nettled by St. George's continued patronising attitude towards Elizabeth. On the fifth day after the Elliots' ball, Lord St. George was telling them a piece of gossip, which included familiarly dropping the names of several peers in the Prince Regent's circle. He stopped part way through the story and said to Elizabeth, with a deprecating smile, "I am sorry, my dear cousin, I should not bore you with stories about people with whom you are not acquainted."

Georgiana interjected austerely, "Indeed not, Cousin, it would be abominably rude of you to do so."

She smiled sweetly at him and he had the grace to look a little ashamed. He turned the conversation to another topic and left after a few minutes, scrupulously polite to both ladies in his farewells.

The setdown did not keep Lord St. George from their door the next day, however, and he was still with them when the colonel, resplendent in his regimentals, finally came to call in the afternoon.

"I apologise for neglecting you, Cousin Georgiana," he said after he had greeted both ladies, "but I was needed at the palace and was not able to absent myself." He turned to his brother and added in a cooler tone, "What a surprise to see you here, Brother."

"Yes, I have been enjoying making the acquaintance of my new cousin-in-law and renewing my acquaintance with Georgiana while you have been playing soldier," Viscount St. George drawled, with just the faintest hint of condescension in his voice.

"How thoughtful of you, my dear brother," the colonel said smoothly. "I am surprised that your busy schedule allows you to pay afternoon calls."

"Well," he said as he smiled at Georgiana, "one must not neglect one's family, especially not such attractive family."

Georgiana thought she saw the colonel bridle slightly, but he quickly brought himself under control, although his face was far from having its usual pleasant expression. He appeared to her... she struggled for the apt description—stiff and uncomfortable and possibly, deep down, resentful of his brother. The viscount left after a few minutes and the colonel followed soon thereafter. She tried to keep him longer by putting a hand gently on his arm and saying, "Must you leave so soon, Colonel? You just arrived."

"I am truly sorry, my dear cousin, but duty calls me. I need to speak to your brother this afternoon, but I wanted to stop in and let you know that I haven't forgotten you," he said hesitantly then bowed and left the room abruptly.

Georgiana stared at the door for several moments after he left.

"Well," Elizabeth ventured after a pause, "at least he did not call you 'little cousin.'"

Georgiana finally found her voice and said, "Please excuse me, Elizabeth, I am going to have a fit of hysterics and I don't wish you to witness it, so I will go to my room."

She walked stiffly out of the drawing-room and up the stairs.

Elizabeth could not help smiling to herself, in spite of her worries over Georgiana. Having a sister who went calmly upstairs to "have hysterics" was a considerable change from the Bennet family in which every passion was inflicted upon all of the relations. She sighed at the perversity of mankind and went to her room to rest. She could not help Georgiana keep her spirits up if she was so exhausted that she was in a state of collapse.

In the library, Fitzwilliam sat forwards in his chair and said in a hushed voice, "Darcy, I gave those letters to someone who gathers information for Lord Liverpool, and he was most appreciative. He has a network of informants who bring him facts, rumours, and stories and he sits like a spider in his web and collects and sifts the information to squeeze out a few truths for his master. I suspect that he gathers information on the Prince Regent as well. At any rate, he is the man who first brought me the rumour of a possible assassination attempt on the Prince Regent by this group of arms smugglers.

"I suppose Perceval's assassination two years ago made them think that it might be possible to reach the Prince Regent as well, and there are any number of people who dislike the prince's influence on society. If they could escape without being immediately identified they might succeed and the entire government might be destabilised, allowing Napoleon to rise again and re-form his army." He gave his cousin a sharp look. "The arms business would remain brisk."

Darcy, who had been watching his cousin over his steepled fingers while he spoke, nodded his understanding and the colonel continued.

"This aide of Liverpool's has gathered enough confirmatory evidence related to the clues in the letters to suggest that Captain Blackman is indeed involved in smuggling arms to France. On the twelfth he had a quiet talk to the captain and convinced him that it would be in his best interest to help them put his associates out of business. He finally admitted the plan and gave them the meeting place and time in Calais. Unfortunately, either the captain managed to warn the lady or she had spies of her own posted. In either case, she did not keep their engagement, and the captain has been quietly arrested and is being held very closely; he is sweating now, but has not yet given them the names of his associates. From what they have gathered, the lady seems to be the leader and has shown an organisational ability and lack of moral squeamishness far beyond what one might expect from one of the female sex. That is all I have for now, but I thought you might be interested to know the importance of the letter you appropriated."

"Have you given any more thought to Walker?"

"I have, but I have not resolved yet how to deal with him. Did you speak to Sir Robert?"

"Yes. I was finally forced to send him an invitation to dine and hope that Walker did not hear of it and become suspicious. I arranged a private room at the club and, as you might imagine, it was a damned awkward interview. Sir Robert was understandably shocked and very distressed about his sister. Walker is pressing for a quick wedding and Miss Blake is very eager to marry, but Blake thinks that he can influence her not to rush into marriage. From what he said, she has been desperate to find a husband and frustrated by the lack of opportunities in the country. Her family's continued association with trade has held her back socially in spite of their fortune, and he believes that she accepted Walker as the answer to her prayers for a husband with an ancient family name to cleanse her of that taint. Now that she is engaged to be married, she will hopefully be amenable to enjoying her status through the rest of the Season before planning the wedding.

"Fortunately, Blake has control of her dowry, so he has a powerful inducement for Walker to submit to his pressure. Apparently, Blake's father left everything to Sir Robert and left with him the responsibility to provide for his brothers and sister. If necessary, he can inform his sister about the true character of her fiancé, but he is hoping that she will see through him on her own and break off the engagement. Blake will be alert, of course, to any hint that Walker has convinced her to marry without his consent, but it would seem unlikely that Walker would risk the loss of her dowry."

"Good. At least he knows what Walker is. I must return to the palace. I will keep you informed."

Darcy lifted his glass of wine to his cousin and the colonel departed.

Georgiana worked out her feelings with Beethoven, concentrating on his most dramatic and, occasionally, disturbing pieces. An hour later, she was very warm and stopped to cool off. Elizabeth came in the music room and said, "How are you doing, my sweet?" as she brushed a few damp hairs back from Georgiana's brow. "Are you feeling calmer now that you have had your hysterics?"

Georgiana gave a weak smile. "Yes, I am… I am sorry to be so out of spirits lately."

"Compared to some of my sisters, you are a model of serenity, my dear." Elizabeth smiled reassuringly. "Sometimes I feel that it is a shame we women cannot relieve our emotions by participating in some of the more violent sports," she reflected. "There have been times in my life when I have felt that a few rounds in a boxing ring would be just the thing to restore my happiness."

Georgiana laughed until she had to wipe the tears from her eyes. "My dear Mrs. Darcy, you never cease to surprise me. I wonder if I will ever be able to predict what you will say next."

They both laughed then, and Georgiana felt better as she went upstairs to dress for dinner. They were to dine at Longford House before going on to a party at a friend's. The dinner was to be a family party only and the colonel was expected to be there, as was Lord St. George. Lady Whitwell had told Elizabeth, when she extended the invitation, "We will have a nice quiet family dinner.

Georgiana probably needs to recoup her energy after her first round of parties."

Elizabeth told Georgiana that she had agreed that a quiet dinner would be a good idea, although she privately wondered whether she would get one with the two sons of the house present.

The Darcys arrived early at Longford House and gathered with the family in the drawing-room before dinner. Lord St. George clung tenaciously to Georgiana's side and made small talk, but Georgiana eventually allowed her attention to lapse and looked for the colonel. He was the last to appear, and he saw his brother and Georgiana and immediately made his way towards them. Georgiana turned to him, turning her back to St. George's chatter, and the colonel greeted her formally with a bow.

"How charming you look tonight, Georgiana."

She looked into his eyes and managed a half-smile.

"I thank you, Colonel," was the best answer she could form, her mouth suddenly dry.

Lord St. George cleared his throat to regain her attention, and she glanced up at his petulant expression.

"What were we discussing, Cousin?"

Before St. George could speak, a footman announced dinner and Lord Whitwell led Elizabeth into the dining-room, followed by Viscount St. George and Georgiana, and Darcy and Lady Whitwell. Colonel Fitzwilliam brought up the rear of the procession with Mrs. Appleton, a very elderly cousin of Lord Whitwell's, on his arm. Georgiana noted acidly to herself that this was a rather apt demonstration of the status of the younger son of a noble house.

Georgiana was seated between Lord Whitwell and Lord St. George and she divided her time between the two, listening quietly and nodding occasionally as the conversation demanded but not saying much in return. She managed to glance covertly down the table towards the colonel, who was talking abstractedly to Mrs. Appleton. Georgiana thought that Lord St. George seemed far too absorbed by her conversation, and she tried to distance herself by speaking with her uncle as much as she could without rudeness. She did intercept a speculative look between Lord and Lady Whitwell when they saw that their son was vying for her attention, and her ears caught the querulous tones of Mrs. Appleton asking the colonel, "When are you two young men going to get married? It is time that you both did your duty to the family."

The colonel gave her a wan smile but managed to deflect the attack, agreeing with her that it would be a desirable action on his part but saying that he would not want to act precipitously.

"A little more precipitance would perhaps be advisable in the case of yourself and your brother. Neither of you is getting any younger, you know," she returned tartly. Then with a wizened smile that took the sting from her words she added, "However, you must forgive an opinionated old lady for prying into your affairs. Marriages and deaths are meat and drink to someone as old as I." She chuckled at his expression and patted his arm. "You must take some pointers from your cousin," she said, nodding towards Darcy, "and find yourself a pretty young woman before they are all married off."

The colonel chuckled halfheartedly, glancing at his brother and Georgiana. His mother turned the conversation in another direction, and the colonel seconded her efforts with relief.

The ladies soon rose and adjourned to the drawing-room, where Mrs. Appleton engaged Georgiana's attention with a lively account of her own coming-out almost fifty years earlier. They were well entertained until the gentlemen joined them and they poured out the tea and coffee. Lord St. George requested a song from the ladies, bowing impartially between Elizabeth and Georgiana. When Elizabeth demurred, Georgiana rose and went to the pianoforte, where she selected a sonata and began playing. Lord St. George turned the pages for her and seemed rapt in the music—or at least in the musician.

The colonel joined them at the instrument and stationed himself where he could see Georgiana's face and where she could in turn see him when she glanced up from her music. During one glance upwards, her gaze caught his and she stumbled over a note before she could look down again and find her place. Lord St. George gave his brother a sardonic look and drawled, "Brother, you should find another place from which to enjoy the music. You disconcert our cousin hanging over her like a carrion bird."

Georgiana gave him a piercing look and said astringently, "I know of no one who resembles a vulture less than your brother, Lord St. George; and if I was disconcerted by being watched while I played then you would be at fault as well."

He chuckled gently and murmured, "I would not want to do anything that would make you uncomfortable, my dear cousin."

She looked away and continued playing until it was time to leave for their party.

As she closed the pianoforte, Lord St. George took her hand and said, "I hope that you will allow me the first pair of dances again this evening, my dearest cousin."

She bowed her head slightly in assent and turned to Colonel Fitzwilliam. Interpreting her look, Lord St. George added to his brother, "If you want a dance with our lovely cousin, Brother, you should speak now, for I will be keeping her quite busy this evening."

The colonel bowed and said, very formally, "I, of course, wish to dance with you as well, Miss Darcy. Perhaps I could have the second pair of dances?"

Georgiana bowed her head again, this time letting a smile play at the corners of her mouth. The colonel smiled in return, and the group left the drawing-room for the party.

The entertainment that evening was at the home of another of the debutantes, this one a rather plain girl who was the eldest daughter of a baronet as well as a friend of Georgiana's. The girl had a lively intellect, which made her popular with her friends, but her family was a large one and of only moderate fortune, so her father made sure that he hosted several parties each Season to attract as many eligible young men as they could.

Jane and Bingley had decided to remain at home this evening, so the Darcys chaperoned Miss Bingley and Kitty as well as Georgiana. The baronet had kindly invited all of them, in spite of the additional competition they provided for his daughter, because the presence of Miss Darcy would ensure that the wealthier young men would attend as well. The house was of moderate size but furnished in an elegant style, and the refreshments were lavish.

Georgiana left her family to dance the first dance with Lord St. George. She danced with little conversation, merely answering her partner's comments with a small smile or brief comment of her own and then gazing remotely over his shoulder as she thought about her next partner. When St. George escorted her off the dance floor, she curtseyed briefly before moving off with some other young women.

The colonel immediately claimed her for his two dances. She put her gloved hand gently on his offered arm and glanced up at him, briefly meeting his gaze. During the dance she smiled and gazed steadily at him when they were facing each other, still not speaking much but very aware of his every movement and expression. Each touch of his hand burnt through her gloves and she could feel herself flushing. She could see that he was flustered by her steady regard, and soon his easy conversation died and they danced in silence. She could not find any topic of conversation which was not either trite or far too revealing of her state of mind, so she kept quiet, silently blessing Elizabeth for her advice on maintaining an enigmatic silence when unable to converse sensibly. When the first dance finished she thanked the colonel, pitching her voice low and putting as much warmth as she could into her voice, "Thank you, Colonel. Could we sit out our second dance? It is a little too warm in here tonight."

"Of course, Georgiana, if you wish. Could I bring you something to drink? Some punch, perhaps?"

"That would be lovely, but I will come with you. Perhaps there is a quieter and cooler place where we could sit and drink it."

The refreshments were in a small parlour next to the ballroom, which was provided with a cluster of chairs for those who preferred to escape the music for a while. They had barely settled themselves when Lord St. George appeared in the doorway with Justina Dalrymple. The two settled themselves noisily next to Georgiana and the colonel. St. George immediately asked Georgiana about the progress of her first Season, and Justina flashed her dimples at the colonel and teased him.

"Colonel Fitzwilliam! No regimentals tonight?"

"No, Miss Dalrymple, I am a private citizen tonight."

"What a shame. And you look so handsome in them. Do you not love a man in uniform, Georgiana?"

She glanced laughingly at Georgiana, drawing her into their conversation and causing St. George to pout as the attention moved away from him.

Georgiana examined the colonel with deliberate care.

"Indeed, a uniform is a handsome addition to a man's appearance… however, I have noticed that my cousin does not need the assistance of regimentals to turn the heads of the ladies."

Justina squealed with laughter and turned an adoring gaze on Colonel Fitzwilliam.

"Indeed he does not."

The colonel blushed and shook his head but managed to answer in a light tone. "You young ladies will swell my head. Please have a care for my susceptible heart."

Lord St. George inserted, "And what about me? I am told that my brother and I are much alike. May I not receive my share of praise, Miss Dalrymple?"

After a few minutes more of Justina's lavish praise for the two gentlemen, Georgiana gave up and said to the colonel, "Could we have our second dance now, Colonel?"

The colonel bowed briefly and answered, a pensive look on his face, "My pleasure, Miss Darcy."

In spite of her own preoccupations, as Georgiana looked around after their dance she noted that Edward Blake had come with Colonel Fitzwilliam and was happily dancing with all of the young ladies, but when he was free he came back to talk to Kitty and danced two sets with her during the evening. Sir Robert Blake had come late to the party and Georgiana, who at that moment was talking to Elizabeth about the frustration of her attempts to talk to the colonel, had an inspiration and said impishly, "You know, I think that I will introduce Sir Robert to Catherine Freemont. He looks far too grave tonight and they would make a lovely couple. She can cheer him up."

She saw her cousin St. George coming towards them and added, "Elizabeth, why do you not introduce Miss Bingley to my cousin St. George? Since the count is not here tonight she can keep him busy."

She went to find her friend and took her over to Sir Robert and introduced them. Sir Robert bowed courteously and talked with both of them for a few moments. A young man came to claim Georgiana for a promised dance, and Sir Robert apparently asked for Miss Freemont's hand for the next set, for they moved onto the dance floor immediately after Georgiana and her partner.

Elizabeth did as Georgiana suggested and introduced Lord St. George to Miss Bingley. Caroline was charmed and danced and talked with St. George with evident enjoyment through the set, and afterwards she and Georgiana both accepted refreshments from him. Lord St. George preened himself before the two ladies, Georgiana looking on indifferently and Miss Bingley hanging upon his every word.

Halfway through the evening, there was a sudden ripple of excitement among those standing near the entry. Georgiana, who was talking quietly to her friend Catherine about Sir Robert, did not notice the raised voices immediately. Her first inkling that there was something disturbing the controlled gentility of the ballroom was when she saw Catherine suddenly stare over her left shoulder, her eyes wide. Georgiana turned and saw Lord Byron awaiting her notice. He bowed gracefully and said, "Miss Darcy, would you honour me with the next two dances?"

Georgiana curtseyed. "Th-Thank you, my lord."

Byron turned away and it was not long before a crowd of girls surrounded Georgiana.

"Do you know Lord Byron?"

"Have you met Lord Byron, Georgiana?"

The gabble of their voices obscured the questions and Georgiana thought that it was time to try the regal silence again. She gave them a half-smile, took Catherine's hand, and calmly walked through the gathered debutantes to the other side of the room, leaving them with their mouths open.

Lord Byron came to claim Georgiana for their dances and she glanced at her brother and sister, who were both staring intently at them from across the room. She gave Elizabeth a fleeting smile and faced her partner across the space which separated the lines of dancers. He gave her his seductive half-smile and they began the figure. Byron was a good dancer, in spite of his crippled foot, and while they awaited their turn to go down the line he conversed about music.

"I understand that you are a very accomplished musician, Miss Darcy."

Georgiana wondered with whom he had been discussing her but answered calmly enough, "I enjoy music, my lord. I do not know if I would call my efforts accomplished."

"I suspect that you are overly modest, Miss Darcy."

She gave him a brief smile, her attention distracted by the sight of the colonel dancing with Justina Dalrymple. He seemed to feel her gaze and looked over, almost missing a turn with his partner. He recovered smoothly and again attended to his partner, but Georgiana could see that his mind was not on his dancing. She smiled to herself, and Lord Byron, who seemed to see her interest in the other couple, said, "Does your cousin Colonel Fitzwilliam often attend the debutante balls?"

"Pardon?" Georgiana forced her regard back to her dance partner.

"Your cousin seems to be very interested in Miss Dalrymple."

"Yes, I suppose so." She pulled herself together and said, more strongly, "I do not know how often he attended in past years, but he is my guardian along with my brother. It is possible that he attends more this year because of that." She managed to shrug indifferently. "He has danced with Justina Dalrymple often. She is a very good dancer and her fortune is large. She will make someone a splendid wife."

"Indeed she will." Lord Byron watched Miss Dalrymple.

Justina Dalrymple was whispering in the colonel's ear as they paused at the top of the form. When her partner turned in the middle of her compliments to stare at his young cousin and her partner, her vanity was pricked and she narrowed her eyes at him for a moment. She deliberately turned to watch the two dancing and commented with honeyed sweetness, "Do not worry, Colonel Fitzwilliam, Miss Darcy will not fall for Lord Byron. She is already in love with her handsome cousin."

He turned and stared at Justina.

"I hope you are wrong, Miss Dalrymple."

She tossed her head and said, "Trust me. A woman can tell."

When Georgiana and her partner finished the dance, Lord Byron made his way across the room to Justina Dalrymple, who turned her back on the colonel's final bow. Georgiana could see Justina beaming at the poet, and soon they were dancing and carrying on a lively conversation. Georgiana smiled to herself and sought out Catherine Freemont again.

The evening slowly ran its course with the formal movement of gentlemen and ladies as they met off the dance floor, bowing and curtseying, telling a small joke or anecdote, smiling, sometimes with their mouths alone, sometimes with their eyes as well. It was an endless parade of young men and women showing their looks and their grace, displaying their wealth by their elegant and fashionable clothing and caught in an elaborate dance as formal as any taking place on the dance floor. Georgiana suddenly realised that she was extremely fatigued.

When the evening finally wound to its close and they were on their way home, Georgiana and Kitty sagged like wilted flowers in the carriage, but Miss Bingley looked alert and satisfied with herself. Georgiana's last thought when they left Miss Bingley at her brother's house was that she looked like a well-fed cat, and she wondered what mouse she had eaten that night.

Chapter 21

But still the great have kindness in reserve.

—ALEXANDER POPE, "AN EPISTLE TO DR. ARBUTHNOT"

FINALLY THE DAY CAME FOR ELIZABETH'S AND JANE'S PRESENTATION at court. Although she was nervous about making a faux pas in front of the court, Elizabeth confessed to Jane and Georgiana that she was eager to see the Prince Regent, about whom she had heard so many scandalous tales.

"I realise that I am showing a rather prurient interest in his activities, but he seems to be a man who inspires many different emotions in those around him and I long to make my own judgement in the case, so I hope he is there today."

Jane chuckled nervously, and Elizabeth reassured her.

"Do not distress yourself, my dear sister. With your beauty and grace you will charm the court. I, on the other hand, hope that I do not disgrace myself by laughing inappropriately at all of the pomp and ceremony."

Jane smiled more easily at her and kissed her on the cheek. "Dear Lizzy, you always make me laugh at myself."

Georgiana added, "My dear, if I, the most fearful young woman ever, can survive it you will have no difficulties at all." She kissed Jane on the cheek and they embraced for a moment.

Lady Whitwell arrived and checked their costumes to see if they were perfectly correct and then had them demonstrate their curtseys in front of her and Georgiana. She would be Elizabeth's sponsor and a friend of hers, Lady Southaven, would be Jane's, since court protocol forbade Lady Whitwell from presenting both of them herself on the same day. Georgiana kissed them both and wished them luck before sending them off with her aunt.

The carriage ride to St. James Palace seemed far too short to Elizabeth. The day was a little cool and threatened rain, but they were able to leave their wraps in the carriage and enter the foyer of the palace without mishap, their trains draped gracefully over their arms. Lady Southaven awaited them in the entry, and after greeting her they made their way to the anteroom of the reception area. There, the lords-in-waiting lined up all those who would be presented in order of their rank. Elizabeth and Jane were separated since Darcy, although untitled, had a much more ancient name and fortune than Bingley, whose wealth went no further back than his grandfather, who had been in trade (a fact that Miss Bingley conveniently forgot when she was being superior).

Elizabeth prepared herself for an interminable wait since the line was long, but she, as Georgiana had before, consoled herself with the knowledge that it was, fortunately, an ordeal that need only occur once. Lady Whitwell stood with her and they occasionally exchanged remarks, but mostly they waited in silence, for the room was too noisy with the nervous chattering of the debutantes being presented to make conversation easy.

After they had been waiting a good while and the din had quieted somewhat, Lady Whitwell turned to Elizabeth and said in a low voice, "While we have the opportunity of being relatively unremarked, I must thank you for all you have done for Georgiana." Elizabeth blushed and started to shake her head, but her sponsor continued, "Do not try to modestly deny it, my dear. I have seen a most remarkable change in Georgiana's poise and maturity since you and Darcy married. Although he and Edward have done their best as her guardians, two men more than ten years older than she is are much better suited to manage her financial affairs than they are to manage her development into a graceful young woman.

"Unfortunately for Georgiana, although her brother loves her dearly, she has had no female relatives, until now, to help guide her and provide a model from which she could learn. I have several times regretted that I could not spend more time with her, but having only sons I am not sure that I would have been able to do nearly as well as you. I confess that a year ago I was doubtful whether she would be able to face presentation and the Season. She has always been an intelligent and courteous child, prevented only by the excessive shyness she developed a few years ago from shining in the company of others. But she has now blossomed into a confident woman, and I thank you."

She patted Elizabeth's hand as she said these last words. Elizabeth glanced up at her and said diffidently, "If I have been in any small way able to help Georgiana in the last few months, she has amply repaid my efforts with her kindness and affection. I am delighted to claim her as a sister, and I do not look forwards to her marrying and leaving home with any anticipation. I will miss her dreadfully."

Their further conversation was interrupted as the line moved forwards, and they arrived at the front more quickly than Elizabeth had expected. Lady Whitwell gave Elizabeth's card to the lord chamberlain, and in a few too-brief moments he opened the chamber doors for her and bowed her in. One of the lords-in-waiting spread her train out behind her and she approached the throne.

The Prince Regent, when her name was read, sat up a bit straighter and observed her closely as she walked sedately up to the throne and curtseyed deeply to Queen Charlotte and then to the prince. The Prince Regent nodded in his turn and, after the lord-in-waiting draped her train back over her arm, she backed out of the room, unable to keep her amusement at the false solemnity of the ritual from showing in her eyes above her studiously serious mien. She thought for a moment that she saw a small answering smile play over the Prince Regent's face, but it was gone in an instant and she was sure that she must have been mistaken.

When she had managed to back out of the room without mishap, she looked at Lady Whitwell and gave a small sigh of relief. Her sponsor's eyes crinkled in amusement as she led her to a bench in the anteroom where they could relax and wait for Jane to finish her presentation.

Eventually the ordeal was over and, after thanking Lady Southaven for her sponsorship of Jane, they returned to their carriage—not forgetting to turn sideways at the carriage door to get their hooped skirts inside.

At Ashbourne House Darcy, Georgiana, Kitty, and Bingley were all waiting in some anxiety. Georgiana had just begun to pour tea when they heard the carriage arrive, and they jumped up to congratulate Elizabeth and Jane on their presumed success.

Georgiana, after they had all given their congratulations, put on a solemn face and said, "I am so proud that you have both succeeded in this most important milestone in your life."

This provoked all the laughter she was seeking, and Elizabeth and Jane entered the house with lighter hearts than when they had departed in the morning. After the footman had taken their wraps and Burton had congratulated them, they were more than ready for tea, but first they wanted to change out of their court dresses and into their ordinary gowns for, as Elizabeth pointed out, "If we sit down in these gowns, there will be no place for anyone else to be seated. Whoever created this style must have had investments in the furniture industry and planned to make a vast fortune enlarging all of the furniture in the country so that more than one lady could fit on the settee."

Bingley choked on the tea he had just sipped and, while Darcy was pounding on his back, she and Jane swept grandly upstairs to change.

The rest of the day passed in a much more restful fashion than had the morning and they dined at the Bingleys' house that evening. They had not accepted any invitations for later in the evening; they would need an early night tonight, for tomorrow was Lady Whitwell's ball.

Chapter 22

What, my dear Lady Disdain!

—William Shakespeare, *Much Ado About Nothing*

They had no special plans during the next afternoon and spent it relaxing. Georgiana went to the music room and worked on her new Beethoven sonata, which she had not had a great deal of time to practise. After she had worn herself out with the new piece, she played another piece at double speed and then stopped, a little breathless. Elizabeth, who was sitting with her and doing some desultory work on her embroidery, smiled at her choice of composers.

"Feeling in a Beethoven mood again are you, Georgiana?" she queried.

"Yes, Mozart or Handel would simply not express my feelings properly, although perhaps the 'Rondo Alla Turca' would be quite good," she said, with an abashed smile.

"You are fortunate to have a pianoforte on which to express yourself; the harp would probably not be sufficiently emphatic, but on the pianoforte you can pound without fear of alarming the servants."

They both laughed, and Georgiana took out "Le Coucou" and played it molto vivace before covering the keys and taking up her needlepoint.

The day dragged slowly by until Lord St. George visited in the early afternoon. Georgiana acknowledged his bow politely when he entered and then rang for tea. She sat down next to Elizabeth in a chair facing St. George and he settled on the sofa, where she had been sitting before his entrance. He began the conversation by discussing his mother's ball that night and by again engaging Georgiana for the first pair of dances.

"Although," he said with a charming smile, "I don't suppose my mamma will give either of us much choice in the matter, since she will expect us to open the ball." He smiled at her winningly and continued, "Still, I would like for it to be a matter of choice rather than merely a duty."

Georgiana smiled slightly and nodded her acceptance of the engagement then turned the conversation to the happenings around town, about which he knew a great deal, and he was happily occupied with retailing various bits of gossip until the door of the drawing-room opened and Darcy appeared with Colonel Fitzwilliam, both looking pensive. They exerted themselves to put off their dour moods, greet the ladies and Lord St. George and join them for tea. St. George finished the story he had started before their appearance and then gracefully made his excuses and departed.

"What did my esteemed brother want today, Georgiana?" Colonel Fitzwilliam asked, looking at the door where his brother had just disappeared.

"He wanted to engage me for the first two dances tonight, although he pointed out that my aunt would force us to open the ball anyway, so I did not seem to have much choice in the matter," she said with a spark in her eye.

"I very much doubt whether he worded his request in quite that fashion," the colonel said, turning to her with an amused smile, "since, for all his faults, his manners in public are generally acceptable, if supercilious."

She smiled impudently and acknowledged the truth of his statement, and they finished their tea companionably.

When the colonel made his adieux Darcy saw him out, and by the time he returned to the drawing-room Georgiana had gone upstairs. He sat down next to Elizabeth and asked her how she was feeling.

"I am well. However, I feel like a spring is wound up tight inside me, waiting to explode. I cannot but be influenced by Georgiana's tension, although she covers it very well. Perhaps too well. She has been far too polite and genteel throughout the Season. I sometimes think that if she would scream and cry and get it over with, as some of my younger sisters would do, it would be like a storm passing, leaving fresh air in its wake—however, that is not the Darcy way." She smiled at him, her eyes twinkling. "So she has had to resort to Beethoven, which I believe has been somewhat efficacious."

"Yes, I could hear her battle with the pianoforte from my library this morning. Perhaps we should contact Herr Beethoven and commission a work: 'For the Reduction of Tension in Young Ladies during Their First Season'—but possibly we could find a more romantic title."

"Perhaps." She paused and then ventured, "Is there something worrying you, my love? You and the colonel both looked fairly grim when you came in to tea."

"We were just discussing some business concerning his work upon which the colonel wanted my private opinion. Nothing of importance to the rest of the family."

"I see." Elizabeth kissed him and tugged on the hair tumbling over his brow then went upstairs to rest until she needed to dress for the ball—while attempting to reassure herself that all would be well with Georgiana.

While Elizabeth was resting, Darcy went back to his library and picked up his book again, his thoughts reverting to the news which the colonel had brought him today. It was little enough, but had a few points of interest. Horace Blackman was now willing to give up his fellow smugglers if the government would not charge him with treason as well as smuggling, thus eliminating his risk of being hanged for his crimes, and Lord Liverpool was impatient to buy his information. As proof of his good faith he had revealed that one of his partners was a "society gent" who seemed to know his way around the gambling hells of London. Darcy wondered if any of his own acquaintance were either desperate enough or stupid enough to turn traitor. There were any number of young gentlemen of the *ton* who might consider such a venture a lark and not think of the implications of smuggling guns to their country's enemies, or else they might assume that their family connections could rescue them from any consequences of their dangerously foolish behaviour.

It could even be someone in the prince's circle; Darcy knew that this was what concerned Colonel Fitzwilliam. A society buck who felt slighted in some way, or who simply had no morals, and became involved with a group of men who wished to enhance their arms business by assassinating the Prince Regent could pose a serious danger to both the prince and to Darcy's cousin Fitzwilliam. Darcy pulled himself up. It did not do to allow his imagination free rein. With any luck, Blackman would reveal his accomplices very soon, and it was likely that his associates had abandoned their assassination scheme, if it existed, after Blackman's arrest.

He shut his unheeded book and replaced it on the shelf before he went upstairs to change into his evening clothes.

Elizabeth and Lambert went through the same routine they had used before the Elliots' ball; with the older maid taking charge of Georgiana's hair while Durand watched attentively and assisted with the details.

Since Georgiana had worn her sea-green gown to the earlier ball, Elizabeth had helped her select material for another to wear to her aunt's ball. It was a magnificent monochrome creation of translucent gold tissue and lace with a white lining, low cut in the bodice and with puffed sleeves that ended just above her long, satiny white gloves. It would make a perfect frame for Lady Anne's diamonds, which she wore again around her neck and on her ears, with a diamond brooch to embellish her hair. After Georgiana was ready, Elizabeth hurriedly dressed in her wedding gown and her sapphires, which were among the jewels which had been refashioned, and they were both ready by the time the carriage pulled up to the door.

They arrived at Longford House a half hour before the ball was to start so they could take their places in the reception line when the guests began arriving. Lady Whitwell informed them that she had sent a routine invitation to the Prince Regent for the ball and had been surprised when she received an acknowledgement informing her that His Majesty would pay a call during the ball.

"His Majesty will give our ball significant cachet, but we must now delegate one of the servants to watch for his carriage so we can greet him properly." She added dryly, "I cannot imagine that our little ball would hold much interest for His Majesty, so most likely he will stay only a few minutes." Turning to her niece, she added, "Georgiana, my dear, you look lovely. It will be a long night for you, so let us go into the library; a very small glass of wine will fortify you for the tasks ahead of you."

After a few minutes, Lord St. George appeared from upstairs and joined Georgiana where she sat next to the decanter sipping her wine while the rest talked in the hall about the arrangements for the ball and Lady Whitwell instructed them in their roles.

"My dear cousin Georgiana," St. George said suavely, "I am happy to be able to spend a few minutes alone with you. I have wanted to talk to you for some time."

"Really?" she asked acerbically, her brows lifted.

He did not appear to notice her repressive tone and continued with an affectionate smile, "Yes, my dear. I have been quite over-come since seeing you again after our long separation. You are a beautiful woman, Georgiana, and I am deeply in love with you. I hope that you will consent to be my wife."

He looked at her longingly and awaited her answer.

"I am sorry, Cousin, but I cannot," she said quietly.

He started and stared at her. "What?"

He made a motion with his hand as if he wished to recall his exclamation.

"I said that I will not marry you," she enunciated slowly.

"And why not, may I ask?" he said, his voice rising.

"I do not think that we are compatible, Cousin," she said, looking at him steadily.

"What are you waiting for, a duke?" he said with a curl of his lip. "I cannot imagine why else you would reject my suit."

"No, I do not imagine that you can, and that is part of the problem with your proposal," she said coldly.

"Well I hope you are not waiting for a duke to ask you, because, my dear cousin, you are neither rich enough nor beautiful enough to capture one," he hissed.

Georgiana looked at him with a steely eye that caused him to momentarily quail then she said, very quietly, "I fear, Cousin, that you have forgotten how you treated me when I was a child; however, I have *not* forgotten any of the times that you pushed me, or pulled my hair, or maliciously broke my toys. I also suspect that you now find my company acceptable only because my husband will be the recipient of £30,000 when I marry. I, on the other hand, have no desire to marry a spoilt child who will throw away his patrimony and my dowry on gambling and dissipation."

Lord St. George glared at her speechlessly for a moment then attempted to gather the shreds of his dignity and said distantly, "Well, I would not want to pressure you into a marriage that was distasteful to you, Cousin."

"Excellent," she said and immediately set down her half-filled wineglass and left the library.

When the first carriage pulled up, Georgiana had rejoined her family in the hall and appeared to be ready to greet their guests, but Elizabeth was surprised to see that her colour was high and her eyes glittered darkly. She did not have time to talk to her before the first couple appeared, but she watched her covertly during the long reception line. Whatever had upset Georgiana, she did her part correctly, if not with perfect ease, introducing Elizabeth to those guests who had not met her previously. Elizabeth turned from making conversation with an arriving family she had met at an earlier party and realised that the colonel had also arrived and appeared to have been there for some while. She was diverted to see that he had taken a place at one side of Georgiana, while Lord St. George stood stiffly at her other side.

As the first rush of guests passed, Lady Whitwell signalled the orchestra to start the dancing. Lord St. George claimed the first dance with Georgiana, bowing very formally to her. After a preliminary short number while the dancers sorted themselves into lines, with Lord St. George and Georgiana at the head, they struck up a lively dance. Elizabeth and Darcy had been placed within sight of the refreshment table where they could inform Lady Whitwell if it needed attention, and Elizabeth watched Georgiana with veiled apprehension. Her eyes were again glittering above her thin smile, while her partner's face was an unreadable mask, his feelings betrayed only by the equally narrow line of his mouth.

"I think Georgiana and Lord St. George must have quarrelled," Elizabeth whispered to Darcy.

He turned his attention to the dancers and, after watching them for a few moments, nodded. "I think you must be right. What do you suppose they are quarrelling about?"

"I do not know," she said vaguely as she stared at them and then added under her breath, "but I could make an educated guess."

The first dances finished. Lord St. George bowed stiffly again to Georgiana after leading her from the floor, while she returned the bare minimum of a curtsey. Colonel Fitzwilliam came to claim the two dances for which he had engaged her, and she turned to him with a slow smile, which continued to play about her lips all during their dances. She again lifted her eyes to his each time they faced each other in the figure. The colonel seemed pleased enough with his partner but glanced frequently at his brother, a slight frown between his brows. Lord St. George was partnering Miss Bingley and she, at any rate, seemed very happy with the attention and her face was wreathed in smiles during the dances.

Georgiana tried not to let the quarrel ruin her evening, and she managed to avoid meeting Lord St. George off the dance floor. St. George and the colonel did their duties as the sons of the house and made sure that every young woman had her share of partners, but she was greatly relieved when the colonel asked her for a second pair of dances before supper. As soon as their dances finished, Georgiana gathered her courage and said, "Shall we go out on the terrace for a few minutes? It is quite crowded in here and the night is beautiful."

He bowed and offered her his arm and they made their way around the dance floor to where several French doors opened onto the terrace, which was flooded with light from the ballroom. Georgiana saw Lord St. George coming towards them with a deter-mined expression and she flung a pleading look across the room to Elizabeth, who caught her eye and immediately assessed the situa-tion and intercepted St. George.

"Lord St. George! We were just discussing the prospects for the racing season. Do you have an opinion?"

St. George politely turned to her and found himself drawn into the discussion, and Georgiana gave a sigh of relief. She boldly led the way through the French doors and onto the terrace, where marble benches attracted the many couples who needed a breath of air. They could sit and talk in relative privacy without being completely unchaperoned. The colonel led her to a bench in full sight of the ballroom and sat next to her. A nervous shiver ran through her as they sat in silence. When the colonel finally stirred and spoke, his voice was barely above a whisper, "So, Cousin, have you recovered from your terrible experience at the beginning of the season?"

She looked at him; his face was outlined by the moonlight, but its expression was hidden.

"Oh, yes. I am very well. I just wish that I could be sure that Mr. Walker would not bother us again. I-I had nightmares after you rescued me, but they are fading. I suppose only marriage will release me from the fear that he will try again."

She could see his eyes close for a moment, his face giving nothing away.

"I wish that I could assure you of your safety, my dear cousin. I hope it will not be long before we are free of him."

A thought occurred to her and she urgently leaned towards him.

"You would not do anything to punish him yourself, would you, Colonel?"

He sat up a little straighter and looked searchingly at her.

"You are not concerned about Walker, are you, Georgiana?"

She took a deep breath to calm her racing pulse. Quite deliberately, she put her trembling hand on his arm and looked directly into his face, hopeful that the moonlight which hid his visage would illuminate hers.

"No, I am concerned about *you*, Colonel. Much as I long for vengeance against Walker, I do not wish for you to risk your freedom and your reputation by dealing with him yourself. Justice will out, and he will undoubtedly receive what he deserves without our intervention."

"I suppose. It is a very unsatisfying resolution, however, when I feel so murderously angry about his actions."

Georgiana smiled at him, hoping that the dim light hid the flush on her face.

"Do not worry, my dearest cousin. As soon as I am married my dowry will belong to my husband, and Walker will have no reason to make another attempt against me."

The colonel stared at her for a few seconds, his eyes searching her face. Before he could say more, a lull in the music sent half a dozen couples onto the terrace in search of cool air and Georgiana gave a silent sigh of frustration. She wished she had the courage to ask him what he was thinking behind his unreadable countenance, but she feared that she would not want to know his answer to the direct question.

After a moment, Colonel Fitzwilliam said, "Shall we go back in? Supper will be served very soon."

She tried to smile. "Yes, let us go in."

Later, after supper had finished and the dancing had resumed, Georgiana happened to glance over at Lady Whitwell just at the moment when a footman approached and whispered in her ear. She quietly signalled the orchestra leader and they struck up "God Save the King" just as the Prince Regent and several of his retinue entered the ballroom. The family all greeted him very formally, and he spoke with each of them for a moment. When he reached Darcy and Elizabeth, he raised her from her curtsey and said, "Ah, dear lady, I believe that we met not two days ago." He glanced at Darcy with a rather malicious look in his eye. "I hope that your esteemed husband will forgive me if I beg for your hand for the next dance."

Elizabeth raised one brow slightly but consented with a graceful smile and nod. Darcy bowed to his ruler to indicate his approval of the invitation, but his face was a polite mask. Elizabeth advanced to the dance floor, her hand on the Prince Regent's arm, and stood at the head of the line for the start of the dance.

The Prince Regent was a personable man and, in spite of his corpulence, his smile was attractive and he seemed to put himself out to be agreeable to Elizabeth. Georgiana watched as her sister answered his conversation politely, but rather warily, her face showing nothing but calm interest in her partner's conversation, but she was sure she saw a sardonic twinkle in Elizabeth's eye.

She glanced over at the family group and saw Miss Bingley standing with Viscount St. George. Miss Bingley's eyes were narrowed and she whispered rapidly in the viscount's ear. Darcy was watching the Prince Regent without expression until Elizabeth smiled at him across the room; his face relaxed and he sketched a small bow in her direction.

When the dance finished the Prince Regent escorted his partner off of the floor to where Darcy was standing and thanked her for the pleasure of dancing with her. She gave him a reserved smile and curtseyed as she said, "I thank you, Your Majesty, for the great honour."

After a few more minutes of conversation with selected guests, the prince and his entourage left and the ball went on, unchanged except for the murmurs of wonder around the room over the honour conferred by the appearance of the Prince Regent, and the fact that he had danced with Mrs. Darcy.

When the dancing had resumed and the guests' attention had turned away for a moment, Elizabeth whispered to Darcy, "And what am I to make of that situation? I am perplexed as to why the Prince Regent chose to ask me to dance."

Darcy smiled wryly. "I think that His Majesty was curious about you. He also occasionally likes to show his power as an arbiter of fashion and has apparently decided that he endorses your entrance into the haut monde. His approval will give you entrée into all levels of society, should you wish it."

Elizabeth gave a small shrug and went back to watching the dancers.

After the Prince Regent's visit a number of the guests who had barely acknowledged the Darcys when they arrived came over to talk to them. Several of the women proffered invitations to tea to Elizabeth, and some of the gentlemen suddenly seemed to recognise Darcy, inviting him to ride or to meet them at their club for a glass of wine. Both Darcys responded with all the courtesy required, but noncommittally, and soon the sycophants faded away again.

Late in the evening, Georgiana looked around for the colonel, but she could not see him. She saw Elizabeth having a glass of punch at the refreshment table and made her way over to her through the crowd, "Have you seen Colonel Fitzwilliam, Elizabeth?"

Elizabeth glanced around the room. "I am sorry, Georgiana, I have not seen him in quite some time."

Georgiana looked disappointed, although she tried to hide her chagrin. "I was hoping to dance with him again tonight."

Elizabeth was about to reassure her sister when a sudden wave of dizziness overcame her. Georgiana saw the colour drain out of her face and said in alarm, "Are you unwell, Elizabeth?"

Darcy turned from where he had been talking to a group of gentlemen when he heard his sister's voice.

"Elizabeth? Are you ill?"

Elizabeth tried to subdue the dizziness but finally said in a whisper, "My dear, could you please help me out of the room?"

He took her arm and they left unobtrusively, leaving Georgiana standing in the ballroom with a worried frown on her face. As soon as they reached the hall Elizabeth could no longer hold herself up, and she sagged on Darcy's arm. He lifted her and carried her upstairs to one of the sitting-rooms before gently setting her down on the settee. As he put a small cushion under her head he said firmly, "Elizabeth, I am calling the doctor."

She protested weakly, "No, I am feeling better already. The ballroom was simply too warm. If I just lie here a few minutes I will be fine."

Lady Whitwell entered the room. "Georgiana told me that you were feeling faint. I have sent for the doctor and he will be here soon."

Darcy thanked his aunt while she put her hand on Elizabeth's forehead. "She does not seem to have a fever. Are you still feeling unwell, my dear?"

"I am better, thank you," Elizabeth said as she tried to sit up. "It was just a momentary dizziness."

Darcy and Lady Whitwell both said "No" firmly, and she was unable to oppose their combined wills; she reclined again.

The doctor arrived in a quarter hour and the others stood by while he spoke with Elizabeth for quite some time and took her pulse. When he finished Darcy asked anxiously, "How is she, Doctor?"

The doctor smiled wryly, "She is fine. She needs to rest."

When Darcy looked rather perplexed the doctor added, with a slightly ironic smile, "You are going to be a father, sir."

Lady Whitwell murmured, "I suspected as much" before she thanked the doctor and escorted him out.

Darcy crossed the room and sat at Elizabeth's side; she smiled beatifically at him and took his hand.

"I am going to have a baby."

He put his arms around her and kissed her tenderly on the forehead. "How soon?

"The doctor thinks in about five months."

He kissed her again, and they both forgot about the ball in their happiness and in his relief that she was not ill. After a few minutes, Darcy suddenly sat back and chuckled.

"What are you laughing about, my love?" Elizabeth said with a quizzical smile.

"It just occurred to me that I should have been prepared for this. It was very unlikely that you would let your sister Jane perform an act as significant as having a child without you joining her soon after, as befits the younger sister."

She laughed with him and admitted the truth of his observation.

Darcy called for their carriage and arranged for his aunt to bring Georgiana home after the ball before he escorted Elizabeth carefully downstairs. Georgiana was hovering near the door to the ballroom and saw them come down. She floated over to them with a beaming smile and embraced first Elizabeth and then her brother.

"I am so happy for you both that I cannot even begin to tell you. Are you taking her home?" This last to her brother.

"Yes. I think an early evening would be prudent."

"Undoubtedly. I will see you both tomorrow." She kissed them and hurried back to her ball.

On the way home, Darcy told Elizabeth about the Prince Regent's interest in her during his audience in March, which he had forgotten until the ball. She was amused that their marriage could have an effect so opposite to Lady Catherine's dire predictions.

A thought seemed to occur to him, and he asked, "Did you have time to talk to Georgiana and find out why she and St. George are not speaking?"

"No, I am afraid that I forgot," she said.

"Well," he commented philosophically, "if it is important, I am sure we will eventually find out." The matter was dropped.

The next day found a great increase in the number of invitations that were received at Ashbourne House. Darcy cynically discarded most of them as bids to gain their favour after the Prince Regent's actions the night before. One of them, however, he held for a moment, his lips pursed.

Elizabeth was writing a letter to her friend Charlotte and telling her about her expectations, but she looked up at him and asked curiously, "What is it, my dear?"

"An invitation to a party at Lord Rathburn's this evening. He is a member of the prince's coterie and was with him when he came to the ball last night. My initial impulse is to discard it with the others, but Rathburn was at Cambridge with me and was not a bad fellow. We have not kept in contact, but perhaps we should attend; it might be interesting for you to see how the highest circles entertain. I would not want to take Georgiana into those circles until I see how they behave these days, but she has a party this evening with my aunt and uncle. Some of the *haut ton* affairs can be rather decadent but we can always leave if it is too warm for our taste."

"I am almost afraid to ask what sorts of things go on at these affairs," Elizabeth said dryly.

"I would not even mention some of the things in the presence of a lady; however, Rathburn's invitation says that it is 'an evening with a few friends.'"

"I have no objections if you wish to go, dear," said Elizabeth, and she continued to sort the visiting cards that had been received the day before.

After Darcy had left the room, Georgiana said, "Elizabeth you must tell me about your party. I will be eager to hear what it was like."

"And you must tell me about your evening with your aunt and uncle."

"I can already tell you about that. We are dining at a distant and ancient relative's house because my aunt does not want her to feel left out of the Season. We will then go to a small party hosted by my uncle's brother, where there will be no guests under age fifty. It will be tedious but a great relief to not have young men on all sides pressing me for a dance. Particularly since it is usually those with whom I do not wish to dance who exert the most pressure."

The next morning Georgiana and Elizabeth met in the music-room after breakfast to discuss their respective evenings. Georgiana summarised hers by saying, "My evening went exactly as predicted, except that my aunt's distant cousin is a sprightly octogenarian who entertained us with slanderous stories of the royal family from when she was young while my aunt and uncle tried to change the topic to something less daring. She was delightful!"

Elizabeth laughed and said, "My evening was a bit more complicated. We arrived at Lord Rathburn's residence a half hour after the start of the party and were greeted by our host before entering the drawing-room. Lord Rathburn is unmarried and his cousin does the honours as hostess. He received us with courtesy, although his speech was somewhat slurred—which was explained by the champagne glass he held while greeting his guests—and, in turn, introduced us to his cousin, Miss Foster, before handing us over to a footman who bowed us into the salon. The crush of people in the room was incredible, but we managed to make our way slowly to the refreshment table, hampered by frequent stops to greet your brother's acquaintances and to introduce me. I could hear music in the adjoining room and presumed that there was dancing but could not see over the sea of heads between me and the door. The refreshments were piled high on the table and the champagne was flowing very freely.

"After obtaining a cup of punch for each of us, Mr. Darcy led the way to the inner room in search of breathing space."

"So much for 'a few friends,'" Georgiana murmured.

"Quite. The dance floor was sparsely filled as a cotillion began and we managed to find two seats near a window where we could observe the dancers and find some relief from the suffocating heat. I did not recognise any of the people in the two rooms through which we had passed, and your brother did not stop except to briefly introduce me, so I assumed that he had not found any acquaintances to his taste. It would have been difficult to converse in either of the rooms in any case because of the terrific clamour of voices and music. It was absolutely deafening.

"After watching the dancers and greeting the occasional associate or old schoolfellow for about half an hour, Mr. Darcy, looking very bored, offered to fetch me another drink, which I accepted gratefully. I was very warm and was happy to cool myself with my fan and look out of the window at the full moon rising over the treetops.

"He had not been gone long when the string quartet struck up a different sort of tune than those that had preceded it. I looked around at the dance floor and my eyes nearly stood out of my head as I saw the dancers pair off in couples. Although I had never seen it danced, I realised immediately that they were starting a waltz. I was put completely out of countenance, as you might imagine, and debated with myself whether it would be preferable to remain where I was and have it thought that I condoned such activities or to try to make my way quietly towards the salon and risk losing Mr. Darcy in the crowd. As I hesitated, trying to appear both detached from the dancing and unconcerned, I saw a movement to my right from the corner of my eye and turned with relief only to find myself confronted with—not my husband as I had expected but—Lord Rathburn. Our host bowed unsteadily, clearly much the worse for drink and requested my hand for the dance. As I paused—I was too shocked to answer immediately—he mumbled, 'C'mon Mrs. Darcy. I'm sure your husband wouldn't mind you dancing with an ol' schoolfellow.' His tongue stumbled over the final words, but he managed another wobbly bow."

"Do you mean that he thought that you would allow a complete stranger to touch your… your *person* while you danced? That is unbelievable!" Georgiana gasped.

"Without a doubt. I was finally able to exert myself enough to say, 'I am sorry, I do not waltz, my lord,' and was frantically racking my mind to find a way of extricating myself without causing an unpleasant scene when relief came from an unexpected quarter. A voice behind me, filled with disgust, said sharply, 'Rathburn, you are disgracefully drunk or you would not even consider insulting a lady such as Mrs. Darcy with your offensive suggestion.'

"I turned and was face to face with Lord Byron.

"Rathburn attempted to draw himself up in affronted dignity but only succeeded in throwing off whatever precarious balance he still possessed and was forced to lean on Lord Byron to remain upright.

"Our host started to say, 'I say, Byron, you've no right...' but Lord Byron interrupted him. 'I have the right of any man of culture and manners to prevent an insult to a lady.'

"He stopped a young lady in a scandalously diaphanous gown who was passing and said heartily, 'Mrs. Carleton, our host desires to waltz with you but is too modest to ask. I beg you to indulge him.'

"The woman smiled and eyed Rathburn before she said, 'I am not sure that Lord Rathburn is up to the waltz at this moment, Lord Byron.'

"Lord Byron pleaded with her, 'Do try, please, for my sake. He will be desolated if he does not waltz tonight. I would be most grateful.' He gave her an intimate smile and she finally agreed, taking her partner's hand and steering him carefully onto the dance floor.

"He turned to me and began to say, 'I apologise for Rathburn's behaviour, Mrs. Darcy. I am sure that if he was not in a drunken stupor he would not behave like such an idiot...,' when Mr. Darcy suddenly reappeared behind his left shoulder, to my intense relief. Following my gaze, Lord Byron looked around at your brother, who towered over him, and greeted him coolly. Mr. Darcy bowed courteously enough, but I saw his eyes blaze for a moment and I knew he had seen my predicament and come to rescue me from both my host and my rescuer. I decided that the best thing I could do was to extricate us all from this embarrassing situation, so I stood up and turned to Lord Byron and said, 'I hope that you will excuse me, my lord, but I am not feeling very well. The heat is stifling and I was only waiting for his return to ask my husband to take me home.'

"He returned with, 'I am desolated, Mrs. Darcy, but I hope that you will feel better with some fresh air. Perhaps we will meet another time under more auspicious circumstances.'

"I managed to say, 'Perhaps. I thank you for your assistance.'

"Mr. Darcy took my arm and, as we were walking away, said, just barely loud enough for Lord Byron to hear, 'I apologise my dear, you should not be in such a crowd in your delicate condition.'"

Georgiana gasped and covered her mouth. "No, I do not believe my brother would say such a thing!" A giggle broke through and she glanced at the closed door.

"I would have laughed, too, if the situation had not been so embarrassing. We left the room as quickly as we could through the throng, which seemed even more crowded than when we had arrived. Our host was still struggling through the waltz with his partner and his cousin was hidden somewhere in the crowd, obviating the need to say goodnight. When we were safely in the carriage your brother began to whisper furiously, 'I am absolutely livid that disgraceful rake had the audacity to ask you to waltz with him! How dare he insult you with his disgusting attentions!'

"I tried to calm him for several minutes, since there had really been no harm done, and I do not think that our host was trying to offer me an insult. I suspect that Lord Rathburn thinks any woman would be eager to waltz with him. After all, his patron, the prince, has given the dance his tacit approval.

"Finally, when Mr. Darcy's anger did not abate, I said archly, 'Well, I certainly learnt how the haut monde enjoys itself, did I not?' and that seemed to bring him to himself. It was quite an evening. We both agreed that we were glad you were not with us!"

"How disgraceful their behaviour is!" Georgiana breathed.

"It is. There were, however, plenty of couples who were waltzing, so there are obviously some who think that it is acceptable. And truthfully, it would not really be so shocking if all of the couples were married."

Georgiana lowered her voice and glanced at the door. "What does the waltz look like?"

Elizabeth walked over and peeked out of the door to make sure there was no one to interrupt them, shut the door again then took Georgiana's right hand in her left and put her right hand at Georgiana's waist, standing about twelve inches from her and facing her. She tried to imitate the steps but they kept tripping over each other's feet, so Elizabeth tried to show her by herself, turning in graceful circles as she swept around the room.

"I am not sure if I have the footwork down, but this gives you an idea. It actually would be quite beautiful to watch, if it were not so scandalous to see unmarried couples dancing that way. And... Georgiana?" She stopped dancing and looked intently at her sister.

"Yes?"

"Please do not tell your brother that I told you about last evening or showed you the dance—I believe that he would not approve of this conversation. However, I feel that it is better to know how to avoid society's pitfalls than to pretend that they do not exist."

Georgiana smiled impishly and said, "Of course, Elizabeth, I would not *dream* of mentioning this to him."

Chapter 23

So he passed over, and the
Trumpets sounded for him on the other side.

—JOHN BUNYAN, *THE PILGRIM'S PROGRESS*

LATE THE NEXT MORNING, GEORGIANA WAS SITTING ALONE AT the piano again working on her new sonata. Elizabeth had retired upstairs to rest, and Darcy had gone to his library to meet his man of business. The house was silent, except for the occasional sound of a quiet footstep as the servants went about their duties. Georgiana was surprised when Burton announced Colonel Fitzwilliam. She felt her cheeks redden a little in both trepidation and embarrassment but greeted him politely and asked Burton to bring them some coffee. When she rose to move away from the instrument he exclaimed, "No, do not move! I'll pull a chair up next to you."

She sank back down on the bench but picked up Lucky, who had been sitting beside her, and put him on her lap with her fingers in his hair to conceal their trembling. She stared at the keys, feeling as if a hand was twisting her stomach into several knots. The colonel asked her how Elizabeth was feeling, and she was about to answer when the coffee arrived. She thanked the footman breathlessly, following him with her eyes as he departed, and closed the door. The colonel cleared his throat as she turned back to stare again at the pianoforte keys and, after a long pause, said, "Georgiana... I am glad that you are alone this morning because I wanted to talk to you."

He seemed to lose his voice momentarily, and Georgiana glanced up at him quickly and then back down at the keys. His face was flushed. He pulled at his collar, cleared his throat again, and finally said, "I want to tell you that, well, that I-I love you." He took a deep breath and hurried on "I mean, I, of course, have always loved you as a cousin, but now, in the last few weeks, I have come to realise that you are the most important person in the world to me, and I wanted to know if you would consider... if-you-would-do-me-the-honour-of-becoming-my-wife..."

He stopped in confusion and then leapt to his feet as her face blanched white and she closed her eyes.

He stammered in dismay, "Are you all right, Georgiana? I-I am so sorry; I did not mean to upset you..."

Her face suffused with colour again, and she opened her eyes and turned to him. She took his hand and looked up at him with a smile of such happiness on her face that he was unable to support himself; he sank back down onto his chair as she whispered, "I thought that you would never ask."

Interpreting this correctly as an assent, Colonel Fitzwilliam took her hand, placed it gently against his heart, and said, "Georgiana, my darling, I have been in agony for, oh, I do not know how long—it seems like an eternity—trying to decide if I dared tell you how I feel. I was so afraid that you would say no, or, worse yet, say yes only because you felt an obligation to me as your guardian."

They talked for some minutes, he of how he had gradually come to realise that his feelings for her were not those of merely a cousin or a guardian, and she of how she had grown to love him and how his rescue during her kidnapping made her realise that his veneer of calm and ease concealed a man of deep feeling. She also revealed how she had struggled to try to make him see that she was no longer a child. The colonel finally said, still a little diffidently, "I have been walking around the last few weeks feeling very strange. When I see myself in a glass I look exactly the same on the outside as I ever have, but inside I feel rather like the vase over there would look," he pointed to a bouquet on the table in a crystal vase, "if you struck it with a hammer."

"Shattered?" she whispered with a small smile.

"Indeed, yes, shattered is the perfect description of my state. I wondered that it was not visible to everyone I met. I left the ball early last night, risking my mother's displeasure, because I could no longer bear to see you dancing with so many men who were younger, richer, and more handsome than I am. I have so little to offer you beyond my devotion, and you deserve everything good in the world." He added grimly, "As your guardian, I also felt that you could do so much better than a soldier with no patrimony."

"Ah, but the problem with these younger, richer, and more handsome men is that I do not love them. I do not care about anyone but you, dearest Edward."

He kissed her hands affectionately and softly continued, "I was particularly afraid that my brother would make you an offer and that you would accept him," he said. "He has so much more to offer you in the way of fortune, but it would be unbearable to me to see you married to him when I would meet you frequently as a close relative—and you would be the wife of another man, one not nearly good enough for you." He smiled sadly. "Not that I have even a fraction of your worth, my dearest cousin."

Georgiana turned to him with a small smile. "Lord St. George did make me an offer last night before the ball." Fitzwilliam sat up straighter in surprise. "I turned him down. Your brother seems to think that I am unable to remember how badly he treated me when I was a child," she said tartly. "It was understandable that a young man of more than twenty years would not be interested in spending time with a little girl fourteen years younger than he, but he was always scornful and cruel to me when you and my brother were not present. I am afraid that I don't believe his character has undergone any revolution since then, in spite of his compliments and attention." She added in a softer tone, "You, on the other hand, dear Edward, were invariably kind to me."

"I hope that you have not agreed to marry me merely because I was not unkind to you when you were six years old."

"I am afraid my gratitude to you for teaching me to ride my pony does not extend that far!" she exclaimed.

He kissed her hands again and then went on to tell her, "I felt for a long time that I would rather risk losing you than to take the chance of putting a wall between us forever if I was mistaken about your feelings; but I finally realised that the years would stretch out in an eternity of regret if I did not at least try."

They soon agreed that he would go speak to her brother immediately and ask for his consent. He left the room just as Elizabeth was entering and bowed to her with a distrait expression on his face. She turned to Georgiana with a questioning look when he had shut the door. Georgiana promptly threw herself into her sister's arms and burst into tears.

When the colonel appeared quietly at the library door, Darcy was reading some documents but was alone at his desk, his man of business having left some minutes before.

"Darcy," he said, and his cousin looked up, startled. "Darcy," he said again, his voice tight and strained, "I have asked Georgiana to marry me and she has accepted me. I hope that you will give your consent."

Darcy rolled his eyes heavenwards and closed them briefly before saying in a pained voice, "Good God, man, what took you so long?"

He opened his eyes, laughed briefly at the sheepish look on his cousin's face, and added more seriously, "I will most happily give my consent, Fitzwilliam."

The colonel began to say, not very fluently, that he knew that he had nothing to offer Georgiana in the way of fortune, but Darcy stopped him with an upraised hand, saying quietly, "Except yourself, Fitzwilliam, except yourself. If marriage with you is what Georgiana wants then it is enough."

They shook hands with all the warmth of their many years of mutual regard and respect and then returned together to the drawing-room where Georgiana was sitting silently, holding tightly to Elizabeth's hand and waiting for them. When she saw their faces, she ran to her brother and embraced him, shedding a few more joyous tears, while Elizabeth warmly shook the colonel's hand and wished him joy. When the congratulations were finished and everyone had expressed their pleasure in the prospect of the cousins' marriage several times, the colonel finally recollected himself and said, "I had better go to Longford House and tell my parents. They will be very happy to finally have one of their sons bring home a bride, especially one with such an irreproachable family background." He grinned at Georgiana.

They all repeated their congratulations and, after extracting a promise to join them for dinner that night, sent him away.

Georgiana spent the next few hours in a state of happy distraction, quite unable to believe that all her hopes had been realised. Even Lucky had to resort to barking at her several times to get her attention when she was staring into space instead of rolling his ball for him to chase. She finally gave up her attempts to remain calm and had Durand escort her to Freemont House as early as she could decently call. When Catherine came down she said, "Why Georgiana! How good it is to see you!"

Georgiana clutched her friend's arm and said, "May we go to your room?"

Catherine raised her brows, but said, "Of course, my dear."

She directed Durand to the servants' hall and took Georgiana directly upstairs to her sitting-room.

"What is it?" Her face was eager.

Georgiana took a deep breath and said, "I am engaged!"

"What?"

"Yes." She nodded emphatically and grinned at her friend. "I am engaged to my cousin, Colonel Fitzwilliam."

"The Colonel! You astonish me, but I am very happy for you, my dear! Tell me all about it. I had thought that the elder brother might be the one; do not think that I missed his attentions to you!"

"Actually… Lord St. George did ask me, but I turned him down." Georgiana swept St. George away with a flick of her fingers. "Somewhere, somehow, this spring I realised where my affections lay; and it was not with my elder cousin! I suppose when I compared the gentlemen of London to my tall, handsome, easy-tempered, gentle, and completely exasperating cousin I realised that I no longer wished to be his 'little cousin' any more."

Catherine embraced her friend and then swung her around the room. "You sly thing! I saw you watching him, but I had no idea that you were sizing him up for matrimony."

Georgiana laughed, but her expression was a little wry. "It happened rather suddenly… a bit like falling off of a horse, a combination of pain and the pleasure that one has survived the experience! But truthfully, I tried to be circumspect until I had an idea of his mind. Just when I was ready to despair he appeared on my doorstep—or at least in my brother's drawing-room—and laid his heart at my feet." She grinned at her friend. "But, perhaps you would have noticed if you had not been so deep in conversation with Sir Robert Blake."

Catherine endeavoured to smile mysteriously but was too over-come by delight to tease her friend. They talked for almost an hour, until Elizabeth came with the carriage and gathered up Georgiana to visit the Bingleys; there was much to tell them.

Jane was surprised and delighted at Georgiana's news, and Miss Bingley was warmly congratulatory to "dear Georgiana," although she had a rather speculative look on her face as she wished her joy.

That evening Colonel Fitzwilliam came early while the ladies were dressing for dinner and drew Darcy into the library. Darcy looked at the expression on his face and said, "What in the world is the matter, Fitzwilliam?"

"I just wanted to let you know," he said uncomfortably, "that I went home this afternoon to tell my parents that Georgiana and I were engaged." He clasped his hands behind his back and stared over Darcy's head at the books behind him. "They, of course, were very pleased with the news—however, my brother was also there. He was astounded when I told my news and said 'I do not believe it!' So I asked him to what he was referring. He said that he did not believe that Georgiana could be so stupid that she would marry me."

"And what did you say?" Darcy asked quietly.

"I foolishly said, 'Do you mean because she would turn you down for me?'"

"Did she?" Darcy said, glancing up in surprise.

"Yes, she told me this afternoon. He asked her to marry him before my mother's ball and was sure that she would not turn down the Viscount St. George, future Earl of Whitwell," Fitzwilliam said bitterly, starting to pace around the room. He suddenly stopped and looked at Darcy with a ghost of his usual mischievous grin. "Actually, I gather from the little that Georgiana said, and from his reaction, that she gave him quite a dressing down. I wish that I could have seen it. Seeing my dear brother receive such a set-down would have been salutary."

Having been the recipient of such a dressing down himself, Darcy felt a brief pang of sympathy for St. George; however, he roused himself to say, "Elizabeth noticed that she looked fairly put out when they rejoined us before the ball, but she did not have a chance to talk to her before the guests arrived. Georgiana seemed to be fine after greeting the guests and Elizabeth did not pursue the subject. So, what did you do after St. George's comments?"

The colonel stopped pacing and stared up at the ceiling, looking embarrassed. "I asked him to go outside with me for a private conversation. I then told him that I did not ever want to hear him say such a thing about my fiancée, or any other respectable young woman, again. He sneered at me and asked me what I was going to do to enforce that demand—so I hit him."

"You what?!" Darcy sat up in his chair.

"You heard me. I am deeply sorry that Georgiana's name should become involved in such a sordid display, but I can at least say that there were no witnesses to it." His lip curled as he added, "My brother, however, will not be partaking of the gaieties of the Season for the next week or so, until the black eye that I gave him fades."

Darcy murmured, "*A verbis ad verbera.*"

Fitzwilliam gave his cousin a sharp look and continued, "My parents are absolutely furious with him. My mother is not speaking to him and my father took him into the library while St. George was still holding a wet cloth to his eye and told him (in a booming voice that I am sure all of the servants heard) that he was ashamed to call him his son and that if he could prevent him from inheriting the estate and title he would. I have never seen my father so angry. He also cut off his allowance, which he does have the discretion to do. St. George is furious and unrepentant, and you know how stubborn he is." He sighed deeply. "What a mess, and just when I was ready to be happily engaged and enjoy my loss of freedom. How did he get to be like this?"

"I do not know, but I know that your mother and father have always seemed to be excellent parents and have tried to make him be a responsible adult. Still, if you recall, he was always very self-centred. I can only think that he must have been born that way. The two of you have always looked very much alike and been the complete opposite in temper. Do you remember when we found him throwing rocks at the barn cat he had tied up at Whitwell Abbey? He just shrugged when we yelled at him and asked why we were so angry: 'it was just an old cat.'"

"Yes, I remember that and a thousand other things. What upsets me the most right now, however, is that I will have to tell Georgiana something about it; she will wonder why St. George isn't at any parties over the next week or so."

Darcy drummed his fingers on the desk. "Very true. You will have to tell her. She will probably be embarrassed that you were fighting over her, but on the other hand, you can't leave her in ignorance; she may have more embarrassment having people asking her where he is or saying something inadvertently." After a moment of silence, he gave his cousin a sly smile. "Besides, what woman would not be secretly happy to have her fiancé proved to be a knight in shining armour, willing to battle for her honour?"

Colonel Fitzwilliam blushed and then grimaced. "I will talk to her this evening and tell her something."

"I suggest that you tell her *everything*. As Elizabeth once pointed out to your father, my sister is not one to be overcome by the truth, even if it is unpalatable, Fitzwilliam. She would not thank you for trying to 'protect' her from reality to that extent."

Fitzwilliam silently nodded his agreement.

The ladies came downstairs for dinner, and Jane and Bingley and the Gardiners arrived. Elizabeth had invited them to dine a few days before, and now there was a particularly happy reason to have the family gathered. Georgiana was wearing the green gown she had worn to the Elliots' ball, but with her pearl necklace and earrings and the bracelet the colonel had given her for her birthday, and she was flushed with happiness as she accepted their congratulations.

Colonel Fitzwilliam smiled and kissed Georgiana's hand before leading her into the dining-room at the head of the line, a position of importance that pleased Georgiana greatly.

Later, after the gentlemen had rejoined the ladies in the drawing-room, the colonel took Georgiana to the far end of the room and began talking earnestly to her. While the Gardiners and the Bingleys sat and drank their tea and coffee, Darcy asked Elizabeth to play for them and he sat next to her at the piano-forte so that the two lovers could talk in privacy. Elizabeth was halfway through a sonata when Georgiana burst out giggling. She and Darcy both looked over; Georgiana had her fingers covering her mouth and Fitzwilliam had a chagrined expression on his face. Then Georgiana took his hand and said something very quietly in his ear, which made him smile foolishly at her.

Later, when they went upstairs, Darcy explained to Elizabeth what had happened at his uncle's house, and she also laughed.

"It serves St. George right!" she exclaimed.

"It does indeed. I cannot believe that my cousin would behave in such an ill-bred fashion, particularly saying such things about Georgiana. I have half a mind to blacken his other eye!" he said scornfully.

Elizabeth laughed again. "That would be very satisfying, no doubt; however, it might be difficult to keep it hushed up if everyone in the family takes a turn at blackening his eyes."

"Unfortunately," Darcy said seriously, "there has always been a great deal of competition between my two cousins, on St. George's side at least. It is rather odd since he is the one who will inherit everything, while Fitzwilliam will get little or nothing. I suspect St. George realises that, for all his wealth and prospects, Fitzwilliam has always been the one whom everyone likes. When we were young boys, Fitzwilliam and I always went off to play without him, because even then he was an arrogant braggart who always wanted to rub our noses in the fact that he would one day be an earl. It bothered him very much that neither of us seemed much impressed by him."

"I had wondered why you never mentioned your elder cousin when you are such good friends with the colonel. It is very surprising to me that the colonel is as happy and easy as he is after having to deal with such treatment from his brother for his entire life."

"Well, his parents have always tried to improve St. George's temper and make him face the responsibilities that go along with his status, and Fitzwilliam has always been relaxed and easy; it is just his temper to be contented. My aunt must be very happy that he is marrying Georgiana."

"I am sure she is. She sent Georgiana a long note this afternoon telling her so. She wants us all to dine with them tomorrow night, if you have not made other plans."

Darcy chuckled suddenly.

"I wonder if St. George will dine with us."

They both laughed heartily.

Georgiana carried her candle to her bedside table and pulled out her diary. She had neglected it of late; she had been fearful that any words she put down would be engraved on her heart forever. Until she knew of the success or failure of her bid for the colonel's affection she had not dared to reveal more of her feelings, even to herself. Tonight, however, she could pen the love that threatened to burst out of her:

> *6 June: I can finally take up my diary again, my old friend who has stood by me through everything. Today I am the happiest of women. Today my dear Edward asked for my hand, and in a manner so warm, so passionate that I could wish for nothing more to make my happiness complete. I do not yet know when the wedding will be; we were so absorbed that we did not get to those details, but we will have plenty of time to decide those details and the rest of our lives to show how much we love each other!*

She put her pen and her book away and blew out the candle.

The next evening the Darcys arrived at Longford House for dinner, and Georgiana was embraced and kissed by her future mother- and father-in-law. Darcy and Elizabeth were told how happy they were that they would be even more closely related. They had a very enjoyable dinner and Georgiana was bubbly and talkative in her happiness. Lord St. George did not put in an appearance and was not mentioned by the family.

When they had a moment of privacy in the drawing-room, Lady Whitwell told Elizabeth how pleased she was about the engagement.

"Edward has always been my favourite son, although as a mother I should not admit it. I have been concerned about his future, since almost the entire estate is entailed; his marriage to Georgiana answers all of my concerns and, of course, makes me very happy for them both. I wish I could feel as sanguine about my eldest son's future," she said, looking rather sadly towards the staircase that led to the upper floors.

Elizabeth took her hand and patted it reassuringly. Lady Whitwell sighed for a moment and then seemed to pull herself up, smiling at Elizabeth.

"Thank you, my dear. I might as well not discuss it. I do not want to put a damper on Georgiana and Edward's happiness tonight, so we will just let the future take care of itself, shall we?"

Elizabeth agreed, and they quietly listened to Georgiana playing the pianoforte.

After they dined, they were all to go to the Bingleys for the party Jane had been planning with Kitty's help. It would be Jane's first foray into entertaining during the London Season, and Elizabeth hoped that all would go well and help establish her sister in her rightful place in society. It was to be a small party, with friends and relatives, and they would have dancing and cards and would conclude with a late supper. They hurried over their coffee and tea so that they would not be late and then left for Berkeley Square.

Chapter 24

This man of clay, son of despite.

—JOHN MILTON, *PARADISE LOST*

JANE'S PARTY WAS AN UNQUALIFIED SUCCESS. THE GUESTS included Bingley's relatives—the Hursts and Miss Bingley—as well as a number of friends of Bingley's. The Comte de Tournay was there as well, at Caroline's request Georgiana presumed. When the Darcy party entered, Miss Bingley asked whether Lord St. George was with them, and Lady Whitwell told her without hesitation, "I am so sorry, Miss Bingley, my eldest son is not feeling well tonight and so could not come. However, I am sure that he will be better soon."

Miss Bingley quickly covered her disappointment and spent the evening being charming to the count. The Blake family was at the party and Kitty was kept happy dancing and, in the intervals, talking with Edward Blake. Georgiana's friend Catherine was also there, as she and Jane had become well acquainted during the Season, and she spent the evening conversing with Sir Robert Blake when she was not with Georgiana. A whist table was set up in the small parlour adjoining the salon for those guests who could not, or would not, dance, and the dining-parlour offered a variety of refreshments. Jane had been fortunate enough to find a house-keeper for the town house who was highly respectable and very competent, and the arrangements for the party were most elegant.

The guests finally trickled out of the door at around one o'clock, leaving the host to relax with one last glass of wine in the company of his nearest relations while Jane rested her feet on a footstool. She looked pleased with the success of her little entertainment, and Elizabeth bolstered her feelings with her own compliments.

"I had a delightful time, my dear sister. Now you can relax for the remaining days of the Season and let other hostesses work to entertain you, although your triumph sets a rather high standard for them to maintain."

"Dearest Lizzy! You are always so good to me!"

"Indeed I am not! I am only stating the plain truth of the matter," Elizabeth returned with spirit as she gathered her things for the ride home.

The next morning Darcy went to his club and ran into the colonel.

"Darcy, I hoped I might find you here." He grasped his cousin's arm and drew him into the club's small library, where they were the only visitors.

"What is it, Fitzwilliam?" Darcy asked, his alert eyes scanning his cousin's face.

"I have two things to tell you, Cousin. The first is that my brother left town this morning and would not say where he was going. He merely told our father that, since he no longer had an allowance to enable him to live like a gentleman in London, he was going into the country." After a moment he added, "I wonder where he has gone?"

"And I wonder what his creditors will think of this turn," Darcy commented.

"I know not. My parents are very upset and are hoping that he will not do anything to discredit the family name."

"I think that your brother thinks more of the family name than he does the well-being of its members, but it is difficult to predict what a man will do when he is angry," he said grimly. "Unfortunately, there is not much we can do about it, whatever his plans, but I am sure your parents are going to have a disagreeable time until he reappears."

"No doubt."

Darcy started to turn towards the door, but the colonel detained him.

"You have forgotten that I have two pieces of news for you. The second is that my informant at the palace revealed to me that Captain Blackman finally told him the names of his co-conspirators in exchange for his life. I mentioned to you last time we spoke that Lord Liverpool has been pressing for a conclusion to this possible threat to the prince." He paused and looked at his cousin for a moment. "The 'W' in the letter was Jonathan Walker."

"Really?" Darcy stared at him in shock for a moment then walked over to the window and stared out, thinking about the possible ramifications of this development. "Has Walker been arrested?"

"Not yet. I have kept out of this investigation, for which I am now eternally thankful. I would hate to be examining my conscience to try to decide if I had jumped to conclusions because of my desire to implicate Walker."

"What do you think will happen?"

"My informant told me that they will arrest Walker. If he is convicted of treason it is likely he will hang. His property has already been confiscated."

"Walker does not have any property except what he administers for his father."

"Well, we will see."

"Mmmm." Darcy's mind was reeling with the news about Walker. He waved vaguely when the colonel told him goodbye.

When Darcy came home he told Elizabeth and Georgiana the news about St. George with a bleak face. He held back the information on Walker. Better that he and Fitzwilliam have no part of that. As his cousin had implied, they were both too close to the situation to be objective. Elizabeth was surprised at St. George's defection, but Georgiana shrugged indifferently.

"At least I will not have to meet him in public."

"There is, unfortunately, not much we can do about his plan, whatever it is, but I am sure that my aunt and uncle are going to have an unpleasant time over the next few weeks."

Elizabeth agreed that this was likely but could see no hope of improving the situation except to be a support to Lord St. George's parents. Darcy agreed and decided to visit his uncle that afternoon.

Several days went by without news of Lord St. George. The colonel was divided between his happiness with his engagement and concern over his brother and what he might do in the heat of his anger and resentment. He put the situation with Walker firmly out of his mind, and Georgiana tried to keep his spirits up and his mind off Lord St. George, with some success, and they both basked in the good wishes of all of their friends.

Catherine Freemont called on Georgiana often and showed a lively interest in her friend's happiness. As always, Georgiana took delight in her company and was pleased to hear that Sir Robert Blake continued to be attentive when they met at parties and dances.

Georgiana even received a letter of congratulations from Lady Catherine de Bourgh after the engagement was published in the papers, which she showed Elizabeth:

> *My dear Niece,—*
>
> *Congratulations on your engagement to Colonel Fitzwilliam. The match is highly suitable and I am very happy that you, unlike some people, are willing to do your duty to the family. Give my regards to the colonel and his family.—Sincerely,*
>
> *Lady Catherine de Bourgh*

"My aunt would not be quite so pleased had she known that I turned down Lord St. George to marry the younger son of the family," Georgiana stated smugly.

"I am surprised that she is not angry because she might have got the colonel for her daughter. After all, a younger son and an heiress with no brothers or sisters: what could be better?" Elizabeth smiled mischievously at her.

Georgiana responded with a roll of her eyes and they moved on to more agreeable topics.

The next day, the Darcys were at breakfast when Burton announced Mr. Bingley. They all looked up in surprise at this early call. Bingley's eyes were sparkling as he, at Darcy's invitation, sat down at the table. After the footman had laid his place and retired from the breakfast-parlour, Bingley burst out with, "I thank you. I ran over without breakfasting in order to bring you the big news. I wanted to let you know that Caroline accepted a proposal of marriage from the Comte de Tournay."

They all exclaimed over this and demanded further details.

"He trotted up to me while I was taking my morning ride around Rotten Row this morning and asked for my permission. He apparently asked her during a party they both attended last night. She must have given up on your cousin when he left London. I feel very odd, by the way, giving permission as the head of the household for my sister to marry someone old enough to be my father," he said in some embarrassment.

They all laughed at him and gave him their congratulations, and Elizabeth added that she and Georgiana would call on Miss Bingley later in the day to convey their felicitations to her in person.

As Darcy was seeing him out after breakfast, Bingley added quietly, "Caroline is absolutely indecently happy about her engagement. I am sure that she has never forgiven you for marrying Elizabeth instead of her, and she is gloating over the fact that she will be a *comtesse* while Elizabeth is a commoner. Oh, she hasn't been so vulgar as to say it aloud, but I can see it by the look in her eyes."

Darcy smiled and answered, "Well, I hope that she gets all the enjoyment of her title that she deserves," and, after Bingley gave him an ironic glance, sent him on his way.

That afternoon, Elizabeth and Georgiana called on the Bingleys and gave Miss Bingley their best wishes. She was very condescendingly gracious to both of them, and Elizabeth later told Darcy, "I felt rather like a peasant who was noticed by a royal personage—far more so than when I danced with a true royal."

Georgiana could tell that Elizabeth was very amused by Caroline's preening during the visit and had difficulty keeping her countenance serious and sincere, but she, noticing her sister's waning control, squeezed her arm under the cover of her shawl. That captured Elizabeth's attention, and she was able to sip her tea and control herself, although she refrained from looking at Georgiana for the remainder of the visit. When they were safely in the carriage, both of them relieved their feelings by giggling uncontrollably for several minutes.

"I must thank you, my dear sister, for pinching my arm," Elizabeth said as she dabbed at her eyes with her handkerchief. "I needed something to draw my attention. I am afraid that you will think me very ill-bred for being unable to keep my composure; however, Miss Bingley and I have a long history. I fear that her pride and condescension will be boundless now that she will have a title." She sighed and shook her head.

"Yes, I expect that it will. Well, I hope that a title is enough to ensure her enjoyment of a life encompassed by marriage to a man who is twice as old as she and who has no fortune." She coloured suddenly in confusion, realising that some ill-natured gossips might make similar comments about her engagement. She finally said with downcast eyes, "I hope, at least, that there is some affection between them. They have not known each other very long."

Elizabeth took her hand. "I hope so too, my dear."

They finished their ride home in silence and spent the rest of the day quietly reading; they had another ball to attend that night as the Season wound down to its finish. They would leave town in only a week and return to Pemberley. Georgiana was looking forwards to returning to the retirement and serenity of the country where they could relax and rest and get away from the soot of London.

> *10 June: I can hardly wait to leave for Pemberley, although I am not certain that my dear Edward will be able to accompany us. He is attempting to finish his duties so he can spend at least a fortnight in the north, but he has several important things in hand which must be concluded. There is something on his mind which he will not share with me; I do not know if it is his brother St. George or if it is a problem at the palace. (I cannot believe how close-mouthed this man is whom I always thought could talk the birds out of the trees!) Certainly, St. George's behaviour is explanation enough for his lack of spirits.*

Georgiana enjoyed the ball that evening and, on the way home, Elizabeth commented on the evident relief of her fellow debutantes that she had not taken one of the elder sons, but Georgiana merely shrugged off the lesser feelings of her acquaintances.

"They, of course, do not realise that I was never competing with them for the heirs once the Season actually began and that they are welcome to any future lord or landholder that they can enchant, with my blessings."

Elizabeth patted her hand fondly.

Lord Whitwell came to see Darcy the next morning and was closeted with him for about an hour in his library. Later, Darcy told Elizabeth about the meeting.

"We discussed what we wanted to do for Georgiana and the colonel. My uncle would like to give them Longford House. I had not realised that it is not included in the entail, but he purchased it himself years ago and held it out of the entail because of his concerns even then about his eldest son's behaviour. My aunt and uncle prefer to spend most of their time in the country, and Longford House is large enough to accommodate them as guests when they come to town. They have a smaller house near Berkeley Square, just around the corner from the Bingleys' house, which is leased out and is included in the entail and will go to St. George when he inherits. I thought that I would see if I can find a small estate near Pemberley to give them for a wedding present so we could see them often and Georgiana can benefit from your society when the colonel must be in town."

"That will be lovely! I am sure they will not want to be near Whitwell Abbey when your cousin inherits."

"No, my uncle felt, as I did, that it would be better for them to be in another part of the county, and settling near Pemberley would solve that difficulty. My uncle is trying to decide what to do about St. George. They have still not heard from him since he left town. My uncle is quite exercised in his mind; he is struggling to determine how to be fair to both of his sons. He is hoping that St. George is somewhere quietly thinking about his iniquities and resolving to change but fears that it is not so."

"Well, however the problem of St. George resolves itself, it will not affect Georgiana's happiness. She tells me that they want to wait until next spring to get married, soon after she turns eighteen. Lady Whitwell would like them to have a big society wedding at St. George's in Hanover Square, but Georgiana and the colonel have not yet decided if that is what they desire. I think Georgiana would prefer to have a quiet wedding, but she has plenty of time before she must decide."

Darcy smiled. "Hopefully, Fitzwilliam will be able to get to Pemberley often this summer, once the Season is over and the turmoil from Napoleon's defeat dies down. Now that Napoleon is on Elba, the situation in Europe should stabilise and the prince's cronies will settle back into their usual spiteful gossiping and backbiting."

Chapter 25

…Virtue solely is the sum of glory,
And fashions men with true nobility.

—CHRISTOPHER MARLOWE, *TAMBURLAINE THE GREAT*

As the week neared its end, the Darcys were beginning to prepare for their return to Pemberley. There was much to do in the way of packing and planning after such a long stay in town, and Elizabeth and Georgiana were kept busy supervising the servants. After several days of bustle they were finally ready to depart and planned to leave early the next morning. Georgiana was rather downcast to be leaving her fiancé, who still had some unfinished tasks, but she was trying to keep her spirits up by anticipating how beautiful it would be at Pemberley this time of year and how many lovely walks she would be able to take with Elizabeth and Pilot and Lucky. On their last evening they were engaged to dine with the Bingleys, who would also be leaving town in the next day or two and taking Kitty with them to Netherfield for a visit. The colonel was, of course, included in their invitations and arrived at

Ashbourne House an hour before dinner. He was announced to Darcy, who was in his library reading, and said, "I am sorry to interrupt your plans to leave, Darcy, but the Prince Regent wants to meet you tomorrow at one o'clock."

"Whatever for? We have no further business to conduct since I last saw him," Darcy said shortly.

"I know only what I have told you, Cousin," he said, holding up his hands in submission. "I am, once again, merely acting as a messenger."

Darcy sighed and said, "All right, I will be there. I can hardly refuse, can I?"

Georgiana and Elizabeth were disappointed that they were to put off their departure, but they would have an enjoyable dinner with the Bingleys that evening. They then would all leave London on the same morning.

Georgiana spent her evening tête-à-tête with her fiancé while he whispered the usual sweet flattery in her ear. Miss Bingley, on the other hand, was a picture of vivacity as she fawned over the count, who was also present, until even Elizabeth's good-humoured countenance became rigid with boredom.

The next day was spent in waiting. Darcy left the house in good time for his engagement at the palace and was gone for more than three hours. All of their trunks were packed and ready to go on the carriages, but they must await the pleasure of the Prince Regent. After she had played her pianoforte until her fingers hurt, Georgiana finally came down to the drawing-room with Lucky in her arms and plumped herself on the settee discontentedly. She was hard put not to comment on the prince's rudeness in waiting until they were almost in the carriage before he demanded to see her brother, but Elizabeth, correctly interpreting her sister's expression, just shrugged silently.

"Would you like to play a game, Georgiana? It might keep our minds off our grievances."

"I suppose. What would you like to play?"

"Backgammon?"

"It requires too much attention. How about draughts?"

"Perfect. I will set up the board if you will order tea."

They both played badly, but the game at least gave them something to do with their hands.

❦

When Darcy returned to Park Street, accompanied by the colonel, the door was opened by Burton himself instead of one of the footmen. He bowed deeply and murmured, "Welcome home, my lords."

Darcy stopped in astonishment and stared at the old butler as Fitzwilliam burst out laughing.

"How did you know, Burton?"

Burton just smiled smugly.

"Does everyone in the household know?"

"No, my lord! Of course not!" the butler said, shocked, "I would not say anything until I had your permission! I sent the footmen to the kitchen when I saw you returning."

Elizabeth and Georgiana were in the music-room practising a duet after finishing their unsatisfying game of draughts when Darcy came in with the colonel. Georgiana looked up and saw that they were each holding a piece of paper in their hands, and her brother had a rather odd look on his face: a combination of amusement and chagrin.

"What in the world is the matter?" she asked in surprise.

Darcy merely handed her the paper, and Elizabeth and Georgiana read it together. It was a letter of patent renewing the title of Earl of Winslow and bestowing it upon Fitzwilliam Edward George Darcy, "for his support and assistance to the Crown." Elizabeth's mouth dropped open for a moment and she was unable to speak while Georgiana stared at the letter. Darcy obviously noted the rapidly changing expressions on their faces as they comprehended all of the ramifications of his title, for he started laughing, but soon controlled himself and gave them the details of his afternoon.

"The Prince Regent evidently felt that he owed me a debt after this spring, and this particular gift costs him nothing—there are no lands with it or other benefits beyond the title because they all devolved to the king when the title fell out of usage, and he is not giving them up."

He paused for a moment, looking over their shoulders at the letter and then added with a crooked smile, "In fact, I am sure that he particularly enjoyed giving me this, since he knows that it means that I will have the duty to become a member of the House of Lords and come to London when Parliament meets and he knows me well enough to know that I will not shirk my responsibility, however repugnant I find London society. I believe he also means it as a snub to my aunt, Lady Catherine, since she will be absolutely livid to find that, instead of being ostracized by society, we are moving up to the nobility—particularly so since the title was originally her father's. Fitzwilliam tells me that the Prince Regent is not very fond of our aunt's domineering nature. He knew her husband well and always felt pity for the poor man's being attached to her, however noble her birth. Because of her respect for his title, the Prince Regent has, fortunately for him, been relatively safe from her personal criticism of his behaviour, but he nonetheless finds her a trial."

"But why did he give the title to you, Brother?" Georgiana asked, a frown creasing her brow.

"I am afraid, my dear, that I cannot tell you that."

"It has something to do with that time you were gone, before my presentation, does it not?"

He kissed her on the top of her head, but did not answer.

Elizabeth finally overcame her shock and breathed, "I am... absolutely astounded."

"There is more. Georgiana, this concerns you." He pushed the colonel forwards and said, "He made the colonel a baron and gave him an estate not five miles from Pemberley."

"Truly? That is wonderful! Where is it?" She could not understand the odd looks on their faces.

"It is the Walker estate."

She was startled, thinking she had misheard him. "I beg your pardon?"

"Yes. This is, I am afraid, very shocking," the colonel said, his face grave. "As you both know, young Walker has mortgaged the entire family estate to try to keep up with his debts while he looks for a rich wife. Apparently, things came to such a difficult pass that he decided to take more direct action to relieve his financial distress and joined a group which was smuggling English arms to the French and their supporters. When the government agents caught them, his estate was confiscated."

"But it did not really belong to him yet... his father was merely letting him run the estate," Elizabeth protested.

Colonel Fitzwilliam shrugged. "I presume that, since one of the charges in this case was treason, they had the powers necessary to take it. Ultimately, that is for the courts to decide. It is possible that the elder Walkers could make a claim to have it returned to them, but they are absolutely destroyed by their son's actions and have retired to a small cottage near Derby, where they can hide their shame in anonymity and still see their daughters and their grand-children. They will have to disown their only son to save some semblance of their good name and a future for their grandchildren in even the lowest level of good society. It is a tragedy." He shook his head regretfully.

Elizabeth shivered and said, "Those poor people. I never did like their son; he reminded me too much of another worth-less young man of our acquaintance, although less bad in a way. His face smiled, but his eyes were cold and calculating—unlike Wickham, he was unable to dissemble well enough to hide his true nature, which was beneficial to the rest of us since it allowed us to detect his schemes more easily. The elder Walkers, however, always seemed very friendly and forthright."

"At any rate," Darcy said, picking up the thread of the story, "my cousin is now Lord Lambton, and the estate was given to him. I will have to think what I should do about his creditors and about the elder Walkers." He turned and grinned at his sister. "Georgiana, I had thought to find a country estate near Pemberley for the two of you for a wedding present, but this has saved me a great deal of money."

Georgiana looked at him indignantly, but he went on, point-edly ignoring her glare, "The house could, I believe, be made very charming with some modernisation and, of course, the location could not be better." He walked around the room, tapping his leg with the beaver hat which he still held in his hand, having forgotten in his astonishment at Burton's greeting to give it to him when he came in.

Georgiana spoke again, sadly, "I feel very bad that my good fortune is at the squire's expense." She paused for a moment and then her eyes opened wide and she said, "What about Miss Blake?"

"I do not know what will happen to her. Presumably she will break the engagement. Thank God they had not yet married. They seemed to be in a hurry when they became engaged, but Sir Robert was apparently able to discourage too precipitous a marriage after our conversation. Do not worry, my dear, I will do what I can to assist the elder Walkers without offending their pride, but if the colonel refused the estate it would merely go to someone else, and you and Fitzwilliam would have no income to support the responsibilities that come with his title. Also, even if the Walkers applied to the Crown for the return of their property, it was mortgaged for its entire value, and they would never be able to pay it off."

"I suppose that is true, but I still do not feel quite right about it."

"Perhaps if I approached them and said that I know that they could probably obtain the return of their property—but that I would like to buy it, not wanting my sister to be uncomfortable in her home—they would sell it to me. I will want to pay off those that hold the mortgages, at any rate, so you do not have any problems with them in the future and can enjoy your home in good conscience."

"You are so good, my dear brother!" she said, embracing him, "I would feel much better about it if you could try to do that." She turned to her sister-in-law. "Elizabeth, could we go see Miss Blake as soon as we get back to Derbyshire? I assume they will be home soon."

"Of course, Georgiana, we will go as soon as we can."

Darcy kissed Georgiana on the forehead and escorted the two ladies upstairs so that they could all dress for dinner, while the colonel settled himself in Darcy's library with a book. Jane and Bingley were coming tonight with Kitty, so they would have one last evening together before both parties left town. The colonel had managed to finish all his duties and so would also stay for dinner and would travel north with them as well, allowing him to delay as long as possible his separation from Georgiana. They would have an early evening since everyone was travelling at first light the next morning.

Later, when Burton announced the Bingley party in the drawing-room, Bingley burst out as soon as the door had closed, "So it *is* true, Darcy! I heard just before we left the house that you had received a title this afternoon! Burton looked as if he could die from happiness when he said, 'I will announce you to his lordship and her ladyship.'"

The Darcys and the colonel joined him in his laughter and spent the rest of the evening telling the Bingleys that part of the story which was open for discussion. Their enjoyment was tempered by the sad tale of the Walkers and their son, told without, of course, mentioning his criminal behaviour towards Georgiana. Eventually, Georgiana confessed that she was becoming interested to see the house and what work would need to be done on it.

"I already know one thing that absolutely must be done; we must get rid of those horrible yews that are overwhelming what might otherwise be an attractive house. They are so dark and dank looking! I suppose we shall have to find another name for it once the yews are gone, however."

Darcy and Elizabeth both laughed but agreed that cutting them down was a good first step towards making the house their own. They stayed up later than any of them had planned since this news did not wear out its interest quickly, but eventually their guests left and the inhabitants of Ashbourne House retired for what rest they could get before they must rise and travel.

They made the trip to Pemberley in three days, travelling at an easy pace. The weather was warm but not too uncomfortable, and Georgiana could feel the tension of the last months gradually leaving her as they drew nearer and nearer to home. They arrived in the early afternoon of the third day and were greeted enthusiastically by the staff, who had already heard from Burton of their master's elevation to the peerage. Smithfield was smiling proudly as Darcy and Elizabeth led the way into the hall, while Georgiana and the colonel paused to speak to Mrs. Reynolds and receive her congratulations on their engagement and his new title and estate. When she finally entered Pemberley House, Georgiana gave a sigh of relief. They were home.

Chapter 26

How sharper than a serpent's tooth it is
To have a thankless child.

—WILLIAM SHAKESPEARE, *KING LEAR*

THE SUMMER WAS IN FULL BLOOM IN DERBYSHIRE, AND
Georgiana was happy to breathe the fresh country air after
the coal smoke that hung like an eternal fog over London. She had
almost forgotten how clear and green the hills were in Derbyshire.
The first two days they were home Darcy needed to catch up
on the estate business, and Georgiana and Elizabeth rode over
to Coldstream Manor with the colonel to see Miss Blake. In the
carriage, Georgiana said to her fiancé, "I would like you to take
Sir Robert out of the room if I am able to see Miss Blake. I hope
that it will not embarrass you if I tell her about my stupidity with
Wickham, if I think that it will help her."

He smiled at her. "You may do as you see fit. I trust your
judgement, my love. Indeed, I am hardly in a position to question
it, am I?"

"I hope not, my dear," she returned with an affectionate smile.

When they arrived, the butler told them that Miss Blake was out, so the colonel asked for Sir Robert. They were shown into the drawing-room and Sir Robert came almost immediately. After greeting them he started to apologise for his sister's absence, but Georgiana stepped forwards and gently held up her hand to stop his awkward speech.

"We came, Sir Robert, to give Miss Blake our sympathy for the distress which she must be going through. If there is some way that we can help her, I hope you will please tell us."

He gave her a bleak smile. "I am most grateful for the friendship that you have shown my sister, Miss Darcy, but she has refused to see anyone since we returned." He thought for a moment and then said hesitantly, "I believe, however, that if you do not mind waiting I will take advantage of your visit and see if I can coax her downstairs. I do not think it is healthy for her to shut herself away from all those who might comfort her."

"We would be most happy to wait," Georgiana said with a gentle smile.

Sir Robert left the room, and was gone about fifteen minutes. When he returned he gently supported his sister on his arm. Her face was pale and thin, and she sat on the sofa next to Georgiana and looked down at her hands in her lap. Sir Robert looked at them in mute appeal, and the colonel said, "Sir Robert, perhaps you could offer me a glass of wine."

"Of course, of course." He escorted the colonel from the room with patent relief.

Georgiana took Miss Blake's hand and said, "We are most concerned about you, Miss Blake, and we hoped that we could bring you some comfort in your hour of distress."

Miss Blake abruptly put her hands over her face, her shoulders shaking with her violent sobs. Georgiana put her arms around her and let her cry, patting her shoulder and crooning soothingly. When the young woman's tears had abated somewhat Georgiana said, "You must not let this overcome you, my dear. In time, the pain will fade a little and you will be yourself again."

Miss Blake said, with a voice that was harsh with grief and tears, "I suppose so. I am so humiliated to have not seen what kind of man he was. I did not know about his criminal activities, of course, but I find now that he probably only wanted my dowry to pay off his debts. It is very unlikely that he cared about me at all, and I did not see it. I was so eager to have a husband that I blinded myself to his character."

She sobbed again, and Georgiana looked at her keenly for a moment then said, "You are not the first woman who has been taken in by a scoundrel, my dear. I myself almost made the same mistake two years ago, except my fault was much worse than yours. I actually considered eloping with him, as he wanted me to do. Fortunately, my brother saved me from myself. I can look back now with amazement that I ever thought that I loved that blackguard."

Miss Blake looked up, surprised. "Does the colonel know about this?"

"Oh yes. Perhaps you do not realise that he has been my guardian along with my brother since my father died. He knows every detail, as does Elizabeth. She nodded at her sister-in-law and then smiled at Miss Blake, who gave her a watery smile in return.

"Thank you. Thank you for coming and thank you for telling me this." She looked back down at her hands. "It is good to know that I have some true friends."

Georgiana patted her hand and stood up. "You probably have more than you realise. I will leave you now, but I will come see you again in a few days if you will allow me. My dear sister has acted as my confidante on many occasions, and you may trust her absolutely, as you may trust me, if you wish to speak confidentially with either of us."

"Oh… yes, please do come, and thank you again." She managed a more genuine smile as she dabbed her eyes with her handkerchief.

While they were riding back to Pemberley, the colonel put Georgiana's arm through his and patted her hand.

"So what was the result of your visit?"

"I told her about my sordid past." She smiled ruefully at him and then added, "I believe that she felt somewhat better when I left.

"Did you tell her about your kidnapping?"

"No, I did not see any point in blackening Walker's name further. I thought the episode with Wickham illustrated my point sufficiently about recovering from stupid mistakes. I feel better now about owning the Walker estate."

"Shall we go this afternoon and look it over?"

"I would love to. Would you like to join us, Elizabeth?"

"Thank you, but I believe that I will rest this afternoon."

"That is an excellent idea." She smiled at her fiancé, the dimple in her right cheek appearing briefly. "I believe we will be able to cope with only Lucky to chaperone."

"The house seems in good condition, but I would like to have you look at it with me," the colonel said to Darcy after he and Georgiana had examined the house from attic to cellar. "Perhaps you could recommend a builder who can check its structural integrity for us."

"Of course, Fitzwilliam, I would be happy to. I know a builder in Kympton who is a capable fellow and, just as importantly, is reasonably honest. I will send him a note to meet us there tomorrow and he can inspect it with us."

Georgiana added, "All of the Walkers' furniture and belongings are still there. Is there some way we can determine if they wish to have them?"

Fitzwilliam answered, "Legally everything in the house belongs to us, but I would prefer to clear the place out before we redecorate. I doubt if you want to use Mrs. Walker's silver hairbrushes, Georgiana, and we will need more space for your pianoforte in the parlour. Darcy, perhaps you could write to the Walkers and see if they would like any of their possessions returned."

Georgiana shuddered. "It would be like having the Walkers' ghosts creeping around our house having everything unchanged from when they lived there."

Darcy nodded thoughtfully.

Georgiana broke the resulting silence by turning to Elizabeth. "There is the sweetest little parlour at the back of the house. It is connected to the drawing-room where we sat when we visited by a double door so we can open the two rooms when we have company, but when I just want to practise by myself I can close it off and have complete privacy. It is just big enough for a pianoforte and my harp."

Elizabeth smiled. "It sounds delightful, Georgiana. I cannot wait to see it."

Several days later, the weather was beautiful and Elizabeth and Darcy were visiting some friends, so Georgiana suggested to her fiancé that they take a short rest from their planning for their house and have a picnic. They set out just after noon, Fitzwilliam carrying the picnic hamper and Georgiana a rug to sit on. They walked slowly and stopped frequently to look at the beauty of the changing views. She took him up a path that led in easy stages over the ridge in back of the main house, following the stream until they lost it into a curve of the hills. The gravelled path was wide and smooth, but the way was ever upwards, requiring that Georgiana stop often to catch her breath and cool herself with her fan. When they came to the top of the ridge, she could see down into a little glen adorned with a small, rocky stream that formed a pool below a tiny waterfall. In the summer heat the glen was very shady and cool looking.

"I have always loved this place," Georgiana remarked. "It is so close to civilisation and yet so isolated. It has always been my special place." She gave her fiancé a sidelong glance and said, "This is where I would always go to hide when you and my brother would not let me play with you, except, of course, when I secretly followed you... Perhaps I should not have shown you where my refuge is."

"Your secret is safe with me, Miss Darcy." Fitzwilliam put down the picnic hamper and drew her to him. He brushed back two stray curls and kissed her on the forehead. After a few minutes, he whispered in her ear, "Shall we walk down to the stream, my love?"

She sighed contentedly and turned down the path.

There was a small clearing next to the stream that was flat and dry and would make a fine place to sit and eat. Georgiana spread the blanket on the ground and then knelt down and looked into the hamper to see what the cook had sent them to eat. There was a loaf of new bread, sliced thin, cheese and apples, a bottle of wine, and tiny fruit tarts for dessert. As they ate, Fitzwilliam commented, "I feel very decadent sitting here eating in the woods. I fear that Zeus will send down his thunderbolts from Mount Olympus to punish us for our audacity in having a picnic next to his sacred pool. There is definitely something uncanny about these woods—or perhaps it is the unusual sensation of the two of us being totally alone."

"So, I take it that you want to go back to the house?" She pretended to start to her feet.

"I think not yet, Miss Darcy," he said with a laugh.

They finished eating, and Fitzwilliam settled himself against the bole of a tree at the edge of the glade, patting the blanket next to him. Georgiana took off her bonnet and curled up beside him in the crook of his arm, resting her head on his shoulder. The woods were very quiet except for the sound of birdsong. They might have been a hundred miles from the nearest settlement instead of a mere quarter mile.

After a few minutes, Georgiana said, "This spot does not remind me of Zeus so much as Shakespeare. I had almost forgotten until now:

"And this our life, exempt from public haunt,
Finds tongues in trees, books in the running brooks,
Sermons in stones, and good in everything."

"That is quite appropriate; this could be the Forest of Arden. 'Are not these woods more free from peril than the envious court?'"

She lifted her face to smile at him and he kissed her again on the forehead, moving slowly down to linger on her lips. Eventually, they somewhat breathlessly resumed their enjoyment of the verdant scene and listened to the quiet chuckling of the water as it trickled over the rocks and into the pool. When they had been sitting in this attitude for most of an hour, Fitzwilliam gave a gusty sigh and said, "I suppose that we should gather up the remains of our alfresco party and make our way back to the real world."

Georgiana echoed his sigh and said wistfully, "It *is* wonderful to be alone with you, even if only for a few minutes."

Fitzwilliam raised his brows in mock surprise. "You admit to preferring the company of your future husband to the gaieties of society? I am quite shocked."

"To such depths have I fallen," she admitted ruefully.

"Well, in that case I must make sure that we return to this idyllic spot as soon as possible. We will do so on the next sunny day."

He helped her up and repacked the hamper while she put her bonnet back on. Hand in hand, they made the climb up the ridge and stopped for a moment at the crest to look down at Pemberley House. They saw the carriage far down the gravelled drive, returning Darcy and Elizabeth from town, and started slowly down the path. By the time they emerged from the woods the elder Darcys were in the drawing-room having a cup of tea and discussing their purchases, so the colonel and Georgiana joined them until it was necessary for Darcy to withdraw for a meeting with his steward.

Elizabeth dozed on a chaise longue set in the shade of the folly that afternoon with Pilot lying in the shade of her chair. She awoke to see her husband approaching, an unopened letter in his hand.

"It looks as if you have received a letter from your friend Charlotte, my dear."

"Oh, how nice. You did not need to bring it yourself, my darling," she smiled up at him.

"It was my pleasure, my lady."

She opened her letter while he settled himself on the bench next to her chair. After a few moments' reading she gave a sharp gasp.

"What is it?" Darcy asked, sitting up abruptly.

"Charlotte writes her congratulations to us and says that they are all well and little Catherine is now five weeks old." She raised her brow and added, "I won't sport with your intelligence by explaining why she is named Catherine." Darcy rolled his eyes heavenwards and she continued, "She then goes on:

> *...We have been rather lively in Kent in the last few weeks as Mr. Darcy's cousin, Lord St. George, has been visiting his aunt, Lady Catherine. He is very pleasant and seems to be much taken with his cousin, Miss de Bourgh. We have been called to make up the table at cards several times since his arrival (as you are aware, Miss de Bourgh does not play whist), and we have found his lordship most amiable...etc.*

"So... Lord St. George is in Kent, happily ensconced at Rosings Park and playing up to Lady Catherine for all he is worth while his relations are all worrying themselves sick about him." She said, with a sudden frown, "I hope that my suspicions about his motives in going to Rosings are incorrect."

Darcy looked very grim. "I am very much afraid that my suspicions echo yours. He must be making a play for my cousin Anne's hand so that he can have the Rosings estate."

"Poor Miss de Bourgh. Do you think he would go that far?"

"I would not be at all surprised. Lady Catherine is probably not aware of what went on in London this spring, since my aunt and uncle would not want to have the news of their son's ill behaviour bandied about. And even if she was aware she might overlook it for the chance of a titled husband for Anne."

"I pray that we are wrong," she said softly.

"So do I, my love, so do I; But I must give the colonel this news as soon as possible, so that he can inform his parents. He and Georgiana are still at The Yews with Mrs. Annesley. I think that I should ride into town and see if I can catch up with him."

"Yes, my dear, go and find them. This is a very unpleasant reflection on your cousin's character, and I dread to think of the distress that he will cause his entire family!"

He kissed her hand briefly and hurried to the stables to order his horse then ran into the house to change into riding clothes. By the time he was back downstairs his horse was ready, and he sprang into the saddle and rode off at a brisk trot. Elizabeth was left to her book but it could no longer hold her attention. As the day warmed, she moved into the drawing-room, while Pilot retired to his usual spot in the library to continue his nap. The time seemed to creep by interminably as she awaited Darcy's return.

Finally, after two hours had slowly ticked by and she had reread the same passages at least three times, she gave up and ordered tea. She had barely emptied her cup when the entire party returned together. The colonel was in a state of barely controlled agitation when he came in and immediately ran upstairs to have his man pack his things. The others joined Elizabeth in the drawing-room, where a fresh pot of tea waited, and Georgiana said, "I cannot believe that my cousin St. George has been at Rosings all this time without giving his family a single hint as to his whereabouts! I hope my brother's assumptions about St. George's desire to marry our cousin are incorrect. The colonel feels that he must go to Whitwell Abbey and tell my aunt and uncle this news in person so they can discuss what recourse they might have."

"Can you think of any other reason for his secrecy about this extended visit to Rosings?"

"No, I am afraid I cannot, unless he is just hiding to cause his parents grief and punish them for cutting off his allowance, like a spoilt child."

"I would not put it past him, but Charlotte says that he seems 'quite taken with his cousin Anne.' Here is the letter."

She handed Georgiana Charlotte's note.

"Hmm. Yes, much as I would like to disagree with your conclusions, I cannot."

Elizabeth turned to Darcy, who was sitting silently, staring blankly at the teacup in his hand.

"Perhaps you should go with him, my dear, so that you may offer your thoughts on the matter. They will need as many clear heads as possible if they are to think of a way to avert this misuse of their niece."

Darcy sighed. "Perhaps I should. I cannot say that I am eager to leave you again, just as we have arrived home." He picked up her hand and kissed it while Georgiana rather pointedly busied herself putting milk and sugar in her tea.

In the end, Darcy did decide to go with his cousin. After a tense evening in which they could find little to talk about in front of the servants, they all retired early. Georgiana mused over her diary for thirty minutes before she wrote,

25 July: We received startling news today: St. George is at Rosings Park and being very attentive to our cousin Anne. My stomach turns over with the thought that my refusal could have such a violent effect on St. George's actions, and I am sure my brother feels the same about his refusal to marry Anne. The Darcys seem to have conspired to deprive Anne of any happiness in life, but I do not see how we could have done otherwise. I know I really should blame the person ultimately responsible for this problem, and that is my cousin St. George.

The gentlemen rode out first thing the next morning and Elizabeth received a letter from Darcy the next day assuring her that they had arrived in safety, but with no further news. While Darcy and the colonel were at Whitwell Abbey, Elizabeth and Georgiana attempted to keep to their usual routine of walks, music, and needlework; but in actuality they spent the first three days of solitude revisiting the problem of Lord St. George, with nothing but discouragement to reward their time.

A few days after the gentlemen had departed, their depression of spirits was raised when Elizabeth received a letter from her sister Jane. She had not heard from her since leaving London, and she eagerly opened the envelope and read:

> *Dearest Lizzy,—*
>
> *I am sorry to be so dilatory in my correspondence; I know that you will understand how busy we are reopening Netherfield after the Season and your generous heart will forgive me. It has taken longer than I would have liked to*

have the household functioning properly as the Wickhams joined us unexpectedly not long after our return. In addition, I am beginning to feel rather like that elephant that we used to look at in Papa's African animal book when we were children. I am becoming more and more nervous about my confinement but will be glad to have the ordeal over. Mr. Bingley assures me that I am as beautiful as ever, but I do not feel beautiful in the least. I do, however, appreciate his tact.

I must tell you, my dearest sister, that returning to Hertfordshire after this extended absence has made it very clear to both of us that we cannot stay at Netherfield permanently. After the superior company of yourself and all the Darcy relations, it is difficult to tolerate the excesses of our own family. I know that you will forgive me for speaking so plainly, but I find myself blushing constantly over the manners and attitudes of many of our relations. You will not be surprised to hear that Lydia is unchanged after a year of marriage and talks only of parties and schemes when she is not complaining about how poor they are. Because of all these factors we have decided to quit Netherfield as soon as we find a suitable estate to purchase, and we are hoping to find one near enough to Pemberley that we can see you and Darcy, and Georgiana and the colonel, frequently. I must go now and visit our parents; our father has missed both of us very much and I feel rather guilty to be contemplating a move, but we feel that it will be for the best.—Give my best regards to…etc.

Elizabeth shook her head over this epistle's reflections upon her family, and Georgiana asked her what the news was. She read the relevant parts of the letter to her, and Georgiana was very pleased that the Bingleys were, hopefully, to move closer to Pemberley. This topic gave them something more enjoyable to converse about than the sins of their cousin, and they spent many hours in pleasant speculation over where the Bingleys might find an estate in Derbyshire, temporarily at least forgetting Lord St. George, except to eagerly watch for the post each day.

Five days after their departure, Georgiana finally received a letter from Colonel Fitzwilliam.

Dearest Georgiana,—

We have spent the past five days discussing nothing but my brother's plans and whether we could or should try to take action in the matter but have been unable to find an answer. My father was at first inclined to think that his eldest son was finally showing a sense of responsibility, but when Darcy and I gave him the full particulars of our cousin Anne's state of health, he was shocked and dismayed. He could not convince himself that his wayward son would marry a woman who was a complete invalid except for the most venal reasons. My parents have still had no word from St. George or Lady Catherine regarding his presence in Kent. Since we cannot think of a way to influence either party without giving a grave insult to Cousin Anne or Lady Catherine, which would further estrange them from their family, my father has reluctantly decided that we should do nothing at the present time for fear that a move would precipitate events. Darcy and I will arrive at Pemberley the day after you receive this letter.—With all my love,

Edward

Chapter 27

...There's nothing in the whole universe that perishes, believe me,
Rather it renews and varies its substance.

—OVID, *METAMORPHOSES*

AFTER DARCY AND THE COLONEL RETURNED FROM WHITWELL Abbey, they told Elizabeth and Georgiana about their discussions with Lord and Lady Whitwell. They were all dismayed and shocked by the situation, but in spite of numerous talks, none of them could construct a solution that would solve the problem without causing many others. It consumed the thoughts and devoured the sleep of them all, and only the need to appear as usual in front of the servants forced them to give up their interminable rounds of talk. But finally, as the weeks of summer advanced, they began, slowly, to let go of the problem and to wait, as Lord Whitwell had recommended. The beautiful park at Pemberley was of great service in this regard, as the sunshine and warm breezes tempted them out-of-doors most days, and their difficulties diminished in the beauties of nature. Colonel Fitzwilliam reluctantly returned to his duties at St. James, and Georgiana kept her spirits up in front of her brother and sister but confessed her true thoughts to her diary:

> *9 August: My dear Edward left for London today and I already feel his absence acutely. We all still ache for my cousin Anne's plight, but I believe that we must allow the mistress of Rosings to make the decisions for her daughter, no matter how repugnant. My poor brother feels the pain of his cousin's plight most keenly because his refusal to marry her has left her vulnerable to the mercenary plans of her mother and Lord St. George. I, too, feel guilt in the situation because of my harsh refusal of St. George, but I pointed out to my brother that ruining our happiness with regrets was not going to protect her from her mother's future matrimonial ambitions. My brother has been riding hard over the estate and working himself into a state of exhaustion to forget. I find my dear sister Elizabeth a great solace in my pain.*

Eventually, Georgiana found herself, after many days had passed, able to attend to the sermons of the parson of Lambton church. Instead of being caught in an endless cycle of dismay and concern for the anguish that Lord St. George might introduce to his family, she could listen to and comprehend the message and confine her internal thoughts to a small prayer at the end of the service for the protection of her cousin Anne in whatever the future would hold.

Finally, one Sunday in mid-August the parson, Mr. Woodson, preached a sermon on the acceptance of God's will. Woodson was a rather small and timid-appearing young man who was hampered in village society by extreme shyness. He appeared to best advantage when speaking from the pulpit, putting on the ancient dignity and authority of the Church like a cloak. His message that day was a simple one: "Find God's will and, when you do, accept it as your own." Georgiana felt a silent sigh shudder through her brother and she, too, felt great solace in the words.

They were in the carriage, returning from church when Elizabeth suddenly sat up straight and turned eagerly to Darcy, as if they had been discussing aloud the problem which occupied their thoughts.

"I do not know why I did not think of this before! I do have one suggestion that might be of service to Miss de Bourgh."

"Please tell me; I could use some good news, my dear," he said, raising his brows questioningly.

She hesitated just a moment. "I do not know if you will be entirely pleased with this idea, but do you not think that you should write to your aunt Lady Catherine and try to re-establish relations with her?"

He frowned. "I am not sure that I want to do that after her entirely uncalled-for behaviour towards you, my love."

"I believe that you should give her another chance, if only for Anne's sake, dearest. You do not need to apologise for your actions—I, for one, do not repent of them at all," she said with a brief smile, "but if you can merely open the door slightly it may allow you to be of some use to your family in their concerns, whereas now you are persona non grata to Lady Catherine and have not the smallest influence over her."

Georgiana's eyes had brightened while she was talking and she said to her sister, "I think it is an excellent idea, Elizabeth." She turned to Darcy. "You have nothing to lose, my dear brother."

"My aunt has always been a woman to give advice rather than

accept it, but you are both right: I should try to recover my status as her nephew, if only for the comfort of the rest of the family."

When they returned to the house, Darcy shut himself in his library to compose the letter. After more than an hour, he finally finished and sought out Elizabeth and Georgiana in the music room so they could read it before he posted it.

> *Dear Lady Catherine,—*
>
> *I am writing to let you know that Elizabeth and I are well, and she is expecting our first child in November. As you are, I believe, aware, Georgiana's presentation and debut went very well this spring, thanks to the efforts of Lady Whitwell and Elizabeth, and she is engaged to Colonel Fitzwilliam, now Lord Lambton. They are planning to marry in the spring. She is very happy decorating the house on the estate given the colonel by His Majesty along with his title and it should be ready for them to move in by the time they marry. Lord Whitwell is giving them Longford House for a wedding present, so they will also have a house in town. If you are able, in the future, to visit Pemberley, you and Cousin Anne are always welcome.—Sincerely, etc.*

"It is not the most gracious letter I have ever written, but it was the best that I could do under the circumstances, unrepentant as I am," he said sheepishly.

Georgiana said briskly, "It will do; she will either accept it or not, and I doubt if she would respect you if you grovelled. This at least allows her the opportunity to reopen your acquaintance without admitting that she was wrong, which I very much doubt that she will ever do. She is the one who must decide how important her family is to her own happiness."

"Well, I will send it off and we will see how she responds. I have also written to Lord and Lady Whitwell to inform them of our actions."

The letters went out the next morning, and since they could take no further action until they received a response (if any) they returned to their accustomed activities. Elizabeth spent hours helping Georgiana decide upon the decor of her future home. The structure had been found to be sound, but most of the house needed a great deal of updating, so they had an enjoyable time picking out papers, carpets, and furniture. Georgiana commented one day when they had made many selections, "Well, we have made great progress, and I am quite satisfied. I must say that this intensive shopping is like a narcotic: it dulls the pain of family problems, if only for a few hours. We must find a new name for our home, however, now that those horrible yews are gone."

She later wrote,

16 August: Elizabeth and I spent a great deal of time at the house today, and I am very pleased with the progress on the drawing-room. The paper is exactly what I wished for. Our main topic of discussion today was the new name for the house, and Elizabeth suggested Bellamy, which I adored. I will write to Edward immediately and see if the name is agreeable to him.

Georgiana wrote her letter and received her answer by return post:

"...I think Bellamy would be a perfect name for our home, ma belle amie..."

Darcy had paid off the mortgage on the estate so the creditors had dispersed; but the senior Walkers had refused any payment for the property, telling him with dignity that it would not be right for him to pay for the unconscionable acts of their son and wishing Georgiana and the colonel every happiness in their new home. As they were very firm in their decision, he was compelled to accept their word, however reluctantly.

As September approached with the anticipation of slightly cooler temperatures, Elizabeth received a letter from Jane inviting them to Miss Bingley's wedding to the Comte de Tournay:

> *Dearest Lizzy, Mr. Darcy, and Georgiana,—*
> *Caroline has asked me to assist her in writing the invitations for her wedding, so I am writing to the Darcy family first of all. They will be married on September the first at St. George's, Hanover Square, at ten o'clock in the morning. We would very much like you all to stay with us until we travel to London for the wedding, …etc.*

Elizabeth's physician in Lambton felt that she could safely go, as long as the trip was taken in easy steps and she was not over-tired. Her own confinement was not expected for some time yet, so, although she was beginning to feel rather ungainly, she thought that she could travel in reasonable comfort, and of course Darcy would be with her and make everything easy. She wrote to Jane to let her know that they would be arriving in a few days, and the servants spent the day packing for the trip.

Georgiana was delighted to have this unexpected opportunity

to see her fiancé for the first time in several weeks. They had been corresponding almost daily as the work on the house progressed, discussing changes to their plans and how quickly (or not) the work was progressing, but she longed to see him in person.

They left for Netherfield the day after Jane's invitation arrived and spent three nights on the road, as the coachman kept the horses to a sedate trot. Georgiana tried to watch her sister covertly to make sure that she did not become too tired and she caught her brother's eye several times as he did the same. When Elizabeth saw their concern she laughed and said,

"Please relax, my dears! You may trust me to tell you if I am not feeling well. I am neither an invalid nor a Dresden shepherdess."

Mrs. Annesley just smiled calmly.

They drove decorously up to the front door of Netherfield in the late afternoon of the fourth day and Elizabeth and Georgiana embraced Jane. Her slender figure was swollen by the new life within her, and she led them to the drawing-room and immediately sat down, breathing heavily. Georgiana noticed that she had dark smudges under her eyes and her face appeared strained as she said, "Please pardon me, my dears. I do not have much energy at the moment, but I am truly happy to see you!" She burst into tears and clung to Elizabeth, who patted her back and soothed her; Elizabeth caught Darcy's startled eyes over Jane's head and jerked her chin towards the door. The two gentlemen arose hastily and disappeared into the billiard-room, Bingley peering back through the doorway for a moment in concern.

After they had started the game, Bingley leaned on his cue. He glanced back towards the drawing-room again then cleared his throat and said, with an attempt at his usual good humour, "I have wanted to tell you that Caroline was absolutely livid when she heard that you received a title. I really thought for a few moments that she was going to have an apoplectic attack, Darcy—or would you prefer it if I call you Lord Winslow now?"

Darcy snorted derisively, and Bingley grinned and went on, "I believe that is why Caroline is hurrying her wedding, so that she can be addressed as 'my lady' as soon as possible."

Darcy shook his head in mock reproach at his friend's levity, and they continued their game.

In the drawing-room, Jane had dried her tears and was telling her sisters that she was really feeling very well, just tired, but she would be happy when the baby arrived.

"I am very happy that you felt well enough to come, Lizzy, because, as I think I told you, I am getting rather nervous as my confinement approaches. Mamma has daily been filling my head with all the terrifying occurrences that she has seen or heard of when women have their lying-in. I try to reassure myself that she had five children without any difficulties, but I am unable to ignore the tales. I am not sleeping much because I am not very comfortable, so it does not take much unease of mind to keep me awake all night. It also does not help that my poor husband is very worried about me; this is all new for him too, after all. I feel better already having you here to keep me sensible, Lizzy," she finished as she dashed a remaining tear impatiently from her eye.

In a little while Jane retired upstairs for a rest, and Elizabeth said to Georgiana, "I wish I could reassure Jane, but I am no more experienced in this area than she is. However, I am determined to prevent our mother from frightening Jane further, if at all possible."

"Could your father assist in this matter?" Georgiana asked, hesitantly.

"I will speak to him. I am also concerned about Jane travelling to London in her condition. She is far too close to her time. I will need to talk to her and possibly enlist her doctor's help. What do you think, Mrs. Annesley?"

Mrs. Annesley immediately answered, "I would not recommend travelling at this time, my lady."

Elizabeth talked to Darcy, and the next morning, when she had a chance to see Jane alone, she put her opinion before her sister— offering to stay with her while Bingley, Darcy, and Georgiana went to London for the wedding. Jane considered very briefly before she agreed to the idea.

"Yes, I am sure you are right, Lizzy, that I probably should not travel. I just hate to let Caroline down on her wedding day."

"I am sure she will understand, Jane," she said. Then she added tartly, "Consider this: if she really wanted for you to be there, she could have put off the wedding for a couple of months, now could she not? Bingley will be there to give her away and she will be as happy as can be with her society friends around her to give their congratulations."

Jane smiled her agreement and went to tell Bingley their plan. Later in the day, while Jane was resting, Bingley sought Elizabeth out in the music-room and sat next to her, saying,

"Thank you, my dear sister, for staying with Jane while we go to London. I was very worried about her travelling, but I did not like to leave her here without a family member to take care of her, either. You have eased my mind greatly."

"I am happy to be of assistance, although I hate to forgo Caroline's society wedding." She gave him an impish smile and he laughed.

"Yes, I hope everything goes as she plans it, or she will be fit to be tied. I have already begged Darcy to allow me to stay at Ashbourne

House so that I do not have to live through Caroline's wedding-day nerves. I am not sure that I am strong enough to survive it."

"What are their plans for their honeymoon? Will they stay in London, or travel?" Elizabeth enquired politely.

"They are planning to drive directly to the count's estate, which is near Windsor, so it is not terribly far from town."

"Has Caroline seen the house yet?"

"I don't believe so, but the count has described it to us. It is a small manor house that is about seventy years old. He told me that he wants to use Caroline's dowry to buy more land to add to his estate and provide steady income."

"That sounds very sensible. Well, I hope they will be very happy. Make sure that you convey our best wishes." Elizabeth's eyes twinkled and Bingley smiled back at her for a moment. Then his brow furrowed.

"I will, but please send an express if anything should happen while we are gone. I can be here in three hours on a fast horse."

"Do not worry, I will send for you immediately after I send for the doctor."

When Elizabeth told Darcy of her plan, he approved it immediately.

"I think it is an excellent plan, my dear. Is she still nervous about her confinement?"

"Yes. My dear mamma has been filling her head with lurid tales of death and disaster."

"Could I propose a change of plan? Would you, perhaps, like to stay until Jane is over at least part of her confinement? I am sure that she would feel better with you here, and Georgiana and I could stay in London so that she could be with the colonel for a couple of weeks. It would give them a chance to undertake any business relating to their house, as well."

"That would probably be a good idea. If nothing else, I can keep Mamma from terrifying Jane. It would be nice to see Papa for a longer period, as well."

"We will plan on staying in town for about a fortnight, then, until you write to us that your sister is well enough for us to bring you home."

"Thank you, my love. I will miss you. At least I have the consolation at *this* separation that I will know where you are!" She grinned up at him.

He responded with a cocked eyebrow and a kiss on her forehead before he joined Bingley for a ride over his temporary demesne. Elizabeth rejoined Jane and Georgiana and told them of the completed plan. Georgiana's eyes glowed when she realised that she would be able to spend an entire fortnight with her future husband. They spent the afternoon trying to relax and make Jane as much at ease as possible, but she was too uncomfortable to sit still for long.

The tedium was broken when Doctor Porter called to see Jane late in the day. After he had examined her in her room he came to Elizabeth, who was waiting in the drawing-room, and told her that all was well and that the baby could come at any time.

"It is well, then, that she is not going to her sister-in-law's wedding in London the day after tomorrow."

"Oh no, my lady, that would not do at all; she must certainly stay at home!"

"She will, and I am planning to stay until she has her lying-in and has recovered."

"That will be of very great assistance to your sister, I am sure, my lady."

"Thank you, Doctor."

The Bennets came to dinner that evening, and Jane felt well

enough after a long afternoon rest to join them at the table. Mrs. Bennet's eyes glittered brightly all evening as she carried on about her pleasure at becoming a grandmother.

"I am so excited! By the end of the year I will have three grand-children! I hope that everything goes well, Jane, my love. Mrs. Long's eldest niece just had her lying-in, but, poor thing, the baby died a few hours later." She conveyed this news with ghoulish satis-faction, oblivious to Jane's ghastly pallor. "The mother developed a fever and they almost despaired of her life, too."

Knowing that Georgiana was now becoming acquainted with all of her mother's weaknesses, Elizabeth felt herself blush several times, and for Jane's sake was desperate to stop her mother's flow of talk. Darcy finally saw her worried looks and engaged Georgiana and Kitty in talking about London, including Bingley and Jane in the conversation. Elizabeth was able to turn to her father, plunging into the first topic that came to her mind.

"Papa, have you heard from Mr. Collins lately?"

"No, my dear, I have heard nothing from him. What are your plans for the time you are here?"

She glanced down the table to make sure that they were not overheard. "I am hoping to keep Mamma from scaring Jane to death with her talk," she said quietly, "and to keep Jane quiet and as rested as may be until her lying-in."

"That is an admirable plan, if you can carry it out, my love," was his wry response. "I will attempt to divert your mother when she becomes too indiscreet."

"Thank you, Papa."

The next afternoon Bingley, Darcy, and Georgiana left for London after Bingley had spent the morning hovering over his wife in poorly concealed concern.

When their mother came to call in the early afternoon, Elizabeth determinedly kept the conversation to the latest news from London and what fashions they had seen during the Season. Jane seconded her efforts gamely, and they were able to keep their mother on trivial topics for the entire visit.

Elizabeth received a letter the following day from Darcy telling of their safe arrival, but it was not until two days later that she received an account of the wedding from Georgiana.

Dearest Elizabeth,—

Well, my dear sister, the wedding is over and the newlyweds are now at the comte's estate near Windsor. The day was sunny and rather warm for the season, but not unpleasantly so, and we arrived at the church early as Mr. Bingley was, of course, to give away the bride. Miss Bingley was dressed in a beautiful gown of cream silk, with yards and yards of Belgian lace. Her bonnet was of cream, with ribbons of silver, and her bouquet was of cream hothouse roses surrounded by small fern leaves. The church was about a quarter full of society people, and Miss Bingley was very gratified by the number who attended in spite of the unfashionable date.

Everything went off very smoothly, and Mr. Bingley was smiling and gracious, as always, when he handed his sister off to her husband-to-be. The Hursts had a wedding breakfast for the newlyweds, and they stayed for about an hour before retiring to change into their travel clothes.

They went to his estate immediately after, and we visited for a short time with the other wedding guests and were back at Ashbourne House in time for dinner. Colonel Fitzwilliam joined us for the wedding and reception (looking very handsome in his regimentals I might add), but his duty required him to return to the palace afterwards, so we did not have much time to talk.

I would tell you who was at the wedding, but I am afraid that I did not notice once my dear fiancé arrived. He will join us for dinner here today. He told me that he received information from someone at the palace that Jonathan Walker was sentenced to hang, but the judge then commuted (if that is the correct word) his sentence to life imprisonment at the penal colony in New South Wales. Apparently the judge felt that Walker should not lose his life when his superior in the smuggling scheme was able to save his own life by giving up his comrades. I am glad his life was spared. As much as I resent and abhor his behaviour towards me, I would not wish for his parents to live with the knowledge that their only son had been hanged.

My dearest sister, I do not know how I will bear waiting until spring for our wedding. It seemed like a sensible plan two months ago, but now the spring seems an eternity away. I will not complain any further, however! My best love to Jane and I hope that she feels very well.—Love, etc.

Elizabeth was entertained by Georgiana's letter, which she thought was probably quite accurate, and read it to Jane.

The heat was abominable for the rest of the week, with storm clouds piling up in the west but no rain to give them relief, but Georgiana did not notice. She was too happy spending whatever time she could with the colonel to be bothered by other things. They shopped in the London warehouses and spent their evenings at the few theatre offerings or dinner parties available at that time of year, but most of their evenings were spent at home at Ashbourne House. Mr. Bingley had returned to Hertfordshire immediately after Miss Bingley's wedding so Mr. Darcy frequently resorted to his club to give him a place of refuge away from the lovers, while Mrs. Annesley had a great deal of correspondence each evening.

A few days after the wedding, Georgiana received a letter from Elizabeth:

My dear Georgiana,—

I am delighted to tell you that my sister Jane was delivered of a beautiful, healthy baby girl today. Both mother and baby seem to be thriving, and I feel a great weight of worry lifted from my shoulders. Mr. Bingley almost went mad with waiting and was as white as a ghost when he was finally allowed in to see his wife and their new daughter. Once he was assured of Jane's well-being, however, he regained his spirits (although I suspect he fortified himself with a stiff brandy when he left us!). The Bingleys surprised me by telling me that they are naming her after me, so there will be another Lizzy in the family. I anticipate that I will be able to leave Hertfordshire in about a fortnight without concern for my sister. I am hoping the unseasonable weather will cool and we will all be more comfortable. Give the colonel my best, my dearest girl.—Your affectionate sister,

Elizabeth

Georgiana was relieved to know that Jane was well, but knowing the time limit of her current happiness depressed her spirits. She voiced her discontent in her diary that night:

5 September: Only two more weeks before we travel north, leaving my love in town. I thought it sensible to wait to marry until I turned eighteen and we would have time to prepare the house and the wedding at leisure, but the closer our parting comes, the less my plans please me. I talked to Edward tonight about planning the wedding sooner and he admitted that next March seemed very far away. He also commented that he "wasn't getting any younger," which amused me. Anyone less elderly than my Edward I cannot imagine! I will write to Elizabeth immediately and ask for her opinion: could the arrangements be moved forwards, or are we being precipitous?

Fortunately for Georgiana's temper, Elizabeth wrote to her by return post:

My dear girl,—

Talk to your brother and order your wedding gown as soon as may be. The only arrangements that are of importance are yours and the colonel's.—With all my love, etc.

When she had been at Netherfield for nearly a fortnight and Jane was recovered enough that Elizabeth no longer had any fears about her health, she received two letters. The first, from Darcy, said that they would return from London the next day:

My dearest Wife,—

I am happy to hear that Jane is feeling so well and that your namesake is healthy. It seems like months since we left Netherfield and I can hardly wait to see you. I know that Georgiana has been corresponding with you, so this will come as no surprise, but she and the colonel have decided to marry as soon as possible. They will both return to Netherfield with me tomorrow, and I am hoping that we can return to Pemberley within the next week. They will be married in the Pemberley chapel, probably a week after we return. I hope that you are feeling well and that your nursing duties with your sister have not tired you, my darling.—With all my love, etc.

The second letter was from Georgiana:

Dearest Elizabeth,—

We have talked with my brother and our wishes have prevailed (not that there was much opposition in the case!). My gown is not quite finished, but the seamstress will deliver it to Pemberley within a few days of our return for the final fitting. I will describe it to you when we get to Netherfield, which will be in the early afternoon tomorrow, and a week after our return to Pemberley we will have Mr. Woodson marry us in the Pemberley chapel. I did not expect a year ago that I would be married so soon, and I must confess that I feel rather giddy! I will see you very soon.—Love,

Georgiana

Chapter 28

She is your treasure, she must have a husband.

—William Shakespeare, *The Taming of the Shrew*

WITHIN A WEEK AND A HALF THEY WERE BACK AT PEMBERLEY. Both Jane and little Lizzy were doing very well when they left and Georgiana could see that Elizabeth had regained her equanimity. She told Georgiana, "I naturally have fears about my own lying-in, but I refuse to allow myself to be out of spirits for the next two months."

This resolution was the more easily kept since the plans for the upcoming wedding gave them all much to talk about during the long drive home. The air when they reached Derbyshire was noticeably cooler and more comfortable than that in Hertfordshire, and Georgiana could already see a few yellow leaves peeping out from amongst the green along the highway.

After they had climbed with relief from the carriage and greeted Mrs. Reynolds and Smithfield, the housekeeper handed Darcy a letter. It was from Lady Catherine and had arrived while they were still in Hertfordshire; it had been directed to Pemberley and held there, since Mrs. Reynolds knew that they would be home the next day. Darcy read it and handed it silently to Elizabeth, his face a cypher. Georgiana peered over her sister's shoulder. Lady Catherine mentioned none of the previous unpleasantness, but her tone was as militant as always:

> *Lord Winslow,—*
>
> *I thank you for your letter and will wait upon you at Pemberley on the second of October. Anne will accompany me, and we expect to stay a fortnight. I am sorry that we cannot make a longer stay, but you may not be aware that your cousin Anne just became engaged to Viscount St. George and we must hurry back to Kent to finish the arrangements for the wedding, which will be quite soon.—I am yours sincerely, etc.*

Elizabeth, startled, looked up at Darcy as he stood over her while she read. "The second of October. That is today!"

"Indeed it is," he said and then added acerbically, "We are fortunate that we arrived at Pemberley before she did. It would not have improved our relationship if she visited and we were not at home!"

Georgiana's eyes looked rather wary, but the colonel's only response was to say, with a sigh, "I had better warn my parents about my brother's engagement."

Lady Catherine and her daughter arrived just before they were about to have a cup of tea, so Elizabeth and Georgiana had the tea things to occupy them when their guests came down from their rooms after changing from their travel clothes. Miss de Bourgh and her companion, Mrs. Jenkinson, arrived first and, as usual, Miss de Bourgh sat on the couch like an inanimate object while Mrs. Jenkinson fluttered around her. Lady Catherine seemed surprised to be the last to arrive in the drawing-room and, as soon as the courtesies had been performed, resentfully carped, "How did you and Anne get down before me, Mrs. Jenkinson? I came down almost immediately."

Mrs. Jenkinson seemed to quail before her and stammered that it did not seem as if they had hurried. Georgiana thought a deflecting tactic might help and turned to Anne and said, "I understand that you are engaged to be married, Cousin Anne. I congratulate you."

Anne thanked her quietly and resumed her mute posture.

Georgiana turned to Lady Catherine and added, "It is very fortunate that you have come at this time, Lady Catherine. The colonel and I are to be married next week. I was afraid that our plans would not allow all of our family to be present at the ceremony, so I am very pleased that you are here."

Lady Catherine launched into a harangue on the preparations that were necessary for a proper nuptial and pointed out firmly that they must not have their wedding until after Anne and Lord St. George were married as they were the elder cousins and had precedence. Georgiana and the colonel both nodded gravely at each point she made until she finally ran down and sipped the tea Elizabeth had poured her.

Elizabeth gave a slightly desperate look at Darcy and he took up the thread of the conversation.

"It is quite some years since you were at Pemberley, Lady Catherine, is it not?"

"I was last here in the year before your father died. This tea is too weak, Lady Winslow. You should tell your cook to steep it longer."

Elizabeth nodded graciously, but Georgiana noted that her lips were compressed as she passed a cup to Mrs. Jenkinson. Those were the only words Lady Catherine addressed to Elizabeth the entire evening. Georgiana tried to engage her aunt in conversation again by telling her about the colonel's estate in Lambton. This diverted her attention for about half an hour while she told Georgiana how many servants to hire, what kind of paper to put on the walls, and how the gardeners should arrange the shrubbery. They all listened attentively (or at least with the air of attentiveness), although Georgiana soon felt as if her eyes were glazing over.

Eventually Lady Catherine gathered up her daughter and Mrs. Jenkinson and they went upstairs so that Anne could rest for an hour before it was time to dress for dinner. Elizabeth sighed and went up to her own room, followed by Georgiana.

"What are we going to do, Elizabeth?" she whispered angrily. "She is going to make our lives a misery if we try to marry next week."

"Calm down, my dear." She put her arm around her sister's shoulder. "We need to talk to your brother and the colonel. Let us go back downstairs and find them while Lady Catherine is still in her room."

They found the gentlemen collapsed in comfortable chairs in the library. They had already begun discussing the wedding problem.

"Georgiana, my dear," the colonel said ruefully, "I do not see that we have any alternative but to put the wedding off until after my brother's wedding. I really care not what Lady Catherine's opinion is, but it would be unfair to force my parents to choose between us."

Tears welled up in Georgiana's eyes but she forced them down and answered, "I do not see any alternative, either, but I just want you all to know that I am going to be *seething* inside the entire time that my aunt is here."

The colonel took her hand, kissed it, and said, "When the disaster that is my brother's marriage rites is finished, I will marry the bravest, strongest, most understanding woman on earth as soon as can possibly be managed." His eyes twinkled at her until a reluctant smile appeared on her face.

When the crisis was over, Darcy insisted that Elizabeth go back upstairs to lie down. She finally consented, saying, "Even though my lying-in is due more than a month in the future, I feel enormous. It is clear that Lady Catherine's visit will be a great challenge to my amiability so I should rest while I can."

Georgiana also went upstairs to sit in her room and control her anger. When she had struggled with her emotions for quite some time, she gave up and pulled her diary out of her drawer.

2 October: Lady Catherine has arrived at Pemberley the same day we returned home, her letter announcing her intention to visit arriving after we had already left Netherfield Hall. I am so angry with my aunt that I feel as if I could explode into a million pieces! She insists, in her usual forthright manner, that the colonel and I wait until after Anne and St. George's marriage before we wed. She feels that the elder cousins should have precedence and my dear fiancé does not wish to force his parents to decide between their sons' weddings. I know that my aunt speaks as she finds, but it is unfortunate that she finds so much... Now that I have expressed my fury I feel better prepared

to behave in a ladylike fashion to Lady Catherine. I hope
that my manners will hold up until her departure.

When the gong rang for dinner, Georgiana knocked on Elizabeth's door and accompanied her, but it took all of her fortitude to draw herself up and glide down the marble staircase with a pleasant smile upon her face.

When they reached the bottom of the stairs, Darcy stepped forwards from the doorway of the drawing-room to kiss his wife's hand and offer her his arm solicitously, a sardonic tilt to his lips, which he smoothed into a bland smile as he offered Georgiana his other arm and they turned to enter the room. Georgiana smiled at her brother and found that she could face their aunt with calm, if not with joy. They survived the evening by sitting mutely while Lady Catherine held forth on various topics; nodding at the appropriate times in the conversation.

When they finally retired, Georgiana went upstairs with Elizabeth, and whispered, "I find it incredible that my brother tolerated that woman for all those years. I hope that this attempt to ease my family's relationships bears fruit because we are all making a great sacrifice having Lady Catherine here. You, especially, my dear sister, are sacrificing the serenity of your home and I want you to know that we all appreciate your efforts."

"I can only blame myself, since it was, after all, my idea to invite her. I have to say that I am happy she does not really want to talk to me; it at least relieves me from too much of her intrusive attention. You and the colonel will probably receive most of it because there are an *infinite* number of pieces of advice that Lady Catherine can give about your wedding and new house."

Georgiana giggled in spite of her pique. "And I am sure we will hear them all."

As expected, the fortnight of Lady Catherine's visit was a perpetual challenge to Georgiana's good nature, but they finally reached the end of it. Darcy dealt with it by staying continuously by Elizabeth's side, offering her every courtesy and keeping her arm through his—mute testament to Lady Catherine of how excessively happy they were. Georgiana also bore up under her invasive scrutiny, courageously inviting Lady Catherine to see her house and garden so that her aunt could have ample scope for her forthright advice. She also attempted to converse with her cousin Anne about her wedding when Lady Catherine went upstairs for a few minutes, but it was uphill work. The only real comment that she received in response to her questions was, "It doesn't matter; I will still be living at Rosings."

This was given in such a flat tone that Georgiana was unable to determine if her cousin considered staying at Rosings as a benefit or otherwise. At any rate, Anne did not complain of ill-usage in the arrangement of her marriage. At Elizabeth's suggestion, Georgiana played the pianoforte and the harp as much as possible so that there would be less time available to converse with Lady Catherine. Her aunt praised her playing and admired her drawings excessively and also spent a great deal of time talking about Anne's wedding, which was to be the first week after their return, in Kent.

One morning, before Lady Catherine had appeared for breakfast, Georgiana commented to Elizabeth, "I would be much more elevated by her praise if I did not realise that she is trying to disparage your accomplishments by excessive praise of mine, my dear sister. She is really very much like Miss Bingley—pardon me, the Comtesse de Tournay—in that respect. My aunt at least confines herself to giving instruction rather than whispering sarcastic comments behind one's back, so I suppose that I should be grateful for her attention," she finished with unusual acidity.

Elizabeth had to smile at this assessment but added, "At least she is correct that your musical accomplishments are excellent, my dear."

Georgiana just smiled and shook her head pityingly at her sister.

When the day came for the Rosings party to leave, Lady Catherine condescended to acknowledge Elizabeth with a brief curtsey as they made their farewells.

"You will be coming to Anne's wedding next week, I am sure," she said abruptly to Darcy.

"I doubt if my wife," he said, stressing the word slightly, "will be well enough to travel that far in her delicate condition, and I would not want to leave her at this important time, but perhaps Georgiana could come with Lord and Lady Whitwell." Georgiana nodded agreeably to this, as if she and her brother and sister had not discussed it the night before with the colonel.

The required farewells finally completed, the Darcys and the colonel waved them off from the front terrace with artificial smiles and then returned to the breakfast room to enjoy their morning tea in unbroken silence.

With the departure of Lady Catherine, life at Pemberley returned to its usual peaceful tenor. The fair, cool weather of early October was exchanged for days of cold, sleety rain in the middle of the month. Georgiana and Mrs. Annesley travelled to Whitwell Abbey with the colonel before they were to go into Kent for the wedding at Rosings Park. Georgiana wrote often to keep her brother and sister apprised of the situation. Her aunt and uncle, Lord and Lady

Whitwell, continued to look very grim when the subject of the wedding came up, so they all avoided speaking about it as much as possible. She also wrote to Elizabeth:

> *...We will be leaving tomorrow morning for Kent. I must admit that I am apprehensive about this wedding, not only because of my cousin St. George's underhanded pursuit of my cousin Anne's fortune, but because of the strain it is putting on my aunt and uncle. They have still not heard from St. George; all of their information about him has been received from Lady Catherine, and that of only the most general sort. Colonel Fitzwilliam has already left for Kent in the hope that he can find an opportunity to talk seriously to his brother—not, of course, to dissuade him from the wedding, for it is obvious that it is too late for that, but to attempt to make him acknowledge the seriousness of his responsibility for Cousin Anne's health and happiness. Well, we will see how the situation lies when we get there. I will write when we arrive safely.—With much affection, etc.*

Elizabeth sighed when she read this epistle and handed it to Darcy. He read it silently then refolded it and left the room. She shook her head sadly, a small crease between her brows, as she listened to his footsteps fade away and heard the tiny click of the door of his library. The next few days he was very tender and gentle to Elizabeth but quiet and abstracted. At the end of three days, they received two letters from Kent: one to the both of them from Georgiana, and one for Darcy from the colonel. They opened Georgiana's first:

Dearest Sister and Brother,—

The wedding went off very calmly at eleven o'clock yesterday morning, without any demonstrations of acrimony but also without any great joy, excepting that of Lady Catherine. Cousin Anne wore a magnificent cream-coloured satin dress covered with Venetian lace, and, although her gown fitted her well, she seemed to disappear into all of that elaborate lace and become almost invisible. She stood up next to Lord St. George and looked like a child playing at dress-up, or possibly a doll. Lord St. George had a smug but defiant look on his face as he watched his bride walk up the aisle on the arm of his father, who gave her away. His eyes met those of his father, and they briefly locked in a visible struggle until St. George dropped his gaze. The other guests, of whom there were few, naturally did not realise that this was occurring, as my aunt and uncle and the colonel all maintained a dignified façade in front of them.

Lady Catherine had a wedding breakfast for the newlyweds after the ceremony so that the guests could congratulate the couple and, although St. George took Anne around on his arm to accept the best wishes of the guests, not once did I see her smile. Some of the guests, especially St. George's friends, looked rather shocked when they saw how tiny and ill-looking the bride was, and most gave their muted congratulations and faded away. The breakfast was over in just under an hour. Lady Catherine had a lavish supper laid on for the family that evening, but Lady Anne left halfway through the meal as she was exhausted by the exertions of the day. St. George stayed until we were finished, drinking a great deal of wine and talking to his mother-in-law with determined jollity while she preened herself over capturing a lord for her daughter, both seeming insensible of Anne's departure.

The gentlemen spent very little time over their port, as you might imagine, and they rejoined us in the drawing-room with faces like stone. We all retired very soon after they came in. I pray that Lady Anne will be well taken care of by her husband, but I continue to have grave doubts. The one minuscule piece of good news is that with all of St. George's greater sins to think about, I completely forgot to feel self-conscious in his presence, although this was the first time that I had seen him since we had our argument before the ball.—With my dearest affection, etc.

Darcy sat for a moment staring at the rain beating on the long windows of the salon then seemed to shake himself and opened the colonel's letter. After he read it he handed it to Elizabeth, saying, "I am not sure that I should let you read this, since I would like to preserve some sense of dignity for my family. However, you already know so much of it that I suppose it cannot be made any worse."

She took the letter curiously and read,

Darcy,—

Well, the wedding farce has concluded and St. George and Anne are married. As you know, I arrived in Kent two days before the wedding in the hope that I could drive some sense into my dear brother. He managed to evade me until the day of the wedding, when I bearded

*him in his lair before he was dressed. He continues to be
as intransigent and defiant as ever and, although I spoke
to him very calmly (much more calmly than I felt, I am
sure you can believe), he would not listen. He admits
that having an invalid wife will be a bore but says that
he will not need to spend much time in Kent. He scorns
Anne's weakness and frailty and does not respect his
mother-in-law. I am ashamed to be associated with this
deed, but we all held up our heads and behaved with as
much honour as the situation would allow us. We are
leaving this morning after breakfast and will be back at
Pemberley as soon as we are able. Lady Catherine will
be coming with us, as well as my parents, so tell Mr.
Woodson to have his surplice at hand, because Georgiana
and I are not waiting any longer. To my happiness at
marrying Georgiana is added the immeasurable bliss of
having an irrefutable excuse for leaving the presence of
Lady Catherine as soon as we are married.—*

Fitzwilliam

These communications left them both subdued and thoughtful,
and they did not discuss them but quietly went about their business, making sure that all the wedding preparations were finished
by the time Georgiana and their guests returned.

Chapter 29

Rise up, my love, my fair one, and come away.
For lo, the winter is past, the rain is over and gone.

—Song of Solomon, 2:10–11

THE WEDDING TOOK PLACE TWO DAYS LATER, BUT IT WAS NOT until late in the afternoon of the wedding day that Elizabeth had time to sit down and write to Jane about it:

> *My dearest Jane,—*
> *Well, this morning Georgiana and Colonel Fitzwilliam were married in the Pemberley chapel. Lord and Lady Whitwell and Lady Catherine came directly to Pemberley after the wedding in Kent, so all of the closest family members on both sides were present, excepting only Lord and Lady St. George. Lambert and I helped Georgiana dress, as we had done so many times in London. Her maid is coming along very well, but she did not feel that she could take all of the responsibility for*

disabled

such an important occasion. Georgiana told me that she would have liked to be married in her sea-green or her gold gown, since she feels that the occasions on which she previously wore those gowns were the turning points in her (as she puts it) "pursuit of the colonel's heart." Since those gowns would be somewhat unconventional and she does not want to give Lady Catherine anything more to talk about, she chose instead to wear a beautiful creamy white silk gown with no lace or other adornment. The skirt was made of several layers of the sheerest silk that you can imagine, and it floated around her as she came down the aisle like gossamer. Her hair was curled around her face, and she wore a white bonnet with a short veil and her pearls and the bracelet that the colonel had given her for her birthday and she looked like an angel come to earth.

After she was dressed, I went down to the chapel and found that Lady Catherine had planted herself in the first pew. Since there was not room for the entire family in front, I sat in the second pew, and when Lord and Lady Whitwell came in a moment later they sat with me, leaving Lady Catherine in solitary splendour. Mrs. Reynolds and Smithfield, and a few of the other upper servants, sat in the back pew. When the organist started the processional, Lady Whitwell reached over and took my hand. I looked up at her and she smiled at me, but she had tears in her eyes, as did I.

Georgiana glided down the aisle like a ship with all her flags flying and her eyes only for the colonel. I have never seen a bride more unwavering than Georgiana.

Although she never showed the slightest loss of temper after the initial upset of their plans, when they returned from Kent I believe that any difficulties put in her way would have fallen before her determination like straw before a flame.

Mr. Darcy tells me that the colonel was fidgeting in the library all morning until it was time for him to dress for the wedding—he almost drove my poor husband mad—for fear that the wedding would be put off again, but of course it was not. We had a lovely wedding breakfast, and the bride and groom left at one o'clock for Bellamy. The colonel was able to push the workmen to make the house liveable for them by finishing enough rooms for the comfort of themselves and their few servants. They will stay only a few days and then travel back to London, where they will stay at Longford House; the colonel will finish turning over his duties and then resign his commission. They expect to be back in Derbyshire within a month.

The one sad note for Georgiana was when Mrs. Annesley told her on the way home from Rosings Park that now that Georgiana did not need her she wished to take a position with Sir Robert Blake as a companion for his sister. It is an excellent plan since Georgiana will be able to visit Mrs. Annesley and not feel as if she has abandoned the friend who helped her so much over the past two years. Dear girl that she is, she does not want anyone to lose by her happiness.

Our guests left not long ago and already the house seems empty without Georgiana. I am glad that she will be close once they have settled all of their business in London. I hope that your search for an estate near Pemberley goes well, my dear sister, for I long to have you near me as well. I must go now; Mr. Darcy and I are going for a short walk—the weather has finally cleared after almost a fortnight of rain and we both feel the need to breathe some fresh air out-of-doors (and breathing is about the only part of a walk that I can manage at the moment!). Love to Mr. Bingley and my dear little Lizzy and, of course, to you, my dearest Jane.—Your Loving Sister,

Elizabeth

She folded her letter and sealed it with a melancholy sigh.

At Bellamy, Georgiana was at the pianoforte, her husband sitting in a chair next to her, while she played the Italian love songs which she had performed for Elizabeth and Jane in London the previous year. The colonel watched her hands as they fluttered over the keys, her long fingers stroking the keys tenderly or pounding them passionately. Her hands fascinated him. They looked slender and delicate at rest, yet strong and sure when she played. When she neared the finale of the piece, Fitzwilliam noticed the ringlets at the side of her hair dancing as she reached a crescendo, and suddenly felt the desire to keep them dancing, so he softly blew on them, pleased with their swaying. When she finished, Georgiana turned on her bench to face him.

"Is there some reason that you are blowing on my neck, Cousin?" she asked dryly. "Are you bored with the music?"

"Not at all, but I confess that I am more interested in the

musician at the moment." A mischievous grin spread over his face. "And I suddenly recall that you had an extremely ticklish neck as a child."

"Oh no… do not even think about tickling my neck," she said, giving him a dangerous look.

"Why not, little cousin? Do you not want to play?" his tone was ingenuous, but she was stern.

"I commented to Elizabeth at one time that I desired to slap your face when you called me 'little cousin.'"

Fitzwilliam smiled blandly for a moment, in apparent surrender and then, without warning, grabbed her waist. She gasped as he effortlessly swung her around onto his lap and cradled her in his arms like a baby. He offered his cheek to her and said, "Here it is, little cousin, do with it what you will."

She abruptly reached up and ran her fingers across his cheek, making him flinch at her sudden movement, but she merely laughed and walked her fingers up the side of his face and into his hair then grasped his head with both hands and turned it to face her.

"I can see that I must educate my husband in the properly respectful manner to treat his wife."

Still holding her, he put his hand on his heart and declaimed, "If I may paraphrase, my lady: 'Georgiana, love on and I will tame my wild heart to thy loving hand.'" In his normal voice he added, "And you thought that I had wasted all my youth tormenting my tutors instead of studying my books." He offered his cheek to her again. "So what is your verdict, little cousin?"

"Perhaps, Cousin, I have changed my mind," she said softly then tugged his head down and kissed him.

Historical Notes
on the Regency Era

ALTHOUGH MR. DARCY'S COVERT ADVENTURE IN PARIS RESCUING the Prince Regent's letters is fiction, the secret marriage of the Prince of Wales to Mrs. Fitzherbert, a young Catholic widow, is fact. As Prince of Wales, Prince George was subject to the Acts of Settlement of 1701 and the Royal Marriages Act of 1772, which required that he obtain the approval of his father, King George III, to marry. For Prince George to marry without his permission would make him ineligible to inherit the throne, and the king would never consent to his marrying a Catholic. This was a prejudice that was codified in the law and was the result of a long history of strained relations between Catholic and Protestant Christians in England that began with Henry VIII and his break with the Pope over his divorce of Catherine of Aragon in 1532.

In 1784, when Mrs. Fitzherbert was first introduced to Prince George, she had been twice widowed and had lost an infant son to the many infectious diseases prevalent in the day. The prince was immediately transfixed by her attractive face and demure nature, which contrasted greatly with the sophisticated and scheming ladies of the court. Her refusal to bow to his wishes and become his mistress or, later, his wife inflamed the desire of the prince and he pressured her indefatigably until she finally decided to flee to the Continent to escape his importunities. The prince fought this move, even up to the point of stabbing himself in the leg and claiming that he had attempted suicide over his despair at her pending departure. In order to calm him, she agreed to marry him but instead left for the Continent at daylight the next morning.

After almost a year and a half of the prince's passionate letters urging her to marry him, Mrs. Fitzherbert finally agreed and they were wed with the utmost secrecy on December 15, 1785, by a Church of England minister; he had been languishing in debtors prison and was willing to commit a felony (for the illegal marriage was considered such under the law) for financial relief and promises of future preferment.

Unfortunately for the cause of true love, the prince continued his dissolute lifestyle and frequent philandering after his marriage and finally, in 1793, his relationship with his wife had deteriorated seriously. The prince's advisors strongly urged him to take a royal Protestant wife to quiet the rumours about his marriage to Mrs. Fitzherbert, trusting that this would convince Parliament of his desire to do his duty to his country and they would then vote to give him some relief from his debts. He finally agreed to marry his cousin, Princess Caroline of Brunswick. The prince, however, was repulsed by the princess's looks and personal hygiene when they met, and he lived with her for only a very short period before he could tolerate her no longer. The princess conceived during this brief period of cohabitation and bore the prince a daughter, Charlotte, who lived twenty-one years before dying in childbirth, leaving the prince without a legitimate heir. The Prince and Princess of Wales spent the greater part of their married life separated.

Prince George became Prince Regent of England in 1811 when King George III was declared permanently insane. The king had suffered from a similar fit of madness in 1788 to 1789—most likely, according to modern medical historians, the effect of porphyria, an inherited disorder of haemoglobin metabolism—and Parliament had subsequently passed laws allowing for a regency in case of a recurrence of his disorder, primarily because Parliament needed the king's permission to sit and when the king's first bout of insanity began Parliament was not in session and could not meet because their ruler was thus unable to give them that permission. King George III's insanity indeed did recur in late 1810 and the prince was declared regent in early 1811. The king did not recover, and the Prince of Wales continued as regent until his father's death in 1820, when he became King George IV, ruling until 1830.

During the Regency period and the years preceding it, England was a member of various coalitions formed with other European countries to oppose Napoleon's efforts to conquer most of the countries of Europe and bring them into his empire. On March 31, 1814, the Sixth Coalition forces occupied Paris and on April 6 Napoleon abdicated in favour of his son; then, at the insistence of the Coalition, he unconditionally surrendered on April 11, 1814. He was exiled to Elba, an island in the Mediterranean off the coast of Italy, and remained there until February 26, 1815, when he escaped and rejoined what remained of his army. He was finally defeated by the Duke of Wellington at Waterloo on June 18, 1815, and was exiled to the remote island of St. Helena in the southern Atlantic Ocean. He remained there for the six years until his death.

George Gordon Byron, Sixth Baron Byron, was one of the major poets of the Romantic period, which included the years of the Regency, and from his name is coined the phrase "the Byronic hero," of which he was the epitome. In spite of his slight stature and a limp caused by a birth defect, he was notorious for his dissolute lifestyle and numerous affairs; some historians number them in the hundreds, and many were the wives of prominent men. One of these well-known affairs was with Lady Caroline Lamb in 1812, who famously described him after their breakup as "mad, bad, and dangerous to know." His poetry was popular during his life, but he was compelled to flee England in 1816 after the breakup of his marriage because of rampant rumours of incest and homosexuality (which were by most accounts quite true)—rumours assisted by the jealous Lady Caroline Lamb, who had lasted only a few months in his affections but who continued to be obsessed with her former lover, stalking him through London (often in the guise of a young man) for months after he rejected her. After his flight, Byron became involved in the Greek struggle for independence from Turkey and he died at Messalonghi of a putrid fever in 1824. He is considered to be a great national hero by the Greeks because of his support, including almost single-handedly making the Greek navy an important force in the conflict.

English property law was based on the concept of *primogeniture*, or inheritance by the eldest son. Most landholders left their entire estate to their eldest son to keep the property in one piece, because property that was divided each generation among all the sons would eventually be unable to support a family. Large estates also provided the family with power and influence because of the wealth they produced, and dividing the land also divided the power of the family. If a gentleman died intestate, his entire estate would legally go to the eldest son, as well. The *entail* was another method of protecting the property by making it into a single legal entity that would pass to the eldest male relative and could not be sold. If a family had no sons, as in the Bennet family, the nearest male relative might be a cousin, nephew, etc., whoever was the closest male relation. The entail prevented irresponsible sons from gambling away or selling their patrimony as they could raise money only on the income and not on the property itself. Entails lasted three generations but could be broken by two generations agreeing to do so (as Mr. Bennet had hoped to do if he had a son). After it expired, the current owner could renew the entail or leave it unencumbered. Rosings Park, Lady Catherine de Bourgh's estate, was not entailed and her husband left it to Lady Catherine, who would then pass it to Miss Anne de Bourgh. This is the reason Anne was such a desirable match to Lord St. George—instead of only a dowry, she would be the owner of a vast estate and when she married, her husband would have complete control of her estate. Single women could own property, but if they married the ownership passed to their husbands.

The presentation at court of young men and women of the nobility and upper gentry as they reached adulthood was fraught with strict tradition and protocol. The young women were presented at court Drawing-rooms and the young men at Levees. A woman who had not been presented at court before her marriage and who qualified for presentation because of her husband's status could be presented as well; and protocol required presentation before she could attend any court social functions.

The dress for a man when presented at court was not significantly different from his typical formal wear, except that he was required to wear a sword. The ladies, however, had an elaborate set of instructions for their dress, and until the Prince Regent became king and changed the requirements they were required to wear clothing much like what we normally picture Marie Antoinette and her French court wearing. This included a tight, fitted, low-cut bodice over a corset, with the mantua, or wide hoops, that had been fashionable in the mid-eighteenth century. They must also wear a train exactly three yards in length and an ostrich plume in their hair at the back of their head. Married women added a tiara to this costume. Those being presented were not allowed to wear any type of shawl or cloak; no matter how cold the weather they were required to leave their outdoor garments in their carriages before entering the palace, unless they had a physician's certification stating that their health would not permit it.

When the Prince Regent became King George IV, he changed the court dress requirements to fit more into the then-current fashion (except for the requirement for an ostrich feather plume in the hair, which remained). This trend of having court dress reflect contemporary fashions continued until the mid-twentieth century, when Queen Elizabeth II dropped the court presentation ritual completely and substituted a less formal

Garden Party, which relieved much stress for the young ladies of the gentry and nobility.

Hyde Park is located to the west of the posh Mayfair district in London. It was originally purchased by Henry VIII in 1536 and fenced as a royal hunting preserve. It became a public park in 1637, and in 1689 William III built a road along the south edge between his home at Kensington Palace and St. James Palace. The road was known as the *route de roi* (the king's route), which was eventually corrupted into "Rotten Row," the most popular location to see and be seen in the nineteenth century on horseback or in a carriage. The park has numerous walking paths and is divided by the meandering, shallow lake called the Serpentine.

Angelica Catalani, the soloist the Darcy party listened to at their first night at the theater, was an Italian soprano who came to England in 1806 and was for seven years the undisputed prima donna of English opera. She left to manage the Paris opera and continued to tour until her retirement in 1828. She eventually moved to Florence and started a singing school. She was notorious during her years in England for her sexual misbehaviour, including providing young women from the chorus for her male friends, including Lord Byron.

For further reading I would recommend the following:

David, Saul. *Prince of Pleasure.* New York: Grove Press, 1998. (A biography of the life and regency of Prince George.)

McGann, Jerome J. *Lord Byron: The Major Works.* Oxford: Oxford University Press, 1986. (The introduction includes an extensive biography of Lord Byron.)

Orczy, Baroness Emmuska. *The Scarlet Pimpernel.* New York: Simon and Schuster, Inc., 2004. (The classic story, first published in 1905.)

Acknowledgments

This book would not have been published without the encouragement and assistance of my husband, Eric, and my sister, Dana Van Brocklin. Thank you!

About the Author

C. Allyn Pierson is the nom de plume of physician Carey A. Bligard, who has combined her many years of interest in the works of Jane Austen and the history of Regency England into this sequel to *Pride and Prejudice*. She lives in Fort Dodge, Iowa, with her family and two dogs. Visit her on the web at www.callynpierson.com.